# ECHO FROM
# A BAYOU

## ONE MAN'S JOURNEY TO CONFRONT HIS OWN MURDERER...

## ALSO BY J. LUKE BENNECKE

JAKE BENDEL THRILLERS

*Civil Terror: Gridlock*

*Waterborne*

*Blackout (Coming Soon)*

# ECHO FROM A BAYOU

## J. LUKE BENNECKE

J. Luke Bennecke
www.jlukebennecke.com

Jaytech Publishing
PO Box 421
Beaumont, CA 92223
www.jaytechpublishing.com

Ordering Information:
Quantity sales. Special discounts are available on quantity purchases by corporations, associations, and others. For details, contact the publisher at the address above.
Orders by U.S. trade bookstores and wholesalers. Please contact Jaytech Publishing at www.jaytechpublishing.com.

Printed in the United States of America

Publisher's Cataloging-in-Publication data
Bennecke, J. Luke
Echo From A Bayou / J. Luke Bennecke
p. cm.
        ISBN 978-0-9657715-5-9 (paperback)
        ISBN 978-0-9657715-7-3 (eBook)
1. The main category of the book — Thriller — Suspense.

This book is a work of fiction. Any references to events, real people, or real places are used fictitiously or are the products of the author's imagination. Any resemblance to actual persons, living or dead, or actual events is entirely coincidental.

Advanced Reader Edition
10 9 8 7 6 5 4 3 2 1 AR

Interior Design and Typesetting by Bridget Bennecke
Cover Design by Hristo Kovatliev

*For my beautiful wife and soulmate, together forever in this life and beyond . . .*

# CHAPTER 1

## John Bastian

*November 8, 2016 - Mammoth Mountain, CA*

Never had I seen so many angry trees in one place.

Through a gondola window covered with spider cracks, ominous mountains loomed in the darkened distance. One peak in particular, a white, snowcapped giant, laughed at me with his frozen face and pointed pines, pompous with knowledge he had risen to life, fallen, and rebirthed his dominance over countless millennia.

Ignoring the familiar tug to spiral down another rabbit hole of negativity, I instead envisioned myself racing down a crazy-steep, treeless, triple black diamond slope at the summit of Mammoth Mountain: Huevos Grande.

Passengers continued to pack inside the already-full car, oblivious to our collective need to breathe oxygen, already limited in the high altitude air that smelled of sweaty gym socks.

"And I don't see *you* wearin' no helmet," Kevin said.

"Enough about Sonny Bono already, that was a long time ago," I said, glancing down at Kevin, who, at a foot shorter than me, sported matching black ski pants and jacket with a rainbow-colored voodoo doll embroidered on the back. The snowboarding boots boosted his height by two inches, bringing his height up to five feet five inches.

My closest friend for the last two decades and best man at the wedding of my disaster of a marriage, we'd met at track practice during senior year of high school.

With my last shred of patience wearing thin, I waited with Kevin in the front corner of the room-sized orange cube, near the sliding doors. Skis propped and steadied with one hand, I gave his down-insulated shoulder a friendly punch with the other and said, "Stay positive, man. We need as much optimism as we can handle."

"Glad you finally gettin' your head outta them clouds," Kevin said. "Sooner you forgive Margaret, sooner you can get on with your life, Johnny Jackass."

"You know I hate it when you call me that."

"Exactly."

Two months ago, he'd suggested this trip to some of California's highest slopes in order to check off the last item on our mid-life crisis bucket list.

One final group of skiers jammed inside, jerking the box that would soon glide us up to the peak of peaks. My heart flopped around inside my chest as I ignored the instinctive urge to go back to our room and down a double bourbon. Instead, I adjusted my black beanie, giving Kevin a forced smile. A tinge of alcohol withdrawal headache pinged my noggin. I dug out two Tylenol gel caps from my inner jacket pocket, popped them into my mouth and swallowed without water.

I tightened my lips and turned my head, glancing through a different gondola window, up to the 11,000-foot peak riddled with wide, white, invincible slopes.

But a shiver crawled up from my legs to my neck, deflating any remnants of confidence.

I tapped open a weather app on my phone. "This might be the last run. That huge storm front's almost here."

"Word."

We both enjoyed the occasional humorous embellishment of stereotypical hip-hop culture, even though Kevin had two masters' degrees from Berkeley, one in American history and another in theater arts.

After separating from Margaret three years ago, the entire divorce process continually marinated in my head, but I wanted—needed—to lick my mental wounds, get on with my life, and find a new purpose. Hence my agreeing to this trip.

Heads bobbed among the other snow enthusiasts, along with a colorful assortment of mirrored goggles and insulated garments. My height allowed me an unobstructed view of my fellow sardines.

"Think of all the times they said it was supposed to rain back home in Newport Beach," I said. "Nothing. Just a few drops here and there. Damned drought's horrible."

A man with dark, heavy-lidded eyes stood five feet away from us in the rear of the gondola, wearing a baby blue sweater and black jeans. Then for no apparent reason, he started tapping his forehead repeatedly on the gondola wall.

Dude wore no ski jacket.

No ski pants.

*Odd.*

Short and thin-framed, as he rubbed the nape of his neck, his entire presence screamed of fear and anger. Black-rimmed glasses sat atop his nose, above a thick Freddy Mercury mustache, his face flushed red.

Kevin bounced up and down several times, arms crossed, rubbing his outer shoulders, probably to increase his blood flow. Too much caffeine for him. Again.

"So tell me 'bout this good news you got," Kevin whispered, shivering. The primary reason we'd listed this ski trip on our bucket list five years ago was an excuse to spend some "bro" time away from work, away from our real lives. Now it served as a way for me to hide from my memories of Margaret.

But it wasn't working.

Leaning in close to Kevin to make sure nobody else heard our discussion, I said, "We got a big real estate deal set to close on a sweet piece of beachfront commercial property. Killer views. And with that single commission, I'm planning to rebuild my brokerage."

A thought wandered into my mind, of creamy smooth whiskey flowing gently over my tongue and down into my gut. Something to sooth my frayed nerves.

Kevin smiled with his huge, toothy grin and jumped again. "That's what I'm talkin' about."

I don't know why, but the overall appearance of the mustached man in the corner, coupled with his darting glances and multiple throat clearings, gave me the willies. I turned away, trying to ignore him and his negative vibes. Finally, the line to the gondola had shriveled to two skiers, a mother and her young son. The kid had a smile the size of a crescent moon as he crossed the threshold from the loading platform to the gondola. But his boot snagged on the lip of the doorway. He landed hard on his knees in front of me and, with a loud grunt, rolled onto his side.

I leaned down, extended my arm, and helped the hundred-pound fella to his feet.

The kid smiled, thanked me, and I patted him on the back. "No worries."

His mother placed her hand over her chest and gave me a thankful glance. A pleasant warmth filled my heart.

The lady in charge of the gondola stuck her head inside and gave a brief speech about the trip lasting fifteen minutes, staying inside the safety areas, avoiding out of bounds markers, and something about having fun.

"What's up with this cracked window?" a man interrupted with a raised voice, pointing to the rear corner.

"Scheduled for repair tomorrow."

"Jesus," the man muttered to himself, waving off the woman.

Seconds later, the doors slid shut and we started our ascent.

Halfway up to Mammoth's highest ridge, the inside of my right shoulder started throbbing. Strong. Like never before. After dropping forty pounds over the past six months, every joint of my now two-hundred-pound body ached and moaned whenever I moved. I hoped the Tylenol would work its magic soon.

A loud metal-on-metal screeching noise filled the air and with a thundering thud, the haul cable crashed to a dead stop. Everyone covered their ears.

Our car continued its forward momentum. We swayed up, peaked, and arced backwards, like a giant, slow-moving pendulum on an old grandfather clock.

Passengers screamed.

I braced my back against the gondola wall and scanned the surface of the tiny sea of forty or so shuffling, mumbling human souls, all of us suspended mid-air and clinging to life by a thin, wobbly, and probably frayed cable.

I craned my head and peeked downward and immediately wished I hadn't. My stomach lurched. A jagged, rocky crevasse stared back up at me from hundreds of feet below us.

"I knew we shouldn't have come up today," a woman said.

Emergency amber lights flashed and a broken tin-can voice shot from inside a wall speaker. *"... worry ... got ... down ... soon. Sorry for ... thank you ..."*

Human voices mumbled. Our car continued to sway back and forth. Kevin stared at me with rapidly blinking eyes.

Wire tension ebbed and flowed, bobbing us up and down .

The mustached man standing in the opposite corner of the gondola rubbed his temples, bared an assortment of mangled teeth, and banged his fist several times against his forehead. His eyes darted left to right. He squatted and I lost sight of him behind a rather hefty woman wearing an all-pink jumpsuit.

I leaned toward Kevin. "Something's wrong with that dude."

# CHAPTER 2

Kevin glanced toward the mustached man in the gondola. "Something's wrong with us." He jerked his arms and legs, squirming. "This ain't cool, man. We ain't supposed to be hangin' up here in the damned sky like this. I'm 'bout ready to freak my ass out right now."

The car started free-falling toward the earth, filling the gondola with terrified screams and giving me a weightless feeling. But only for a split-second. Another boom, then we slammed to a sudden stop. I struggled to overcome g-forces that easily doubled my weight.

The mustached man stood, wiped his brow, grabbed at his chest, and hammered his head three times against the gondola wall. "Stop it. Leave me alone, Jacques. I can't breathe," he yelled to absolutely nobody. "Need air."

Arms above his head, he'd rotated one of his skis horizontally above him, ramming the front tip through the cracked rear window, shattering the plexiglass. More screams. He threw down his ski and, climbing onto the hand rail, punched out the remaining shards and grabbed the inside of the window frame, pulling his head and upper torso through the opening.

A burly, bearded man from the crowd grabbed the guy's leg, but took a boot to the face and landed hard on his ass, blood pouring from his nose, lips and chin.

Kevin and I bolted toward the escapee, trying to seize the man's flailing legs and wrestle him back to safety.

Before we could pull him inside, the car jolted back to life, yanking us all sideways. Kevin and I fell off balance, both losing our grip on the man's legs. The gondola continued its trek upwards toward the peak, the inertia sucking the rest of the man's body out the window.

I jumped and thrust my entire upper body through the window opening. Looking straight down the side of the car, I fully expected to see a falling body. But instead, the man dangled from the side, gripping the sill with one hand. His glasses slipped from his face and plummeted toward the canyon below.

Then he looked at me. We connected.

Fear engulfed us both. Pure, primal panic.

The distant rocks below made my vision spin. Finding untapped internal strength, I somehow managed to grab hold of his right wrist and forearm with my gloved hands and told myself to focus. "Hold on. I got you. Give me your other arm."

Legs flapped in the open air, he struck the side of the car, bouncing and slipping along the wet metal. Someone grabbed my waist and secured me. But I wiggled my way further out the window another couple of inches, waiting for the right moment to let go with my right hand and grab the left wrist of this crazy man.

My abdomen slid against plexiglass shards still embedded in the window sill, sharp pieces scraping along my jacket, poking, pushing, prodding into my belly. The padding in my gloves only handicapped my grip, my forearm muscles pulsating and burning to quit.

"Stop messin' around and pull that dude back inside," Kevin said from inside. "Before we get to the next support tower."

Both my forearms begged to release their grip. I doubled my efforts to maintain a solid hold on the dangling man while turning my head, looking forward to the other side of the tower where the canyon rose steeply and the gondola car would only be a dozen feet above a patch of soft powdery ground. A landing spot. If I could manage to hold onto this guy another few seconds and let go, the drop would be non-lethal. Maybe a fractured ankle. Maybe nothing.

Or I could try to pull him inside.

Now.

The man waved his left arm around, making it impossible to grab. "Relax so I can grab ahold of your other hand." He slapped his free hand against the steel wall. *Now's my chance.* In a split second, I let go of his arm with my right hand and grabbed his left wrist, squeezing with every ounce of strength I could muster, knowing my focus, determination, and strength were this man's only connection to life.

With both arms secured, I turned my head upwards. "I got him! Hurry! Pull us back in!"

My left forearm cramped. More pain surged through my right shoulder. A fresh jolt of adrenaline provided strength to continue another second.

Our eyes locked dead. "I got you," I said. A sense of confidence washed over me, knowing I could heave the man up and inside. "Talk about your fucked-up Mondays." The man blinked, confused. "First round's on me when we get back down."

A tiny smile appeared in the corner of his mouth.

But my body slid further out the window portal, sucked downwards. All remaining optimism popped like a water balloon. My belly continued scraping against the bottom of the windowsill as my lungs continued pumping, laboring to provide the oxygen I needed to complete the rescue.

The gondola swept upwards onto the final support tower. As we made our way across most of the pulleys, the cable we hung from jerked us around, shaking the entire car sideways, blasting up and thrusting our mass down.

With both forearms completely numb, physical control of my grip became impossible.

When our cable connection slid and bounced across the final pulley, the car slammed down and stopped. The g-forces tried to tear my body in half. But an instant later, the crazy man released his grip on my arms. The only thread tying that poor man to life snapped.

His eyes stared directly at me, into me.

A primal scream.

He fell, belly-up, arms and legs thrashing in a futile effort to save himself. The plummeting body shrank with each microsecond until his body thwacked onto a jagged rock protruding from the snow, forcing his right leg to wrench behind his back, crimson red instantly covering the surface of his once pale face.

Kevin and several others sucked me back up inside the gondola.

"Why'd he let go?" I asked mostly to myself, the world spinning, staring at the aluminum floor and failing with numb gloved hands to wipe saliva from my lips. "I had him."

Kevin patted my back. "Not your fault, man. You tried. You almost died trying."

# CHAPTER 3

**A** few long hours later down at base camp, as I sat back in a plastic chair, a policewoman appeared and slipped a business card into my hand.

"Call me if you remember anything else, Mr. Bastian," she said. I gave a weak nod and she wandered away.

Local authorities had interviewed all the passengers from the gondola. Rumors of an investigation popped up here and there.

"We're good to go, man," Kevin said. "Let's hit the bar. We gotta digest all this shit."

*No.*

The fog in my brain evaporated, replaced by several questions.

"What time is it?"

"Four," Kevin said.

"And the storm?"

"Not here yet."

"The gondola's fixed?"

"They got more than one gondola, dog."

*We can still do this. We have time. But it's got to be now.*

I slid on my gloves and stood, grabbing my skis.

Kevin blocked my way before I could step toward the closest chair lift. "Uh-uh. We goin' to the bar."

"Dude, we've been planning this for months. This is the last day of our trip. We don't do this now, it's never gonna happen."

"A man died today, John. Died. You watched his ass fall. Going skiin' ain't what you do after experiencing something like that, man. We need alcohol. Lots and lots of alcohol."

Point taken. The pull to knock back a double bourbon tugged strong at my belly. But something different inside me overrode my alcoholic urge. I still wanted to make the run. No, I needed to make the run. Prove to myself I was still worthy. Still alive. "Yes. A man just died and it was his time to go. But that's even more reason for us to do this. Right now. Before it's our time." I took a step closer to Kevin. "We'll drink. Yes. Digest and talk. Yes. But after the run. I gotta do this. We gotta do this."

He pulled his head back and curled his shoulders over his chest. "Dammit." He wet his lips and pressed them together, then scooped up his snowboard. "One final run. But that's it."

The authorities had allowed Mammoth to re-open the gondola. At least until the impending storm came. Nestled inside our car, we crossed the area where the mustached man had fallen. Eyes closed, my stomach churned as I pictured him laying there, broken and bloody.

The policewoman had told me the dead guy's name was Blake Lynds. In my mind's eye, investigators worked the jagged rocks below, cleaning up the man's remains, taking measurements, doing whatever those crime scene people do. I had no desire to see all that. Just wanted to get to the top and do one final run.

In that moment I realized how short our time on this planet really is. Any of us could check out any minute. Every second should be treated as a precious gift. Even more reason to make it down that mountain. Stop looking backwards. Jump start my life. Move forward. Heck, this entire experience might even enable me to finally forgive Margaret for all the pain she'd inflicted.

My life depended on this run.

Five minutes later, we approached the station perched atop the peak of Mammoth Mountain. As the gondola slowed, pulled in and stopped, my eyes shot open, staring northwest to the early sunset. A cloud front approached, black and ugly, stretched across the entire sky. Thin rays of horizontal sunshine played hide-and-seek behind the storm clouds, but tight trails of light bounced off the slopes, enough for us to make the run. Perfect. In ten minutes, the entire resort would be shrouded in darkness. This needed to happen now.

Someone grabbed my upper arm. I swung around.

"Sorry, pal, all slopes are closed," said a tall, husky man wearing a red uniform with a white "plus" symbol on the upper front side.

Ski Patrol.

"We're expecting white-out conditions later. C'mon, you need to ride back down with me."

I jerked my arm free and drove my poles into the snow, propelling myself away from the man, past the rear of the summit cafe.

The man yelled something about stopping, avalanche conditions, not safe, et cetera.

Kevin hobbled along next to me, carrying his board, huffing, and said, "This is a bad idea, man. We need to go back down on that gondola. We're losing light and some crazy-ass ice storm is headed in. Plus, I don't like the idea of getting arrested."

"Then we better hurry and get down the hill," I said, thrusting myself further along the ridge.

The ski patrol dude stayed put. Probably not worth the pursuit. At a safe distance away, Kevin plopped onto a snow seat, ratcheted both boots tightly to his snowboard and followed me down a mild slope along the ridge.

"OK, man, but you better not be dragging me into some kind of suicide mission. My agent finally got me hooked up with a sweet-ass TV gig."

Although crisp, the cold air smelled clean, fresh. Snow crunched beneath my skis, smooth, with a whooshing sound permeating all around us. But at eleven thousand feet, I found myself breathing like some damned rabbit, lungs straining for oxygen.

"You're telling me this amazing, life-changing news right now?"

"Was gonna tell you tonight. As a surprise."

"Don't worry. We're up here to live. Sounds like that big-time success you've been chasing for twenty years is right around the corner. Just one more run."

"I know. It's gonna happen this time, dog. I can feel it, too. Gonna make America laugh."

"I'll believe that when I see it," I said with a wink before sliding on my rainbow-colored reflective goggles.

We continued slogging along the narrow barren ridge, dark clouds growing more intense as flashes of lightning peppered the sky. Heading east, I glanced down here and there in search of an optimal drop-off point. And I tried to shake the eerie, lonely feeling of skiing somewhere normally packed with people, now completely void. Dead. The downward face of the smooth treeless slope, a massive bleached white ice wall a quarter-mile wide, begged me to jump. Intimidated, not having ever skied down anything so impossibly steep, I managed a hard swallow as my heart rate soared and the urge for bourbon tugged at my entire body.

Kevin slid past me then slowed, pointing to a takeoff area a hundred yards in front of us. "Huevos Grande is up there."

The top ridge of this mountain scared the hell out of me, but I chose to feed on the fear like a wolf devouring a juicy buffalo thigh. I wanted to face my fears, prove to myself I could make this happen. *Fear is weakness.*

Of course, it certainly helped knowing the faster I got to the bottom, the sooner I could throw back a couple shots of whiskey.

My legs and arms trembled, but I wanted to feel invincible, no fear. I needed to lean in to this challenge. Before I knew it, something inside me had made the decision to go. "Here goes nothing," I yelled, jumping onto the slope way steeper than the Huevos Grande.

Kevin yelled at me to stop, but I'd already committed.

My stomach soared up into my throat. Ice-cold wind slapped my frozen, numbing face. I struggled to stay in control, leaning back on the slope, trying to slow down.

In that moment, thoughts of Margaret, my brokerage business, and the mustached man falling to his death all took a back seat. My head cleared, focused only on getting down the extreme vertical face of this slope. I felt alive. More motivated than ever.

Fly-sized pellets of ice speckled my goggles, which I quickly swiped away as I flew down the hill faster than fifty miles an hour. Seconds into the run, I sailed into a thick cloud of swirling snow and fog.

The ground in front of me merged with the surrounding whiteness, killing my senses of depth and direction.

In a panic, I initiated a skid to stop. But at the beginning of the rapid turn, as several small saplings zoomed by, the snow beneath my skis turned into thick, ungroomed powder.

*Shit. Out of bounds.*

My turn to stop failed and my skis straightened out, pointing back down the hill. I was going too fast to make an emergency stop.

A massive, curmudgeon of a pine appeared out of the fog, coming directly into view in front of me. A transparent, ghost-like image of Blake Lynds hovered between me and the tree. His face was contorted with a fearful scream, exactly the same as it had been the moment he'd let go of my hand. But no sound, only a deadly silence.

*Time's up.*

I flew through the vision or apparition or whatever the hell the damned thing was, slamming headfirst into the angry tree. Intense pain shot through every bone in my body, but only for an instant, along with a loud, crunchy thud. Then everything went black.

# CHAPTER
# 4

An annoying beeping noise repeated over and over and over in never-ending darkness. I floated through unknown space. Time slowed. No. Time had stopped. There was no sense of up or down, no pain—only pure freedom and joy. Between the beeps, distant voices faded in and out. Strings of incomprehensible words floated all around.

". . . not sure, but . . . been out for three days now . . ."

*Beep. Beep. Beep.*

"His eyes are moving under his eyelids. Good sign," a voice said.

An instant before the joyful weightlessness disappeared, a rush of memories slammed into my brain. Bright memories appeared of a young, redheaded woman, floating in the darkness front of me. She smiled, tilted her head, and extended her arm toward me. *Those eyes. I know them.* They were as familiar as my own.

Rays of light glistened behind her in a pulsating glow. She drifted toward me. A comfortable, generous love flowed from deep inside her.

The woman faded backwards into the dark beyond, away from me, replaced by a grand treasure of gold coins buried deep in some swamp, then an angry man leaned over my body, pummeling fists into my chest and face as I lay on the moist earth, defending myself. Pain.

The sharp blade of an axe dug into my right shoulder.

Filled with unfounded betrayal mixed with pain, I yelled into the open space, "No! How could you?"

Blood spurted. The axe had severed my arm, now resting beside me on a bed of dried leaves.

All joy washed away, my heavy eyelids fought to stay closed. But with every ounce of strength available, I triumphed.

A blinding light appeared. Confused, I put my hand to my forehead. Stark white walls surrounded me, one with a windowpane and a broad oak door. I grabbed the sheet beneath me with balled fists.

A portly woman with kind eyes, a wrinkled face, and streaks of gray in her dark brown hair stood over me, staring. A name badge hung from her navy blue smock like the ones nurses wear.

"Shh. Shh. Shh. John, everything's fine," the woman said. "You were in a pretty bad skiing accident and have been in a coma for three days. Just relax."

John?

A stabbing pain shot through my neck into my brain. I rubbed my hand across my forehead and winced. Mouth dry as a distant desert, my voice came out deep and raspy as I said, "Thirsty. Water."

The nurse disappeared for a moment and returned with a cup of crushed ice. "I'm gonna get the doctor, but tell me how you're feeling."

"Muh head feels like it's trapped in the jaws of a gator." After performing a quick internal body survey, I moved my legs, back, arms. No paralysis. No broken bones. Whew. Normal. "Yee-up, only muh head."

"I believe the doctor has you on a morphine drip. Just press the little button right here if you feel any pain." She handed me a gray, plastic joystick with lights and a red button on top. "I'll be back in a minute. The doc will explain more."

Moments after pressing the funny little button, a warm sensation made its way up my neck and tempered my headache. *Yessiree. The magic of opioids.* I smiled, feeling even more drowsy.

The instant my eyes closed, the redheaded beauty from the earlier dream returned. Crystal clear, the vivid details of her face were as realistic as if she were sitting on the bed. Her striking blue eyes complimented a warm, loving smile and soft, smooth, fiery red hair. Charlie perfume awakened my tired blood. I spoke her name. "Tammy." My entire body tingled at the familiarity, so I repeated "Tammy" aloud several times.

Every bit of my being was drawn to Tammy by an unbreakable bond of love. But the specific relationship eluded me as I simultaneously sensed a complete lack of logic. In all honesty, I had never felt anything that strong in my life. In fact, the bond resonated with my true inner spirit as pure, unfiltered love. Overwhelming joy enveloped me and a loud laughter poured from deep within. I reached my arm out, trying to touch the mystery woman, but the moment I tried to touch her, she vanished, my hand merely swiping at air.

My shoulders fell back into the soft pillows.

Shuffling footsteps approached. "Mr. Bastian, how are you feeling?" A different woman's voice, deep but brimming with empathy.

Startled, I threw open my eyes and drew my arm back. Some gear switched in my head. The name Bastian sounded both familiar and unfamiliar.

"Bastian?"

The woman flipped open an aluminum chart case and squished her eyebrows together. "Yes. John Bastian." The crisp outer edge of her red lipstick, black-rimmed glasses and her hair pulled back in a low ponytail combined to give her a pleasant, studious look. As hard as I tried to look into her eyes, an odd, jittery feeling came over me when I did, so I averted her gaze, darting my eyes back and forth between her and every other damned object in the tiny room. She spoke again. "I'm Dr. Willis, lead neurologist here at the hospital."

"I don't know no Bastian fella."

She studied the papers inside the chart, now pushing her eyebrows into a "V". "Your driver's license says John Bastian, from Newport Beach."

Name sounded familiar, but nope, not me.

Still unable to maintain eye contact, I said, "Sorry, ma'am, but m'name's Jack Bachman from Baton Rouge, Louisiana. I'm a commercial pilot. Pleasure to make your acquaintance."

She wrinkled her nose. "Interesting. Well, let's talk about what happened. Can you hear me okay?"

Before I could respond, a young boy, maybe nine or ten years old, hustled into the room and stood next to the thin-framed doctor. Wearing a green patient gown, the kid had no hair, but amazing, piercing blue eyes, chapped lips, a tiny body covered with pale, paper-thin skin. He stared at me while wrapping an arm around the doctor's waist and resting his head on her white lab coat.

"Yep," I said.

"Very good. You're at Mammoth Hospital. In California. You say your name is Bachman and you're from Louisiana. Tell me what you remember." She scribbled some notes in her chart. "What you were doing recently?"

I thought for a moment. Nothing. No recent memories. My shoulder itched, but when I reached across my chest to scratch, an explosion of electricity shot through my lower back. Even though I was already on a hefty morphine drip.

I glanced back at the little boy and his eyes bored deep into my soul as he nodded and spoke in a sweet, angelic voice. "You know what to say."

I rubbed my chin and shot a short glance up at the doctor, but she continued staring down at me, waiting for a response to her questions and oblivious to what the boy had just said. Seemed odd for her to ignore a young patient that way, almost rude.

She leaned over me, checking my heartbeat and respiration, but the touch of her stethoscope felt more like the thump of a hammer, and I jerked my chest, rotating my upper torso away from her.

"Does that hurt?" she asked.

"Yes. But no," I replied, knowing I'd never had issues with my shoulder like this before. But maybe I had. Conflicting memories swirled in my mind.

She pulled back slightly, her silky black hair sprinkled with strands of white reflected light from above.

"It's just a stethoscope. I'm not trying to hurt you, but I need to check your vitals. Is this okay?"

I nodded, studying the boy further as she repeatedly touched the cold metal disc to my chest.

Tears formed in the boy's eyes. Exhausted with confusion, I finally said to the doctor, "Maybe ya didn't hear what the boy said cuz ya got the earbuds of the stethoscope jammed in your ears, but please tell me ya heard what he just said."

The doctor paused, drawing her head back as she extracted the stethoscope earpieces. "I'm sorry, who?"

"Him," I said, pointing at the young patient. "That boy."

The doctor stood erect, furrowed her brow, glanced down around the room, then shrugged.

"I'm sorry, ma'am, but somethin' don't feel right havin' him here in my room."

"Excuse me?"

I knew the boy's name and his relationship to the doctor. *I'm either losing my frickin' mind or that morphine be gettin' the best of me.*

The boy stepped forward and clung to her side. Again, I stared deep into his eyes, and in an instant, he'd communicated several thoughts to me without a sound. Like some form of human Wi-Fi.

"It wasn't just leukemia." The words came before I could stop them.

"Mr. Bastian, who are you—"

"No. I ain't gonna tell her nothin' more," I said to the boy, without breaking eye contact. "She'll think I'm plum nuts."

She stared down to her side, where the boy stood, and narrowed her eyes. "I'm sorry. Not going to tell me what?'

"Mark. Your son, he wants me to—"

The doctor put her hand up and cut me off. "Hold on." She surveyed my face, then leaned toward me again. "How in the world?"

The little boy scowled at me, then started sobbing. My eyes shot back and forth between the crying boy and the confused doctor. She looked as jumbled as I felt.

"Mark's tellin' me he gonna be alright. Boy say he's close to finishin' his mission. You lost him eighteen years ago. To leukemia. He spent a lot of time in this very room," I tugged on my ear. "He's standin' right there next to ya. Says he loves ya and . . ." I paused to contemplate what the little boy wanted me to say next, somehow absorbing his thoughts. "You sure?" He nodded. I looked back to the doc, who's eyes had started to water.

She took a step backwards, shaking her head, glaring down at me. "Mr. Bastian, I have no idea how—" She trailed off, then tilted her head.

"Says he's got something ya need to know. Somethin' 'bout his daddy."

The doctor let out a noticeable gasp. "I need to order some extra tests and, uh . . ."

The boy ran out of the room. The doctor paused, blinked several times, then pulled up a chair and sat next to me.

"I don't want to know anything about Mark, but hold on, you're speaking with what sounds to me like a Southern accent, and you think you are someone with a different name than what I show here on your chart."

My voice sounded normal to me. "Not sure what kinda game you're playin' here, ma'am, but I can tell ya, I'm married to . . ." I stared up at the T-bar ceiling tiles. *No, wait, I'm divorced.*

She flinched slightly, rubbing her throat.

I continued. "Boy was standin' right here next to ya. Just as sure as you sittin' next to me."

"Mr. Bastian, there was never any boy in here. Not my son. Not anyone. Only you and me." She blinked rapidly. "This entire time."

Dizziness overpowered me. I closed my eyes. Tammy reappeared, along with the treasure of gold coins, the bloody axe, and details about some swamp, or bayou . . . something.

The doctor tapped my cheek, which felt more like a punch in the face, snapping me back awake. "Like I said, your driver's license says your name is John Bastian and you're from Newport Beach, California."

*That can't be right. Is it? Wait.* I closed my eyes again.

A finger-snapping sound popped in front of my face, forcing my eyes open. With an intense gaze, the doctor bit her inner cheek. "Stay with me. Don't fall asleep. I need you awake."

"The treasure." I held out my hand, making the little sign with my thumb and index finger. "I was this close to findin' it." In my head I pictured a chest filled with gold coins. Thousands of gorgeous, gleaming metal discs. "I know exactly where to find the treasure. In the middle of an island in a Louisiana river. I gotta find it. Gotta get to Tammy before he does. Ya gotta help get me outta here."

As I tried to sit, my relationship with the redheaded woman came into focus. *Tammy's my wife.*

I knew vivid facts. Entrenched in my soul. Someone had murdered me, but I had no idea how. *Wait. I'm still alive.*

I had never known any information to be so real, so absolute and true.

Ever.

Like someone transplanted memories straight into my brain.

The doctor gently put her palm to my chest. "I'm sorry, John. Please lay back down and help me understand what you're talking about."

"My wife," I said, leaning forward and double-fisting the lapel of her white lab coat. "Need ya to tell me she's okay." I tried again to get up from the bed, but this time, the doctor put both hands on my chest and forced me back down, which felt like a sledgehammer thud to my chest.

"You're not going anywhere."

Various images swirled in my head. I released my grip on her, then touched my hands to my mouth and face.

"Again, your driver's license and medical insurance card indicate you are John Bastian," she said. "According to medical records, you've been divorced from a Margaret Bastian, also of Newport Beach, California, now for three years."

I rubbed my eyebrows and bit my lip as a different set of facts, a different persona, different history, downloaded into my head. Another mental gear shift. "Yes, of course. John Bastian. I'm a commercial real estate broker. I live in Newport Beach." I remembered images of the crazed gondola man, Blake Lynds, falling to his death. My stomach turned over. "I'm . . . wait . . . sorry."

The frequency of the beeping noise on the heart monitor increased.

The doctor stood, crossed her arms and frowned. "Now your Southern accent seems to have disappeared. You sound like any other typical Californian."

"Not sure I understand what you mean," I said. "I sound the same."

"A moment ago you had a Southern accent and were behaving borderline manic. Now all that appears to be gone."

I tilted my head.

"Take a deep breath, Mr. Bastian. I need you to rest for now."

As hard as I tried to stay conscious, my eyelids closed. But an unmistakable desire to love that beautiful, sweet, caring redheaded woman remained, pulling me back under into the dreamworld. A warm energy filled my heart, focusing one hundred percent of my attention on her, needing to be with her at any cost. Nothing else mattered. The sweetest name rolled off my tongue one final time— "Tammy."

# CHAPTER 5

**Jack Bachman**
*November 8, 1975*

I brought my push lawnmower to a stop, leaned down, flipped the "off" switch and used the back of my hand to wipe a cup of sweat from my forehead as the pitter-patter of the Briggs & Stratton engine wound down. My lungs pumped in and out as I stood in the quaint front yard of our southern Baton Rouge home, sunshine beating down everywhere. A street sign stood proud and tall in the corner of our lot: Ferndale Drive and Orchid Place.

"Anybody thirsty out here?" my wife asked.

The woman gave me pause as she held the serving tray supporting two glasses of iced tea and a refill pitcher. Her red hair flowed gently in a subtle breeze, her loving smile gleaming out to the entire neighborhood of post-World War II suburban houses.

She carefully set the tray on a round metal table sitting on the front porch. I walked toward her, across the trimmed bluegrass toward our red-bricked home, absorbing the pleasant scent of the freshly cut lawn mixed with blooming gardenias planted in a row beneath the white frames of the front windows.

The latest Doobie Brothers song floated out through the open front door from the living room,

"...old black water...keep on rollin'...Mississippi moon..."

We sat, then I drained half my drink in three gulps.

"Jesus, Jack." She tapped my hand. "You're an insane, primitive hominoid maniac," she said, working her soft, smooth hair around the top of her ear. "You know that, right?"

I set the glass on the table top with a clank and let out a long sigh.

Throughout my life to that point, I'd made every effort possible to avoid any sort of unwanted touching, especially from strangers. A strong scream would erupt deep inside me any time a friend, coworker, or random person at the grocery story bumped into me. Making eye contact during social interactions felt completely unnatural and during high school I'd been called everything from "freak" to "loser" to "queer" because of my atypical behavior whenever someone touched me. The military doc who interviewed me prior to the Vietnam war said I might have schizophrenia, but decided against it since he also discovered my intelligence test scores were off the charts. Apparently, schizos and brainiacs are mutually exclusive.

Nonetheless, I'd struggled my entire life to contain the scream, trying to conform to societal norms.

But not with Tammy. Her touching had the opposite effect and every moment away from her was like a booming stereo without speakers.

I gazed down at her hand on top of mine, enjoying every second, before looking up to her ravishing beauty. "I can't be that crazy. Or primitive. I married you," I said with a wink before sucking down the other half of my iced tea. She poured me another glassful and I admired her wedding ring she'd worn every day. Two small emeralds snuggled up against both sides of a oversized diamond.

"You're too good to me, baby," I said, staring deep into her eyes, overcoming yet another challenge for me with everyone except Tammy.

"I know," she said, leaning in toward me, nuzzling her nose against mine. "But you've got a lot of potential and are lucky I'm so patient."

We both chuckled and sat back.

A wave of appreciation, love, and admiration washed over me. Goosebumps appeared on my forearms, forcing the tiny forest of blond hairs to stand upright.

Our black and white tuxedo cat pushed its way through the front screen door, wandered over, and jumped onto my lap before climbing onto my shoulders and plopping down like a lazy rag doll.

"I love how she loves lying on your shoulders."

The smooth, relaxing sound of the kitty's purring engine tickled my ear as she licked my earlobe. A small, instinctive laugh erupted from my belly and I moved my head away, petting her slowly.

I surveyed the neighborhood, absorbing the warmth of the day before letting my eyes land directly back onto my wife.

"Uh-oh," she said. "You have that look."

I paused, leaned in and cupped my hands in hers. The cat jumped down onto the grass below.

"I think we should have a baby. You'd be the best mama ever."

# CHAPTER 6

### John Bastian

*November 13, 2016*
*Five days after the crash in Mammoth*

**M**y legs trembled as I rocked back and forth in a wicker chair. From my Newport Beach patio, I enjoyed watching the setting sun reflect off the various harbor yachts and multi-million-dollar homes scattered along the perimeter. On a typical day, the comfort and familiarity of sunshine and this place helped me to relax. Today, however, two days after waking up from a three-day coma and twelve hours after Dr. Willis had told me the battery of tests showed absolutely nothing wrong and the pain in my head and chest had disappeared, I chalked up the experience with the little boy, Mark, as a drug-induced hallucination.

Morphine has been known to do that.

And Dr. Willis had not asked about her son or how I'd known his name.

*Lucky guess, perhaps.*

My thoughts turned back to Blake Lynds, the man who fell to his death on the gondola. I craved a hefty swig of bourbon—or rum, or vodka, anything—knowing it would help erase the grisly images splashing in my mind's eye over and over. Coupling those graphic images with the primal urge to be with the woman in my dreams caused my brain to short-circuit. She was so close, so real, yet I had absolutely no idea where to find her.

Or when.

But Dr. Willis had given me strict instructions: no alcohol for at least a week.

I'd had suicidal thoughts many times since the divorce. Now that path seemed like a crappy option. Killing yourself is what failures do. I wasn't a failure. Or was I? I wanted to live. But the enormity of pain throbbing deep inside my heart made it hard to catch my breath. I seriously needed a drink to calm my nerves and process what was happening.

My doorbell rang.

I poured a double shot of my favorite Bayou Rum over two ice cubes, gritting my teeth. My hands shook as I raised the clear glass to my lips and downed half. Not a single living soul on this planet would want to be with me in this current life. I was a miserable failure. No wife. Failed businesses. No legacy. No purpose, really. But thoughts of Tammy sparked a renewed sense of being, motivating me to change all that. But how could a woman I'd never met could help me be a better person? To live a more fulfilling life?

*I'm definitely losing my mind.*

Again, the doorbell rang.

I gulped down the rest of the rum.

"I know you're in there, man. Lemme in," Kevin said before a pause, then more banging. "John, lemme in, man."

"Coming," I shouted.

Additional strength filled me before I shuffled over to the entryway and yanked open the door. There, my best buddy stood, taking in my appearance. He tried to hide a cringe after seeing me with baggy flannels, an old San Diego Chargers t-shirt with dried paint flecks splattered across it, and a grimy Newport Beach baseball cap hiding several days of greasy hair.

He tilted his head, gave me a muted smile that hid his normally shiny white teeth, then put his arms out toward me. We embraced, a sense of calm fell over me, and I invited him in.

We headed out onto my back patio. He noticed the rum, but he knew me. He sensed my pain. Empathy and compassion were ingrained in my old friend, hardwired. For a moment, I assumed he'd get angry, but he stayed calm, staring dead straight into my eyes.

"Drinking your ass into oblivion ain't the solution, man." He scooped up the bottle. "At least, not all by yourself."

He jogged into my kitchen, snatched a second glass, hustled back outside, poured himself a double shot of rum, then filled my glass.

"I'm here for you, man. Tell me how you feeling." He sat in the chair opposite me and scanned the harbor. "Get some of that shit off your chest."

We sipped our rum while gazing out at the harbor, but each time I tried looking Kevin in the eyes, a new, odd sense of restlessness surged inside me, forcing me to look elsewhere.

"I'm telling you, something happened up at that Mammoth hospital," I said. "Can't describe the feeling. It's like nothing I've ever experienced before. I've changed. But can't explain how, exactly."

Kevin took a sip. "The doc told me your ass almost died, dog. Lotta people get in accidents like that and they have crazy out-of-body experiences."

"Maybe. I'm pretty sure you have to actually die to have a near death experience. But probably something else because I didn't die, man. I had some kind of . . . vision."

"There we go. Now tell me about that."

A white yacht with navy blue striping sailed past in front of us, with an elderly tanned man in Speedos casually chatting to several bikini-clad beauties lying around the deck. Normally, out of curiosity I would've grabbed my binoculars to take a better look, but not today. I could only focus on the new memories—I called them that, but they were more like images from a recent, vivid, traumatic experience—of Tammy, an island swamp, a treasure, and an angry, faceless man whacking away at my shoulder with an axe. I shivered. I'd always hated axes. The memories continued playing in my head like a broken, fast-forward slide show.

"The memories, or whatever, are all mixed up. Like a huge knot on a fishing reel. I can't make sense of any of them."

I explained the dreams I'd had about Tammy, how I had this unshakable sense I was married to her, the same way I used to be married to Margaret. And I'd loved Margaret, but the love I was feeling for Tammy was much stronger. I shook my head, staring down into my glass.

"Memories from a dream, maybe," Kevin said.

"No, man. Real memories."

"You need to go tell your shrink all this shit you been dealin' with."

I nodded. "Got an appointment with her *mañana*. Enough about me. Let's talk about you. I want to hear all about this TV deal your agent hooked you up with."

Various lights around the harbor flickered in the sunset. A yellow speedboat zipped past.

"Wasn't sure you'd remember I told you or not. We sealed the deal right before Mammoth."

I raised my glass and toasted with a clank, then set my gaze back onto the idle, parked boats floating gently in the harbor.

Kevin continued, "As long as I can remember, I've wanted to be a star. A comedian. Big time. Y'know what I'm sayin'?"

I raised my eyebrows and chuckled. "No shit."

"I was fifteen when me and my mom moved out here from Louisiana. She left a pretty decent job as mayor for the City of Hammond."

"You never really talked much about your life before coming here to California." I shook my head. "Never heard of Hammond."

"I guess I never really wanted people to know I was from there. I wanted to be Californian. Born and raised, but hell, I ain't getting any younger and the more I pass through life, the less I care about all that."

"Feels good to hear you open up." After finishing up with everything offered by the Groundlings Improv and Comedian School in L.A. back in the 90's, Kevin had been working 24/7 to make his dream come true.

"Don't you be gettin' all mushy on me, man. Hammond is like, forty-five minutes east of Baton Rouge. Beautiful place." He waved his arm. "Along I-12, there's Denham Springs, followed by a bunch of trees and marsh land and bayous, then Hammond. Mom grew up there. Got friends all over the state. But she ain't never goin' back. Loves California and the retired life too much."

"A bayou's like a swamp or something, right?"

"Google it. But yeah."

My phone pinged. A text message from my mom asking how I'm doing and if she can come visit to hear about the details of the skiing accident.

"Anyway, now I got my shot. My agent set me up with—check this out—my homeboy Jimmy Fallon on the Late Show."

"No way."

He nodded, clinking our glasses together again. I texted back to my mom I'm doing fine, not to worry, and I'd try to come visit her over the weekend.

Kevin told me he'd waited to tell my parents about the coma. I'd already woken up before he'd told them. I'd asked him to let me tell them the details, not wanting to add stress to their marriage already on thin ice. Worrying about their son getting into a skiing accident would only add fuel to their troubles.

"Headin' to New York next month. Got you a front-row seat for the gig. It's a four-minute stand-up routine and a short interview. Gonna be dope, I can feel it." He smiled his big white toothy grin, which contrasted appropriately with his dark chocolate skin. Every time he smiled, I had to do the same, even in my current state. His laugh and sense of humor were contagious.

"Right on, man. Thanks. Sounds like fun. I'm super happy for you and glad you came over. Feeling a little better already."

We paused and continued enjoying the harbor view for a moment before he continued. Sparks of hope and joy ignited inside me.

"Now let's talk more about this redheaded chick. What was her name again? Tara? Tina?"

I took a sip of rum. "Tammy."

"Right. I still say it was all a super-cool, super-intense dream."

"Dude. I've had intense dreams before. We all have. This was different."

"Hmmm." He polished off the remainder of his rum and poured another shot onto his ice.

I closed my eyes and thought about the possibility of humans having different places in our brains for different types of memories. Normally, we effortlessly distinguished between dream memories and ones that formed based on real-life events. My memories of Tammy, the treasure, and of dying were stuck deep in the reality side, although logically the memories made absolutely no sense. In my world, there was no Tammy. No treasure. No murder, axe, blood, or a mystery bayou. Only frustration.

"Seriously. I'm thirty-nine and have spent the last three years trying to get over my ex-wife. For the first time since I can remember, I don't feel sad. I feel great, actually. Just confused as hell. I thought maybe I was doomed to be one of those perpetual bachelors, but for some inexplicable reason I'm feeling hopeful right now. Not sure why, though."

"I ain't married. I'm happy."

"Yeah, but you're . . . you."

"Hell yeah, I am."

We both laughed and toasted again.

"I might be losing my mind."

"Dude. You overthinkin' everything again. Always do. Chill for now, enjoy the view we got here, and spill your guts out with your therapist."

One final golden glimmer reflected off a window in the distance before the sun went to bed beneath the horizon.

"I'm telling you, the treasure is real."

"They ain't no treasure."

Two seagulls flew overhead before landing on the edge of my roof overhang.

"What do you think having all that money would be like? Not having to worry about making a living."

Kevin choked a tad on his bourbon, coughing, laughing. Catching his breath, said, "Sweet, fo' sure. I'd definitely blow every penny gettin' all freaky-deaky." He set his feet atop the footstool, crossed one over the other while taking another sip.

"You can be so stereotypical sometimes."

"Just messin' with you, man."

"Multiple partners and crazy sex would get old."

"Probably right. Eventually," Kevin said.

I stood, sauntered to the edge of the porch, and leaned my elbows onto the railing when an epiphany hit me.

"I know exactly what I'd do with a billion dollars. And it would have nothing to do with sex. I'd start a foundation. Philanthropy. Help close the gap between the haves and the have-nots. Give most of it away to people who need it the most, like kids and people with special needs."

# CHAPTER 7

**Scott Jones**
*November 15, 2016*

From its sky arc peak high above, the sun shone down onto Scott Jones, treasure hunter, as he waded through a thin layer of water, mud, cypress trees, and various green and brown waist-high bushes. Deep in these thick swamps outside Baton Rouge, the stench of rotten eggs and composting grass—enough to wake a dead man—bored into him.

Out of nowhere, a six-foot long, hundred-and-forty-pound alligator snapped at Scott's left foot, forcing his attention away from the smell of death. The alligator's potential lunch jumped back, pissed for allowing himself to become distracted, even though the gator missed by several inches. The bayou threat was real: lose focus for a second and risk being eaten alive by primitive Louisiana wildlife.

He remembered the wise words of his LSU archaeology professor back in the 70's: *in a bayou, your life depends on each and every step, so make 'em count.* He alternated focus between the surrounding swamp, immediate landscape, and the carefully preserved, antique, one square foot cotton map in his hand.

A single sign of man's existence presented itself in the form of a forty-year-old elevated freeway four miles to the south, shuttling vehicles over the swamps.

Nobody else would ever find this godforsaken place. Now was Scott's time to shine. His turn to find glory. For good luck, Scott rubbed the gold nugget key chain nestled at the bottom of his jeans pocket. The treasure had to be close. With each wading step, the soft, spongy bottom gave way. The same alligator appeared along with a second, smaller one, both dozens of yards to his right. After deeming both beasts non-threatening, Scott continued his northerly trek through the bayou.

Three loud bangs echoed off a nearby tree cluster and across the water's surface. He turned, crouching on instinct. An airboat headed straight at him with two men aboard. The man at the steering wheel aimed a pistol and fired again. Another three shots echoed all around, one round ricocheting off a nearby, half-submerged boulder. Pulse racing, Scott scurried behind a tree, hoping to God another gator wasn't there waiting to bite off his leg. He whipped out his trusty Springfield .45 from its holster and pointed the weapon skyward, near his ear, waiting for the right moment to shift from defense to offense. The airboat engine and spinning fan roared louder and louder as it approached, then went idle.

"I know you're out there, Scott. No use fighting us anymore," said David Brickheimer, Scott's former partner and now treasure-hunting adversary. "You stole something valuable from me. Give it back and I might let you live."

The idling sound of the airboat engine filled the swamp as a blue heron coasted overhead on a cushion of air.

Continuing to hide amidst the reeds, Scott removed his brown leather fedora, wiped his bald head and rotated his regrettably short, stocky frame, stalling, waiting for his young partner, Mike Bixleton—the other passenger on David's boat—to make a mistake. Scott's wrinkled hands still held enough strength to fight, but instead, he folded the map and stuffed the crinkled cloth into his shirt pocket. Fist fighting was for the *youngins*.

With absolutely no intention of letting David taunt him, Scott had come too far to let some amateur hack get any portion of the awaiting prize. Plus, he flat-out hated David. And the guy's breath smelled like a sewer rat had died from an overdose of chewing tobacco. David's angry temperament and entitled attitude disgusted Scott. How the two men had once been willing partners remained a mystery.

But the double-cross would be over soon.

Scott had a plan.

Already set in motion.

Two more shots, laughter, then a splash. A wave of relief swept over Scott, who stuffed his pistol underneath his belt buckle and rolled out from behind his tree shield.

Three feet away from the boat, a body floated face down in the brown water. Tiny circular waves rippled outward.

Mike, with his curly black head of hair and dyed-black goatee, sat in the driver's seat behind the tiny boat's windshield, revving the engine as he put his arm up, smiled to Scott, and waved him over. The aluminum craft surged toward the ten-foot diameter "island" Scott now stood on and Mike ran the front of the boat aground onto the sand.

Scott adjusted his jeans and stepped to Mike, noting the snake-like eyes before the two men embraced.

"That cocksucker's finally out of our shit. Now we can find this damned thing ourselves," Scott said. "Jesus, I just realized I've been hunting this goddamned treasure now for all of forty years." He looked at the ground, rubbed his shiny head, and threw on his brown fedora. "Never been closer. I can taste it."

# CHAPTER 8

**John Bastian**
*November 15, 2016*

Stabbing pain surged throughout my body as the man's axe cut deep into my right shoulder—tearing through cartilage, bone, tendons and muscle—all ripped apart by the sharp steel blade. Blood spurted everywhere. Next to me on the soggy, leaf-strewn ground, my lifeless, severed arm lay inches from my body. The image of the amputated arm etched itself into my soul. A forest full of ancient eucalyptus trees faded into oblivion as my brain strained for oxygen and I passed out.

After awaking from the night terror at 2:03 am—now exactly one week after my unfortunate meeting with that Mammoth tree—I grabbed hold of my upper right arm and squeezed.

Still attached.

A throbbing sensation pulsated deep inside my shoulder and when I tried to wiggle my arm, the entire length was partially numb, paralyzed for at least five minutes before my fingers started to tingle back to life. I lifted my limb up toward the ceiling and swirled it around like a windmill fan. The thought of having a paralyzed arm scared the crap out of me more than the damned dream.

I had experienced nightmares before and assumed everyone had. If a person was confronted in a dream by a psychopathic pirate, an abusive spouse, a curious or lost ghost with unfulfilled earthly business, a hungry alligator, or whatever, the entity would seem real to us at the time. Our fight-or-flight mechanism would kick in and we'd feel scared, but wake up and realize the experience was only a dream. A trick of the mind. Normal people would calm themselves down and cope by getting out of bed, hitting the bar and guzzling down a stiff drink.

Well, at least, that's what I would do.

But that night I experienced a terror so intense with a level of realism tenfold over any nightmare I'd ever had, it reminded me of those new virtual reality machines, with 3D video and seven-channel surround sound.

Following my own advice, I poured myself a bourbon and, sipping the drink, wandered into my living room. The tip of the moon peeked up over a distant hilltop out beyond the Newport harbor.

I closed my eyes, returning to the vivid image of Tammy, which only served to pique my motivation about finding answers. Wanting nothing except to be with her, an abundant energy flowed through me, the source of which both scared and excited the hell out of me. An attraction to her radiated from within, spreading throughout my entire being for this Tammy person. Except, from a purely logical standpoint, she was nonexistent, created only from a morphine-induced stupor, or, more likely, a broken set of neurons damaged when my head rammed into that damned tree.

I poured and downed two more bourbons, or three, or four, then fell back into a deep, dreamless sleep less than an hour later.

# CHAPTER 9

## Scott Jones
*November 15, 2016*

Scott threw his pistol down onto the sand and wiped his brow, scanning the bayou for landmarks and comparing them to the crumpled map in his hands.

"Our boat'll handle the weight of the treasure," Scott said. "I'm guessing five hundred pounds of pure gold."

Mike shook his head, staring at Scott with pointed eyebrows. "Hate to break it to you, boss, but this ain't the place. That map right there is just another fake. I got David to admit he'd set this whole thing up as a trap. He wanted to get you out of the way."

"No. No. No!" Scott yelled into the foliage, kicking a gallon of slurried sand into the air.

"Sorry, boss." Mike patted him on the shoulder.

"Dammit," Scott said, out of breath. "When you showed up, I figured we'd be heading back today with the loot. But no, we're back at square one. Great."

"Not exactly," Mike said, also scanning the bayou, probably for potential threats. "We still got the witch."

Police sirens crackled throughout the swamp, derailing Scott's train of thought and snapping both men to attention.

"We ain't gonna make it if we run," Mike said.

In less than a second, Scott scanned the sand, weeds, and trees, searching for a hiding place. "Ditch our boat in these bushes and reeds and stay put. I'll take care of the body."

Step by step, Scott waded deeper into the waist-high water, toward the floating corpse of his former rival.

Two white Air Ranger police airboats, each with blue stripes inches above the water line, crept toward Scott and Mike. Local sheriffs. A flood of rotating blue lights painted the midday shadows a ghostly gray, pulsing in tandem with his racing heart. Two boyish, armed officers, probably relatives of the sheriff, stood straight in each boat. One of the dumbshits scanned the area through binoculars.

But stupid or not, they were the law.

Now at David's body floating in a pool of crimson-colored water, Scott grabbed a hold of blood-soaked shirt and pulled the corpse under. Air from David's lungs bubbled up, splashing deathly water droplets onto Scott's face.

With only Scott's head peeking above the surface, he evaluated the risk of a brown recluse spider bite or attack from one of the other swamp creatures against the decades he'd spend in jail if the police caught him trying to dispose of a dead body. Alligators could smell blood from several meters away. It was only a matter of time before the two gators from earlier would return.

*Don't look at his face.*

Scott imagined David's pale face, forever frozen with shock and betrayal.

Underwater, Scott extracted a short rope from inside his knapsack, tied a loop around David's waist and felt with his foot along the soft bayou bottom for a well-anchored tree root. Nothing but old, dead, rotting foliage.

The boats inched closer. One of the officers turned toward Scott and looked his way but only for an instant before searching in a different direction.

Scott kicked a thick root, then gave it a solid yank with his hand to confirm an acceptable attachment to the ground. After drawing in a deep breath, Scott submerged his head and worked to slide the rope beneath the root, anchoring it to the body. He rose slowly, peeking his head just above the water surface to make sure they hadn't spotted him, then took another deep breath, went under again, and yanked up on the rope, careful to keep David's body at sufficient depth to avoid visibility from the surface. With David's body fully submerged, tiny critters would chew, pick and gnaw at the corpse. Over the next few months, the entire thing—including the traitor's bones—would be consumed into oblivion.

Out of instinct, Scott made the mistake of looking down through the water to David. The face staring back at him, with dilated eyes and a gaping mouth, begged to deny the betrayal. Black burn marks surrounded the bullet hole in David's left temple. Raw cheekbone and jaw muscle protruded from the right side of his face, dangling where the bullet had exited.

Scott's stomach lurched as he pinched his eyes closed, inhaled a double lung-full of the stagnant air and resubmerged. Holding his breath underwater, Scott held onto the rope tying David's body to the tree root and waited. Both police boats floated directly toward him from fifteen yards away. For sure, they'd see him if he came up for air. Eyes burning from god-knows-what waterborne organisms picking away at his raw, exposed eyeballs, he thought of the consequences if they caught him red-handed holding Scott's body. No way he could talk his way out. He'd spend the rest of his days rotting in some godforsaken jail.

Thirty feet away. Twenty feet.

The air inside him drew thin, lungs begging for more.

Ten feet.

Scott swallowed as muffled voices filtered through the water. Seconds passed, but felt like hours. Scott squinted his burning eyes and exhaled half his air to keep his breathing reflex calm. Bubbles floated upwards, sliding along his facial skin. But he needed oxygen. The swooshing sounds of both boats swept right above him and stopped. More voices. His field of vision started to close, blackening from the perimeter, which meant—based on previous experiences holding his breath—he was now seconds away from passing out. He fully opened his eyes. David's face stared back at him, inches away.

Scott craned his head upward and squinted. He fantasized about the treasure and the immense joy he'd feel, finally getting the life he deserved. But at that moment, everything he'd dreamed of slowly slipped away. He remembered all the mistakes he'd made along his four-decade treasure hunting journey. The excitement, the thrills, the failures. Everything led up to this point. He needed to stay put, but the instinct to breathe proved too powerful to ignore any longer.

Engines roared, pulsating waves of energy through the swamp surface. Scott pushed down on the soggy soil and shot himself up out of the water, sucking in one massive breath of swampy air. The spinning world around him slowly came to a stop, coming back into focus, blackness receding and clarity returning. Both police boats headed north. Away from the crime scene.

Scott spit into the water several times as he waited. After a minute, he finished knotting the rope to the root, waded his way back onto the sandy island, then crouched among the curtain of reeds. He retrieved the hidden pistol and stuffed the weapon into the rear waistband of his jeans.

"I say we stay hidden here for another twenty minutes, then split," Mike said.

Scott coughed. "Yeah. I got that bastard David tied down real good, so even if they stop us, we can play dumb. Get your fishing gear out in case they come by for another pass."

"To hell with this forgery. We need to get the real map from that old crazy witch, then come back tonight and get us some treasure."

"Agreed, but we'll come back when we're sure we won't get caught. The treasure has been out here for 150 years. Damned thing ain't gonna disappear anytime soon."

"You're the boss."

Scott liked the sound of that. He'd set up the backstabbing effort between Mike and David several months ago after Mike had approached him and negotiated a piece of the action. Scott had been wanting to remove David from the equation for years, but never had the balls to murder the guy.

Scott and Mike climbed back into their boat and set up their fishing gear while sitting and waiting for several minutes. The sound of the police boat engines continued to wane, ultimately disappearing. Scott pushed the throttle button full forward, thrusting their boat onto the water and speeding them south to return to the dock two miles away.

But at a half mile from shore, police sirens blared. Again. Scott turned around. Both police boats tailed them from fifty yards back.

"Play it cool," Scott said, pulling the throttle back to idle. "I'll do all the talking."

The sun disappeared behind a dark patch of gray rain clouds, casting a shadow on the bayou.

The police boats crept up on either side of Scott's fishing boat, with the two dummies tying on with a half-inch nylon boating rope. The tallest of the four lawmen, sporting a thick salt and pepper mustache, chunky cheeks, and wearing a black baseball cap with yellow letters, hammered his foot onto Scott's boat and spit a spoonful of brown tobacco yuck into the water, then wiped his chin with his forearm. The buttons on his black shirt seemed ready to pop open from the beer gut pushing out from inside.

"Don't s'ppose you boys'd mind tellin' us where y'all headed in such a hurry . . . oh hey, Scott, didn't realize it was you," the sheriff said, his nicotine-stained hands on his hips.

Scott gave a playful grin. "Howdy, Sheriff Cook. Nice to see y'all. We had 'nough for the day. Been out since 'fore sunrise. Ain't catchin' nothin.'"

"You pretty wet," the sheriff said. "Gotta be mighty cold in that black t-shirt. Y'ain't supposed to be that wet when you's out fishing in these parts."

Scott chuckled. "Had a big one on the line. Stood and lost my balance. Fell in the damned water. Embarrassin', really, but another reason we's headin' in."

The sheriff glanced at their fishing gear, head bobbing up and down, wheels turning inside about something. "Fishin'. That's good. Y'all hear any gunshots back where ya came from?"

"Yessir, sure did. Whole bunch of 'em," Scott replied, looking at Mike, who, with his arms crossed, nodded in agreement.

"One of the reasons we figured we'd split and head back in," Mike said.

"Don't s'ppose y'all found, er um, caught anything else out in these parts," the sheriff said, looking straight into Scott's eyes.

Scott shook his head slowly. "Not one bite, Sheriff. Bad bait."

The sheriff turned toward his three deputies, then scanned the swamp. "Whatch'all usin'?" he asked, tilting his baseball cap back.

Scott glanced to Mike, then back to the Sheriff. "Chicken livers and chopped chad," Scott said. "Tryin' to catch us some catfish, but I guess they ain't hungry today." He shrugged his shoulders, said, "Somethin'," then turned around and bent over to show the sheriff their bait. When he did, the butt end of the Springfield poked out from behind Scott's shirt.

"Gun!" a deputy yelled. The three young deputies took action, assuming the typical firing position, wide stance, pointing their guns at Scott, who stood upright and put his hands in the air.

The sheriff put his hand on top of the pistol nearest him. "Goddammit, boys," he said, shoving the gun downward. "What I tell you 'bout gettin' all trigger happy? Put them guns away 'fore I shoot y'all myself."

Scott and Mike froze as the three deputies holstered their weapons. The sheriff winked at Scott and boarded their craft. He reached low behind Scott and retrieved the weapon. "Forty-five. Tell me just what the hell you doin' with this," the sheriff said, sounding more like he was complaining than using a voice of authority.

"Last I checked we got ourselves a second amendment right. Matter fact, got my permit here in my wallet, sheriff," Scott said with a smile. "Always take my pistol out with me when I'm fishing. Ain't no law 'gainst that. Never know who—or what—you gonna run into out here."

The sheriff whirled his hand, motioning Scott to retrieve the permit. As slow as a turtle, Scott slid his wet wallet out from his pants, found the permit, and handed the laminated cardstock to the officer.

"Getting cold, officer."

The sheriff gave it a quick glance—not enough time to read anything—handed the permit back to Scott, and stepped back onto his own boat. "We didn't hear no forty-five. Reports were of a thirty-eight, or maybe a nine-millimeter. Plus your gun ain't been fired in a while, looks like."

"Hope y'all figure out what the hell happened," Scott said.

"You and your buddy watch out for gators," the sheriff said. "Had two deaths last week. Grisly. I lived here in these parts my whole life, ain't never liked them gators much. Give me the creeps." He glanced to his deputies, then back at Scott. "Y'all come across anything else s'picious, give us a call." The sheriff handed his business card to Scott.

Scott and Mike nodded, said goodbye to the officers, throttled their engine back up and continued toward the shore.

"We go back when I say," Scott said. "David's boyfriend will probably file a police report tonight about his missin' companion. The police'll figure out the shots they heard today are related and they'll comb over this whole area next week like ants on a honey-covered hill." His shirt was starting to dry out while he navigated through the final few tree-lined waterways near the shore.

They pulled in to the concrete docking ramp and loaded their boat onto Mike's trailer.

Scott walked toward his brand new, black 5-series Mercedes, hopped in, and sped toward town. Mike followed in his dark gray F-250, with the boat in tow, to his home near Louisiana State University, LSU. As he drove along a country road, the orangey-pink sun sank behind a small forest of eucalyptus trees. Scott slid his hand in his pocket, rubbed his lucky gold nugget and smiled. *People are gonna treat me different, especially Tammy, once I'm a billionaire.*

Once at Mike's house, the two men unloaded the boat in Mike's driveway.

Scott's phone rang.

"Ms. Petitpont, I—" Scott said. He paused, listened, and pressed his lips tight. "Okay, fine. Call me when you get into port." He ended the call.

"Sounds like that crazy old witch is coming into town," Mike said.

Scott rubbed his lucky gold nugget again.

"We're goin' fishin' for treasure."

# CHAPTER 10

**John Bastian**
*November 16, 2016*

I slept until eight in the morning, stumbled out of bed and dressed for my nine o'clock therapy appointment with Dr. Kelly Carpenter. The drive to her office on the other side of Newport Harbor took two minutes as sunshine peeked through scattered rain clouds. I parked, wandered into the waiting room, and plopped down in a hefty, soft brown leather recliner.

At 9:05, echoes of her footsteps from the hallway preceded her entrance and seconds later she appeared, gleaming full of positive energy. Her professional attire radiated an overall calm demeanor as big, inviting eyes above raised, prominent cheekbones that alleviated my anxiety. I stood and followed Kelly into her room, watching her long, natural brown hair swing with every step. As I'd done many times over the last two years—starting a year after my divorce—I sat on the well-worn, beige couch and crossed my legs and arms. A box of tissues sat on the end table, within arms' reach.

Repeatedly, I balled my hands into fists as I inhaled long and deep, trying to rid my body of the excess tension.

Sitting across from me in the center of a three-seat couch, she pressed her lips together, forcing her face into a slight grimace. Somehow I managed to make eye contact—more challenging lately and occurring more frequently—as she set down her iPad and drilled a curious gaze my way. "You're different today, John. Tell me about that," she said with a reassuring smile.

Somehow, she felt my pain. The memories. Her training and three decades of experience had likely enabled a magically heightened sense of empathy.

When we had first started sessions, she referred to herself as an "intuitive feeler" or "idealist," one of the four primary temperament types in some psychology model. Since then, I'd worked hard to push my depression away and gain back the mental strength I had back in my twenties, before I entered into the ten-year marriage to Margaret. Throughout my teenage and adult years, I'd been socialized—movies, commercials, magazine ads . . . hell, any bar in America—to believe real men drowned out their sorrows with alcohol. But she'd helped me realize—partially—the futility of numbing my existence with beer and whiskey. Talking about my pain, facing it head on, would do a much better job getting those negative emotions out. Overall, I had been getting better lately, but I obviously still had further to go.

Especially after the skiing accident.

Tears filled my eyes. I broke down again, sobbing like a pathetic baby, before any words could make their way out. I grabbed some tissues and blew my nose.

"It's okay, John. I'm right here. Crying is good."

But I only heard my dad's voice. *Real men don't cry, son.*

I tried focusing on her voice, though, which had a soothing effect, further reducing my anxiety.

After nodding, I found myself rocking slightly left and right, continuing the loser sobbing for a moment before taking in a slow, deep breath, and finding my ground again. "I'm just so confused. I feel like I'm never going to find true love. Makes me feel really sad." I blew my nose again, the urge to cry subsiding. "But, uh, something happened recently."

"It's not your fault Margaret was infertile."

I gave a weak smile. "It's not that, I just—"

"John, we've discussed your marriage in previous sessions and how there was disconnection at all levels. Tell me how knowing about this disconnection can serve you, when what you seek is a deep connection?"

I bowed my head. Whatever. Margaret was the last thing I wanted to talk about today. So, I changed the subject.

"I got in a skiing accident last week. Knocked my head good and hard into a tree. Was in a coma for three days."

She inhaled fast and covered her mouth. "Wow. And you're here. Amazing. Tell me about that."

The rocking motion stopped. I explained as many details as I could about the Mammoth trip, the guy falling from the gondola, and the goddamned tree that showed up out of nowhere.

"Doctors say I'm fine. Physically, at least. Ran a ton of tests and apparently there's no permanent damage. Got a follow up appointment with some neurologist tomorrow."

She grabbed her iPad and started tapping notes.

But as I continued, the rocking motion returned and I found both my arms wrapped around me, hugging myself while struggling to maintain eye contact with Kelly. "Something weird is happening, from the coma. I've been having conflicting thoughts—memories, I think—about a woman." I paused, trying to figure out the best way to describe the sensations I'd been having. "I feel like I'm grieving for her? Which doesn't make any sense because I don't even know who the hell she is. But at the same time, I'm borderline manic about finding her. I keep having . . . visions."

She raised her eyebrows and leaned forward, cocked her head to the side, leaned back, then took some more notes on her iPad. "Continue. And?"

Again, every damned time I tried to look Kelly in the eye, some urge forced my gaze to avert, instead looking to other items in the room, the bookshelf, a desk covered with books and papers, beige shag carpet beneath my feet. "Ever since I woke up from the coma, and this is gonna sound crazy, I feel like . . . a different person. Like I don't belong in this body. The Mammoth hospital doctor wrote in her notes I spoke with a southern accent. I told her my name was Jack Bachman. She said I gave her a bunch of details about her dead son, which absolutely does not make any sense to me."

"Why's that?"

"First of all, I don't even remember talking with her. Second, I don't recall any details about the boy, except he seemed cute, but sad."

Kelly continued plunking on her tablet, making notes. "Please continue."

"My parents raised me strict Catholic, as we've discussed, which is part of what caused my failed marriage and my depression. But there's nothing I'm aware of in that entire religion that helps to provide answers for what I'm going through. This is some crazy weird stuff, Kelly. I'm scared because—"

An ear-piercing, whining siren blared above us and we both covered our ears.

The room went completely black.

Strobe lights flashed.

# CHAPTER 11

"Come with me, John," Kelly said with uncanny calmness as she stood amidst the chaos of blinking lights. She led me from the therapy room, down the hall, to the outside at the back of the building, where we clustered together with another half-dozen frightened souls.

Gray clouds hovered above and light rain started falling, but of course nobody had an umbrella. Californians brought umbrellas as often as frogs wore sun bonnets.

With everyone's hair thoroughly soaked, fire truck sirens finally approached from a distance. A minute later, a massive red fire engine pulled into the side driveway and, with the energy of flashing red lights piercing the calm, two paramedics wearing blue uniforms hopped out. Three others, all wearing their fire-proof suits, equipped with full facial oxygen masks and yellow tanks affixed to their backs, trotted into the office building—nothing more than a rezoned, converted residential house.

With no evidence whatsoever of smoke, I sensed more danger from standing out in the rain than from potential fire or explosion.

A handful of people stood in the parking area near me, probably in my same predicament, seeking remedies for their mental obscurities. In addition to Kelly and the firemen, I counted five others. A likely mixture of therapists and clients. They muttered amongst themselves and I heard one mention something about "Xanax," another mumbled "night terrors, hallucinations and lack of sleep." Hearing every conversation simultaneously, I had trouble distinguishing them from one another, an issue I'd never had before. It was impossible to focus only on one conversation as my mind automatically bounced from one to the other to another, jumbling it all together as noise.

Without warning, a ton of sensory input clogged my brain all at once: the scent of multiple varieties of perfumes, various nearby flowers, the neighbor's grass, dripping oil from a parked car on the street, and every movement among the people, passing cars, the firemen, birds flying above, tree leaves rustling in a slight breeze. My vision started spinning.

I turned toward Kelly and a sixth person, a man, had appeared, seemingly out of nowhere, with perfectly dry hair. And a familiar face.

As he stepped immediately to my right, his eyes fully open. Still dizzy and struggling to maintain consciousness, I glanced away toward the other people. My upper torso began that weird rocking motion again. Air forced its way into and out of my lungs, faster, as a strong sense of awkwardness enveloped the entire area. I wracked my brain, trying to recognize the man's face.

Then it hit me. My entire body shuttered.

Mammoth.

Gondola.

Blake Lynds.

I swallowed hard, wiping newly formed drips of rain from my brow, sneaking another look at the man who'd slipped from my hands and fallen to his grisly death. Eyes still opened wide, unblinking, he stared at me and leaned in.

My leg muscles tightened and I fought the urge to run.

Leaning closer toward me, he said in a whisper, "Listen to the sage. She knows."

I furrowed my brow and froze, panting like an over-heated dog.

Desperate to find out if anyone else in the group was seeing the dead guy, I darted my gaze away from the man for a split second to the other bystanders. Then the firemen climbing into their truck.

Back to Blake.

Gone.

Questioning my sanity, I watched the lead fireman exit the side door to the office as he said to Kelly, "False alarm." After removing his helmet, he gave a bitter smirk. "Someone was probably smoking too close to your smoke detector. Getting tired of these false alarms. You have any idea how much time we waste? Could be out saving lives . . ." He pressed his lips tight, turned and walked to the fire engine.

Kelly stood her ground as though nothing had happened, hands clasped below her waist, giving no response.

I twirled around to scan the scene. Still no sign of Blake. No way he'd survived the fall. Even so, *people can't disappear into thin air. Right?* I thought about the boy in the hospital and questioned the entire memory of my failed heroic efforts up on that gondola.

Blake died. Definitely. No doubt about that.

Wonderful. Now I was officially losing my mind, hallucinating again, but this time, without morphine as an excuse.

Kelly motioned for everyone to funnel back inside the building. A minute later, I found myself sitting on the same comfortable couch, with my therapist once again digging into my mind for information.

"So sorry about that, John. Nobody here smokes. Especially not inside. Maybe I need to get our smoke detectors checked. Anyway," she said, "let's pick up where we left off. You were saying you were scared."

I debated with myself whether to share the experience from outside with Kelly. I needed to talk about Blake's death and how he'd just appeared outside. I needed to talk about the mysterious ghost boy. I needed answers.

"I want to talk about Tammy," I said, rubbing the palms of my hands on my thighs, holding my breath, and closing my eyes. "This sounds crazy, I know, but I'm totally, head over heels in love with a woman named Tammy."

My eyes popped open.

Kelly raised her eyebrows and two dimples appeared in her cheeks. "That's wonderful, John. How did you two meet?"

I bit my lower lip and squinted. "We haven't."

"I'm confused. Help me understand what you mean by that."

"Exactly." I paused for a moment, staring at a floor-to-ceiling bookshelf full of self-help and psychology books, trying to come up with the best way to explain all this to her. "I only know her from the coma and what I would consider to be dreams. Extremely vivid dreams, almost like memories. Real memories. Maybe like the way you now have memories of that upset firefighter. I have, what I would bet my life on, memories of Tammy and me doing all sorts of things together."

"Such as?"

"Picnics at a park. Long walks along a beach, holding hands. Car rides, talking, laughing. Making love over and over and over, knowing every intimate detail of her body, her likes, dislikes. Vivid memories." My voice sounded bubbly to me, almost giddy. "Traveling to different countries like France, England, Canada, and Mexico. Discussing plans for having a family. We were trying to make a baby." The thought of the treasure—one that, at least in my visions, is a hefty wooden box full of old, valuable gold coins pouring out—popped into my head. "Oh, and there's a treasure. Massive. Left long ago from a ship that crashed in a huge storm. And I know exactly where it's been hidden for over a hundred years."

"You say all that so nonchalantly. A treasure. Fascinating," she said, scribbling more notes on her iPad.

"I feel like if I could go to this one spot, a place I've never been to but know exists, I could find my way to the treasure."

The door burst open and a woman poked her head into the room. "I'm so sorry to interrupt, Dr. Carpenter, but with the fire alarm, I need to know what to do with your next patients."

"I can go," I said, starting to stand.

Kelly motioned with her hand for me to sit. "Nonsense. We're not done yet," she said to me with a smile before checking her watch.

# CHAPTER 12

Kelly turned to the woman. "Please give me fifteen minutes to wrap up here and we'll get to them soon afterwards. And thank them for their patience."

I sat, put my hands between my knees, and continued. "The scary part is that I keep having these extremely graphic visions of a super intense fight with some angry, faceless man. I'd give you more details, but everything's fuzzy. And the eczema on my right shoulder is worse now than ever. And now when I find myself in a group of people, I feel like I'm having sensory overload. I hear every single conversation. Smell every perfume and cologne. It's overwhelming, like a filter in my head got deleted, or like I'm losing my grip on sanity. Maybe I'm a schizo."

"John, you are certainly not suffering from schizophrenia. Please don't worry about that." She crossed her legs. "Now, tell me about the boy from the hospital."

I gave her a full physical description and telepathic communications.

"Have you ever had these visions before? I mean, before the coma?"

"Nothing."

"How do you feel?"

I scanned the room, the bookshelf, her desk piled with files, and the rotating ceiling fan. "Oddly enough, I don't feel sad anymore. I feel . . . in love, but at the same time in mourning. And energized to take some kind of action, but nothing too extreme because I seem to get panicked easily and then I get frustrated."

"And why's that?"

I shook my head. "I have this urge to do something, but I have no idea what."

Kelly set her iPad on her thigh, smiled, and nodded. "I have a suggestion. I'd like you to—"

I couldn't hold it in anymore, had to blurt it out. "Oh, and in addition to the boy, I'm having hallucinations of the ghost of the man from the gondola."

She paused, leaned forward and studied my face for several seconds.

"John, I wish you would have started with these two. You seem to be exhibiting behavioral traits of someone on the autism spectrum and we need more time to explore, to do a deep dive into all this, but we're almost out of time for today. I'm so sorry."

We talked about my meds.

"John, this might be hard for you to understand, but I think you're in a position where some new ideas, a different way of looking at the world and our existence here on Earth, will be good for you to hear. I'm going to tell you some theories and I want you to be open-minded about them, okay? Can you walk through this with me?"

I nodded, with no expectations. And nothing to lose. "I'll try."

"John, you're not alone in this. I'm here."

I looked down at my twiddling fingers, still struggling to make eye contact.

"The ghost sightings aside, I believe what you are experiencing are actual, real memories from a past life. Are you familiar with the concept of reincarnation?"

I wondered if I was dreaming and never thought a professional like Kelly would even mention something so ridiculous. How could she suggest something as totally nuts as reincarnation? Only crazy people believed in that crap. My level of confidence in her dropped like a rock through water.

"Oh, come on. You're joking."

She remained silent, staring at me.

I continued, "You mean like Shirley MacLaine reincarnation where we all supposedly have lived in past lives as cows or ants?"

She chuckled. "Well, not exactly. Again, I want you to keep an open mind here. New scientific research has come out over the last decade—strong evidence—that many of us have lived several hundreds of past lives as humans. Somehow, when we die, our soul goes to a different dimension, one we cannot see, hear, measure, et cetera, and it stays there until we are ready to either move into our new human body or pass on to a different, more advanced realm. Sometimes with people who died of non-natural causes, as you might have in a past life, something about the extreme emotion of the event triggers memories for them as children in their future lives."

*Great. My therapist is a total wacko.*

I thought about Blake plummeting to his death from the gondola. Non-natural causes.

"I don't know. My parents raised me Catholic," I said. "I studied in Sunday school what happens when we die. We used to chant every single Sunday about the afterlife. When we die, our soul goes to heaven or hell, depending on what type of life we've lived. What you're talking about could be considered satanic. Blasphemous."

She sat up straight, not threatened by my growing hotheadedness. "Not that I care. But over the centuries people have been murdered, burned at the stake, gutted, for saying stuff like that."

"John, you agreed to try and keep an open mind about this. You're free to reject the whole notion of reincarnation."

I scanned the office, searching for Blake's ghost.

"C'mon, this is pretty far-fetched stuff, you gotta admit. I expected you to tell me I might have brain damage or something."

"All I'm asking you to do at this point is consider this as a possible reason for your visions. That's all. We only have a minute left, but I would encourage you to explore this phenomenon and decide for yourself if it fits or not." She snatched a notepad and scribbled something. She tore off the top piece of paper and handed it to me. "Here. These are a couple of books I suggest you read. There's also a wealth of information available online. Explore this. I want you to search and find the answers. The message in these books is not widely accepted, but there's something there. I feel it."

She walked to the massive bookshelf and studied rows of texts for a moment, tapping the tip of her index finger onto her lower lip before pulling out two books and handing them to me.

In a few seconds, she summarized one of the stories— apparently true—about a psychiatrist who regressed his female patient and discovered hidden secrets about past lives and our purpose here on planet Earth. The other book had dozens of supposedly true stories about children who claimed to have memories of past lives, with evidence to back up their claims.

Key word: *supposedly.*

At that point, I completely rejected reincarnation. But I also wanted to be polite, so put out my hand and accepted both books.

I glanced at her notes. "Okay, but I want you to know, I'm one-hundred and ten percent skeptical of this crap." I wadded the paper, stuffing the crumpled mess into my jeans pocket while standing to leave.

"I understand. You're a rational thinker, an intuitive, logical person. I expect nothing less from you, John. Skepticism is perfectly normal. Now you say you have this woman's first name, Tammy, and you know where this so-called treasure is located, yes?"

"Absolutely, but right now it's all more of a feeling than anything. A hunch."

"Oh, and one more concept I need to quickly make sure you get," she said before describing something called "genetic memory," in which animals—including we humans—have memories embedded in their genetic codes in the absence of an actual sensory experience.

She explained a new theory about how this might be where instincts and phobias come from. It's how cats automatically know how to land on their feet even though they were never trained to do it.

There was a study about mice, trained to fear certain smells, which passed on their aversion to their offspring.

She said, "Carl Jung, a famous psychologist, postulated that 'racial memories' are inherent when we are born that contain feelings, memories, and ideas from our ancestors. He referred to the concept of the 'collective unconscious,' where all the ideas and structures included in each of our unconscious minds are shared among all humans. This is apparently where archetypes, such as a hero, mother, mentor, et cetera, live."

We took several steps down the hallway toward the waiting room as my mind brushed off most of what she'd just said as nonsense.

She added, "Do you have a last name or maybe where she lives?"

I stopped, closed my eyes and let the images come into view. Tammy crinkled her eyes and nose, forcing me to chuckle to myself.

"I think so. The vision says her last name is Bachman and she lives . . ." Some of the images appeared from the blackness, coming into focus. "In Louisiana somewhere, maybe near a bayou, which is also where the treasure is."

A clap of thunder thudded against small office building. I opened my eyes and glanced up at the ceiling.

"There are thousands of reincarnation stories out there. Real scientists. Real data. Real doctors tracking these people. It's not something the counterculture dreamed up on an acid trip in the sixties. It's a real thing."

I raised my eyebrows, confident she was full of it. "Sorry, I don't buy it. We die and the game's over. Poof. We're gone. Our spirit goes to heaven or whatever."

She stopped walking, turned directly at me, and placed her hands on my shoulders. "At great risk of sounding like Yoda, I suggest you search your feelings. Look deep inside your being. The truth is waiting for you."

She was trying to help and believed everything she was saying, but to me, sounded less like a shrink and more like a random hippie in a psychic reading room. Or Ben Kenobi from Star Wars.

Outside, walking toward my car, I surveyed the area, half expecting to see the ghost of Blake.

Nothing.

I sat inside my Beemer and cracked open the first book.

In my gut, I needed to disprove Kelly's ramblings about reincarnation. But I also wanted to see Kevin, talk about the ghosts, have a few drinks, and find some much-needed direction, since Kelly was not much help.

Pulled out my phone and dialed.

After inviting myself over, I flipped on my turn signal and entered traffic.

"Sure, c'mon over," Kevin said. "My mom's here cookin' up a storm."

While zooming away from Kelly's office toward Kevin's place, the image of Blake appeared in my rear-view mirror, standing in the middle of the street. He waved goodbye to me as a car drove right through his semi-opaque body.

# CHAPTER 13

**Scott Jones**
*November 16, 2016*

The Boeing 747 descended through ten thousand feet above the Atlantic coast, heading westward toward New York's JFK airport, when the pilot radioed back to the tower.

"Roger that, Approach. Niner four delta heavy with Echo, twenty miles east, tuning to one-three-four-three-five." He turned to his copilot, Jimbo. "Five bucks says Laurie's gonna kick you to the curb if you try to tap that tonight."

The copilot, an Italian man in his late thirties, with thick black eyebrows and full lips, four days of tightly trimmed stubble blended into long sideburns, and more brawn than brain replied back, "You're on. She's a sure thing, man. You know how hot that babe gets with pilots."

"Yeah, but not with you. I'd loan ya my good luck nugget, but I need a little special help myself tonight," said the pilot, chuckling and tapping an index finger on his chest through a

pressed white captain's shirt.

Jimbo smiled as their speed slowed through one hundred sixty knots and applied ten degrees of flaps.

"Landin' gear down," said the pilot, shifting the gear flap knob down. "Goin' fishin' this weekend with my buddy Mike," said the pilot.

"Nobody cares. Just shut up and get us on the ground in one piece."

Before the pilot could respond, their plane jerked upward and back down. The stall warning buzzer sounded. Out of instinct, the pilot pushed forward on the yolk and pushed the throttle knobs forward to add thrust. A few moments later, the plane stabilized, and the two men checked off each task on the landing list before gliding the plane safely to runway 22-R at JFK.

After the passengers disembarked, both men grabbed their overnight bags, walked toward the airplane door and the pilot said to his mate, "Bet ya ain't never had stall on descent like that before."

"You know, Scott, you can be a real dick sometimes," Jimbo said. They stopped walking, allowing one of the flight attendants to pass. "Hi Laurie," said Jimbo with a wink. Her lips parted and she smiled back.

Scott shook his head. "Don't get no mo' cheesier than that. Surprised ya get any of that at all."

"Like I said, a real dickhole," Jimbo said, walking off the plane.

Scott fished his phone out from his pocket, pressed the on switch, and headed straight to the first class lounge bar. Hands shaking, he ordered a double bourbon to calm his nerves. Once the liquor had kicked in, he closed his eyes and imagined the Lafayette treasure, as he stood proud wearing his leather fedora hat, leaning on a shovel, his muddy black boot hiked up onto a corner of the chest full of gold coins. A wave of excitement washed over him when he envisioned the headline in the Baton Rouge Advocate that would read, "Local Commercial Pilot Finds $1B Treasure After 40 Years of Searching." Then he fantasized about lying on a white sand beach of some random island in the Caribbean he had purchased with a portion of the gold, sipping a Hurricane drink, watching two young, tan, gorgeous bikini-clad honeys bouncing up and down in the water, their wondrous assets flopping about. His insides stirred as he raised his hand and ordered another double.

# CHAPTER 14

**John Bastian**

*November 16, 2016*

Thirteen years ago, the dream life I'd always wanted had become a reality. My marriage to Margaret had been on solid ground. Or so I thought. We had been trying to have a baby. My brand new navy blue five-series Beemer drove like a slice of heaven. And I had more real estate deals rolling in than I could handle.

How short-lived that all had been.

Since then, my marriage had dissolved. My wife and I never had any kids, my real estate business bordered on the brink of bankruptcy, and money crawled in at a fraction of the pace of earlier years, with more going out than in. But I held on to a thread of hope: a big commercial real estate deal with my business partner, Karl Cannon, would boost us financially into the stratosphere and the top fraction of the one-percenters. All we had to do was close escrow.

We both needed the money to rebuild our failing business. Commissions on the number of closed deals, which was the only way we generated revenue, had floundered since my divorce, mostly because I had let my client relationships go stale. But Karl had lost interest, too. We had simply failed to give our business the level of love, energy, and commitment it needed to grow and succeed.

The aggregate of these stressful conditions was tough, but it didn't help that my BMW had transformed into something from a Mad Max movie. Newer model BMW's had Bluetooth, back-up cameras, and all the cool modern tech. Mine had a belt of rust creeping in around the bottom few inches of the body, the new car smell was gone—replaced with a wonderful odor of spoiled milk thanks to Margaret spilling her double espresso latte three years ago during an argument—and a spider crack inched across my front windshield.

I headed several miles inland from the coast towards Kevin's house, where he lived with his mom in a neighborhood filled with houses one-third of the price of the ocean-front properties like mine. Their green single-story bungalow with white trim had a clean green lawn, though, and simple landscaping, but he enjoyed the minimal upkeep.

I strolled up to the door, knocked once, and he let me in.

"I need to borrow your computer to check out a few things," I said.

"You got an iPhone, use that," he said, wiping his hands with a dish rag.

"Screen's too small for looking at maps," I replied, walking over to Kevin's home office to wake up his PC.

"Honey? Someone here?" asked his mom—whom, out of immense respect, I'd always referred to as Mrs. Traylor—from the kitchen.

"Yeah, mom, it's only John."

A few moments later, as I sat in the office chair, his mom popped her head in. "Well, there's the handsome young white boy. How's my favorite real estate agent doing today?"

I smiled politely. "Fine. Something smells amazing in here."

"Rustlin' up some good ol' fashioned Louisiana cookin' for my baby. He gonna be on the TV soon. The Jimmy Fallon show. Gotta make sure he good and fed," she said before heading back into the kitchen.

Kevin and I shared a wonderful, warm laugh. He stood, leaning on the doorway and shook his head. "Sorry, man. I told her not to call you white boy anymore, but she thinks it's cute."

"It's all good. Doesn't bother me," I said, firing up a web browser and starting my research on reincarnation.

Kevin pulled up a chair and watched. "Don't look like real estate, man."

I gave a crisp nod and did my best to explain some of the reincarnation concepts my therapist had shared with me. We spent the next several hours educating ourselves on the phenomenon. Kelly had nailed this.

In fact, my level of ignorance shocked me.

We downed a couple of energy bars around noon and later that afternoon, stumbled onto one website that had a review of one of the books Kelly had recommended, the one about thousands of young kids having memories from past lives.

The more I read, the more some teeny tiny part of me became convinced Kelly's reincarnation crap might be rooted in some level of truth.

But no way in hell could it all be true.

Reincarnation flew in the face of everything the church had taught me and the one billion plus other Catholics and Christians. Same thing with the one billion plus Muslims and Jews. Reincarnation had no place in these three Middle Eastern religions, ones followed by over half the population on planet Earth. None whatsoever. No wonder the idea was far-fetched.

We dug through piles of research and studies. Scientific data. Multiple statistical analyses. Videos of children and their shocked parents. Audio files. Proof on top of proof. I discovered that the explorers of the phenomenon were still searching for answers because not all the pieces to the proverbial puzzle had been discovered.

But they knew way more than I had assumed. Still seemed ridiculous to me, though.

Mostly bullshit. Had to be.

But then I read the story of a boy who, starting at the age of three, had told his mother about his previous life as a pilot in the South Pacific during World War II. He describe in stunning detail to her how he'd died in a plane crash, his name was Rick Larson, his best friend's name was Ralph—also a pilot—he flew a Corsair plane that had shot down fourteen "Jap planes" before his demise, and how they stationed him on the carrier USS Natoma. As the respectable mother and devoted member of a Southern Baptist church, hearing these details from her young son horrified her. She wondered how he, at the age of three, had learned about death, the derogatory term "Jap" for the Japanese people, the name of a pivotal aircraft carrier in World War II, World War II itself, et cetera.

To her surprise, when she and her husband, both of whom were highly educated, researched their son's claims, nearly every single one of the child's assertions were true, according to the newspaper clippings and first-hand stories from veterans.

Sure enough, a pilot with the same name had, in fact, been stationed on the USS Natoma Bay. And the pilot's friend was named Ralph, they both flew Corsair planes, and Rick Larson had been shot down in a dog fight with the Japanese Army over the South Pacific.

"Bet you a hundred bucks this is all part of some elaborate hoax, man," I said to Kevin.

"Yeah, but what are the odds of all this shit being a coincidence? Insane, right? No way some little kid made up all this. Especially not some three-year-old."

Sure, the chances were minuscule that this one, single story had somehow manipulated or falsified. But there were similar stories. And not just a few more. Thousands more.

I held fast to my one and done religious belief—each of us lives a single life, dies, and that's it—but right then, made a conscious decision to keep an open mind. Theoretically, according to my Catholic upbringing, they were setting up a spot for me in hell just for thinking about reincarnation, but my curiosity managed to overrule the Catholic threats.

"Check this out," said Kevin, pointing to the screen. "Says here that twenty-four percent of Americans, across all religions, believe in this reincarnation stuff."

"Seems high," I said, continuing to read. "Look, this psychologist here says these kids are describing false memories," I said. "It's a bunch of hooey, nothing more than a psychological phenomenon."

"Dude, imagine if all this were true," he said, rubbing his chin and looking down at the beige carpet. "Say we mess up in this lifetime, what if we do get another chance again. In the next life. If that's true, holy Jesus."

"Here's another one," I said, tapping at the screen. "Some kid says he woke up in the middle of the night screaming and telling his mom he was homesick." I continued to read. The article talked about how, in a previous life, the boy was a small-time actor in a 1932 film called Night After Night. Somehow, he knew details about the man he supposedly was in a previous life: birth date, friends, his age when he died, how he died, and a ton more.

"Some crazy shit. Look here," said Kevin. "This other one's about a girl in India who woke up one day speaking fluently in a dialect she'd supposedly never heard before." We both stared at the computer monitor, reading, absorbing. "Now you tell me how the hell that shit is possible if reincarnation ain't a real thang."

I shrugged, pursing my lips.

# CHAPTER 15

After another hour of research, Kevin's mom popped her head in our room. "Anyone hungry for some good ol' fashioned Southern grub?"

To my surprise, working on researching, contemplating, and evaluating trippy reincarnation stories had built up a strong appetite. We hustled into the dining room, where the feast included Creole jumbalaya, Southern oxtail soup, eggs Sardou with gulf shrimp added and of course, my favorite, grits, which all made my mouth water.

During dinner, his mom asked, "What you two boys doin' in there? Better not be watchin' any of that nasty porno stuff."

"Kevin's helping me do research."

She finished chewing a bite of Cajun shrimp. "Do tell."

I looked at Kevin. He scratched his cheek and gave a tiny shake of the head.

"About reincarnation," I said, immediately reaching for my glass and gulping down a pint of water.

Kevin closed his eyes.

His mom stared at me, over to Kevin, and back at me. "I thought you was a good Christian boy, John."

"Oh, I am, don't worry," I said, not wanting to argue.

"Jesus did not put us on this earth to research the work of Satan. You boys best stop while you is ahead."

Before I could stop myself, I asked with a raised eyebrow, "You don't believe that reincarnation is possible?"

She narrowed her eyes as a surge of energy jolted the entire house like a bomb had gone off down the block, with thundering low rumbles rolling across the dining room. A glass picture frame fell from a nearby wall, shattering onto the hardwood floor. Then, nothing for four seconds, until the house rumbled again, stronger this time, with rolling waves through the earth beneath us. We ducked, more like fell, under the table. As a native Californian, I had been through my share of earthquakes before. Hundreds. But never anything this strong. The floor acted more like a small fishing boat than something setting on solid ground. The eight-foot pane front window shattered, car alarms blasted sirens outside, and dishes slid out of cupboards, slamming onto the tile floor below.

I struggled to suck air into my lungs, forcing myself to focus on my chest, making my lungs expand, a task which proved difficult to do in the middle of a massive earthquake. Mrs. Traylor screamed as we all white-knuckled the wooden table legs.

That minute in hell dragged on for what felt like an hour of terror.

Finally, the rumbling stopped.

"I don't feel good," Kevin said, rising, running to the bathroom, and releasing the contents of his mother's home cooking into their toilet.

"You alright, Mrs. Traylor?" I asked Kevin's mom. She sat on the floor with both hands on her chest, trying to catch her breath.

"Hoo, cher, I ain't so sure 'bout California no more," she said, standing on one leg, leaning onto a chair as I helped her to her feet.

"Let me get you some water," I said.

"Bless yo' heart, no, I'm fine. Just need to rest here for a minute."

Kevin returned from the bathroom.

"Yo, dog, that was a crazy ride," he said, wiping his lips with his forearm. "I'll bet we just had ourselves a nine-pointer."

I pulled up the USGS app on my phone. "Five point seven, but the epicenter was right underneath us, on what looks like the Newport-Inglewood fault. Might have been a precursor quake, a baby one before the big daddy hits."

# CHAPTER 16

**Scott Jones**
*November 16, 2016*

Still at the lounge bar, Scott dialed his wife. "Hey babe," he said. She asked how he was doing, but he lied and said he was fine. In reality, he wanted nothing more than to get back to Baton Rouge, steal the map from the witch and finish the treasure hunt.

While his ball-and-chain babbled on and on about her day, troubles doing the laundry, and something about having an issue with her credit card while checking out at the grocery store, he watched the basketball game up on the TV screen behind the bar. LA Lakers were ahead 103-89. "Okay, great, gotta run, love you too, babe," he said, ending the call. "Ungrateful fuckin' cunt," he muttered to himself. The bartender slid the next double to him. Scott scooped up the glass, ice cubes clanking, and tossed half the drink down his throat.

Somewhere deep inside, covered in decades of dust and emotional cobwebs, the love Scott once had for Tammy lay hidden from his conscious mind. A jealous rage would consume him every time he imagined her first husband kissing her. Touching her. Sliding his tiny, hard little . . .

Scott downed the second half of his drink.

Scott's love for Tammy, once shiny and fresh, was now decrepit, with mold and sickness woven throughout. He struggled to hide his pain sometimes, but had to out of necessity. He had to in order to stay out of prison.

For decades now, his suspicions grew that Tammy had somehow discovered what he had done to his best friend, Jack, back in '78.

His loins stirred uncomfortably, caused by the three-day build up since his last release. The empty stomach buzz hit him hard, so he ordered a basket of chicken wings from the bartender, gobbled down the protein and fat, then wiped the grease from his lips. The bartender handed him a glass of water, which he drained before paying the bill.

The Lakers won 115-102. He pulled out his cell phone again. This time, his web browser showed him a map of nearby massage parlors and he only needed one to take care of his needs. His online account allowed him to tap into an enormous database of US massage parlors. The site knew his location and recommended the nearest parlor in Queens, the New Apple Spa. The app estimated a twenty-minute drive.

Sex hormones and bourbon fueled his actions as he exited the terminal, rented a car, and drove to the pseudo-brothel. After parking across the street, he yanked off the pilot shirt, leaving on a white undershirt, then removed his shiny black shoes, slipped on a set of well-worn gray Nike running shoes and walked to the parlor. Pungent ripe bum urine permeated the air seconds before Scott opened the door and entered.

Inside, the hypnotic traces of jasmine and fruit erased the pee smell. The mamasan, a short, elderly Chinese woman, strolled up to him with a big smile pasted across her face, both arms extended out in front of her. "You like massage?" She pronounced it muss-AH-Jee. To his right sat five young Asian beauties, all batting their eyelids and giving him their best "fuck me" smiles. He retrieved a c-note from his pants pocket, handed the bill to the old lady, and said, "One hour, with," he pointed to a young girl wearing a pink laced top and matching panties. "Her."

The girl took his hand, leading him down a dimly lit hallway to an open door on his left. He entered and closed the door behind her. Within seconds, he'd stripped off his shoes, socks, and black suit pants. After sliding down his gray silk boxer shorts, he admired how excited his little buddy was, standing at full attention, ready to thrust deep into the awaiting female meat.

He lay face down on the cloth-covered table, remaining still while receiving a shoddy massage for twenty-five minutes.

She asked him what he wanted. The words left his lips before he could change his mind. "Full service."

He completed the job quickly, enjoying the great sense of relief. A minute later, he'd already paid the girl, thrown on his clothes, and hustled back outside. He hurried to his car, raindrops pelting his hair and face, as cold air brushed against his sweaty cheeks.

Primitive needs met, he could now focus on the treasure. Once inside the car, he called Mike. "Please tell me the witch has come in to port," Scott said. "And don't you lie to me."

"Can't," Mike said.

"Don't be fuckin' around, man."

"I could lie and tell you she's here, or I could tell you I don't have the map. Your choice."

"Goddammit. She said she'd be there by now," Scott said, looking through the driver's side window, covered with water drops, into the rainy darkness of Queens as two thugs walked by the front of his rental car, eyeing him.

# CHAPTER 17

**John Bastian**
*November 17, 2016*

I spent the night at Kevin's, mostly to provide emotional support to his mom, who had her own set of mental aftershocks from the quake.

After a tired start the next morning—their couch felt like it had rocks in it, which left a wonderful kink in my neck—I stumbled into the living room like a cold moron, sunlight pounding my throbbing head.

In the bathroom, I downed a few Advil and bummed a vanilla protein shake off Kevin before falling back into my comfortable little bubble with Tammy, the treasure, and some damned Louisiana bayou.

The thought, albeit remote, of having lived here on Earth in a previous life, in someone else's body freaked me out, dwarfing anything else happening at the time. I had promised my therapist to keep an open mind. And I did, in fact, as various details untangled and I started coming around to the notion.

*How could so many children share—across the globe, across vastly different cultures and religions—such undeniable details of their past lives, all of which appeared to be backed up by facts and evidence, without a reasonable alternative explanation?*

In my current life, the only reincarnation references I could recall were always made by crazy nut jobs. Total wackos.

The simple act of questioning whether mainstream America could accept, or even explore, the concept of reincarnation, was like trying to swim upstream in rough, social whitewater river.

Of course, all these thoughts only spiked my anxiety.

A little after 3:00 pm, Kevin reminded me of my doctor's appointment.

"Let's do this," he said.

We hopped into my dirty Beemer and headed toward the neurologist's office in downtown Huntington Beach.

On the way, we talked more about reincarnation, business, and Kevin's upcoming stint on national TV.

"Dog, you gotta chill about all that, man," Kevin said. "Whatever's gonna happen, it's gonna happen. You just gotta keep your head up. Know what I'm sayin'?"

Once again, my friend was right. In the past, whenever negative thoughts took over my mind and the demons began to creep out from behind the shadows, bad things tended to happen to me. But I was learning that the opposite seemed true for positive thoughts. Of course, easier said than done.

Kevin patted my shoulder. "Take a deep breath, dog. Everything's gonna be a'right."

We parked, headed up to the doctor's office on the fifth floor of the medical building, and waited in the lobby. The nurse called my name, we stood and Kevin gave me a warm embrace. "You got this. Whatever the doc says, I'm right here and we gonna talk when you done."

After a brief fist bump, Kevin scooped up a copy of "Silver and Gold" magazine and had sat and crossed his legs before I started my walk back into an exam room. After a few minutes, the doctor showed up.

The neurologist stood several inches shorter than me with short white hair, rimless glasses, and a slight Indian accent. He handed me a printout with the results of the latest round of medical tests. "You want the good news or bad news first?" he asked.

"Always the good."

He nodded. "Well, we've reviewed all of the data from the tests Dr. Willis ran during your stint at Mammoth Hospital, along with a barrage of other ones I ran on you here, and I'm happy to give you a clean bill of health, sir. It's like you never hit that tree. Never slipped into a coma. It's a small miracle, really. You should feel fortunate after what you went through."

Same damned problem with eye contact. An invisible force made it a struggle to look the man in the eye, but I spoke anyway, averting my gaze to his tie, the window, a leather chair, and a chart about heart attacks. "Terrific. Wait, hold on a second. I—"

"Your coma was considered a nine on the Glasgow Coma Scale, which means you were in a coma, but not necessarily the worst type there is."

"Had no idea," I said, still unable to maintain eye contact.

"Statistically, there was a fifty-fifty chance you'd wake up and live a normal life."

"Wow. You mean I could've died?"

I thought about that angry tree.

He nodded, then glanced down at a chart held in his hand.

"And the bad news?" I asked.

He chuckled. "Oh wait, there is no bad news." He slapped his knee, apparently cracking himself up. Doctor humor.

Something pulled at me and since this was probably going to be a quick visit, and—despite his failed attempt at humor—this guy's medical opinion would be a great sounding board for what had been happening to me, with all of the hallucinations, dreams, and an emotional connection to a woman I'd never met, I asked, "Doc, do you believe in reincarnation?"

His smile turned to a frown before his lips moved to the side. Pushing out his chest as he slid off his glasses, he paused, thinking, then raised his eyebrows.

"Medically speaking, there's absolutely no evidence, at least that I'm aware of, to support reincarnation. That said, I think we as humans still have much more to learn about death and the great beyond. It would be extremely arrogant to suggest it's not at least possible. Why do you ask?"

I bit my lower lip and explained my story to him. "Curious what your opinion is, since you're a brain expert." The scent of rubbing alcohol hit my nose, strong, and I cringed.

He shifted his weight and leaned against the countertop. "Honestly, over my forty-year career as a neurologist, I've witnessed events that are truly unexplainable. As I said, there's much more we still must learn about the brain, death, and spirituality." He picked up a manila folder from the countertop, clicked the top of his black Bic pen, and wrote some notes in my file. "Let me know if you have any more hallucinations."

My need for answers intensifying by the minute, I wandered out into the waiting room and found Kevin. He approached, took hold of my shoulders, squinted, and asked, "How you holdin' up? We need to hit a bar?"

"Apparently, I'm back to a hundred percent. We could go drinking, but for some reason, I don't feel it anymore." I paused, blinking, sensing odd changes inside my body. " I feel like something's about to happen. My skull is tingling and I'm like extra alert. Not normal for me. Must be because I brought you along," I said with a wink before we sauntered toward the exit door.

Outside, in the sun, we approached my Beemer and my phone rang.

"Mom, I'm just—"

"Honey, your father's just been admitted to the hospital. They think he had a stroke."

# CHAPTER 18

## Scott Jones
*November 17, 2016*

Since, according to Mike, the old witch hadn't pulled in to port yet, Scott needed to get his ass back down to Louisiana. In order to meet with Mike as quickly as possible, Scott hopped on a one-way 9:00 pm flight to Baton Rouge, then drove his Benz along Interstate 10 to the Louis Armstrong Airport in New Orleans.

Being an airline captain made a great alibi.

Especially for murder.

"Mike, it's me," Scott said into his phone via Bluetooth while driving down a deserted street in the business district of town. "Got good news."

The radio played a low-volume Doobie Brothers tune from the seventies.

"Yeah? I'm getting tired of you saying we're getting close and not finding nothin'."

"Ya best watch your mouth, son, but either way, the treasure's gonna be in the bag once we got the map. That crazy old witch just texted me. Tomorrow night."

*Black Water* ended and the radio cut to a newscaster, who mentioned something about an approaching hurricane, now shifting direction, and heading for Louisiana. Scott barely heard.

Scott continued, firing up a Marlboro and exhaling out the window before he said, "So you keep your nose clean." His right fist regripped the steering wheel, tight. "Said she's got somethin' better than that map and the compass for us to buy. If so, we'll finally know the exact location and pay dirt. I had to kill my best friend to get to this point and nothing's gonna stop me. That treasure is mine, goddammit, I can practically taste it."

"Ours," Mike corrected.

# CHAPTER 19

## John Bastian

*November 17, 2016*

When Mom told me the news about Dad's stroke, the urge hit me hard to crawl into a hole and assume the fetal position, but instead, I turned my fear into anger and took it out on the road as Kevin and I broke every speed limit law in California to get to the Kaiser hospital in Fontana seventy miles inland.

My parents, Joseph and Louise Bastian, lived in Beaumont, California and had enjoyed several years of the typical baby-boomer retirement life: golf practically every day, plenty of eating out, and the full enrichment offered by a slow-paced life. I tried to visit every few weeks and catch up but had failed miserably the last few months, knowing their relationship was on the rocks. I suspected my mom's drinking had gotten worse, but wasn't sure.

I'd purposely avoided talking to them about my skiing accident. As much as I wanted to share the details, my mom would hit the bottle hard at the simple thought of losing her only child. And if I mentioned to my Catholic dad the possibility of the reincarnation angle, his head would explode.

Dad was the driving force behind raising me with strict Catholic beliefs. But instead of growing up a good Catholic boy like he'd wanted me to, I instead boycotted the entire program, sloughing off the teachings, protocols, and philosophies as religious dogma that made no sense whatsoever. A hundred percent illogical. Although my mom attended church with us when I was young, that was mostly to avoid another shouting match.

Religious manipulation efforts aside, as dad's go, I'd say mine was decent. There was never a shortage of love and dad jokes in our home. Except when he lost his temper, which always confused the hell out of me. One day he'd be this loving, caring role model of a dad. The next day I would be shunned as some evil devil child, completely worthless and the target of multiple lashes with his belt. How could a loving father be so brutal?

"Need to toughen you up," he'd say just before cracking down on my butt.

Toxic masculinity at its finest.

When I went off to college, though, his crinkled eyes anchored a face beaming with pride. As long as our discussions steered clear of religion or spirituality, we stayed on acceptable speaking terms.

On the 91 freeway headed east, I topped out at over a hundred miles an hour during the forty-five-minute drive to Fontana. Kevin and I screeched into the hospital parking lot, checked in with the front desk, and made our way to the ICU.

My mom was seated in a chair next to dad's bed, tears streaming from her bloodshot, puffy eyes. I walked in, gave her a hug and asked how she was holding up.

"I thought we'd have at least another ten years, maybe more," she said with a forced smile. Her words and emotions confused me and I balled my hands into fists at my side.

"Hope it's okay if Kevin visits with us," I said, waving my arm toward my buddy. He gave her a hug, too. "What's the doc saying? Dad's gonna make it, right?"

"Of course I am, sport," my dad managed to choke out with a low, gravelly voice, eyes half-open.

I rushed to his side. He coughed up a mouthful of phlegm.

Seeing my once-strong father in this weakened condition made me question my own strength, my own life force.

Mom crossed her arms and leaned back in her chair. "They say they expect a full recovery." She curled her lip. "He needs rest and time for his head to get better. Apparently, it was a relatively minor stroke, but you never know."

Dad glanced my way and said with a dismissive wave, "Never listen to the naysayers, bud. We'll be back out on the golf course soon enough, you and me."

I pulled up a chair for Kevin, one for myself, and sat. Mom punched me in the shoulder.

"You and your dad, I tell ya."

I managed to fight the urge to avoid looking at my dad's face, but once I did, he'd already closed his eyes. I nudged his shoulder. "Dad?" No response.

Mom spoke up. "He's going to be in and out of it for the next few days they said." She gripped and twisted her wrists, more tears forming puddles in her eyes, threatening to break free any second. I put my arm around her shoulders and gave her a squeeze.

"Worrying you must run in the family, on Dad's side," I said, a failed attempt at humor.

She let out a shaky chuckle, covered her mouth and wiped droplets onto her fingertips from below her eyelids. "You seem a little off, Sweetie. Anything new in your life?"

"Don't worry about me, Mom, I'm fine," I lied, not wanting to concern her with my hallucinations. Or ghost sightings. Or whatever the hell was wrong with me. "Had a checkup today at Huntington and they said I'm a hundred percent."

Her lips parted and she let out a long sigh.

I leaned in and gave her another hug.

"I wish we could rewind a few years," she said.

A nurse popped her head into the room. "Visiting hours end in five minutes."

After a pause, Kevin butted in. "Yo, John, tell your mom about your visions."

My mouth fell open.

Shaking my head, I said, "She's got enough on her plate." I looked to my mom. "Sorry, he shouldn't have said that."

"Said what? What's wrong, Johnny?"

"It's nothing, mom, honest." I scratched my jaw, staring at Kevin.

"You might as well tell me. We have nothing but time right now, even if visiting hours are almost up."

I drew in a deep breath, exhaled, and did what any loving son would do in this situation: change the subject.

"Got a big escrow scheduled to close soon."

"Oh honey, that's wonderful." She tilted her head.

An annoying buzzing noise came from the room next to us, echoing throughout the ward. Hospital staff buzzed around, making shuffling noises, yelling something about "code blue" and a "crash cart." Several of the nurses flocked to the other room.

"Glad we're not in there," I said, with Mom and Kevin both looking around.

Then she shifted her eyes, stared deep into my soul, and patted the top of my knee.

"Your father's on some pretty heavy meds. I say we go get a bite to eat."

I agreed. "If Dad's gonna be out of it for a while, maybe afterwards, Kevin can drive himself home in my Beemer and I'll chauffeur you back to Beaumont so you can get some rest. Plus, we need to catch up on a few things."

"I'd like that."

We left the hospital. While grabbing some food at a nearby bar and grill, we reminisced about the good old days with Dad.

Mom excused herself, said she needed to visit the restroom, but snuck over to the bar instead and ordered a drink, probably her usual: double bourbon, neat.

Two years of sobriety, gone in the snap of your fingers.

While Mom dealt with the stress her way, I whipped out my iPhone and continued researching reincarnation, the curiosity getting the better of my reluctance to use the small screen.

As Kevin caught up on texts from his agent, I read story after story after story about reincarnation. Still highly improbable, though. No way half the planet's human population was wrong about something so critical as death.

After sharing a story with Kevin, I asked, "Maybe all these people made up their own fiction?"

He pulled out some printouts he'd made at his house earlier. "Or wanted attention," he said without looking up. "But you and me, man, we both logical people. Committin' fraud for purposes of getting' media attention and/or money seems feasible. At least for one or two, but for all these people to make up such insane, wild stories just for attention . . . I don't know, man."

Kevin focused his attention to one of the printouts and continued. "Especially parents with zero motivation whatsoever to pull a stunt and put their families through the ringer. I'm talkin' about educated parents, ones with Christian or other religious backgrounds."

According to the stuff online, scientists had proven with factual, physical evidence, beyond a reasonable doubt that thousands of children across the globe—all under the age of six—had been reincarnated.

But it was more likely that ghosts or demons were possessing these poor kids?

Mom returned, along with the scent of booze on her breath and we chatted a bit more as she ate her chicken salad.

At the end of the meal I realized even more how important my Dad had been to me growing up.

We said goodbye to Kevin, then he zoomed off in my Beemer, headed back to his place. In my mom's old Camry, I drove her back to their Beaumont home, another half hour drive east of the hospital.

I pulled up to the outskirts of their gated community and punched in the secret code. The black wrought iron security gate swung open and we rolled toward their quaint, comfortable two-story modern home adjacent to the twelfth hole of their golf course, aptly named "Turnberry" because of all the twists and turns of the various fairways. We pulled into the garage and went inside.

"You can get yourself some water, Johnny, I'm sure you're thirsty," she said. "I need another drink." She climbed to the highest cabinet, swiped a bottle of Kentucky bourbon and continued self-medicating.

I filled two glasses with water, brought both to the kitchen table and sat next to her.

"Now, mister. I want you to tell me everything. We don't keep secrets, remember?" she asked, slurred, but with a smile. Her eyes still showed signs from crying.

I darted my gaze down to my glass, then back up to her. "At Mammoth Mountain, I hit a tree. Was in a coma for three days."

She gasped, covering her mouth with her hand. "Oh my goodness, are you alright? Why didn't you or Kevin tell me?"

"I told him not to. You know how you get whenever I'm injured, plus you were on the wagon and I didn't want to do anything to knock you off. Too late now, I guess. But remember when I was ten, how many people you pissed off at my soccer game when I broke my ankle?"

"I don't overreact. I do what any mother would—"

"The point is, when I woke up, something inside me had changed." I took a deep breath and continued. "This is gonna sound totally nuts, but I saw a ghost, then apparently told the doctor my name was Jack Bachman, that I was married to someone named Tammy, I was hunting for a treasure of gold coins, and an angry man cut off my right arm with an axe—"

My mom gave me such a wide-eyed stare I couldn't continue.

Then the blood drained from her face. Something was wrong. Definitely wrong.

# CHAPTER 20

**M**y mom put her hand on her chest, apparently stunned about something I'd said. Not the reaction I was expecting. Sad. Yes. Worried. Yes. Shocked, but at the same time almost giddy? No.

"Hold on, Johnny, slow down. One thing at a time. You saw a ghost?"

"Honestly, I don't know if I'm losing my mind here, or what."

"Married to a woman named Tammy, too? Interesting . . ."

I read her face as though she'd found a missing puzzle piece.

"I know. Like I said, totally crazy. I tried to chalk it up to some kind of intense dream or drug-induced hallucination during the coma, but that was over a week ago and I feel like I'm still in the dream, like I'm still connected to this woman I've never met, and she's—and this sounds weird, too—in danger. My right arm hurts constantly, at the shoulder joint, where the man cut off my arm in my dream. My eczema there is worse than ever and my senses keep going on overload, which is all freaking me out." I lowered my gaze to the table.

"And you're rocking, too." She bent her neck, then blinked. "Tell me about the ghost."

I tried to stop rocking but couldn't. Without rocking, the same uncomfortable, jittery feeling came over me, just like when I tried to make eye contact. "Two ghosts, actually. So real. I swear. I always thought ghosts would be transparent, like in the movies, but the first one, a little boy, was as real as you or me are right now. Except, apparently nobody else could see him. Only me."

"Maybe it was an actual boy, not a ghost." She furrowed her brow, likely pondering the possibilities like I'd done a thousand times.

"Exactly what I thought, but I somehow also knew things about him. Like how he died. And his age. And his name."

"Odd."

I nodded. "And when he spoke to me, the doctor said she couldn't hear him, only I could. Apparently, the little boy was the deceased son of the doctor helping me recover from my coma, which totally creeps me out."

"I'll bet." She took a sip of water, paused, thinking, leaning back in her chair. "I want to hear more about this Tammy woman."

I stood, walked to the fruit basket on the counter and grabbed an apple. The taste of the crisp red fruit brought back emotions of fall. With my eyes closed, joyful memories flooded in of carving pumpkins, Thanksgiving dinner in a small home in Thibodaux, Louisiana—wait, what? I opened my eyes and rubbed my face.

I sat back in the same chair, leaned in toward my mom, and asked, "Did we ever travel to Louisiana?"

She glanced up at the ceiling. "Nope. Never."

"Anywhere in the South?"

"Nope."

"I remember a Thanksgiving dinner with Tammy and several other family members. There was another guy who looked exactly like me, and an older guy named Bryan, his wife Elaine, and some friends of ours."

"I'm sure it was only a memory of some weird, random dream you've had, honey." She patted my knee, but as she did, my entire focus shifted to her hand, and the touch, and the rough feel of the jeans' cotton on my thigh skin, and my strong urge to recoil, wishing she would remove her hand, which she did after what seemed like an eternity. Normally, I didn't mind when my mom touched me; in fact, it usually felt comforting.

*Odd.*

My respiration had increased, as had my pulse. I shook my head, returning to the discussion. "That's the problem. Logically, I agree with you, but emotionally, mentally, no. This feels like something that really happened."

She curled her lips. "Holy Moly." She put her palms to her forehead and leaned back in her chair, motionless. After several seconds she jumped up, slapped her hand on the table and said, "Just remembered something. Stay here. I'll be right back," then scurried up the stairs. Some muffled banging noises made their way down to me.

A few minutes later, she raced back to the table carrying a gray shoe box with a dusty black lid.

"Have you spoken to anyone else about your dreams besides Kevin and me?" she asked.

"I saw my shrink yesterday and she said the memories might be evidence of a past life, but that seems pretty farfetched." I expected another form of some shocked expression on her face, but no. *What the hell is happening?* "Honestly, I'm having trouble wrapping my head around that as a possibility."

Holding the lid on tight, her voice cracked as she said, "Take a look at the items in this box." She took a hard swallow. "As long as we're sharing crazy stories, you might not believe this, but do you remember not talking until you were four years old?"

I tilted my head. "No way. You never said anything about—"

"Your psychiatrist at the time recommended we drop the whole issue. Said you'd move on and wouldn't remember and it would be best if we never brought it up again."

*My psychiatrist?* I searched my mind for memories of being a mute. None.

"That can't be."

"Swear to God. And you had nightmares. Night terrors, actually. That's what the psychiatrist called them."

I gazed down at my shoes, still wracking my brain for any memories of this. Nothing. "Not once have I ever seen a shrink. Not even a therapist, well, until the divorce."

My mom bit her lip before taking a sip of bourbon and continuing. "Sorry, Sweetie, you did. You couldn't talk, but you had these amazing drawing skills. You communicated to your dad and me entirely with body language and with crayon sketches."

I stood and raked my fingers through my hair. With my other hand on my waist, I turned away. "I have zero recollection of that. And I've never been much of an artist, either."

"The psychiatrist said you'd probably forget everything and would be better off anyway. Said you'd probably repress the memories."

*Repressed? More like deleted.*

"The other kids in your preschool would draw pictures of food, flowers, cars, pets, whatever. But you drew these graphic, horrible images of death. Blood and gold and trees and swamps. Here."

I turned back toward her and leaned onto the table. She swiped a layer of dust from the top of the shoe box and plucked off the lid, exposing a jumbled mess of papers and small colored clay objects.

I sat next to her, then hovered close to get a better view of all the cool little things inside the box.

"Johnny, you started having the night terrors when you were about two and a half and continued until you were around five.

You'd wake up in the middle of the night screaming bloody murder. When I'd come to your bed, we'd spend a good half hour calming you down."

"I swear I have zero memories of any night terrors."

She nodded, rubbing her chin. "That's a blessing, believe me. Weird thing is that the psychiatrist said there's no way you, as young as you were, could hallucinate or have memories like that. Kids aren't supposed to know violence, especially not at the level you drew in your drawings." She held up one drawing and gave a tight-lipped smile. "He was so fond of you; I think he enjoyed the challenge of figuring you out. I remember he told me your condition was unique because you had all of the physical symptoms of post-traumatic stress disorder, even though you'd never had any actual trauma happen to you." She paused again, squinting, looking through the rear sliding door to the golf course outside. "At least not in this lifetime."

She set down the drawing and picked up another one, stared at it for a second, then back up to me, straight into my eyes. I looked away, giving in to that weird feeling again of not being able to look anyone in the eye. I rubbed absently at my arms.

"You'd have dilated pupils," she said, clearing her throat, then swallowing. "Increased heart rate, and all the classic symptoms of what he called hyper-arousal. You were jittery, easily startled by noise, and always had to have your back to a wall whenever we went somewhere."

I blinked rapidly, picking up one of the pictures and studying the image.

"PTSD? At four years old? I thought that's what our military guys have after they fight in war."

"You're right and this might be hard for you to digest, but," she said, taking another deep breath, "you made a bunch of vivid drawings of a man chasing you with an axe. She bit her lower lip again. "Here." She slid the drawing closer to me and shivered. "This one gave me nightmares. Honestly, I never wanted to see this thing again and thought about burning it.

But see here?" She pointed to a little stick figure. "It looks like this guy, whoever he is, or was, cut off your arm and killed you." She winced and continued, with downturned facial features. "Blood everywhere. This shocked the hell out of us. Four years old, Johnny! I couldn't sleep for weeks. I felt so bad for you. Your young little brain thought all of this was somehow real." With shaking fingers, she pointed to several blotches of red crayon splattered on the paper. "And here, look on the left side of the page." Her lower lip trembled as she pointed to another stick figure on my drawing. "This guy's smiling and looks like your friend, but here on the right side, he has fire in his eyes as he's leaning over . . ." Her broken voice trailed off, her hand over her mouth, looking up, tears welling. "Your bloody body." She stood, covered her hands over her face, and wailed out pure dread that had been pent up for decades.

Several curly lines were drawn in the lower corner. White flowers? Gardenias? In a row in front of a brick wall drawn in perspective.

*Can four-year-olds draw in perspective?*

I stood and, with a warm embrace, patted her back. "That could be anybody, Mom," I said, failing to sound confident. "You don't know that's me."

"It's you. Trust me. You didn't speak, but you were a genius at non-verbal communication, especially with all the questions we asked you." She wiped tears from her cheeks, sniffled, and stared back down at the image. "It always amazed me how you'd point your fingers. You'd make hand gestures the same way adults do."

Goose bumps rose on both my forearms, my body somehow knowing all this was true. "Seriously?"

*Could this really have happened?*

We sat again, then after another deep breath, she fished out a different crayon drawing from the box. "This one creeped me out, too." The sketch showed two stick men—one figure held an axe, the other guy had blood spurting out of his shoulder. Green stick trees and brown water surrounded the men.

I shuffled through several other drawings, glancing at each one, absorbing the various messages, all of which depicted different angles of the same scene, telling a story. Incredible. My mind kicked into overdrive and the internal slide show started up again.

Lowering my hand into the box, I retrieved a small shiny metal airplane. "I don't remember this either."

She took another sip. "You had an uncanny familiarity with airplanes. Various makes and models, engine horsepower, speeds. Oddly enough, especially small commercial planes."

Written in black ink on the bottom of the plane: *Johnny, 1983*

I closed my eyes, floating in darkness, trying to access the long forgotten memories. "Somehow I know you're right. I haven't thought about planes for years, but this is a model of a DC-9. I'm sure."

Our fluffy black kitty walked up to me and rubbed her fur across the side of my shin. "Hello Pushkin," I said, picking up the feline and placing the old gal on my lap. She had been in our family for twenty years. We shared a special bond, but for some reason, she didn't want to stay seated. Instead, she climbed up onto my shoulders and plopped down like a lazy ragdoll. Her fur felt extra soft on my palm and fingertips. And she weighed heavier than I remembered, with her purr hitting my eardrums loud and strong, like never before. She moved her nose close to my ear and for the first time, started nibbling on my earlobe, which tickled. Everything about her felt more focused, more intense.

"That's odd. She's never done that before," Mom said.

As I continued petting Pushkin, I enjoyed the sensation of having a cat lie on my shoulders for the first time.

Mom sniffled again, then continued. "You knew stuff about flying that kids your age weren't supposed to know, like millimeters of mercury, bearing, that the foot pedals steer the plane when you're on the ground, and you wrote the number of the speed pilots rotate Cessna 172's when they take off. Right here, where it says 65 kia, with the little airplane on the runway and the rotating arrows."

I crossed my arms. "No idea what 'kia' is." The cat stopped purring.

"I felt like I was losing my mind, not being able to help you, watching you suffer like that, so after the first few episodes, I started a journal of every single one of your night terrors, my interpretations of your drawings, and eventually, the words you spoke once you started talking." She handed me a dried out leather-bound book and I leafed through dozens of pages of hand-written notes detailing my alleged saga. She'd documented over eighty different times when I woke up crying and screaming, all between the ages of three and five. Every few days, another night terror. My brain must have been trying to tell me something.

"I swore I'd never tell you this, but what the hell. Your official diagnosis at the time was possible schizophrenia, which had your father and me as worried as a pair of deaf bats. Once, when we took you to the local zoo, another little boy touched your forearm and you freaked out, total temper tantrum. Like someone was trying to rip your arm out of its socket, and we couldn't calm you down no matter what we tried." She paused again, staring long and hard outside, eyes watering up. "You were always sensitive to touch, almost like you felt pain whenever anyone other than me came into contact with your skin. I had nightmares about what would happen to you if you never started talking, what awful parents we must be for causing you all that suffering, trying to figure out what we'd done wrong. So much guilt." She placed her folded arm on the table and buried her face in the elbow crotch.

I reached out, put my hand on top of mom's and gave a gentle squeeze.

"I'm so sorry you had to go through all that."

Mom looked up toward the ceiling and slid a finger beneath both eyes, catching more tears before they broke free.

"On your fifth birthday, we'd had enough and were desperate. Your father had a friend of a friend, a hypnotherapist, and, even though I was super skeptical, we took you there and over the course of about a month of daily sessions, you slowly started to come out of your little world. Long story short, the good news is by the time you were six, everything weird had stopped. Your touch sensitivity went away, your social skills kicked in, you could make eye contact like a normal person, the night terrors vanished and you started sleeping like a normal boy. You actually enjoyed being around other kids. We enrolled you in soccer and you absolutely thrived. It was amazing to watch the transformation. You were basically autistic, which is supposed to be an untreatable condition, but you somehow grew out of it. Later, they came out with this term I read about that said kids with symptoms like yours are referred to as 'on the spectrum'."

*Same condition Kelly said I might have.*

"I remember playing soccer. Good times."

She drew in a long breath and pushed out a quick exhale, tapping her palms on top of her thighs, then handed me another crayon drawing with a circle with three-hundred-sixty degrees shown, a stick figure steering the plane with his feet, and another '65 kia' above a plane rotating right before lifting off the runway.

"Knots Indicated Airspeed," I said before I realized I'd said anything.

"How do you know that?"

"No idea."

"After you drew this, your father and I went to the library. We looked up 'rotation speed' and the number written here is spot-on correct for a typical Cessna 172."

A rush of fear flowed through me.

"This is freaking me out," I said as Pushkin jumped down onto the tile floor and I stood, turning my back to Mom, walking toward the rear sliding glass door.

Mom came over and rubbed her palm on my upper back. "This was one of the sweeter ones," she said, handing another drawing to me, which showed what looked like a woman with orange hair, blue eyes, and letters scribbled at the top: "T-A-M-I." Bright red hearts surrounded her body and face, she had an oversized smile and appeared to be wearing a ring on her left hand with two tiny green blots and a white one on top of a gold circle.

The Tammy images in my mind gained intensity, with new ones appearing in my mental slide show. Vivid to the point that I could barely see my mom, the golf course, the table, the room, and everything in my reality. Not only was my field of vision filled with Tammy, but I started hearing her voice talking to me as clear as if she had been sitting at the table with us.

"Johnny, I love you," Mom said, hugging me from the side. "And I'll always be here for you, no matter what." Tears pooled in my eyes and broke free down my cheeks. The emotion felt hyper-intense, so concentrated and overwhelming.

"I can tell this is perfectly real for you, but it's not," she said. "You're gonna hate me for saying this, but I think you have to ignore all this and find a way to move on."

# CHAPTER 21

I broke down and wept on my mom's shoulder like some grief-stricken child. My dad would be ashamed. Not the behavior of the man he raised.

"I feel like I'm in a dream and can't wake up. Deep in my heart there's this crazy, throbbing love for this Tammy woman, but at the same time, I'm confused because loving someone I've never met just isn't logical." I knew I was rambling but couldn't help myself. The cat meowed for food.

We ended our embrace. "Come sit back at the table, honey." On the tablecloth, my mom set out another drawing.

I picked up the next crayon sketch. As I wiped baby tears from my face, my mom continued. "This picture here." She pinched the corner with her fingertips, wiggling the paper. "We never figured out what it meant." Apparently, I'd used four different colors of crayon to draw lines, circles, and something that looked possibly like a calculus equation. I rotated the paper to try and make sense of the numbers, but nothing came to me. Mom handed another drawing to me.

"And look at this one, too, Sweetie."

I sniffled, took another bite of apple, set down the previous drawing and took hold of the largest paper in the bunch. On an eleven by seventeen-inch piece of cardstock, my childhood self had drawn a dominant round, bald head, about six inches in width, and two scribbled lines of brown hair. A three-inch gray airplane flew in the background amidst a light blue sky, next to a full-circled yellow sun near the upper right hand corner. Some more chicken-scratch text in the lower left read: "J-A-K--B-A-K-M-A-N."

Goosebumps popped up on both my forearms. Out of the corner of my eye I thought I saw the man from the gondola standing in the kitchen corner. I whipped my head up to see. Nothing.

Dammit.

My legs jittered, the urge to move growing stronger. I had to stand again.

I rubbed my palms up and down on my face, went to the living room and walked in circles.

My mom approached, holding her glass, taking another sip, eyebrows fully arced, and a slow nod. "Pretty trippy."

A thought hit me. "This probably means we're dealing with more than reincarnation. Or maybe something I made up. A fantasy. And getting conked in the head by that Mammoth tree somehow unlocked hidden memories of a fantasy I'd completely repressed. That's all. I'm simply remembering some stuff I went through as a kid. This is nothing real. Just a pure psychological experience." I tried to convince myself of this new line of reasoning, but deep inside me, doubt reverberated everywhere.

Mom wandered back to the shoe box and pulled out a tiny clay figure, a miniature woman five inches tall, with detailed paint covering the entire surface. I stepped back to the kitchen table.

"Maybe. Here." She handed the figurine to me. "You had exceptional skill at making little clay figures like this."

*Why didn't any of these skills persist into adulthood? If I was such an amazing artist and had exceptional drawing and sculpting skills, why am I not an architect or draftsman? Or 3D modeling expert? How did all these skills just vanish?*

Mom continued. "Our first dog tore into this box a long time ago and all were destroyed. Except this one. We somehow managed to save it."

The figurine was an intricate 3D version of the orange-haired woman from the drawing. From my dreams. She wore a light blue dress with white trim. My young self had carved a big smile across the woman's face. "This is Tammy."

My mom nodded. Cringing, she said, "There's something else, too, but I'm not sure you're ready to hear. It's a little creepy."

I finished my apple, chucked the core into the trash can, downed the rest of my water and set the glass hard on the table. After a hard swallow, I said, "You might as well blurt it out. I'm done being shocked for today."

She rubbed the palms of her hands on the tops of the jeans again, clenching her teeth. "When you finally started talking, you caught up. Fast. Thousands of words flooded your brain, as though you'd been talking the whole time. No developmental lag."

"Sounds normal."

"No. Learning to speak that quickly was not normal. Not by a long shot, according to your doctors. But here's what worried us: you had an accent. A southern accent. And boy was it a strong one." She rubbed her chin. "And here's the kicker: they told us the accent was . . . Louisianan."

The air in my lungs escaped and I slapped my chest, sucking in enough oxygen to vacuum the carpet. "You're kidding me."

"And somehow you knew all about Cajun and Creole food. Way more than you should have."

"I can't believe that. This is some kind of scene from Punk'd." In complete disbelief, I pushed myself away from the table, stood, and looked around for hidden cameras. "Please tell me you're joking." I stepped toward her and stared down into her eyes.

She took my hands into hers, giving me a loving gaze full of pain, like she had raised a crazy man. "Listen to me, honey, you grew up here in Southern California, raised by two parents who speak, well, Californian English. Neither of us have a southern accent, your grandparents don't have a southern accent, none of our friends or neighbors did. You never watched any TV shows with anyone with a southern accent. In fact, you'd never been exposed to anything from Louisiana at that point in your life, so your accent came as a total shock. Completely unexpected and inexplicable."

"I don't have a southern accent now. Don't remember having one at all."

"Over about a year, the accent slowly faded. By your sixth birthday you sounded just like the rest of us."

"I'm having a hard time processing all this." I felt tired and wanted to go to bed. "Why did you wait until now to tell me all this?"

She stood, downed the rest of her bourbon, walked over to the fridge, pulled out a Diet Coke and popped open the can. "Honey, your father had a stroke today and we're not getting any younger." She took a sip. "You're having these wild, vivid memories of something that, at least in your mind, actually happened. Your story matches up with what bothered you as a child. From where I stand, I think sharing all this with you is the right thing to do. Before now, though, I had no reason to drudge up all the horrors from the past."

"I'll bet Dad would flip if he knew about what's been happening. This weird connection to my childhood."

She nodded. "Every now and then, your father and I talk about it and although he's pretty much repressed the hell out of what we all went through, I know he's just as curious as I am about what happened and why."

"Maybe we should tell him when he wakes up."

She took a beat to think. "No. Until you have answers, bringing this up now wouldn't go over too well."

"I feel lost."

She took another sip and set the Coke onto the kitchen table, then leaned toward me and rubbed my cheek with the backside of her fingers. "One option for you is simple. Take all this stuff somewhere, squirt lighter fluid on it and toss in a match. Burn all these bad memories and move on. Maybe the universe is trying to tell you something."

I thought about telling my mom about the ghost sighting—or hallucination or whatever—from a minute ago.

She stood, put her hands on my shoulders from behind and squeezed. "I know all I've given you here are more questions," she said with a loving smile, "but you need to move on with your life."

"Don't you think Dad would want me to go find answers? You guys have been waiting over three decades to find out why in God's earth I put you guys through all that trauma."

"I'll admit I'm curious, both of us are, but we don't need answers. Not at the expense of your mental health."

"I want to be here when Dad gets out of the hospital, but this pull, this force to go to Louisiana is like gravity, I can't seem to fight it."

"Honey, I'm sure you can wait a couple of days. I'm trying to manifest that he'll make a full recovery, but you gotta give him time."

I paused, giving my next move serious thought. "No. If dad was awake and knew all this shit, he'd want me to go. I have to find answers about Tammy or else these feelings of anxiety and regret will haunt me for the rest of my life."

Mom's mouth turned downward.

I wet my lips as the decision fully soaked into every cell in my body. "Dad always said, *nothing ventured, nothing gained.*"

# CHAPTER 22

**A**lthough mentally drained, I stayed up late studying reincarnation. Oddly enough, the deeper I slid down into the rabbit hole, the more fascinating it all seemed. And perplexing. I ended up printing out and highlighting several inches of web pages and PDF's by the time my eyes slid shut in the wee hours of the night.

The next morning, and despite the constant worry about my dad, I whipped out my phone and called Kevin to tell him my plan to take a road trip to Louisiana alone.

"I'm going with you, dog," Kevin said.

"That's very generous, but no, I gotta do this alone. I'll be all right. You've got your big gig coming up. Should probably practice your routine."

"Ain't no way you gonna go to Louisiana by yourself. You gotta have someone there to keep your white ass safe. I got your back. Plus, I'll bet my mom knows people who can help us."

I paused for a few seconds, ideas bouncing around in my head.

"Fine. Be over here within an hour or I'm leaving without you," I said, half-joking.

Once on the freeway, I realized we had no idea where exactly in Louisiana to go, but figured we had three days of driving time to find a reasonable destination.

We blazed along Interstate 10, across the California border into Arizona. I reached into the back seat, pulled out the stack of printed docs from the previous night and handed it to Kevin.

"There's a ton more information out there than I thought," I said, patting the top of the pile. I explained how I had initially Googled reincarnation stories, but since most were cheesy with zero science or logic, I had discarded eighty percent of what I had found, easily dismissed as something other than reincarnation. For example, there was the story of the little girl who thought she was Marilyn Monroe in a past life. The story explained zilch about the facts or details, other than what the girl thought. Well, heck, most kids would think they were someone else at some point in their lives. I thought I was Batman when I was seven.

As the desert landscape blurred past us, Kevin pored through the stack of papers, absorbing the information.

Fortunately, deep in the recesses of the internet, hidden between a bazillion HTML and PHP pages, buried way down in the weeds, I'd found several allegedly credible stories written by reputable, educated professionals exploring this phenomenon. These tales from the beyond were well-written by scientists—including several medical doctors—using the scientific method, and offered possibilities besides reincarnation to explain the children's behavior.

More desert landscape sped past as Kevin and I shared ideas and thoughts.

Whether I was experiencing aftereffects of an actual reincarnation or not, my defensive ice shield had melted. The concept had become plausible, useful even. To me, at least.

But I still didn't wholly believe in reincarnation. My religious upbringing was rooted deeply in my head. You die, you go to heaven or hell. No other explanation.

"Some pretty weird-ass stuff goin' on here, man," Kevin said.

From behind the seat, after a brief unintended swerve, I retrieved and handed him the box of clues I had inadvertently sent to my adult self as a young boy. "Dude, my mom told me this crazy story yesterday. Apparently, when I was a toddler, I had night terrors and drew all these pictures about this stuff with the gold treasure, Tammy, and some angry guy killing me with an axe. All the same stuff I've been seeing in my visions, I saw as a four-year-old."

I asked Kevin to pull out the indecipherable drawing with the calculus equations written and stared at the numbers, equations, and images. The center right side had the letters "L-A" scribbled in black crayon.

"Maybe the 'L-A' is an abbreviation for Los Angeles," Kevin said.

"Maybe. But my visions are of a swamp or bayou in Louisiana."

We parked at a roadside rest stop to handle the call of Mother Nature. Walking back to the car, I tossed the keys to Kevin. "You drive."

Back on the road, I took control of the iPad, pulled up a Google Map of Louisiana and searched.

After another thirty minutes of driving eastward, I found a map of the Mississippi River that traversed through New Orleans. A missing piece to the puzzle clicked in my head. The shape of a dark blue wavy line on my drawing matched up pretty well with the scale and shape of the snaking river.

Kevin glanced between the road and the iPad.

Pointing to the drawing, I said, "See how the line here continues up through what would be Baton Rouge, assuming the crayon line drawn by my four-year-old toddler self thirty-four years ago was, in fact, the Mississippi River?"

Kevin looked forward, through the windshield and said, "Yep. West Baton Rouge, to be exact. You drew an arrow that points from that spot to another bunch of scribbly lines in the upper corner. The tiny brown and gold rectangle with gold circles. Maybe the treasure?"

"Gonna do a search for lost treasures in the Baton Rouge area," I said, fingers flying across the keyboard, as we zoomed past a gasoline tanker.

Scrolling through a ton of websites, I summarized to Kevin how Louisiana had been a hotbed for treasure hunters for several decades.

"Who knew?" he asked before I continued, explaining how apparently, the laws of Louisiana allowed the finder of a treasure to keep the discovery, even if the valuables were found on public land.

One particularly fascinating old tale wove itself around an island quest for the lost gold of Jacques Lafayette.

Dark brown, sharp mountaintops peaked along the eastern horizon in front of us.

"Check this out," I read, "according to legend, in 1841 a wealthy French merchant named Jacques Lafayette arrived late one evening to his family mansion." I leaned over, showing Kevin an iPad image, a detailed oil painting of a stern-looking man with a bulbous nose and pork chop sideburns, wearing a shiny black silk top-hat. The man, easily in his sixties, had a certain gaze about him that screamed control-freak.

"Says here he'd lost his wife to cholera a decade earlier, but he dealt with his grief and pain by spending most of his time traveling the world with his daughter, Bridgette. According to the legend, in addition to her stunning beauty, Bridgette had a natural gift for advanced mathematics. She enjoyed the field of astronomy and taught herself geometry, trigonometry, and even calculus, which was unheard of back then, especially for a lady."

My summary continued, describing how by traveling the globe, Lafayette had built up a successful trading company that bought and sold tobacco between the Americans and French. In doing so, he amassed a fortune. A frugal man by nature, he only spent what he needed to live a lifestyle of minimalist luxury. He was known to have been keen on avoiding wasteful spending.

When Lafayette had walked through the front door of his mansion that fateful night, he heard muffled screams coming from the kitchen. Disturbed, he dropped his leather satchel and sprinted across the living room to the kitchen where he saw his beloved daughter lying on her back on the wooden floor, a younger man on top having his way with her. But the rapist was clearly enjoying himself to the point where he did not hear Jacques, who had made eye contact with his daughter as he tip-toed to the counter and slid a razor-sharp cleaver from the knife bucket.

Jacques carefully stepped toward the man. Calling upon the strength of ten men from deep inside his belly—where the grief for his wife had festered and combined with this fresh wave of anger for a man violating his precious little girl—Jacques struck a fatal blow to the back of the man's skull. But it wasn't enough. He had awoken something dark and sinister inside himself, continuing to butcher the rapist's neck, ultimately hacking off his blood-soaked head. Repeatedly, the daughter screamed as crimson poured onto her face and chest. Jacques grabbed a fistful of hair and held the head high, turning the face toward himself as he recognized the dead man as Richard Fatale, the local barber. Next to Bridgette, the man's limp torso fell to the floor with a loud thump. Jacques stood over his daughter, holding Richard's head, eyes full of rage, chest heaving in and out like some crazed animal.

Jacques used his right boot to shove the dead body away from his daughter, who was hiding her face with her hands, crying. Before he had a chance to toss the dripping wet, severed head to the other side of the room, Jacques took one final look into the eyes of Mr. Fatale. But the eyes, suspended in time and filled with surprised anger, only stared back at Jacques and drilled straight into his sad soul, forever haunting him.

Or so the story went.

"A three month long investigation ensued," I said. "The police accused Jacques of murder. During the trial, Jacques made detailed backup plans that included a scenario in case the jury found him guilty, to smuggle his daughter and wealth out of the country."

Way off in the distance, above the eastern Arizona desert horizon, I noticed massive cloud formations appearing high across the entire sky.

Fortunately for Jacques, I continued explaining to Kevin, his peers acquitted him of the crime. However, every so often the apparition of Mr. Fatale would be spotted late at night roaming the halls of their mansion, cradling the decapitated head in his hands.

"So, according to the story, Jacques had that damned rapist ghost trapped in his frickin' house?" Kevin asked.

"You got it."

"Lafayette seemed like a legitimate businessman. But I'm wondering, was the dude being haunted by Fatale or was he hallucinating 'cuz of the trauma of the tragedy? Don't know about you, but I wouldn't be able to get them shitty memories out of my damned head."

"Says here he made arrangements to leave Baton Rouge and sail back to Port-Saint-Louis-du-Rhone, on the southern coast of France."

A highway patrol car sped past us in the fast lane.

I continued. "Lafayette's trading company owned several wooden sailing ships. He brought one ship into port and loaded the vessel with all his worldly assets, planning to transport everything in his estate back to France. But as part of the preparations for his journey, he quietly piled his immense collection of over 70,000 Spanish doubloons into a wooden chest and stowed the treasure away in the cargo hold. The following November, now 1842, on a dreary morning a year after the rape, as a thick fog rolled into Baton Rouge and mere hours before Jacques planned to set sail to France, the ghost appeared. Only this time, the ghost scared Jacques to the point he had a heart attack. The next morning, Bridgette found his body in the upstairs hallway and, after several hours of grieving, her dad's spirit allegedly told her to instruct the sailors to dig a hole and bury the treasure chest near an ancient bald cypress tree along the waterway of one of the bayous. Over time, the treasure became known as the 'Trésor Fatale' and was apparently rumored to come with a curse."

Normally, these kinds of stories seemed silly to me, like forgotten fairy tales. But for some reason, this one resonated deep inside, sending a cold shiver down my spine. And I couldn't explain it at the time, but the entire story felt familiar to me, like I'd had a dream about it, or read about it somewhere else.

Intrigued, I speed read through the rest of the article. "Bridgette had sailed back to France, away from the painful memories of the rape and her father's death and planned to return the following year to find and retrieve the treasure. But her ship ran into a massive hurricane when they rounded the coast of Florida and sank. All crew members and Bridgette Lafayette drowned. Rumors spread that before she died, the young Lafayette woman had made a treasure map that pinpointed the precise location. But with her genius for math and puzzles, and not wanting just anyone to be able to read the map, she added a sophisticated level of complexity. A unique mathematical device needed to be used in conjunction with the map. Since nobody had a copy of the map and the details about the mathematical device were sketchy, the experts assumed the treasure had been lost forever, somewhere in Louisiana."

Kevin glanced between me and the road ahead. "You look pale, dude."

Le Trésor Fatale absolutely had something to do with my journey. Somehow, it connected to my love for this Tammy woman, all of which lit a fire of motivation deep inside my bones.

"Go. Faster. Now," I said to Kevin.

He floored the gas and raced to ninety miles an hour.

# CHAPTER 23

**Scott Jones**
*November 18, 2016*

Scott checked in at the airline counter, performed his exterior preflight check of the 737, and stepped into the cockpit. Same co-pilot as the recent flight to New York.

An image of the massage parlor and that sweet young Chinese gal entered his mind, but he put his primitive urges aside and focused on his job.

"There's my favorite copilot," said Scott to Jimbo, shaking hands before Scott sat in the captain's chair.

The two chatted for a bit about the hot flight attendant, Jimbo bragging how he did, in fact, get the woman into the sack that night. After a high five and a "Guess you're not such an asshole after all," from Jimbo, they put on their headsets, continued their pre-flight checklist and took off on schedule with an easterly heading toward Miami, Florida.

As they ascended through seventeen thousand feet, Scott pushed the "cabin talk" button to speak to his passengers.

"Good evening ladies and gentlemen," Scott said to his passengers. "This is Captain Scott Jones, I'll be flying us to Miami, Florida. The trip will be about an hour and fifty minutes, putting us at the arrival gate at approximately 11:50 pm eastern time. We're going to stay out in front of the hurricane brewing in the Gulf, so y'all don't need to worry none. This here flight should be nice and smooth so just sit back and relax."

Jimbo shook his head.

"They don't need to worry about the hurricane," Scott said. "It's the return flight that concerns me."

"Whatever."

The flight was, as Scott had promised, smooth all the way to Miami. They landed, parked, refueled and boarded the next group of passengers. By now, the hurricane had traveled further north and there was a chance their return flight would be cancelled. Scott checked in with the tower and evaluated the latest weather reports.

"If we fly at max speed, we can make it, but it's gonna be tight," Scott told Jimbo.

Once the cabin had been secured, they were quickly cleared for takeoff, rolled down the runway and jumped into the sky.

"Good evening ladies and gentlemen," Scott said into the microphone to the new passengers on their way back to New Orleans. "This is Captain Scott Jones, I will be flying us to New Orleans, Louisiana. For those of you concerned with the hurricane, not to worry, air traffic has cleared us a nice safe path to travel along our one hour and fifty-three-minute trip. There might be some turbulence, but it shouldn't be too bad. So just sit back and relax, we'll have you at the gate in no time."

But an hour into the flight, over the Gulf of Mexico, someone banged on the flight cabin door. The indicator beeper went off, which meant someone outside the cockpit wanted to chat with the pilot. Scott pressed the "talk" button.

"Captain, there's a man here demanding to talk with you," a woman said with a wavering shrill in her voice. "He has a knife and is holding a lady hostage."

Scott's eyes grew wide as he looked at Jimbo.

The door buzzer went off, meaning Meghan had requested access to the cockpit. Scott moved his hand to switch the cockpit door lever to "Open", but Jimbo grabbed Scott's wrist.

"No. That's not protocol. We have to keep that door locked," Jimbo said.

"No way, we need to go out there and see what's going on."

"That's. Not. Protocol."

"Shut up, stay put and don't move. Your controls."

Scott removed his headset, stood from his seat, walked to the cockpit door, and looked through the heavy fish-eye lens spyhole.

"It's Meghan. She's all freaked out," Scott said as some guy shuffled down the aisle toward the cockpit door, holding a woman in a choke hold with a knife to her throat.

The man banged on the door, grabbed the service phone and spoke into the receiver. Only Jimbo heard the man.

"He's saying he wants us to divert to Cuba or he'll kill the lady. If any of the other crew members come near him, he'll kill her," Jimbo said.

Scott licked his lips.

A hijacker.

"Fucking moron. No way. There's a goddamned Category Four hurricane between us and Cuba. We need to stall this bastard, but don't have much time." He looked at the floor, then surveyed the instrument panel. "Check the weather report, contact ATC, report the crime, then see how much time you can buy us by flying north a bit, away from the hurricane."

"Roger that," said Jimbo, immediately requesting the latest weather report, then notifying air traffic control of the hijacking.

Scott continued to watch the action unfold through the spyhole, then stepped back toward his seat, grabbed his headset, and spoke to the hijacker. "This is Captain Jones. I understand you would like us to—"

"Don't fuck with me, man," the hijacker said, panicked, with a thick New York accent, possibly Brooklyn. "Take me to Cuba or I put this knife through this bitch's neck. End of story."

"I understand. We're turning toward Cuba now. Please stay calm," Scott said.

With the night sky and no horizontal references through any cabin window, the only way someone would know the direction of the airplane was if they looked at the heading indicator, which read 303 degrees before their diversion north. This meant the plane headed in a northwesterly direction.

"Do a 375 degree turn to the right," Scott instructed Jimbo. "That'll put us onto a heading of three-one-eight. Then do the turn at a forty-five-degree bank to throw off his sense of direction. No way his inner ear can figure out which way we're goin' after that."

Jimbo complied.

The plane turned sharply to the right as the g-forces in the plane pulled everyone and everything downward.

Jimbo successfully executed more turns.

Scott spoke to the hijacker and lied. "Okay, we're now heading to Cuba." They were still heading in a northwesterly direction.

"How long 'til we land?" the man asked.

"We'll land in two hours," Scott replied.

Over the next two hours, Jimbo and Scott kept a close eye on the fuel. They headed toward Mississippi and made several minor heading corrections in succession to essentially travel in a circle at 25,000 feet above Louisiana.

The service phone beeped again. "We got to be getting close, man. Tell me where the hell we are," the man demanded.

"We'll be on the ground in ten minutes," Scott said, realizing the hijacker had to be getting tired, still standing behind the hostage in a choke hold.

"That's what you told me fifteen minutes ago, mother fucker! You better not be playing any games with me or I swear to God I'll slit her throat."

"I understand, sir. We're having some minor issues with the weather, but I assure you we will be on the ground soon," Scott said.

"Bullshit," Jimbo said to Scott, mic off. "We're out of time and running low on gas, Captain. We need to either head north and land somewhere in the next thirty minutes, or land now at Louis Armstrong."

Scott leaned against the cabin door, rubbing his chin. The animal instinct in him roared inside and came alive full force. "Right now, this asshole is standing right behind me. Next to the door," Scott said. "It's not like he has a gun or anything. Stay there." I got an idea."

Jimbo shook his head. "No, man. You do that and we are way outta bounds on protocol."

"Don't worry. I can be a prick sometimes, but I'm an ex-Marine and I know exactly how to handle this son-of-a-bitch. Never underestimate the power of the element of surprise, son," Scott said with a wink.

"Tell me why you want to go to Cuba," Scott said to the hijacker, looking through the peep hole in an attempt at distraction.

"Fuck you."

"Seriously. We have a few minutes. I genuinely want to know. Tell me all about it." Scott made sure his voice sounded calm.

The man's eyes darted around. He adjusted his grip on the knife and the passenger.

"My bitch wife cheated on me with some Cuban asshole named Rodrigo. Lives outside Havana."

"Are you kidding me?" Scott asked, trying to throw the man off.

"What?"

"The exact same thing happened to me. Fucking Cuban. Two-year affair. Had no idea."

The hijacker paused, shifted his stance.

"Hers was six months, man. Six months! She was fucking him, sucking him, licking his toes. Fucking sick, man. She promised to love me for life, man. For life!"

"I get it," Scott said. "I promise I'm gonna get you to Cuba and you can find that dickhead and stick that knife into his gut. You're gonna feel so much better. Show him who the real man is."

The hijacker nodded. "Yeah, man. I just . . . I just want Sara back, want her back the way things were before that Cuban asshole fucked everything up." Scott noted a shred of pain in his voice.

"I'm sure it wasn't Sara's fault. She still loves you. Everything's gonna be okay, trust me."

The hijacker loosened his grip on the passenger and let out a wail of grief that bordered on crying. *The first signs of breaking down.* Maybe even a tear broke free, hard to tell through the peephole. But close enough.

In a fraction of a second, Scott thrust open the door, used both hands to grab the hijacker's wrist holding the knife, and kneed the bastard in the balls.

The hostage fell to the ground, screaming, but unhurt.

The two men struggled for the knife. Scott tried to force the man off balance and, although twenty years the man's senior, overpowered him.

He whacked the back of the hijacker's hand onto a metal wall corner multiple times. The knife fell to the ground.

Scott went to work with right-left-right gut punches. He yanked the man's head down onto Scott's upward moving knee, exploding his face with blood, forcing his eyes shut, knees shaking.

Scott grabbed the man's right wrist and twisted counter-clockwise, which forced the man to turn around, then Scott shoved him onto the ground, face first, chest landing with a loud thud.

With Scott's knee in the man's back, he said to Meghan, "Get me the passenger restraints." She turned to her left, opened a compartment, retrieved a set of plastic Tuff-Ties, and handed them to Scott.

Bloodied and limp, the man passed out.

Scott continued wrapping the restraints around the guy's wrists before standing, putting his foot on top of the unconscious man and proclaimed, "All clear, ladies and gentlemen."

The entire plane erupted with cheer.

A man in the third row stood and approached Scott, Air Marshal credentials hanging from his black leather wallet.

"You're in big trouble, son," the air marshal said. Scott wondered why the hell the guy hadn't helped out. "I was waiting for the right time to take this guy down. You violated every goddamned rule in the book with your macho hero shit." He winked. "But let me take care of the worthless piece of cow dung so you can get back to flying." They shook hands.

Scott returned to the cockpit, picked up his headset and sat.

"Tell me where we're at. How we're doing?" Scott asked.

"Wow," Jimbo said. "We got twenty minutes of cruising fuel, more than enough to descend into Shreveport."

"I need to get back to New Orleans," Scott said.

"Sorry, sir, no can do. ATC's diverted us to Shreveport due to the weather. We were airborne too long. The hurricane is already hitting the coast with 100 knot gusts. You're a good pilot, but c'mon. One heroic act is enough for today."

Scott thought about the treasure and how the three-hundred-mile detour would set him back at least another day. He massaged his temples and ran his hand over his head. "Fine. Set our course for Shreveport."

# CHAPTER 24

**John Bastian**

*November 18, 2016*

Kevin and I spent the first night at a Motel 6 in Tucson, Arizona, after a quick meal at a taco shack and some ice-cold beers in our room.

After driving all day, I fell asleep fast.

I dreamt about my twenty-four-year-old-self working as a pilot for a small commercial airline, flying a plane headed to Las Vegas. The man in the dream was me, but as I walked through the terminal, sipping sweet tea, outside to the boarding ramp, crew members kept saying "Hi" to me using the name "Jack."

An intimate familiarity of the inner workings of the DC-9 flowed through my mind and I handled the preflight procedures with confidence before boarding.

After making my way into the cockpit, I placed my briefcase on the floor and continued the preflight checklist with the copilot, same as I'd done a million times before. Or at least it felt that way.

Apparently, three glassfuls of iced tea worked their way through my system and my bladder cried for release, so I sauntered to the rear of the plane, toward the bathroom, passing several passengers, one of whom was reading a magazine with Richard Nixon on the cover. Another read TIME that had an image of dense, green jungle foliage that read "Vietnam: Breaking it Down." The restroom door had a sliding sign posted above the aluminum handle: "Occupied."

A few seconds later, the door opened, a woman exited and stood there in front of me. The most beautiful redhead I had ever laid eyes on, she smiled up at me and time stopped as the angel stepped forward. But she tripped on the doorway and fell toward me. My pilot's hat slid off my head. Although I tried to catch her to land safely in my arms, I missed and she collapsed like a ragdoll, falling hard onto the floor.

*So much for helping my passengers!*

"I'm so sorry," I said, gently grabbing ahold of her wrist to help her up, a move that sent pleasant shockwaves across my skin.

"My goodness, I'm such a klutz," she said with an embarrassed smile and rosy cheeks.

"Not the first time I've seen someone trip on that darned doorway," I replied, picking up my hat and brushing off the top, as if a layer of dust had instantly accumulated.

A woman several rows behind us called out. "Tammy, dear, come sit back down. We're about to take off and I need your help lighting my cigarette."

"Ah," I found myself saying. "Well, Tammy. Welcome aboard, I'm Captain Bachman, er, um, Jack, please."

Her cheeks turned a deep shade of red and with her hands clasped behind her back, she rotated her body back and forth, all the while smelling wonderfully of fresh, spring gardenias.

"Thank you, Jack." Her eyes smiled at me. "My mother has a broken wrist, I'm now her personal cigarette lighter, and I've tried to get her to quit but she says . . . well, um, she's calling me and all these people are waiting for you to take off. I should get back to my seat."

I touched my finger to the brim of my hat. "Of course. Good day, miss." As she walked back to her seat, the lime green dress wrapped snugly around her trim legs and the orange silk scarf around her neck accented her hair just right.

A moment later in my dream we had fast-forwarded two years. Wedding decorations surrounded us and before long I found myself inside a church, standing at an altar next to a Catholic priest. At the rear of the church hung a wall-sized paper banner that read: "September 27, 1975" and below it, another one: "Mr. and Mrs. Bachman". The music changed to an old Doobie Brothers' song "Black Water," instead of the usual "Here Comes the Bride." At the end of the aisle the same young lady from the airplane marched toward me.

Her soft red hair flowed down onto the white satin and lace wedding gown. She glided along wearing silk shoes, carrying a red rose bouquet with her dad as an escort, whom I somehow knew as Robert Schroeder, wearing a black tuxedo. I swear I could smell the flowers. She approached, kissed her dad, and tripped as she stepped up onto the alter next to me, but this time I caught her. She looked up, blushing and smiling at me.

"I'm such a klutz, Jack," she said in a whisper, smiling.

"Just one of the many things I love about you, Tammy," I said, not able to take my eyes off her. "Don't worry, I'll always be here to catch you."

I'd had dreams before that felt real, but I could sometimes sort of "wake up" inside them and enjoy the experience. Lucid dreams, I think they are called. The same thing happened to me that night. I knew this was a dream. But I also somehow knew what I was experiencing was a memory.

My love for Tammy at that moment resonated inside me as real and strong as any love I'd ever had for any woman in my current life as John Bastian.

"I now pronounce you man and wife," said the priest. I went in for a kiss, but a ringing noise stopped us cold as the pinging sound of Kevin's phone alarm snapped me awake out of my warm, love-filled dream, back in the one-star motel room that smelled like old gym socks.

An internal motivation permeated my entire existence. I needed to find Tammy, to be with the redheaded beauty. I shook Kevin awake and an hour later we were on the road again, continuing our trek to Louisiana.

# CHAPTER
# 25

### Scott Jones
*November 18, 2016*

Through the rough winds, Scott managed to safely land the plane carrying 126 souls, including the would-be hijacker. Scott rolled in to the arrival gate and exited the cockpit, watching to ensure the air marshal handed off the hijacker to the other TSA authorities.

Over the next several hours, all passengers were interviewed. Scott personally thanked each one for their patience, but realized from the kind words and body language of everyone that for the most part, they were the ones thanking him.

"Hero in my book," one old timer said, patting Scott on the chest.

In a holding room buried deep inside the internal structure of the airport, federal authorities grilled Scott from every angle, a grueling interview in which he received a strict scolding about how he'd endangered the lives of all his passengers, blah, blah, blah.

Such a huge waste of time, Scott thought. He simply wanted to get back to finding his gold.

He signed some papers agreeing to his testimony and not to speak to anyone about the ordeal until the feds released their official report.

They finally freed him from the room.

From his shirt pocket, Scott fished out his phone.

Fifteen new voicemails.

Seated in the lobby, he listened to them all, wondering not only how the press had discovered what happened, but how they managed to get his personal cell number. Messages from local television and radio stations all requested interviews. Every voicemail complimented Scott, stating he was a hero.

*That's a little more like it.*

He called Mike. "I need you to check around with your people and do a little recon on Adam, see if he's still willing to play ball. The guy we hired to tap his phone said he might be workin' with a couple of treasure hunters. Deal with this however you see fit. Understand? Anything. I'm outta town, but gonna be back in a few hours. I expect ya to get this done."

He had never flown into or out of Shreveport before, so he strolled through the airport, but nothing happened until he exited at the TSA checkpoint, where dozens of media-types, cameras clicking, clamored for his attention.

He walked through the doorway and within seconds, a throng of cameras flashed around him, questions hitting him from all directions.

Total paparazzi chaos.

One reporter, a gorgeous petite, young blonde woman with bright red lipstick, caught his attention. She kept repeating the same question, "Please give us a statement. Were you scared up there?"

Scott spoke and the questions died down. Reporters took notes. The cameras continued flashing. "I'm not a hero. Just another pilot doing his job to ensure passengers get safely from one place to the next. That's all."

The blonde reporter spoke again. "What will you do now that you're a hero?"

"All I want to do is find my way back to Baton Rouge and have a nice glass of wine with my wife." The young reporter tilted her head and looked at him with puppy dog eyes.

"Aww, how sweet," she said.

He asked the young reporter for her card and did the same with several others. The crowd slowly dispersed, but the young reporter stayed behind.

"You got any plans for the rest of the night, captain? It's late," she said.

His insides stirred. Blood flooded to his member. "No, I don't. I uh, just need to get back to Baton Rouge."

"My place is only five minutes from here." She licked her lips, scanning him up and down. "Why don't you come by for a drink? You can freshen up and get some rest before you head home to your wife. I'd do anything to hear all the nitty-gritty details of your story. Make sure we really push the hero angle." She winked.

His heart pounded. Scott's former best friend, Jack, had been labeled a hero in Vietnam, earning the Purple Heart after saving three men from drowning. Now it was Scott's turn to wear the hero suit. Sweat covered his palms as he gave her a long, steady stare. Firm thighs, full natural breasts, sexy eyes and a gleaming bright, gorgeous smile.

What the hell, Mike can wait, Scott thought, scanning the interior of the airport terminal before giving her a curt nod.

"Follow me," she said, taking his coat and suitcase.

Without a word, she led him to her car, and they hopped in. Before long, they arrived at her apartment in downtown Shreveport.

# CHAPTER
# 26

**John Bastian**
*November 19, 2016*

Back on Interstate 10, Kevin drove us east under a high layer of gray Arizona clouds.

"Second day in a row we didn't eat breakfast before we left. I'm starving and I need caffeine," he said, taking the next off-ramp and pulling into a fast food breakfast chain. We scooped up some of the documents, strolled inside, ordered, and sat down with our food.

I sipped my black coffee, but burned the roof of my mouth as Kevin took a huge bite out of an egg sandwich.

"Hypothetically," I said, blowing onto my coffee while looking out the window at the desert landscape partially blocked by a massive 18-wheeler, "if we're somehow able to transfer non-physical data to our kids via genetics, that means humans can transmit memories and feelings from one to another." I pictured a bunch of zeros and ones streaming between a silhou-

etted mom and a baby, like two computers, a gross oversimplifi-
cation. "Assuming of course, there exists some yet-to-be-discov-
ered dimension where this information is stored."

Kevin stopped chewing, raised his thick eyebrows, and
swallowed. "Makes sense, dog, 'specially after reading all that
shit about them kids all over the world having the same kinda
past life thing."

"Exactly. Check this out."

I scooted next to him, flipped through some of the printed
docs, and grabbed one with a title I'd highlighted yellow earlier.
Holding the web page printout—an unsolved murder—in my
hand, I placed the sheet down and read it out loud:

*May 15, 1979 - Clarion Herald*

*Baton Rouge Murder Stumps Law Enforcement Officials*

*Baton Rouge, Louisiana - The alleged murder of a local
commercial airline pilot has been a source of frustration for state
and county police officials. The severed arm of the victim, thought
to be Jack Bachman, was found in West Baton Rouge seven
months ago on November 8, 1978, with enough blood, police
claim, to have been the cause of death. A pilot's ring on the finger
of the dead hand was used to identify the victim. According to his
wife of three years, Tammy Bachman, Mr. Bachman has been
missing, coincidentally, for seven months. "He went out for his
morning coffee, but never returned. I'm lost without him," she
said. No other clues have been uncovered. Police are asking the
public to come forward with any information about this case by
contacting Detective Herbert Benedict at 555-1235.*

"Holy. Crap. Are you kidding me with this?" Kevin asked
through a mouth full of food as he set his sandwich down.

I blinked several times, trying to process the article. "Funny,
I don't remember printing this out."

Kevin slapped his hand onto the table. "These are the same damned names you've been blabbing about all week. This shit just got crazy real."

This article resonated with me as a huge step in the right direction.

We finished our meal and hopped back onto the interstate.

"Can you work your magic and run a records search for Tammy Bachman and see what comes up?" I asked, holding the steering wheel with one hand while unlocking my phone with the other and handing it to him. "Use my Wi-Fi hotspot so we'll have internet on the road."

Even though Kevin had two master's degrees, he had a hard time finding work that paid his bills and also gave him the flexibility to pursue his lifetime passion of becoming a successful comedian. Lately, he'd landed a gig working part-time as a collection specialist, which gave him access to some key databases that might prove helpful to us.

"Boom. Here we go. Marriage certificate between," he said, scrolling down on his tablet, "Tammy Schroeder and Jack Bachman, September 27, 1975." He swiped, tapped, and did his thing.

"I'm logging in to another database," he said. A few minutes later, he snapped his fingers. "Okay, I found a Tammy Schroeder born in Birmingham, Alabama on March 2, 1952."

"This means," I said, "assuming this has anything to do with our search, she would have been what, like, twenty-three when she got married? And twenty-six when her husband was killed in 1978?"

More images swirled in my head, distracting me from driving as an unknown force continued to pull us eastward. My gut told me we were headed down the correct path.

Kevin nodded and put his hand up. "Here's the weird part: if she's still alive, she'd be," Kevin paused, looked up to the ceiling and snapped his fingers, "sixty-four years old. Checkin' the death records now to see if there's anything for her." He whacked away at the keyboard, popped open another window, and did a new search. "Nope, she ain't dead. In fact, I got her address right here." He pointed to an address.

In Baton Rouge, Louisiana.

"My friend," I said with a smile, "I believe you just found our first official stop."

"Check this other one out. Got somethin' else on this Jack character," he said, scrolling down, studying the screen. "Jackpot. Here's a bunch of shit from the original police report."

The sun pushed high into the eastern sky, which heated up the inside of the Beemer. I turned on the A/C as Kevin continued skimming through the report details.

"Here's a crude sketch of where they found the dude's arm." He leaned over and showed the iPad screen.

"The damned thing was half buried," I said, looking at a gruesome photo of the arm sticking up out of the ground, buried to the elbow, death dangling from the limp fingers.

"Like the killer *wanted* the po-po to find it."

"Sick."

"Says here the police assumed the murder occurred here where the arm was found because so much blood soaked into the soil. Definitely not a body part dump." He continued to scroll through the details. "Arm of a white male. No other discernible trauma to the hand or arm, other than where the limb had been severed from the body. At the shoulder."

A twinge of pain jolted through my right shoulder and scurried down my arm. I wiggled my fingers to make sure they still worked. The tips felt numb.

"You look like you just seen a ghost. Oooh," Kevin said, mocking me with his wiggling fingers and bulging eyes.

"Not cool, man. You know I saw the ghost of that boy and the gondola guy and—"

"Hold up. You tellin' me you seen two ghosts?"

"Drop it."

"No, you didn't tell me about no ghosts," he said, glaring at me.

I shared everything with him about the doctor's son in Mammoth and what I saw. He lifted his forearm with goosebumps sprawled across. "Check it, dude. Now you givin' me the willies."

I opened fully opened my eyes and nodded.

"And the dude from the gondola. You seein' that crazy man, too?"

"Let's focus on the treasure for a sec."

He swatted at the air.

"So some crazy old French dude had a bunch of gold coins, died, and his daughter hid 'em somewhere and they ain't never been found."

I nodded. A small piston engine aircraft flew over us to the south, triggering a flood of memories: the interior cabin of a small airplane, filling gas tanks from on top of the wings, the excitement of lifting off from the runway for the first time, and practicing stall maneuvers way up in the sky.

After a quick peek toward the center console where the shoe box sat, I picked up the clay figurine of Tammy, alternating glances between her and the desert road ahead. But I swerved a few feet onto the dirt shoulder. The sounds of pebbles pelted the underbelly of my car, rattling the interior and making the steering wheel hard to control, but I jerked us back onto the pavement.

"Jesus! Watch where you goin', man!" Kevin said.

I stuffed the doll into my jacket pocket and over the next several minutes worked hard to calm my breathing. I soon realized that everything in my entire life, every bit of learned information, everything I'd ever felt and observed about love, every movie, every song, every emotion was all balled up into one tight package inside me, bursting to get out. As though my very existence depended on it, I needed to be with this Tammy woman. My entire being was fully drawn to her on a spiritual and simultaneously primitive, instinctive level.

My cell phone rang from the Bluetooth car phone. My mom. "How's Dad?" I asked.

"Still resting. Hasn't woken up yet from when he drifted off last night with you there, but Johnny, I forgot to mention something."

I stole a glance at Kevin.

"We're listening."

"I know you think you're doing the right thing with your road trip, and you might think you figured how your life fits into this crazy story by looking at your old drawings, but . . ." she stopped.

"It's okay, Mom. Tell me."

I let my foot off the gas pedal, slowed, and merged into the right lane so I could pay better attention to whatever she was going to tell me.

"Since you have these images and feelings back, you need to know there was a dark side to what you—we—experienced. Something I should've tried to explain earlier, but I'm not sure I can."

I pursed my lips. "I know, mom. If there's truth to the fairy tale, a man killed me in my previous life. Violently. And I died and left my bride of three years behind. That's pretty dark."

"Well, yeah, but there's more."

I looked at Kevin again, who shrugged. "Not sure I follow," I said.

"If you study some of your drawings, there are little skulls and crossbones, the kind on pirate flags and poisonous bottles, but different. Look at the sketch with the number three in the upper right corner."

Kevin quickly dug through the box, flipped through and found the sheet and held it up so we could both see.

"Got it."

"Look at the part of the drawing with red, brown, and cream-colored lines and a circles, with red ovals nearby."

"You mean those sticks on the ground next to the icon?"

She paused. "Honey, the red ovals are drops of blood. And those lines and a circle aren't sticks, they're bones and a skull. Buried."

# CHAPTER 27

*November 19, 2016*

Click.

"That was my new best bud, Adam Bachman," said Kevin, ten minutes later, stuffing his phone into his jeans. Outside some random town, I continued speeding eastward on I-10, zooming across the Arizona New Mexico border.

"It's unimaginable how fast you got ahold of the dead guy's brother. It's like you know everyone in Louisiana. Crazy," I said.

"You know my mom—she hooked us up. She still stays in contact with all the key players in our home state."

The cool blue sky arched over us, but the massive cloud formation in the east had grown taller.

Narrow-eyed, I turned to Kevin in the passenger seat. "Yeah, but you don't know the guy like a buddy. He's a friend of a friend or something?"

"Right, but he did agree to meet with us," he said, smiling before staring out his window with a finger pressed to his chin.

"We best see him first before bargin' in to Tammy's place with no warnin'. Means to an end, my friend. Means to an end."

Halfway through New Mexico, we stopped to grab a bite at a barbequed rib joint next to a farm with a massive green and white barn. As we walked toward the front door of the restaurant, I heard someone chopping wood, and looked to my right.

A tall, lanky man, wearing a black cowboy hat and denim jacket gripped a hefty red, shiny axe dangling at his side. He lifted a small log, placed it atop an old tree stump, and thrust down, splitting the wood in two.

My heart leapt from my chest. My irrational, lifelong fear of that particular tool surfaced again, but a thousand times stronger. I yanked open the entrance door, scurried inside the restaurant, and the smell of the cooked beef wafting through the air helped distract me.

We gobbled down two slabs of pork ribs caked with barbeque sauce, crunchy fries, and two large colas. I slouched in my yellow plastic chair, tummy full, and asked Kevin what he thought of all this.

"I don't know, dog. Just don't know." He took a sip of sweet tea, looking out the window toward the barn. Dark clouds had crept in over the entire area. Drops of rain the size of silver dollars splatted onto the sidewalk and parking lot.

"I feel like every breath I take depends on this. My mind says run, but my heart needs to keep moving toward Louisiana. Toward finding Tammy."

On my phone, I checked a weather app, zooming in on the southern part of the US, where a three-state-wide circular cloud pattern—gray with overlays of green, yellow and bands of red—was apparently moving north from the Gulf of Mexico. I showed Kevin and said, "We got a hurricane headed toward Alabama. *Hurricane Carl*, they're calling it. Gonna miss Louisiana. This rain here is just the western tip."

He stood and patted my shoulder. "C'mon. Let's see if we can get to Louisiana 'fore the hurricane beats us there and they try to keep our California asses out."

As we hurried back to our car, the scent of freshly fallen rain soothed my nerves. We wound our way back to the Interstate 10 freeway, but the storm had already moved in. Curtains of rain came down hard. I switched the speed of my windshield wipers from normal to fast, but could still barely make out the road in front of us, so I slowed down to forty miles per hour, plowing through the downpour as best I could.

"This is some crazy-ass rain, dude," Kevin said.

We had traveled about ten miles in the storm when Blake Lynds, the guy who fell from the gondola, appeared, crouched down on top of the hood of my car, staring at me, eyes filled with anger.

And the rain had no effect on him.

Mouth dry and lungs deflated, my hands shook as I somehow managed to eek out a few words. "Dude. Please tell me you see that guy squatting on the hood of our car."

Kevin looked up from his iPad with a crinkled nose, rubbed the back of his neck and said, "Say what?" He looked out the drenched windshield, back at me, and back out front again. "They ain't nobody there. You either been drivin' too long or you losin' your mind."

He could be right. Logically, Lynds was dead. We knew this. Fact. And nobody other than a stunt man could sit on the hood of a moving vehicle, let alone in this torrential downpour. So either I was having another hallucination—which didn't seem likely because I felt fine, was wide awake, not dreaming, not on any medication—or I was literally seeing an actual ghost, which was absolutely not possible scientifically.

I locked my arms straight and stared. White knuckles gripping the steering wheel and my mouth burning like the inside of an oven, I blinked several times. All the water on the windshield was probably playing a trick on me—a simple optical illusion—or there was, in fact, a ghost staring me down.

With his bulging eyes beaming directly at me, the mustached apparition lifted both arms, palms vertical and facing me, he was trying to tell me something. Trying to tell me to stop.

But why?

Before I could figure out what the hell he meant, I let my foot off the gas pedal and the car in front of us—an old, white, sixties-model Ford Mustang—drove through a wide puddle and started to spin. After two full rotations, the Mustang skidded right, into the adjacent lane, and crashed its front end into the left side of an orange van. The van swerved hard right, but the driver overcorrected to his left, tossing the van onto its side before rolling several times and sliding to a stop on its side, perpendicular to the lanes, in the dirt median. At the same time, the Mustang flipped upside down and scraped along its rooftop for several hundred feet before also stopping in the median.

I slowed to avoid crashing into anything. The ghost disappeared, which gave me an unobstructed view of the violent collision before I slammed on my brakes and came to a complete stop.

Heart racing, I told Kevin, "I'll check the Mustang, you check the van."

Running on pure survival instinct, we both raced away from my Beemer, toward the two vehicles, getting ourselves thoroughly drenched in the downpour.

As I approached the overturned car, muffled screams came from inside the vehicle, over the loud, pelting sound of rain pouring down onto the asphalt, dirt, and the Mustang's underbelly. The mixed scent of oil, gasoline, and radiator fluid hit my nose while steam or smoke spewed upwards from the car. I knelt, shoved both palms into the mud and peeked inside a broken side window.

Shouts came from the front seat. "Help us! Please!"

# CHAPTER 28

Two men, held in place by their front seat safety belts, hung in an upside-down seated position. Blood streamed down the side of the driver's head as he reached an arm toward me. The other man was unconscious, with a substantial gash along the side of his neck, his head twisted out of place in a completely unnatural way.

"Cover your face," I told the driver. I lay back and kicked the broken side window with my shoe. A pointed glass tip gouged the top of my ankle. Blood appeared, streaming down my lower leg, but no pain registered, as though it belonged to someone else.

Using my leather shoe as a buffer, I swept my foot around the perimeter of the window to clean out some of the chunks, then quickly repositioned myself and stuck my head inside the car.

The front of the cabin continued to fill with smoke. Between screams of pain the man said, "Save Paul. I'm fine, just save Paul."

"Hold on," I said, ignoring his request and reaching up to undo his seatbelt. With my upper back, I pushed him up in order to get the buckle undone. Click. I wiggled my way back out the window while holding the guy—who was now passed out—by his underarms, sucking him out of the car and dragging him toward my Beemer.

By that time, a small fire had erupted on the undercarriage of the Mustang.

I ran back and crawled inside the burning Mustang from the driver's side, then placed two fingers on the front of the passenger's neck. No pulse. But I still wanted to get him out of the car.

"Let's get you out of here," I said mostly to myself, knowing he was unconscious and probably worse, before reaching in to find his seatbelt like I had with the driver's a moment earlier, but something grabbed ahold of my ankle and shook.

"This thing's on fire, dog, get your ass outta there," Kevin said, yanking at my leg.

"Can't let this guy die here, he might still make it."

The heat from the flames blasted my face, forcing me to squint and recoil. I only had seconds.

"No," Kevin said. "Ain't no time."

The heat was intense, even with the rain falling everywhere. For an instant, I paused and stared at the man's face, absorbing the details of his eyes, nose, mouth, forever etching the visual into my memory before deciding to let him go.

On my elbows and knees, I backed out of the car, then crab-walked backwards several yards, turned over and had started to sprint away from the car as the Mustang exploded with a massive orange and black fireball climbing up into the sky.

The thunderous shockwave blew me away from the car, knocking me onto my back.

I landed on the wet pavement, slid to a stop, then rolled onto my front, covering my head.

My ears rang as I peeked out between my arms at the car. Yellow and orange flames crackled, licking the sides of the fenders.

Soon, the man inside was nothing but a charred black body. Kevin sat to my left, both of us catching our breath, with the unconscious man between us.

Fifteen minutes later, several highway patrol vehicles, ambulances and paramedics arrived, working furiously on the driver, who finally came to, coughing and shouting and crying.

I gave the officer my account of what happened as another paramedic tended to my ankle wound. Kevin and I watched as firemen doused the fire, pried open the burned, blackened Mustang and carefully extracted the stiff, lifeless body from inside.

"I'm guessing everyone in the van made it out okay," I said to Kevin, who leaned up against the Beemer next to me, arms crossed.

"Some of those people were pretty banged up, though. But yeah. All alive."

Another ambulance arrived, gave the driver a shot, probably a sedative, then took him away, siren blaring.

Several hours passed and the rain downgraded into a light drizzle. Eventually the clean up crews mopped up the mess, traffic flowed through the scene and the officer told us we could leave.

Curious, I asked the man in blue, "That guy, what's his story?"

"Those men were married, they lived in Big Bear, California, and were heading to Texas for some sort of vacation," the officer said.

I looked down at the ground, deep in thought about the man whose life I'd failed to save. "Okay." I put my hand out to shake.

"I'll call you if we need any further information," the officer said.

"And please let me know if there's anything I can do."

He shook my hand. "You're a hero, Mr. Bastian. You saved that man's life."

*Hero?*

"I wish I'd had more time to help save the other guy."

He patted me on the shoulder. "My two cents off the record: from the look of the guy, he likely had a broken neck and had bled out before the car caught fire, so he was probably DOA. Been doing this three decades. You do what you can. You save who you can. That's the best any of us can hope for. Trust me, Mr. Bastian. You did a good thing today." He finished shaking my hand, turned and walked toward his cruiser.

After wandering back toward my car, standing on the freeway shoulder, I realized something about myself. I'd been selfish my entire life. Probably why my marriage to Margaret had failed. My life was not about me. Love was not something that happened all by itself. *It's about sharing yourself with another human before our time is up.* Which can come at any moment. Memories flooded my head of how my mom had always put my needs in front of her own. Like how the driver, moments away from death, wanted me to save his partner before him. That's the kind of person I wanted to be. I had to change. I needed to change.

My thoughts turned to my dad, in a hospital in Fontana. I questioned my decision to go on this trip.

Kevin came up to me from behind and put his hand on my back. "Let's go, man. Nothin' more for us to do here."

# CHAPTER
## 29

After a night filled with horrific dreams mixed in with restless sleep, I awoke the next day with zero appetite. I sipped a half-cup of coffee at the diner next to our motel as I watched Kevin gobble down a lumberjack breakfast. Once on the road, I found myself zoning out while driving, but we made our way eastward across the southern parts of New Mexico and into Texas.

Around eleven in the morning, a migraine pounded my head to the point spots appeared in my field of vision. Kevin took over the driving duties for the next several hours while I suffered in the back seat, waiting for two Tylenol to kick in.

We stopped mid-afternoon for a bite to eat, a much needed bathroom break, and gas. I managed to choke down half a cheeseburger with an extra-large Coke, hoping the caffeine would help ease the headache.

I resumed the driver's position and, over the next several hours as the headache slowly disappeared, enjoyed hearing more of Kevin's jokes and what he planned to do on the Tonight Show.

During the afternoon, cruising along the interstate at a pleasant seventy miles an hour, a montage of images paraded through my mind and I swear, sometimes the visions of Tammy's face and those soft, penetrating blue eyes marinated into my soul so vividly I could swear she was real, hovering above the hood of our car, smiling at me.

By late afternoon, we finally passed the halfway point of the 800 mile stretch across Texas. Dark clouds loomed prominently on the southeastern horizon, threatening to overtake the remnants of patchy blue sky. Kevin continued searching online for answers.

"Found more treasure info. That gold's got some kinda eff'd up curse, givin' me the willies just reading 'bout it," he said.

"Exactly why I didn't tell you. You get weird."

I looked ahead, down the two-lane highway winding through the flat, open desert.

Kevin tried to man up.

"Ain't afraid of no curse."

"Sure. Whatever you say, buddy."

He shot a look at me. "Look, man, my dad used to tell me bedtime stories about a deep dark forest, a fishing pond, and angry ghosts living in a shed."

"C'mon, dude, that was a long time ago. You're a grown man," I said. "Tell me about the so-called curse you found."

Countless acres of beige and lime green scrub brush littered the landscape on both sides of the highway as I increased our speed to eighty miles an hour.

"Apparently the curse is French."

"Curses have geographic boundaries? Had no idea."

"Shut up, man. It's cuz the name is French."

"So if we're not French, the curse doesn't apply to us?"

"I'm tellin' you, man, you better shut the hell up and listen," Kevin said, giving me another friendly jab to my sore shoulder.

I forced a smile and reworked my grip on the steering wheel. He stared down at the iPad on his lap, touching and tapping and swiping the screen. "Says here, and I'm paraphrasing, a bunch of folks been killed over the years tryin' to find that Lafayette treasure. All men."

"No women?"

"That's what this shit says. Apparently, each guy died within a week of getting his greedy fingers on some treasure map. One guy had a heart attack, some other dude had a stroke, another hit by a car. And get this: three committed suicide."

"I can see how, maybe, one or two people might have died hunting for the treasure. Coincidence."

"Dude, we ain't talkin' about no one or two of these sons-a-bitches. Twenty-eight of these mo-fo's was killed."

"You're joking. Twenty-eight?"

"Uh-huh. This site has a table with a list of all of 'em, their ages, and how they died. All within a week of touching the map."

"Dates?" I asked.

Kevin scrolled though the web page. "Says here all the deaths happened in the nineteen 40's, 50's, and 60's. Nothing in the last forty- or fifty-plus years. Maybe some chick got the map now, and she ain't affected by the curse."

"Imagine having all that gold. Wow," I said. Kevin shot me a yearning look. "Out of curiosity, how would we sell that many gold coins to get full value? Gotta be a pretty complex process."

"No idea, man," Kevin said.

Our last night on the road, we stayed outside of Houston, Texas, at a small motel in Baytown. The room was cheap. Too cheap. The cracks in the walls and cigarette burns on the sheets of both queen beds told quite the story. Hell, we were too tired to care. We dropped our bags and flipped on the TV. As cheap as it was, there was still a minibar. I grabbed three 50ml bottles of whiskey, and chugged them to settle my nerves before lying down on the lumpy bed and waiting for the jolt to hit me.

Kevin watched. "Damn," he said, drawing out the word while shaking his head.

He stripped to his boxer shorts and hopped into his bed. Kevin flipped through channels.

"You think you can find this box of gold because you have visions?"

Fingers locked behind my neck, I watched the last few seconds of some news report about self-driving cars. "Maybe, but hard to explain. Assuming this is the same treasure, I feel like I could pinpoint the exact location, if I could just get a couple of clues to start. Just that simple."

He threw his head back. "See. That's what I'm talking about. I want to know how you can say something crazy like that. That don't make no sense."

The news anchor introduced the weather woman, who stood in front of a full-screen map, waving her arms at a circular swirling mass of clouds across the southern U.S. and the Gulf of Mexico, with the words "Hurricane Carl" scrolling along the bottom in bold yellow letters. Kevin turned up the volume.

*"Right now, it's listed as a Category 3 hurricane,"* said the weatherwoman, *"with winds up to 110 miles per hour, heading north toward the southern coast of Mississippi and Alabama." A series of arrows pointed toward Mobile. "Our models are predicting an increase in strength as the storm gathers energy from the warm waters in the Gulf and heads toward the coastline. The governors of both states have issued evacuation orders for everyone in the path. We're expecting the brunt of the storm to miss Louisiana, which will be a relief for everyone continuing to recover from the devastation caused by Katrina back in 2005."*

I splayed my fingers over my eyes, raised my eyebrows, and rubbed. "Terrific. I knew I should have left you back home," I said.

"Sure, blame me," he said, smiling. "I'm the all powerful weather god, with power to make big ol' huge hurricanes." He paused. "Shit . . . I'm tellin' you, man, it's the damned curse. Le Trésor Fatale."

We both laughed.

The liquor belted my brain, causing the room to spin, my arms and legs tingled, but the accompanying numbness became my friend and the strength of the visions waned.

After tossing and turning all night and waking up feeling worse than the night before, I managed to corral Kevin to the lobby where we found some donuts and coffee. With enough carbs and caffeine in our bellies for a racehorse to sprint five miles, we hopped back on the road with the goal of hitting Baton Rouge by midday. When we crossed over the Mississippi River, I turned and leaned backwards to the rear seat and made sure we still had my shoebox full of trinkets from my youth, then felt the clay figurine of Tammy in my jacket pocket.

Check.

Inside a French restaurant near Zeeland Place, we sat in a soft leather booth and waved over a waitress to order.

She strolled up and, with a French accent, asked if we'd like some water. I had taken three years of French while attending Cal-Poly San Luis Obispo and earning my degree in business finance, so I thought it would be fun to use my rusty linguistic skills.

"Parlez vous Francais?" I asked.

She smiled. "Oui, monsieur."

In French, I said, "Terrific. What is the special of the day?"

The waitress tilted her head, narrowing her eyes, and responded in French, "You are from around here, yes?"

"Why do you ask?"

"You are dressed like a tourist, but your Louisiana French accent is perfect."

I leaned back in my chair, satisfied I could still speak a little French. In English, I said, "Great observation. I'm from California. This is my first day in Louisiana." I smiled.

She furrowed her brow. "Amazing. Except for your clothes, I would have easily mistaken you for a local." She winked at me.

Kevin tilted his head to one side and pursed his lips.

She held up her notepad and set the pen tip on it, ready to write. "Anyway, what can I get you boys?"

We ordered our food and enjoyed a terrific meal of frog legs, grits, French fries and Cajun shrimp. I sensed I had eaten here before, in this exact town. Inexplicably, every street, every corner, felt oddly familiar. *Must be the past-life memories again.* But the places looked slightly different, bricks where stucco had been, green front walls where yellow had been. Like that.

My phone rang. Unknown caller.

"Hello?" I said.

"This is Doctor Willis at Mammoth Mountain Hospital. Am I speaking with John Bastian?" the woman asked.

"Hi, Doctor Willis. Yes. I'm doing . . . well, I'm fine as far as the headaches are concerned."

I salted up the last French fry and tossed the cut spud into my mouth.

"Glad to hear that, Mr. Bastian. I apologize for calling, but this is about a related, albeit different matter. When you first woke up from your coma, do you remember the conversation we had?"

"Yes, of course. You told me I was in an accident and in a coma for a few days. Why?"

"I'm curious if you remember mentioning the boy—Mark," the doctor said.

I closed my eyes. "Of course, the little boy standing next to you. Your son. Yeah, barely. I must have been hallucinating or something. Probably the morphine."

There was a long pause on the line before she spoke again.

"I'm afraid not, Mr. Bastian, and this might sound crazy, but I don't believe he was a hallucination." I rubbed my jaw and swallowed. "Since you were discharged nearly two weeks ago, there have been two other reports from patients—both of whom also sustained head injuries similar to yours—who've stayed in the same room who claim to have seen the same boy. In fact, even though my nurse told you that you were on morphine, you weren't. I'd prescribed you a different type of pain medication, one with no known hallucinogenic or psychotropic side effects."

I leaned to my right, toward Kevin, and oriented the phone flat, near my right ear, so we could both listen.

"Let me get this straight. You, as a medical professional, are saying I *did* see a ghost?"

Kevin shook his head and took a swig of sweet tea.

"That's what I want to talk with you about," she said. "Again, I realize I'm a little out of bounds on this and it sounds illogical, maybe even borders on malpractice, but—I have to ask. Assuming you did see the ghost of my son, I'd like to find out what he told you. Maybe you've seen him since we discharged you?"

*Is a doctor seriously asking me details about a ghost sighting?*

I searched my recent memories. "No. Only what I told you at the time."

"Well that's the issue," she said. "This is very hard for me to discuss, but if I remember correctly, you mentioned something about him not dying of what we thought, which I'm confident was leukemia. We have all his tests to confirm this."

As sure as if someone were physically whispering in my left ear, I heard, "Tell her I didn't die of leukemia. Tell her my dad is a murderer. Tell her James is fine and waiting for her in the next realm."

I looked around, fully expecting to see someone. Or something. But nobody was there. Nothing. No boy. Confused, I half-asked myself, "James? Who the heck is James?"

She must have heard my rambling. "James was my first husband. Mr. Bastian, I'm sorry, but how do you know about him, too?"

"I honestly have no clue," I said. "I swear I just heard some-one whisper in my ear that they want you to know James is alright and he's waiting for you in the next realm, whatever that means but more importantly, he wants me to tell you—"

The woman on the other end of the line—the one who saved my life and brought me back from a severe coma, some-one I held immense respect for—began to sob.

I heard the same exact words whispered in my ear again. "There's something else you need to know," I said into the phone.

She sniffled.

I continued. "He wants me to tell you his dad was a—"

She cut me off, said, "I'm sorry I bothered you, Mr. Bastian. Goodbye," then hung up.

# CHAPTER
# 30

Our newfound Louisiana contact, Adam Bachman, had surprisingly agreed to drive down to New Orleans and meet us at 4:00. Apparently, Adam lived in Zion City, a small community a few miles north of Baton Rouge.

Kevin rubbed the nape of his neck and said, "Never been there before, even when me and my mom lived here. Seems like a fun place. Always wanted to visit."

Worry about my dad weighed heavily on me. I wondered if he'd woken up yet. But I agreed to meet with Adam, mostly because of Kevin's high level of excitement.

And we honestly had no other decent leads.

With some time to kill, we parked and found ourselves strolling along Bourbon Street in the world famous New Orleans French Quarter, heading toward the agreed rendezvous point: a voodoo shop. Not sure if that was Kevin or Adam's idea. Perhaps Kevin thought it would be funny. In the early afternoon on an otherwise non-celebratory day, measly crowds meandered about the various streets and sidewalks, way fewer people than Mardi Gras photos I had seen over the years.

We stepped into the Tropical Isle restaurant and ordered two hurricane drinks, some local concoction of white and dark rum, fruit juice and grenadine, then continued walking along the streets, amazed at the sheer number of shops begging for our business. Eventually, we wound up standing outside Madam Laveau's, an honest-to-god voodoo store.

We waited until 4:14, when Kevin received a text from Adam: *Can't make it today. Sorry.*

Kevin replied: *Maybe later?*

Adam: *Car troubles. Maybe next week.*

Two women in fancy eighteenth-century French costumes walked past us. Kevin showed me Adam's text and said, "No. We didn't come down here to wait 'til next week."

Kevin texted back: *We'll come to your house. 5pm ok?*

I looked around the cramped street, eyeing several restaurants, bars, and novelty shops.

Finally, Kevin received a response.

Text from Adam: *See you @ 5.*

We turned to head back to my Beemer, but a man stood blocking our way, arm pointing toward the entrance of the voodoo store. He had a French Fork beard, which looked like an upside-down pitch fork hanging from his chin, a tie-dye shirt, and waist-long braided ponytail.

"You need to go inside," he said with a poker face.

Kevin and I exchanged confused glances.

"We got five minutes," Kevin said, raising a shoulder. "Not gonna hurt to look around."

I shrugged and we shuffled inside, following the man. Tattoos of nude women and skeletons decorated both his arms, hinting at a forbidden darkness.

He leaned against a glass display case and asked, "Y'all lookin' for somethin' in particular?"

"Got any good luck charms?" I asked with a smile.

He frowned and shook his head. "Nope."

"How 'bout something to help with spirit communications?"

He looked up and down at Kevin. "Yup. We got dolls that'll help y'all talk with the dead," he said.

Kevin shook his head. "Changed my mind. I'll be outside waiting for Johnny Jackass."

The bearded man pushed away from the counter and motioned for me to follow. Toward the back of the store, we slithered through a slotted black hanging cloth doorway into a candle-lit room that was probably used as a closet for the original building.

"Here they are," he said with a single wave of his extended arm, like Vanna White, across a wall filled with various sizes of dolls.

"Hmmm . . . clay voodoo dolls," I said, putting two and two together.

"Yessir, but ya gotta speak with our medium before buyin' one. She'll help guide ya on your journey."

I wiped my forehead and followed him into a different room, where Madam Laveau sat alone at a circular table. Deep wrinkles crisscrossed the face of an otherwise tiny woman, who wore a red silk scarf over graying black hair. More bracelets than I could count dangled from both wrists as she looked up from a crystal ball atop the center of the table. A stack of tarot cards sat off to the side and the B-movie setting made me chuckle. She smiled, showing off her coffee-stained teeth and requested that I pay the $30 reading fee. From my wallet, I pulled out a $20 and a $10, handed the bills to her and took a seat in the wooden chair.

With a slow, raspy voice, she asked to see my palms.

I hesitated before complying. The tip of her right index fingertip ran sideways along my right palm. Nodding, she said, "Strong life line. You are on a great quest, one that would instill terrific fear in most people."

"I don't believe in this stuff," I said, eyebrows raised, not impressed with the carnival theatrics.

She squinted. "Most people don't. A lot of what's in this shop is fake crap we sell to tourists. But make no mistake, good sir, my craft is real."

While she circled her fingertip around my palm, I scanned my surroundings, noting an assortment of silkscreened t-shirts, talisman charms, colorful tiny oil bottles, and various types of jewelry.

When I turned back toward the medium, a man had appeared, standing behind her and to the right. He stood quietly and looked about ten years older than me. With a long, dark beard, he wore an old-style tuxedo that, if I had to guess, was from the mid-nineteenth century. Possibly earlier. Like the one Abe Lincoln always seemed to wear in his portraits.

All fine and well, but here's the weird part: the man's sclera—the normally white part of our eyes—were pitch black. Both eyes were filled with fear.

"Don't mind him," she said, not looking up from her crystal ball. "He's not really here." And as she waved her hand, her forearm passed through the man like he was a hologram.

I fought the rising urge to get up and run. Instead, I remained seated, darting glances between her and the curly-mustached man. A black silk top hat rested atop the man's head full of medium-length, wavy hair, all slicked back with oil or grease.

She continued. "A wife, a biological daughter, and grand-children await you. I see a long, happy life in front of you. With them."

*Gotcha.* Now I had proof. The effects of the cocktail kicked in and I shook my spinning head. After a brief nervous laugh, I said, "Sorry, lady. I'm divorced and I don't have any kids. And that man is clearly some sort of illusion. High-tech magic trick or something. I don't buy any of this, sorry. But I can't fault you for trying."

I leaned back in my chair, confident I'd figured out her little hoax.

A smile appeared on her roughened face and with a cackle, she said, "That's not what the spirits say." She paused and leaned forward. "Jack."

My heart leapt from my chest and I pushed back from the table, tilting my head. "How the hell you do you know about my other," I swallowed, "I mean, well, my . . ." I looked around to find hidden cameras.

"You see, Jack, in this room, time stands still for us both. I see the past, present, and future. All as one. You may consider yourself a man named John, divorced without any children, but the spirit world paints an entirely different picture of your true self."

The man, or ghost, or hologram, or whatever, slowly dissolved.

Mind racing for answers, I looked down at the crystal ball, to the swirling rainbow colors and auras shooting outward from deep inside. I pressed my lips together and took a step forward.

She continued. "You have been given a rare gift by a wood spirit, one that has prematurely opened a portal for you to the great beyond. You now have the power to see and hear what others cannot. But make haste, you must find your true spirit partner before the portal closes or be forever lost and without love."

The drink churned in my belly, trying to crawl back up, but I choked it down while I set my hands on top of the table, replaying her spoken words over and over in my mind, trying in vain to comprehend the cryptic message.

*Wood spirit? The angry tree I hit?*
*Power? Is this why I'm seeing ghosts?*
*Spirit partner? Tammy?*

With a smirk, she stood. "Good. It appears I now have your attention, so please allow me to introduce you to a specific doll, one that can keep you safe as you move forward down this path in search of your true family." She gently took my hand and led me back into, for lack of a better term, the doll room. After crossing her arms, she put one hand under her chin and surveyed hundreds of dolls. She closed her eyes for a moment, randomly waved her bony arms, opened her eyes and said, "Ah. Here we are." She reached out toward the wall and snatched two six-inch-tall dolls, the first of which, in all honesty, looked like a miniature version of a balding man with a bulging belly.

And the second—*wait a minute!*

The second doll was a woman wearing a light-blue dress with white trim and a big smile.

And red hair.

No way.

I fished out my clay doll—the one I made as a child—from inside my jacket pocket and held all three dolls side-by-side in my open palms. One bald man and two nearly identical dolls of Tammy.

"I don't understand," I said to the old woman. "How did you—"

She curled my fingers around all three dolls. "Keep these with you at all times until you find what you are searching for. The spirit world will tell you what to do when the time comes."

I pulled my brows in. "But I have no idea what I'm looking for," I said.

She smiled, nodding. "Yes you do, Jack. Search your heart. You already know."

I blinked several times and swallowed twice as her so-called advice sank in.

In a daze, I thanked her for her time, wandered back to the front counter, paid the hippie for both clay dolls, and grabbed Kevin.

# CHAPTER
# 31

"We only got a half hour now until we meet Adam at his house," Kevin said, studying Google Maps on his phone. I got him up to speed with the Madam Laveau interaction, the hologram Abe Lincoln-looking dude, and the clay dolls. Or at least I tried to.

We sped north, back up toward Baton Rouge and about halfway there, at a fork in the road, Kevin asked me to pull over and told me about a shortcut. On his phone, he showed me a state highway that wound north/south, more or less parallel to the eastern shore of the Mississippi River. He said it looked like a faster way to head north, meandering along the Mighty Miss.

I shook my head and said, "That's gonna take longer." His proposed route sounded dangerous, too, with all the tight curves and unknowns.

He disagreed. Said it would be fun.

In California, a civil engineer had once told me with the exception of one road near Lake Arrowhead, all their state highways were paved, and California spent billions of dollars each year to maintain those roads.

Reluctantly, I agreed, but soon discovered Louisiana was not like California. Not by a long shot. We headed out onto Point Clair, came upon an abrupt end to the asphalt on the so-called state highway, and were now rolling along on a narrow muddy road, which appeared well-traveled. With fields of plowed grass blanketing the surrounding land, I guessed we were traveling along a typical country road, driven by countless trucks working the surrounding agricultural industry.

"Call and let him know we're going to be late," I said, swerving to avoid a hefty pothole filled with brown water.

Kevin made the call. Adam told us to get there when we could—good ol' Southern hospitality.

Along the dirt road we passed occasional residences and the occasional herd of cows. A substantial earthen berm paralleled the road on our left, a massive barrier between us and our country's second longest, but largest river. The gigantic mound looked like a thirty-foot-high dam that meandered for miles. Kevin said the berm was a levee built back in the 1930's to prevent flooding, where the river at that point was about a half-mile wide.

Kevin's shortcut ended up taking us an extra two hours, but we finally arrived at Adam's house on Paige Street with zero expectations. I honestly had no idea whether or not this would be a stepping stone to Tammy and the treasure, or our first true dead end. I trusted Kevin with my life, so although I had not yet spoken with the guy, Adam had struck Kevin as a friendly man and that was good enough for me.

Located on an ancient prairie, the run-down suburban lot was as flat as a desktop, but shimmered with various shades of green beyond belief to my California eyes. Cypress and magnolia trees dotted the neighborhood, with multiple grass species littering every remaining square foot of land. High-arching, dark gray clouds loomed to the distant south.

One house down from Adam's, we pulled onto the side of the potholed street and parked.

"Getting nervous about this," I told Kevin.

"They ain't nothin' to worry about." He patted my knee. "We just gonna meet the twin brother of the guy you supposedly have memories of and see what he knows. That's all."

"You're not helping."

Kevin opened his door. "After that, we gonna bounce out and head to the bar for a few cold ones because you're gonna need 'em," he said with that winning pearly white smile.

I raked my fingers through my hair and cracked my knuckles. "I feel like I should call my mom, get an update on my dad."

"Sure thing. But let's see what this Adam guy knows first, then you can make some calls on the way to the bar."

If I wanted answers, I had to meet this guy.

I shoved open my door, exited, and, scanning the otherwise quiet neighborhood, strolled across the uncut weed-lawn toward the door. Distant dog barks echoed off nearby houses. From within the home came muffled sounds of broken glass, then a cat screaming, then someone yelling, "Dammit, Bones." A moment later a flustered man opened the door with a drawn-out squeak.

"Sorry 'bout that. Stupid cat got in the way."

"No worries," Kevin said.

"You must be Kevin. Hi, I'm Adam. Nice to meet you," he said, pushing open the screen door and putting his hand out to shake.

Kevin shook Adam's hand and said, "This is my friend John Bastian, the one I told you about," while motioning to me on his right.

"Pleasure to meet you," I said and put my hand out to shake, too.

And that's when the universe gave me another sign.

Time slowed and seconds counted by like minutes.

When my palm connected with Adam's, a colorful display of fireworks and light flashes exploded in my mind. Adam vanished and reappeared repeatedly like bad TV reception.

My right shoulder throbbed with increasingly sharp pains.

But the moment I thought I'd collapse from the pain, when I couldn't take it any more, I shook my head and the blinking visions stopped. So did the throbbing.

At that point, hypothetically, if any of our assumptions were correct—and if my therapist Kelly Carpenter's assessment that I had, in fact, been reincarnated was true—I was shaking the hand of the identical twin brother of my previous body.

I looked at Kevin, expecting confusion, but he only raised his eyebrows as if nothing had happened. No big deal.

*Great. Now my sense of time is out of whack, too.*

"Y'all okay?" Adam asked with a thick Louisiana accent as we ended the hand shake.

"I'm good, thanks," I lied, nodding. My hand and arm were totally numb, and I tried to hide a flinch at the remnants of pain in my right shoulder.

Adam gave me an inexplicable sense of foreboding. Nothing specific, but dark. Brotherly rivalry, perhaps? Or his outdated red and black checkerboard robe covering his well-worn, formerly white undershirt caused my uneasiness, or possibly the three days of unshaved salt and pepper stubble. The few remaining hairs on his balding head shot outward, trying to escape. His meaty fingers held a half empty bottle of Pabst Blue Ribbon. At least the guy liked the same beer we did. He couldn't be all that bad.

"Ahh, pibber," I said, pointing to his brew.

He held up his beer bottle, looked at the label, and said, "Yup. The original. Nothin' like it. Y'all thirsty?"

"Nah, I'm good," I said, noting to myself I had no problem making eye contact with the guy.

He invited us inside and as we entered, he provided a warning about the mess we were about to encounter.

Now, I had heard the term "hoarder" to describe folks with an overwhelming fear of throwing anything away, but never actually considered what the inside of a hoarder's house would look like. To my surprise, a two-foot wide trail snaked between the front door and kitchen twenty feet further in, toward the rear of the home. I stepped as carefully as possible, the entire time feeling like a giant hamster. Steep slopes of trash jutted upward from the floor to the ceiling on both sides of the trail. Several crinkled up fast food bags and empty beer bottles littered the trashy landscape, piled on top of dirty clothes, papers, books, and random nick-knacks.

We entered the kitchen and Adam cleared away several small stacks of old newspapers from a counter, surrounded by trash on the floor, for us to sit on two barstool chairs.

"Seriously, y'all both look like ya could use a couple of beers," Adam said, leaning his elbows on the counter.

"I'm good, thanks," I said, putting my hand up, studying various pieces of junk. But Kevin could never seem to pass up a cold one.

"I'd love a beer, man," Kevin said.

Adam turned around to the fridge, reached inside, tossed a beer bottle to Kevin, leaned back onto the counter and took a swig of brew.

"So, from what ya said on the phone, y'all are interested in talking about my brother."

"Yes, I was wondering—" I started.

"Now, y'all gotta understand somethin'," Adam said, cutting me off. "I don't normally talk about that stuff. That period of time, when he died, was very emotional. I'd even say traumatic. Dark." He looked down at the counter, curling his lips inward. "Messed me up somethin' fierce. I still can't believe he's gone."

Kevin and I exchanged glances.

Adam continued. "But for some reason, a tiny voice inside told me to meet with you guys. Not sure why. Y'all came all the way out here from the west coast to talk to me?"

"More or less. I . . ." But before I could finish my sentence, something caught my eye. To my right, the same top-hatted, translucent man from the voodoo shop appeared, wearing the same black tux. If I discarded the theory of me continuing to have hallucinations, either Adam had the same holographic projector as Madam Leveau or a ghost was standing with us.

Either way, the being's completely black eyes were wide-open, brimming with fear.

# CHAPTER
# 32

Standing in trash up to his knees, what I will refer to as the ghost stood next to an interior wall, still and quiet as a mud puddle. Slowly, he rotated his gaze from me toward a shelf next to the gas stove behind Adam, then lifted his arm and pointed.

Ignoring the apparition and glancing between the two actual living humans in the room, I said, "Sure good the three of us could meet, I really appreciate this."

Kevin looked at me and took another swig, oblivious to the man in the top hat.

On the shelf, a small skateboard-shaped pillow sat undisturbed. Made from faded blue jean denim, the fluffy item had two yellow felt cutouts of human feet sewn on top, like the old Hang Ten logo from the seventies, and four red jumbo marshmallow-sized tires, also felt. A memory appeared of me sitting at a desk inside a classroom full of eight-year-olds, all of us hand-sewing our own miniature skateboard pillows. I stood and stepped toward the shelf to get a closer look, still ignoring the top-hatted ghost.

I pointed to the pillow and with a tilted head, asked, "Can you tell me about this skateboard pillow?"

Adam looked at Kevin and paused, taking another hit from his beer. He exhaled and responded, "My brother made that when we was in third grade. I made one too, a much better version, cleaner design, but our dog chewed the damned thing up a long time ago. I keep that pillow there as a memento." He crossed his arms, narrowed his eyes and gazed at me.

"Mind if I—?"

"Sure," he said.

I reached up and grabbed the pillow. About one foot in length, the surface of it was made of a patchwork of soft, denim squares. On the back, written in black marker: MADE BY JACK B. 1957 MRS. GARDNER'S CLASS

I squeezed the fluff from the pillow, inhaling the scent of old cloth, memories scrolling by of a playground, steel jungle gym, white nylon jump rope, girls with pigtails, lunch boxes, a black and white television, and a young Adam pushing me on a playground.

I closed my eyes to see the memories more clearly.

From the direction of the top-hatted ghost, the words, "Jack Bachman" echoed three times.

I opened my eyes. The apparition had vanished.

With a furled brow, I placed the pillow back on the shelf, walked back to my barstool, and sat.

"I understand you and Jack were twins," I said to Adam, not letting on about how much I knew about him.

"Identical," he responded with a nod.

"Wow. Did you have a special connection? I've read twins can sometimes read each other's minds."

He laughed. "He was the smart one, for sure. And even though we looked the same, the ladies always seemed to flock to him. Anyway, when he passed back in '78, part of me died, too. I know we all just met, but . . ." he hesitated, weighing his words and giving a grim twist to his mouth. "But, I don't know why I'm telling you this." He paused again. "I went to a therapist a few years ago and she told me I haven't been able to move on with my life since the day some bastard killed Jack. After our daddy drowned near an island in the Mississippi back in '65, Jack and I made a pact we was gonna change the world together, me and him. He got married to a gorgeous babe back in '75. We didn't see as much of each other after that, but we did stay close." He looked up to the stained popcorn ceiling. "Feels like yesterday Jack was right here with me, and now . . ."

As I stared at his face, into his pooling eyes, images flashed back to the grisly scene of that man attacking me with the axe.

My right shoulder throbbed, stronger now.

Jolts of electricity shot down my still numb arm.

My fingertips tingled.

"I know this must be hard for you, but since the police referred to his death as a murder, what's been keeping the police from solving the crime?"

Adam tapped his fingers on the countertop and I looked at them, noticing his pinky adorned with a gold ring, a pea-sized red ruby in the center. I glanced down at my hand and, for a moment, saw the same ring on my finger. But before I could register what had happened, I blinked and my ring had disappeared.

"No idea," Adam said, scraping his palm back along the top of his head.

Curiosity expanded inside me like magma in a soon-to-erupt volcano.

"Adam. That pilot's ring on your finger belonged to Jack, right?"

He crossed his arms on his chest. "How'd ya know that?"

The pressure continued to build inside me, cracking the surface, rumbling my chest. "Not sure, but I'm sensing the ring belonged to him. Something related to flying. Was he a pilot?"

Adam gently bit his lower lip, twisted off the ring, and handed the gold piece to me.

The inner inscription read: *Stay safe in the sky, Jack. Love Mom. 1972*

"I never liked flying. But mom had it made for him when he passed his commercial pilot exam."

Wheels spun in my head, resonating strong.

"You mentioned he was married."

He nodded. "Yeah, to Tammy. I think her maiden name was Shroeder. A beautiful woman inside and out. Like two peas in a pod the two of them. Inseparable. In fact, I introduced them . . ." He smiled, looked up, and wiped his eyes again.

My internal volcano exploded.

I knew this was a lie. Jack and Tammy met on an airplane.

"And when were they married?" I asked, ignoring the warning signals inside me.

He drew in a long, deep breath and exhaled slowly, sounding exhausted as he looked back up to the ceiling. "Let's see . . . 1975. Yup."

"So Jack received his commercial pilot certification in 1973, you introduced them between '73 and '75, and he married Tammy Schroeder in 1975, and was murdered by some mystery guy in 1978?"

"November 1978. Yup. Thirty-eight years ago. This month, in fact," Adam said.

Kevin piped in. "You gotta have some idea who his killer might've been."

"I do," Adam said, all joy leaving his face. "I have a very good idea."

I wanted more answers, but could only take the smell of rotting trash so long, as a tinge of nausea bounced in my belly.

"Well, thanks again for your time, Adam. We have to get—"

"Hold on, son, let's go back to the skateboard and ring," said Adam with a close-lipped smile that jutted into his cheek. He swung his arm around in an arc. "I got all this junk in here. My junk. There's only two things in this entire house that used to belong to my brother. Two. Nothin' else." The man's pleasant demeanor withered away.

I choked down a hard gulp.

"I wanna know how in God's green earth you knew the exact two things." He pounded his fist onto the counter. "You tell me that right now."

Kevin took a step backwards.

"To be honest, I don't—"

"You been spying on us? Huh? You working for Scott?"

I shot a quick glance to Kevin, who licked his lips, trembling.

Without warning, another set of memories filled the dark void inside my head.

I slammed my eyelids shut.

A rush of cold swallowed me.

Frozen water. Winter white. I looked down my extended arms to my hands as they pulled a body out of a stream. Or maybe a lake. A wet, pale blue face with closed eyes. Adam. Mouth to mouth. Frozen lips. A red, white, and blue button that read "Nixon's The One!"

Dizziness overpowered me, then the entire scene went blank. Out cold.

When I came to, Kevin hovered above me, tapping my cheeks as I lay on the trash-strewn carpet. Somehow, I powered through a strong urge to sleep.

"John. John. Wake up!" He pulled my arms, supporting my back as he helped me to my feet. Although I felt like I weighed five hundred pounds, I managed to stand and lean against the counter, huffing to catch my breath.

Adam and Kevin stared at me with fixed gazes when the solution hit me.

"You guys better not be some kinda con artists, tryin' to pull a fast one here," Adam said.

"Adam, I don't know anyone named Scott," I said, still out of breath. "But you almost drowned in the late sixties. There was a cold snap and you got stuck in one of the local bayous.

Your brother saved your life. Tell me I'm wrong." I felt faint and rubbed my forehead.

Jack's twin stood still, wide-eyed. "You tell me how in Jesus' name you know that. Nobody knew nothin' about that except me and Jack. Nobody."

"I wish I could explain it, Adam, I do. I realize I sound crazy. Insane even." I debated whether to let out our true intentions. "I just . . . well . . . something tells me maybe your brother is trying to talk to me or send us a message. I've never believed in any of this, but it's like I have some weird psychic connection."

I fully expected him to kick us out of his house.

But instead he nodded slowly, shifting his stance. In a calm voice he said, "Maybe."

"Let's not get carried away," Kevin said. "We ain't got no evidence or know that for sure. We don't know nothin', really."

Adam took a step toward me, standing directly in front, face to face. "Close your eyes," he said.

All of Adam's hostility had neutralized and I shot a glance at Kevin, who raised a shoulder and took a sip of beer.

With nothing to lose, I closed my eyes.

"With no actual body, only Jack's arm, we held an empty casket funeral for him at—"

"Hillcrest Memorial Gardens," I said, finishing his sentence, but completely unsure how.

As if in a dream, I heard droplets of rain and looked down from above a crowd of people gathered around a brown coffin, a standard grave site. A minister preached. I described the scene to Adam. "You didn't cry at Jack's funeral."

"No way you could know that," Adam said.

"And your mom didn't go. You uh," I dropped my head, continuing with my eyes shut, focusing on the images. "You slipped in the mud and nearly fell into the grave," I said, opening my eyes, looking up at Adam.

Adam's mouth hung open, his with eyes blazing into mine as he shook his head before taking a step backwards. He covered his mouth. "Holy. Shit."

I was unable to tell if he was happy or sad. Or shocked. Or all three. Confused.

"Or maybe you are my brother. Reincarnated. You're his same spirit, come back for reasons unknown. And you know who killed Jack."

He leaned forward and continued in a faint whisper. "Like an echo from the great beyond." Looking off into the distance behind me, he paused. "Or from the bayou where he was killed."

# CHAPTER
## 33

Adam gave me a crushing hug, then gripped my shoulders at arm's length. "This. Is. Amazing. Tell me something from our childhood, Jack," Adam said.

"It doesn't really work like that," I said. "But what the hell." I closed my eyes. Nothing. I opened them back up, walked over to the skateboard pillow and tried again, this time inhaling a strong whiff.

Still, nothing. But after several seconds, images began flashing in the darkness: a Davy Crockett hat, a Space Patrol toy rocket, a Gotham electric football.

I rattled off descriptions of these items to Adam, with colors and references to dates when he and Jack had received each toy and specific ways we played with each one. Adam stood with a look somewhere between shock and amazement, grabbed the skateboard pillow and pulled it tightly to his chest. He leaned on the countertop, nodding and running a palm along his balding head twice.

"We got somethin' here, boys," Kevin said, with his big white toothy grin.

"When we played electric football," Adam said, "I always wanted to be the yellow team, and Jack always wanted to be—" We said the next word at the same time: "Blue." We smiled at each other. I felt as though the connection with Adam had always been there, inside me, hiding. And now we'd released our hidden bond into reality.

"You wanted to build your own house back in '75," I said. "A single-story brick home, twenty-one hundred square feet, with a tall, open window in front. And columns, one on each side of the front door."

These uncanny details changed Adam's demeanor to fear. He looked up at the ceiling, at Kevin, then at me.

"I'm speechless," Adam said with trembling lips.

Several awkward moments later, we continued talking and, with a shaking hand, Adam wrote down something on a piece of paper.

"I'd like to ask a favor," I said. Adam rubbed his chin. "I need to confirm Tammy's contact info. Address. Phone number."

I sensed Adam hiding something, but nothing concrete. He squinted then looked to the floor, chewing his inner cheek.

"Not sure that's a good idea," he said.

"C'mon, man," Kevin said. "You said it yourself. This is Jack's spirit inside my boy right here. We can go visit Tammy and see what other trippy shit gonna unfold."

"I don't know," Adam said. "Maybe things are better off left the way they are. Don't want to go 'round diggin' up stuff been buried for four decades, or whatever."

"We already have her address, just need her phone number so we don't show up all creepy and weird like a couple of stalkers. We don't even need to mention your name."

A tuxedo cat ran through the kitchen, bumped into my leg, and bolted into the trash-filled living room.

"Fine," Adam said. He swiped a pizza delivery ad and scribbled something on the back. "Here's the phone number of my former sister-in-law. She remarried back in the early eighties. Need you to promise not to tell her what happened here tonight, otherwise she'll kick you two out faster than a croc chompin' at a toad."

"I have no idea what to say to get her to meet with us," I said. "It's not like I can say I'm an old friend of Jack's."

Adam shifted his stance, thinking. "Well, she likes to travel. Maybe you can use that."

"Got it!" Kevin said, snapping his fingers. "We tell her you're a writer with AAA Magazine, doin' a story on Louisiana."

*No way*, I thought. *That would be an idiot move. Nobody in their right mind would agree to—*

"I like it," Adam said. "Kevin can be your camera guy."

Thoughts of the treasure rushed in. A rotten egg sewage smell hit my nose. I needed to get out of there soon. "Adam, you said earlier you had an idea of who your brother's killer might have been?"

"Jack was hunting for a treasure and died at the hands of someone hunting for the same one he was," Adam said. Looking dead into my eyes, he continued. "Jack told me the night before he died that he'd figured out and knew the exact location of the treasure."

"Some kind of curse?" Kevin asked with a darting gaze.

Adam gave a slow nod.

Ignoring him, I said, "There are a bunch of lost treasures around here. You're saying you know the one he was looking for?" I asked, curious if Adam's memories matched up with mine.

"That treasure was all Jack ever talked about. Especially during his last year. The treasure this, the treasure that."

"Must've been weird for him to spend all that time obsessing," Kevin said.

Adam slid his fingertips over his oily scalp. "You boys ever hear of Jacques Lafayette? From the early nineteenth century?"

I glanced at cringing Kevin, back at Adam, and smiled, remembering the name Blake Lynds mentioned before he died: Jacques. "Matches perfectly with John's memories. We found some info online before we headed here, but weren't sure about it until now."

Kevin said, "We don't know all the details other than the dude saved his daughter, but apparently a ghost gave him a heart attack or some crazy shit like that. Guess his daughter buried a chest of gold coins somewhere?"

Adam shook his head. "Not 'apparently'. Lafayette's daughter did bury a treasure. Never found, neither. All that gold's out there, waitin'." He put his hands on his hips and stared off in the distance.

I assumed Jack had failed to take the time to tell his brother the exact location of the treasure. Otherwise the hoarder would be living in a mansion full of trash instead of the small two-bedroom shack.

"I'm not really supposed to talk about this, but hell." Adam took a wide stance and cocked his head. "Accordin' to legend, there are two clues to the location. The first is a map. One of the hired help drew it for the young Lafayette girl so she'd know where to find the treasure. However, being smart like her daddy, she made sure to draw the map so it needed a special triangulating device to pinpoint the exact location."

"Like a compass or something?"

"Bingo," Adam said with a wink, pointing his index finger at me. "Nobody knows the size or dimensions, but that's the second clue: they called it a double compass, and it's made from wood. So if you got only one tool, either the map or the wooden compass, either one is useless. Y'all need both the map and the wood compass to figure out where X marks the spot. Jack told me he'd finally gotten both, but was murdered and that was that." Adam's shoulders drooped and he looked again at the floor.

I closed my eyes. A map appeared in my mind, floating, rotating. But no wood compass. I pictured the map as clear as looking through a clean window.

After opening my eyes, I asked, "Does Tammy know anything about the treasure?"

"Yeah, but she won't talk about it. Too much trauma," Adam said.

The map image continued to shine bright in my head.

I felt blood draining from my head. Spots appeared in my vision. The room spun.

I needed to get out of that house as fast as possible.

# CHAPTER
# 34

A simple idea tugged at me from deep inside my gut, a possible exit strategy from that smelly home.

To Adam, I mentioned that things were getting late and how I thought we had taken up enough of his time.

He agreed and, in a single file, the three of us traversed back to the front entrance, along the winding valley between trash heaps.

The instant Adam arrived at the entryway, as he reached out to grab ahold of the door handle, someone banged a fist on the door.

The same tuxedo cat darted in front of us before disappearing behind the remains of a ripped cardboard box at the base of a trash pile.

I stole a glance at Adam, both of us unsure what to do. Through three frosted rectangular window panes set in a diagonal pattern on the door, blurry colored figures shifted back and forth outside.

"Open up, Adam," a deep male voice demanded. More pounding.

Adam twisted the doorknob and yanked open the door. He flipped on the porch light, which illuminated a tall, sturdy man in his forties wearing a black leather, double rider pilot's jacket, faded blue jeans, and scuffed black dress shoes.

"Mike," Adam said, raising his hand to tug at his earlobe. "Wasn't expecting to see ya 'til tomorrow."

"Yeah, well I need the, um, object sooner rather than later," Mike said with a moderate Louisiana accent. "So, I thought I'd drop by for a visit." His sunken eyes, with bushy brows hovering above, darted among the three of us. "Didn't know you'd have company."

An awkward moment hung in the air.

"Right. Sorry. These are some friends of mine visiting from California," Adam said to Mike, stepping aside.

Kevin stepped forward and introduced himself. Mike smirked as they shook. I wondered if Mike had a Ku Klux Klan bed sheet outfit in the trunk of his car.

Then I introduced myself, first name only and shook Mike's clammy hand. My shoulder twanged with pain, images flashing in my head of a man holding an axe above me. Then I witnessed a brief memory montage of airplanes, runways, and control towers.

I struggled to stay present, blinking several times, trying to avoid going down another rabbit hole filled with memories of my former life. And pass out again.

Mike licked his lower lip, tilted his head, and stared at me with narrow, intense eyes. "I know you from somewhere?"

My first instinct was to agree. But instead, I gulped and replied with a forced smile.

"No. I don't believe so."

Mike looked at Adam, then back at me. "I do know you from somewhere."

"You ever been to California?" I asked.

"Been to all fifty states. And most countries." Mike cocked his head to the opposite side. "Why?"

I shrugged, sliding my hands into my pockets. "It's a big state."

Another awkward moment drifted past.

"How's your girlfriend doing, Mike?" Adam asked.

"Pain in the ass. Typical. Y'all know women." Mike let out a brief, cocky laugh.

"Yup." We all nodded. The urge to argue grew strong inside me, but I managed to keep my mouth shut.

Mike raised his eyebrows, said, "Adam, I need you to go get it right now. I'm in a hurry. Scott's on his way back."

That was our cue.

"Nice to meet you, Mike," I said, squeezing through the doorway, stepping toward him and slipping by. Kevin followed. Mike scurried into the house.

I turned my head to Adam and we shared a glance. "Y'all have a good trip back to California," Adam said with a nod and a wave before closing his front door.

Halfway to our car, I turned around to take another look at the house. "That was sure enlightening."

"Some crazy voodoo shit you did in there. Got no idea how you knew all them facts and stuff."

We leaned our butts against the front fender of my Beemer. The black and white cat raced across the lawn, then stopped in front of us. With shimmering green eyes, the obese feline stared up at me, meowing. He stepped toward me and rubbed the side of his arched back against my lower leg, begging me to pick him up. I leaned down, lifted the hefty fella to my chest and scratched the sides of his face as he purred.

"You must be Bones," I said to the little fella as his purr turned strong and pronounced, like a rapid bass drum. I craned my head to Kevin. "Yeah, I'm tripping out on how these weird memories keep coming to me. They're real memories, but somehow I know they're not really mine, in terms of my life right here, as John Bastian. They're Jack's."

"What about this dude hookin' us up with his ex-sister-in-law, Tammy?"

The cat wiggled so I set him down onto a dirt patch between the straggling weeds. "We need a plan. The address on the paper Adam gave me matches the one we found during our drive out here. She lives here in Baton Rouge, too."

Kevin gave a slow smile.

"Wonder what those two are talking about in there," Kevin said as he crossed his arms. The neighbor's trees rustled in the wind and several dry leaves floated to the ground.

I had never excelled at hiding. As a young boy, I totally sucked at hide-and-go-seek. The other neighborhood kids always seemed to find me first. And none of them ever wanted me on their team.

Which is why I surprised myself when I agreed to his idea to eavesdrop on Adam and Mike.

Making a physical drawing of the map—one from the image in my head—would have to wait.

I told Kevin to hold tight as I hunched over into a crouch, hustled around to the back of Adam's house and ducked underneath two side windows, stepping like a ballerina over a short berry bush, and tip-toeing to the back porch. Old magazines, newspapers, crumpled beer cans and more trash covered Adam's entire porch. Stifled voices came from inside the kitchen area, where Kevin and I had been only a few minutes earlier. I crept closer to the smudged rear glass sliding door, careful not to cast my shadow and give away my presence.

The volume of the dull voices increased, but were still indistinct, so I leaned onto the exterior wall with my fingertips, turned my head and touched my left ear to the glass.

Every word came through crystal clear.

"...now either ya tell me who the hell those two clowns are or I swear to god, your mom's life support ends today," said one man, who I assumed was Mike.

"I told you, they're a couple of guys from the California branch of AAA, nothing to worry about—"

"That's my treasure. And Scott's. We don't need anyone getting in the way. Too much at stake," yelled Mike.

"They're from California. They don't know shit about no treasure. Trust me. Plus, even if they did, Scott's been looking for this thing for, what, like forty years? They wouldn't get—"

"You keep 'em away from us, y'hear? I swear if I so much as sniff one of those sons-a-bitches, they're dead and your momma ain't gonna wake up. You best get your shit together, Adam."

We'd been in Louisiana for less than a day and already some crazy guy wanted to kill us.

I thought about Kevin, still out front, probably still resting against the Beemer fender.

Not enough time to run back out to the front and drive off before Mike left, which sounded like any second. I whipped out my phone and sent Kevin a text message: *hide in the back of the car!*

Bones appeared. He found his way to my legs and rubbed against them. He meowed several times. I hurried away from the rear porch, back to the side of the house and as I rounded the corner, I heard the rear slider door open with a loud screech.

"Bones, get in here," Adam said, as I circled back toward the front of the house, then peeked into the front yard from behind a hydrangea bush.

A green and white car, with a gold police star pasted onto the front passenger door, turned the corner at the end of the block, heading toward Adam's house.

Sheriff.

As if we'd planned our stealthy exit, Kevin hopped into the back seat of my car, out of sight. The sheriff's car parked across the street. Grabbing a sly look around the bush, I caught a glimpse of the lawman exiting his vehicle.

With each step, his substantial beer belly bounced up and down. He put on a black baseball cap with yellow letters, then ratcheted up his belt buckle and pants before moseying across the street to Mike's car.

Mike walked up to the sheriff and they shook hands as the officer glanced around the neighborhood. They talked for several minutes, but I was unable to make out any words. The sheriff patted Mike on the side of his upper arm, then the two men walked to their respective vehicles and drove off south.

Once they had rounded the corner of the block, I hurried out to my car, hopped in, drove two blocks north, hung a right down some random street and pulled to the side with a screeching halt.

Kevin lifted his head from the back seat.

"It's safe now," I said.

He exited the rear and sat down in the front passenger seat.

From inside my backpack, I snatched out my notebook, tore off a piece of yellow paper, clicked out some lead from my 0.5mm mechanical pencil, and started sketching.

Kevin leaned over to see the paper. "Whatcha mean 'we're safe now'? Seems like a pretty decent neighborhood to me."

"That Mike guy wants us dead."

Kevin jerked his head around, scanning the neighborhood. "Say what? We didn't do nothin' to him. Why the hell—"

"I'll tell you later. Gotta draw this map."

"I need to tell you somethin'."

"Not now, man. Gotta finish this."

"When Mike was talkin' to the sheriff," Kevin said, "I heard him say a word you're gonna be interested in."

I stopped sketching.

Kevin continued. "Lafayette."

# CHAPTER
## 35

**B**ack in our one-star motel room, Kevin watched me finish the sketch of the map based on the vision in my head.

He leaned over. "I never seen a map look so detailed, even got them little trees along the perimeter of the island. And this here look like that earth berm we drove by earlier."

Satisfied with my handiwork, I dug into my jeans pocket and fished out the small white paper Adam had given me, the one with Tammy's phone number and address.

"Punch this into your Google Maps," I said, handing the tiny receipt to Kevin. A moment later we had our next destination, but a strange voice in my head told me that I needed to call Tammy first. Setting up an appointment with her ahead of time would improve our chances of success.

But not for another few hours.

Various details of our journey thus far churned over and over in my mind. I wrestled with the events at Adam's house, the ring and skateboard pillow and what he had said. And that sheriff. And the guy wearing the biker jacket.

Logically, these clues were guiding us down the right path, but for some odd reason, I felt like I should be back in California helping my dad somehow.

Although, overcoming self-doubt had never been one of my strengths.

I had a hard copy sketch of a map from one of Jack's memories. Finding the treasure would require some kind of wooden compass, which I had no recollection of.

At all.

The recommendation from Kevin and a dead guy's twin brother that we call Adam's former sister-in-law to talk—under the guise of being a magazine reporter—seemed absurd, bordering on insane. This conflicted with the fire of curiosity about meeting and talking with the woman from my dreams, which continued to grow with greater intensity by the hour.

I called my mom and asked how Dad was doing, but nothing new. He was still dozing in and out of consciousness. She said they're still hoping he'll make a full recovery, not to worry.

Wanting to know more about this new sketch I had drawn, I asked her if she remembered a wood compass, but nothing there, either.

My mental negativity made its way through the phone line to her. Everything from Tammy not being who I hoped she'd be, to my real estate deal not closing, to the gondola death, to my dad's declining health, to the guy from the desert car accident, to the little ghost boy at the hospital, to the potential of being perpetually broke for the rest of my life and never, ever finding true love.

"Honey, it's not too late to come back home. We can burn everything out in our fire pit. We'll have a nice vodka toast and say goodbye to all that, and everyone can move on from this hell you've been in," she said, with slurred speech. "But you're very smart and you're gonna figure it all out. I'll let you know if anything changes with your dad."

I needed a cold beer. Or ten. Kevin and I tore out from the motel parking lot, sped to a nearby bar, walked in, absorbed the emptiness of the joint, and sat at a small corner table. We ordered a pitcher and I chugged the first brew.

"I been thinking about this shit, man," Kevin said. "We need to call that chick soon."

I checked my phone.

7:05 pm.

"One more beer."

He gave me the thumbs up and poured us another round.

I picked up my mug of liquid courage, took a swig, and turned to Kevin.

"I'm worried about this trip," I said, rattling off my other concerns.

He sucked down half his beer and wiped the foam from his upper lip. "I gotta feeling it's all gonna be okay."

"And you with your Jimmy Fallon deal. This trip's not gonna screw that up, I hope."

"As long as we back near L.A. by next week, it's all good. In fact, while you were playing double-O-seven behind Adam's house, I did some more research on you when you were Jack. Here, check this shit out," he said, shoving his iPad in front of me on the table, swiping through several screenshots.

According to the records Kevin found, Jack Bachman served in the U.S. Air Force during the Vietnam War between 1969 and 1972. The man flew hundreds of missions as a bomber pilot over North Vietnam, was credited with taking out over a dozen grounded fighter planes on one mission and was awarded the Purple Heart.

"That's the one you get if you're wounded or killed in action, but we know he wasn't killed over there," I said.

The waitress approached. "Y'all want another pitcher?" We gave her a double thumbs up before she hustled away.

"Exactly. Says here one of his engines caught fire and the dude had to ditch his F-111 Aardvark over enemy territory.

Apparently, those planes had a fully-jettisonable cockpit capsule, so he and his copilot ejected and landed safely on the ground. But they had to trek over forty miles to make it back."

"Maybe he was injured during the ejection," I said.

"Nope. But it does say right here that the two men ran into trouble and ended up in a fire fight with enemy troops on their way back. His copilot was killed in action and you, uh, I mean Jack, got hit in the right shoulder."

Another shooting pain stabbed through my shoulder. *Getting tired of the shoulder pains!* But it seemed weird how Kevin kept referring to something that happened before I was born, as though it had happened to me.

"Guess my right shoulder was a weak spot. In my previous life, of course."

Kevin scrolled down on the iPad and raised his eyebrows. "Well, it says he lost control of his right arm and the doctors considered amputating, but they saved the limb. A miracle, they called it."

The waitress brought the next pitcher, along with some chips and pretzels to munch on. I grabbed a handful of carbs, then threw some into my mouth, pondering these new facts.

"There's more," Kevin said, opening up another screenshot. "Here we got a copy of Jack's birth certificate." He pointed to the date.

Jack was born on November 8, 1949, exactly the same calendar day as my birthday, but twenty-nine years earlier. I rubbed my chin. "That can't possibly be a coincidence." I slogged another few gulps of brew.

Kevin raised his eyebrows again, slowly shaking his head while opening another file. "Says here Jack graduated from Thibodaux High School in 1967 and lucky for us, they digitized all their yearbooks back to the year 1900, so I pulled up their senior yearbook and from the photos, seems like you and someone named Scott Jones was good friends."

"Unbelievable."

A wave of déjà vu washed over me.

"Maybe best friends. You both ended up becoming commercial pilots."

"Can you please stop saying 'you?' I'm right here. I didn't do any of those things." I paused. "I'm sorry, but this is just freaking me out, man. What happened to this stuff giving you the willies?"

"I don't know, man. Just seems like you're the real deal. Whatever spirit is inside you, this body right here, is the same spirit that occupied the body of Jack Bachman."

He had a point, but it still creeped me out.

"How about a death certificate?" I asked, needing to move on.

"Jack Bachman is either still alive, which we know now is not possible, or he died, and nobody knows where his body is buried. No record of his death."

I grabbed some more munchies and tossed them in, washing it all down with another swig of beer. The pleasant buzz of alcohol swept through me, numbing most of my anxiety, so I punched in the numbers for Tammy's cell and gave her a call.

Voicemail. I hung up. No message.

Kevin's body perked up and he stared at me with insecure eyes.

"She didn't pick up," I said, flicking a potato chip.

We needed an backup plan. One without Tammy in the equation. But my mind failed to cooperate. My noggin wanted to shut down. Time for sleep.

After paying our tab, we wandered back outside to the Beemer and drove back to our motel. The moment we parked, my phone rang and the display indicated an unknown caller.

I answered. "Hello?"

A female voice on the other side said, "Hi, I'm returning a call for someone?"

"Who's this?"

"Exactly. Who is this?"

"This is John Bastian," I said, not knowing what else to say.

Pause.

"I don't know a John Bastian," she responded. "Must be a wrong number."

Pause. I had a fraction of a second to save the call and without any other options, I went with the lie.

"No wait, if this is Tammy, yes, I did call you. I'm with Silver and Gold magazine." I flinched, wanting to kick myself for lying to her. "We're running a story about the lost treasure of Lafayette and as I understand from Adam, you might have some insights into the legend that might appeal to our readers."

Click.

"Hello?" I asked. "Hello?"

"What the hell happened?" Kevin asked.

"That went well." I tossed my phone on my lap.

"We gotta figure us out a new plan if she ain't gonna play ball."

"Tomorrow," I said with little purpose.

I made sure the shoebox of trinkets was still nestled in the back seat. Check.

We exited the Beemer, moseyed into our lost-cause of a room, and I hit the mid-sized fridge again for a few more mini-bottles of whiskey. After watching TV for a few minutes, mostly the weather and shots of the looming hurricane coming our way, I nodded off to another night of restless sleep.

# CHAPTER
# 36

*November 22, 2016*

Chased by someone, tired and in pain, I hobbled my way through a swampy bayou. But this time instead of an axe-wielding man, the little ghost boy from Mammoth Hospital, Mark, ran after me, closing in as I tripped on an exposed root. Instead of thrusting the axe deep into my shoulder, he smiled, set the axe down on the ground beside me, and helped me up. "Stay the course, Jack," he told me with a high-pitched, youthful voice. "Stay the course. All will be revealed in time."

I awoke from the dream gasping for air, realizing how much of a bitch karma could be. Apparently, my right shoulder was destined to suffer. No matter what life I was in. Wondering how or why this was happening, I drifted back into a light sleep as my mind circled for options, trying to find a reason.

After several more hours of tossing around the lumpy bed, I got up late, threw on some clothes and convinced Kevin to join me for some Waffle House grub one block away. We entered, sat, and both ordered All-Star specials with two cups of coffee. He asked me what I'd do if we ever found the treasure.

My head pounded with a minor hangover. "I'd give back as much of the gold as I could to help the children of the world," I said. "To increase the collective consciousness of our youth."

My response surprised me. And Kevin.

"Something's definitely wrong with that head of yours. You're tellin' me you get a billion dollars' worth of gold . . . and you'd just give that shit away?"

I nodded. "We could educate people on the various aspects of spirituality, levels of consciousness, et cetera, and over time the world would be a better place. I know it. There'd be fewer wars, rapes, and violence. Way more empathy."

He chuckled and said, "You talkin' about making love not war," giving my knee a solid slap. "All that hippie-dippy crap."

"Yeah, but what if those hippies were right? I don't know, something to think about. Or maybe I did hit my head too hard on that tree."

He blew the surface of his coffee, took a sip, and grimaced. "Ooh, that shit is bit-ter," he said, dumping several spoonfuls of sugar into his mug and trying again. He grimaced again. "But we wandering around in the dark on this treasure hunt, man," Kevin said. "We need a plan. A strategy."

The waitress set our plates of food onto our table and Kevin dug in, taking several more sips of coffee.

"You ain't gonna eat?" he asked.

"Too nervous. We came all the way out here to talk with Tammy. I lied to her, then she hung up. I feel like shit." I pushed my plate and coffee mug aside. My stomach turned.

"Maybe try some juice?"

Before I had a chance to respond, at three minutes past ten o'clock, my phone vibrated again.

*Unknown caller.*

"Hello?"

"Um, yes, hi, this is Tammy. I, uh, wanted to call you back and apologize for hanging up on you last night."

In my chest, my heart did a 180 as I mouthed to Kevin the caller was Tammy. He gave me a big, toothy grin, and a double thumbs up.

She continued. "I, uh, had a rough evening and, um, well, I owe you an apology. If you'd still like to come over and talk about the Lafayette legend, I'll be happy to answer any questions you might have."

*Jackpot.*

"Sure, we can be over in a few hours, say one o'clock this afternoon?" She agreed to the time and confirmed the address.

I hung up.

"My neck feels stiff. So does my face," Kevin said right before his eyes rolled up and back.

Then his arms and legs spasmed, forcing him to the floor.

# CHAPTER 37

On the low-pile carpet of the Waffle House, Kevin's entire body jerked into an arched position with only his feet and head touching the floor, eyes closed, choking for air.

A dozen patrons appeared, surrounding us.

Like a panicked idiot, I looked around for a doctor, but realized that would be unlikely in a small breakfast restaurant.

I remembered a few tips from first aid training a decade earlier. His respiration felt fine and when I put my fingers on his wrist, he had a strong, fast pulse. I pulled my cell out, dialed 9-1-1, and described the scene to the man on the line.

"Paramedics are on the way," the operator said.

I asked her if there was anything I could do, but she advised only to stay away, give him room.

The people standing around continued to sip their coffee and talk about what a shame this is, how nothing like this has ever happened before, et cetera.

"Clear back," I barked. "Let the man breathe, for god's sakes."

I held Kevin's hand and tried to talk to him.

"It's gonna be okay, buddy, hang in there. Ambulance is on its way."

Kevin alternated between convulsions and unconsciousness. My buddy had volunteered to join me on this journey to help protect me and give me strength, but now, watching him suffer this way, without any way to help, felt like the universe was trying to carve out my heart.

I found myself crying, squeezing his hand with a death grip, and praying to a God I no longer believed in to help give Kevin a tiny bit of relief. Nobody should ever have to watch their friend suffer this way. If I could have swapped places with him, I'd have done so faster than a crocodile's snap.

I asked a husky gentleman to wait outside for the ambulance and to show them in when they arrived, which they did ten minutes later.

An eternity.

Finally, two paramedics wearing white pressed shirts and black slacks hustled in and knelt down to Kevin, performing a bunch of tests before loading him onto a gurney. They wheeled him into the ambulance outside—now raining—doing their best to cover his body and keep him from getting wet.

I asked if I could ride along, but they said no. Several minutes later, I caught up in my Beemer, trying to follow them as best I could.

After a short, frantic drive two miles down the highway, we arrived at the Baton Rouge General Medical Center located just north of the LSU campus. By the time I parked and checked in, they already had Kevin in an emergency room. I hustled through the hallway, searching for someone in charge. Finally, I found Kevin, lying on a bed, resting.

His skin looked pale, almost like a white guy.

While standing near the doorway to Kevin's room, I called Kevin's mom. She freaked out and I tried to calm her down.

Several minutes later a doctor showed up wanting to explain what they'd found.

I lifted my finger to put the call on speakerphone, but another call came in from an unknown caller.

I told the doc to hold on a quick second and answered, putting Kevin's mom on hold and half-expecting to hear Tammy. But no.

Only static.

I needed to get Kevin's mom back on the line and find out what happened to Kevin. I switched back to her and put the phone on speaker.

"Kevin ingested a near-fatal dose of strychnine," the doctor said. "We've informed the local authorities. They're on their way now."

My thoughts turned to the conversation with Adam and Mike and the realization hit me: someone probably poisoned Kevin's coffee.

Attempted murder.

Jesus Christ.

The doc continued, but that goddamned nervousness inside me spiked whenever I tried to make eye contact. "We pumped his stomach and administered a healthy dose of activated charcoal to absorb any remaining poison. We also administered anticonvulsant drugs and injected a unique cocktail of muscle relaxants, so he's resting now. If he continues to show progress over the next twelve hours, we'll release him. We expect him to make a full recovery."

Kevin's mom let out a "Who, Lordy," over the speakerphone and asked me to keep her updated. I thanked the doctor.

"In life," Kevin's mom said, "whenever you come across a stressful situation, just take a deep breath and focus on the positives. Now would be a good time for you to do this, John."

I thanked her for the advice and ended the call.

After speeding back to the Waffle House, I stood in the front entryway. Drenched in rain, I caught the eye of our waitress, the one who had delivered our coffees. All just conjecture, though, because I had no evidence.

Until she dropped her serving tray full of food.

And bolted toward the restaurant rear.

I stepped toward her, but slammed into an elderly woman, knocking us both to the floor. After the briefest of apologies, I continued my pursuit through the restaurant, plowing through a swinging chase door before stopping in a food storage area to get my bearings.

"Hey. You can't be in here," yelled some guy. I surveyed the room, which had nothing more than a dish-cleaning sink and food preparation stuff strewn about. The rear door slammed shut. The waitress had disappeared. Nowhere to be seen.

I ran toward the rear door and pushed through to the outside. I jerked my head back and forth, scanning the gray exterior as buckets of rain drenched the alley.

In the distance, a small shadow ran away from me.

Continuing my pursuit, I splashed through puddles of muddy water in the pot-holed pavement and switched gears to running speed, the one I used in high school football to evade tacklers.

Within seconds, I reached the would-be assassin, grabbed her shirt from behind and wrangled her to the slippery ground.

She struggled, putting up an admirable fight, especially for someone her size. I'd guess five-foot nothing, a hundred twenty pounds.

"Let me go," she said, spitting in my face, but the rain drenched everything and her efforts to disgust me failed.

With both my hands, I grabbed the wrist of her left arm and twisted counterclockwise, flipping her over onto her front and locking her arm behind her back.

"Tell me why you poisoned my friend!" I said, water drops falling from my brow and nose.

Her eyes grew big and she shook her head. "I didn't poison nobody. I swear. I only put the extra sugar powder into your coffee like the man asked me to."

"Why the hell did you run?"

No response.

"Wait a minute," I said, something not feeling right. I helped her to her feet and let go of her arm. "Tell me about the sugar. And the man."

In the pouring rain, out of breath, shoulders slouched over, her hair went sloppy and she pushed her bangs out away from her eyes.

"Dude slipped me a c-note," she said, "and told me to put white powder from inside this little pink paper packet into both your coffees. Said it was just some stupid laxative prank. Y'all went to college together. Some shit like that."

I shook my head in confusion and remembered I didn't drink any of the coffee.

Thank god!

"Tell me about the dude. Height, weight, clothing."

"Man, I ain't no tape recorder."

"My friend's in the hospital dying. Try. It's barely been two hours."

An oily taste filled my mouth. I spit rainwater and saliva onto the pavement.

"I dunno. I think I overheard someone call him Mike, no last name. Tall dude, way over six-foot, thick black hair, athletic build. Goatee. Older guy, maybe fifty. Creepy looking. I swear, I needed the money, man."

A late-eighties model car rolled by us in the alley. Water splashed from a puddle onto our clothes.

"And you had no idea the white powder was strychnine?" I asked.

"Strychnine? Rat poison? Hell no. Uh-uh. I ain't about tryin' to kill nobody. Like I said, dude told me it was a prank. Easy money."

I looked into her eyes as best I could with the water dripping down her face. I'd always been skilled at reading people and my gut told me this young woman was telling the truth.

I told her I believed her and let her get back to work. Thought about calling the local police, but since the sheriff seemed shady, I decided to leave him out of this.

In the front parking lot, I hopped into my car, drenching the leather seats, closed my eyes and let the visions come again.

After scrolling through more of John's memories—still there, thank God—I grabbed an old t-shirt from the back seat, wiped my face and gathered my thoughts. The appointment time for meeting with Tammy was approaching fast.

Crap.

My thoughts turned to Kevin's recovery. And my dad's. I'd never really minded hospitals all that much until recently.

If I never set foot in one again, it would be too soon.

# CHAPTER 38

**Scott Jones**

*November 22, 2016*

After a five-hour drive back home and a few stops for food and coffee, Scott paid several hundred dollars to Uber, along with a hefty tip. He made sure the driver parked a block away from his house, behind a hefty tree.

Carrying his coat and suitcase in hand, he walked around the corner and spied what seemed like the same locust swarm of reporters from the airport. The paparazzi appeared to be somewhat hunkered down, awaiting his arrival and the chance to glean more juicy tidbits of information, possibly another interview.

His ego enjoyed this newfound fame.

He suspected his wife knew the secret. About the murder thirty-eight years ago.

But over the years he'd been unsuccessful with confirming his suspicions with her.

Trusting her for a situation like this, Scott called her anyway and asked her to grab some extra clothes and drive around the corner to pick him up. A few minutes later, her car pulled out from the garage, parted the sea of reporters, and drove toward him. Hiding behind the tree until she arrived, he darted inside, and they sped away.

"Wow, look at you, Mr. Hero Pilot," said his wife, a proud mom and former schoolteacher, with frizzy hair, wearing no makeup.

"Shut up, pull over at the next block and get out."

They both exited, but she sniffed the air as he walked past her and said, "You smell like perfume and sex. I thought you said you wanted to get home to me and have a glass of wine. Looks like you already had your wine, with someone else," she said, eyes dull.

"I'm taking the car to the Hampton Inn downtown. I need to get a shower and get back to work."

"I'm not going to let you leave me here in the rain to walk back to our home two blocks away."

He reached into the back seat, grabbed an umbrella, and tossed it at her.

"Yes you are."

He zoomed away, leaving her standing on the corner, sopping wet.

Fifteen minutes later, he parked at the corner of Main and Lafayette in downtown Baton Rouge, checked in, headed up to his room and downed three cups of coffee. He showered, changed into the fresh set of clothes, strung his lucky gold nugget necklace around his neck, and threw on an LSU baseball cap. He walked out of his room and dialed Mike.

"Hey, it's me. I need an update. Meet me at our usual place in fifteen minutes."

# CHAPTER 39

Scott sped through the downpour, relishing how he'd achieved reasonable success in life by combining his intellect with a deep-seated drive for money. People frequently told him he had a big ego. In fact, one cranky old female passenger had told him a decade ago, "Your ego would barely fit inside my living room."

But Scott's ego had taken him further, faster, and higher in life than he had ever thought possible.

So fuck that whiny little bitch. *Fuck all those naysayers.*

Saving the lives of those passengers from that knife-wielding terrorist added enormous volume to his ego. He put on his best humble act when he spoke to the press, but inside he knew he deserved all the credit, relishing every second of the spotlight.

He had always considered himself the jealous type, especially when it came to his wife. He had married her out of pity.

And regret for what happened all those years ago.

Back in '78, several months after what he referred to as "the incident," Scott had discovered Jack's widow was pregnant with Jack's daughter. Scott had fallen into a severe depression and contemplated committing suicide. After the baby was born, Scott's solution to rid himself of the guilt was to manipulate Tammy into thinking he truly cared for her and her baby girl, and they should unite and make a family together.

Tammy grieved for several years after Jack's death, finding comfort in the arms of his best friend, Scott. Eventually, she moved on from Jack's tragedy and—in accordance with the plan—fell in love with Scott. When they married in 1984, six years after the incident, Scott honestly hoped they'd ride off into the classic sunset and leave the past alone, letting him forget what he'd done to his best friend.

Especially if he could find the elusive treasure.

For a brief period, his life felt complete. He'd managed to bury the guilt way down deep, hidden from everyone. He'd formally adopted Tammy's young girl, Jennifer, and Tammy seemed to adore their small family life together.

Scott truly felt somewhat of a bond with his bride, the former Mrs. Jack Bachman.

Now Mrs. Scott Jones.

But their friendly relationship lasted all of two years. At most.

Over time, the daughter devolved into a needy, screaming little brat. She never did what he told her to do even when he lost his temper, which occurred regularly.

Of course, the first time Tammy stepped in, trying to defend her little girl, Scott had to give the mom a lesson. He tried his best to control his anger and frustration with the two females, but sometimes they would gang up on him for the most idiotic of arguments and he'd lose his grip. After his explosions, the family would wander around speechless for several days. Tammy would inevitably come back to him, apologizing for getting out of hand, always taking the blame, as any obedient wife should.

Scott was the man of the house. He had a duty and obligation to lead with a strong fist.

At times he suspected she knew what he'd done to Jack, but he'd convinced himself he was being paranoid, especially since it happened several decades ago.

Ancient history.

But Jack's death wasn't the only one that haunted him—there was another, more recent loss that ate at him in an entirely different way. One Tammy couldn't possibly know about. He mouthed the boy's name, hoping to forget about it.

Mark.

# CHAPTER 40

Scott could still smell the rubbing alcohol inside Shauna's house.

Twenty-nine years ago, when he was thirty-nine, during a one-night layover in Orange County, California, Scott had flown into John Wayne Airport and on a whim, took a cab north about seven miles to one of his favorite restaurants: Black Angus Steakhouse.

Tired and hungry for a juicy steak, he wanted a high-calorie dinner, a few drinks, and to head back to his hotel for a few hours of shut eye before an early flight. He knew consuming alcohol within twelve hours of taking control of a passenger aircraft was a violation of FAA rules, but he had broken that stupid rule more times than he could count.

He sauntered into the restaurant at half-past six, but there was an hour-long wait for a table. He made his way into the bar area, stopped to find a seat, and spied a gorgeous, lonely creature hunched over a strawberry margarita, twirling the thin red straw. She wore a black shift dress, with lightweight woven fabric and a V-neck as deep as an ocean abyss. The matching leather boots traveled up to the tops of her knees. Her body language signaled sad, desperate for attention.

Easy prey, he thought, jamming his wedding ring deep into his pocket before cozying up next to her.

"You look like you could use some company," he said, smooth as ever.

Without looking up she replied, "Is it really that bad?" and continued her distant gaze into the cocktail.

He took a seat and ordered the same drink, which helped break the ice. Eventually he introduced himself and managed to eke out a half smile from that perfect little piece of lady meat.

"For what it's worth, I've been told I'm a great listener. If you happen to have anything you'd like to talk about, I'm here for you." His bright white toothy grin grabbed her attention. An effective manipulation tool that typically worked wonders on most women in her position.

At first, she hesitated to talk, but he continued to work his magic and once she opened up, she spilled her guts about the recent break up with her long-time boyfriend, how he had cheated on her even though they were talking about getting married and having kids, and how she'd always been attracted to the wrong kind of men.

Putty in Scott's hands.

After a few more drinks, they shared some snacks and she asked him if he was married. He lied, saying he hadn't found the right woman yet. She told him she had a thing for pilots, and he reeled her in.

Under the guise of a night cap, they eventually stumbled back to his hotel room, but once inside they consumed each other with lust. He realized he had forgotten to bring a condom, and although he told himself to be careful, in the heat of the moment he failed to pull out. Damned primitive animal instincts. She kept telling him to give her everything he had.

So he did.

He rested for a few hours, showered and dressed while she slept. On his way out the door, he kissed her cheek and whispered to her to keep sleeping. A taxi drove him to the John Wayne airport, he flew his commercial flight back to Baton Rouge and drove home, already forgetting the encounter.

Another clichéd one-night stand with some secretary. Or teacher. Or maid.

Five months later, while mowing his front lawn, he received a call.

Shauna.

He had no idea how she'd found him.

"Scott, we need to talk," she said.

He had already moved on and could barely remember the chick's name. *So many hot babes, so little time.*

"Look, Shauna, or whatever your name is, I gotta—"

"Scott, I'm pregnant."

He paused, envisioning the possibility of divorcing Tammy, or having a bigamist life as a father and husband. No more one-night stands. No more fun. No way.

"It's not mine. Can't be."

"Scott, I haven't been with anyone since I was with you and my boyfriend always used a condom."

*Condoms fail.* They aren't a hundred percent reliable.

"So you say."

"I'm not lying."

"You're not gonna sucker me into child support payments, the kid's gotta be his."

"I don't understand why you're being so belligerent. All I'm asking is for us to sit down together and talk about how to deal with this. I want you to come out to California and meet with me."

A breeze blew through the trees, ruffling the crinkly leaves, and Scott looked up at the sky, wiping a forearm across his brow full of sweat.

"Look, I lied to you, Shauna. I am married. I have a family here in Louisiana. I'm not going anywhere. You have no proof the kid's mine. You need to deal with this on your own. Good-bye and please don't ever call here again." He hung up and whistled his favorite Doobie Brothers tune, *What a Fool Believes*, as he strolled back outside to finish mowing.

For ten long years, Scott heard nothing from Shauna.

But in '98, the next call came out of the blue on his cell phone while he was driving alone toward a local lake to go fishing with his friends.

"Scott, I know you don't want to hear from me," Shauna said, her crying coming through the receiver.

"You're right, I don't."

Before he had a chance to hang up, she blurted out, "Scott, our son is dying."

He looked up at the interior ceiling of his car and mumbled something about Jesus.

"I don't know what kind of game you think you're playing, but I'm not the father of some kid in California."

"He looks exactly like you, Scott. He has your eyes. Your nose. But he has leukemia and we need a blood donor. A relative. I'm not a match, but you might be."

Scott pulled off to the side of the rural road he had been driving on and rubbed his temples, debating what to say next.

"Fine. I'm not admitting to anything, but I happen to be flying into Los Angeles tomorrow. I'm assuming you're still in the Orange County area, so maybe I could meet you somewhere."

"I moved up to Mammoth Mountain three years ago where our son, Mark, and I have been here fighting for his life. I work at the local hospital and Mark is undergoing hospice care here at my house near the base of the ski slopes. He's received the best care possible."

"I didn't know you were a nurse," Scott said.

"I'm a doctor. Neurologist. You would have known had you asked, but that doesn't matter. Can you come up here or not?"

Scott squirmed in his seat, staring out the window at a flock of birds flying off in the distant sky.

"Text me the address and I'll be there later tomorrow evening."

The next day, Scott parked his rental car along the curb of a mansion-sized log cabin. The forest green roof and matching trim gave the home a rugged look. He walked up the winding front pathway to the front door and rang the bell.

Shauna answered the door. She looked as beautiful, or better, than she had ten years ago. She stepped toward him, staring into his soul. Her puffy cried-out eyes broke loose a few tears that streamed down her freckled cheeks.

"Okay, I'm here. Let's get this over with. I have to get back to the airport," he said, looking down at his wristwatch.

"Nice to see you too, Scott." With a cold shoulder, she turned around and led him through an expansive entryway and living room, down a bright white hallway and around a corner to Mark's room.

Inside, the smell of alcohol permeated the air. Posters of the Los Angeles Rams covered the walls, along with autographed black and white pictures of various running backs, quarterbacks, and wide receivers. Several trophies rested on top of a dark, wood-stained cabinet. A slow beeping noise resonated from a hulking machine jammed into the corner. Scott shuffled in across the carpet and found a tiny boy with no hair and chapped lips lying on a bed, with the covers up to his chest. His pale skin made him look unhealthy, almost dead.

Until the boy opened his eyes.

The two parents hovered over the bed.

"Hi Mom," the boy said, weak and gravelly.

"Hey baby. You wanted to meet your dad. Well, here he is. Scott, this is Mark. Your son."

"I thought I was here for the blood thing," Scott said with narrow eyes.

"You lied to me, I lied to you. Sorry."

"Jesus Christ," Scott said, turning around.

"Mark only has a few days left to live," she said. "I thought you'd like to know so you can see him before he passes. His cancer has taken a turn for the worst." She covered her mouth.

"It's okay, Mommy," Mark said. "Don't be sad, please don't cry."

Scott turned back toward Shauna, putting his fingertips to his lips while he stepped toward his son.

The boy looked up at Scott, furrowing his brow. "You don't look like my daddy. I pictured someone else," Mark said, coughing.

Scott immediately regretted coming to see this kid. He saw nothing but pain in his future. They had no prior relationship. He owed this kid nothing. Scott rubbed his goatee. The boy did not look like a younger version of himself, not by a long shot.

"This is awkward," Scott said, taking a step back.

Shauna's phone rang. "I have to take this. I'll leave you two to talk. Be back in a sec." She took the call, left the room and closed the door.

Over the next fifteen minutes, Mark melted Scott's icy heart and the commercial pilot opened up to the little boy.

*Maybe this kid is mine, after all.*

At one point during the conversation, Scott's ego got the best of him.

He needed to brag about the treasure.

He explained how close he was to finding the gold and some of the details involved with Jack's death. Scott figured he might get some psychological benefit by confessing the incident from twenty years before, especially if the person was a child with only a few days left to live.

*This kid needs to know what a bad-ass I am.*

Eventually, Scott leaned in. "You wanna know a secret? Someone else almost beat me to the treasure once. But I found out, and I stopped him."

"How?"

"Well, I made sure he wasn't around anymore."

"What—what do you mean? Do you mean you—you killed him?" Something was wrong. The joy had disappeared from Mark's face. "You're a murderer. My dad is a murderer? No. No." Mark said, with increasing volume.

"Shhh," Scott said, cupping his hands over the boy's mouth while scanning the room to make sure nobody heard them.

The muffled shouts became louder.

Scott let go, initially not wanting to hurt the dying boy.

But the damned kid kept on screaming. Scott stepped toward the door to leave, but Shauna burst in.

"Help us, something's wrong, he's having some kind of panic att—"

"What the hell's going on here?" she asked.

The beeping noise on the heart monitor had increased to over two hundred per minute. Mark continued wailing.

"My dad's a . . . he's a . . ."

Ten seconds later the screams and wiggling stopped. The monitor went to flat line.

Shauna shook her son.

"Mark! Mark! No!"

She leaned over the bed and laid her head on Mark's chest, weeping.

Scott stepped to Shauna, placed his hand on her shoulder, said, "I'm so sorry. Seemed like a pretty neat kid."

Shauna shirked away his hand, standing. "You did this. You were supposed to come here and help him." Her voice trembled. "Help make him better."

After skirting around questions from Shauna about exactly what had happened, Shauna broke down again.

She called the coroner, who confirmed Mark likely died from a seizure brought on by stress and his leukemia.

Several hours later, Scott said goodbye to Dr. Shauna Willis and assumed she would be out of his life forever. He hoped the guilt he harbored would drift away faster than a mild hangover. But no. That guilty feeling weighed heavily inside him every day thereafter.

Scott had let Mark Willis die there at his home in Mammoth Mountain. Nothing he could do. Fate.

At least that's what he told himself.

He'd driven to LAX and flown back home to Baton Rouge, where he'd spend the last eighteen years trying to forget about Mark.

# CHAPTER 41

**John Bastian**
*November 22, 2016*

My thoughts pivoted to Kevin, my best buddy, and the attempted murder via poisoning. No updates yet from the doctor or anyone at the hospital.

Tammy had confirmed our appointment. Said she was home without a car and had nothing better to do.

But I was seriously doubting the entire trip. If my best buddy ended up dying because I needed to find answers to a bunch of memories—which could all still be some whacked out form of mental illness—I'd never forgive myself.

Despite my growing resentment about the trip, something inside urged me to push forward down the path to the dark unknown. Which, of course, meant meeting Tammy in person to do the pseudo-interview, but without the benefit of having Kevin there to back me up or help fend off one or more maniacs apparently trying to kill us.

I wondered why Adam's associates would automatically assume we were a threat to them, to the point they felt the need to actually murder us. Danger was surely on the horizon, but that also meant I was getting close to something. Perhaps the treasure? Or at a minimum: answers.

After making sure the shoebox was still in the back seat of my Beemer, I drove to the motel, locked the doors, and changed clothes inside our room. I jogged across the street to the Alligator Alley liquor store and bought the latest copy of Silver and Gold magazine, figuring it would help me act the part of a reporter, consistent with the lie. My cover.

The drive to Tammy's house in the Westminster area of Baton Rouge was quick and uneventful, compared to two and a half decades of driving in California, where I had become accustomed to traffic congestion, slugging through every mile of street and highway.

And I half expected someone to follow me.

With no traffic, I arrived early and discovered two local news vans parked along the curb outside the house, so I sat in my car across the street and waited. A male reporter with a mic stood on Tammy's lawn giving a report in front of a tripod-mounted video camera.

Why did Tammy have a reporter on her front lawn? Seeing the guy talking to a camera only served to add fertilizer to my ever-growing doubts.

Tammy's two-story brick home, with green hurricane window shutters and clay tile roof, appeared to be a sturdy structure, but sparked nothing special in my mind. The clean-cut green grass and perfectly trimmed bushes, lush trees, and flowers added a perfect polish. If the house was situated on waterfront property back home in Newport Beach, I could probably sell it for a couple million bucks from multiple offers, and I absentmindedly calculated what my commission would be, even though I hated selling residential.

At a few minutes before one o'clock, I exited the Beemer, ignored the two vans, and strolled up to the front door, pretending as though I belonged there. I stepped up onto the curbed porch at the entryway, stretching my hand out to press the doorbell button when, to my surprise, the door swung open.

A red-haired woman in her early sixties stood in the doorway, hiding one arm behind the door and the other at her side.

My facial muscles fell limp.

My heart fluttered in my chest.

I bounced on my toes.

Jack's memories merged with the gorgeous creature before me.

The woman in my dreams, visions, memories—whatever they were—stood five feet away. Every cell in my body told me with one hundred percent accuracy this was the woman I had been searching for. Beauty resonated from every inch like a roaring fire on a cold, blistery night as I searched for a word— any word—to speak, but my mind went completely blank.

With a burning desire to make a strong first impression, I did what any desperate man on the verge of losing his mind would do.

I smiled.

And whipped out my best version of bullshit.

"Good morning, I'm, uh, John Bastian and—"

My foot slipped off the back of the curbed porch. I lost my balance. With my arms flailing about like a featherless bird falling from a nest, trying to regain my stance, I tripped on a sprinkler and fell into the flowering bushes nearby before hopping back up, shaking my head, and dusting off the front of my clothes.

Tammy covered her mouth, hiding a pair of soft, supple, red lips while letting out the most amazing giggle.

"I'm so, uh, sorry about that, ma'am. I can be a real klutz sometimes," I said with a chuckle. *Way to sweep her off her feet, John!*

"Are you alright? Please hurry inside before any reporters come up," she said with a melodic Louisiana accent, stepping forward to help brush off my shirt with her palm.

She extended her hand, said, "I'm Tammy, pleasure to meet you, John," and we shook. The instant her skin touched mine, something magical happened inside me and for the briefest of moments, sparkling dust and the sounds of laughing children swirled everywhere, while an overwhelming sense of calm permeated my entire body.

A moment later, I snapped out of the clichéd daze when she invited me in.

"Here, you come on inside and we'll getcha a nice glass of my homemade sweet tea." Her Louisiana accent soaked deep into my soul like maple syrup into a tall stack of butter-milk pancakes.

I complied, entering her home with the continued rushed introduction. "Anyway, I'm with Silver and Gold Magazine. We spoke on the phone."

I shared a brief summary of Kevin, the poisoning, and the prognosis he'd be fine.

She gasped, covering her mouth again.

"I'm so sorry to hear that, honey."

Her home was immaculate. Decorations from countries across the globe hung on every wall. Paintings, ceramic sculp-tures, figurines, and books from Singapore, France, Egypt, and what looked like countries in South America.

"Please, have a seat." She glanced out the front window, checking for something. "I'll grab the tea and be back in a jiffy. Make yourself comfortable," she said, motioning to a beige antique couch.

She disappeared into her kitchen. *Real smooth, dummy, real smooth.*

Tammy returned, holding a shoulder-width silver tray with a clear crystal jug full of ice cubes and brown tea, two matching glasses, and what looked like miniature English muffins.

She poured some tea into our glasses, picked one up for herself, and leaned back in her chair. The ring on her right hand sparkled with two emeralds and a diamond.

*Same as the drawing I made as a kid.*

She sipped her tea before asking me several qualifying questions—all of which I'd anticipated—about how long I'd worked at the magazine, where I lived, and more. I'd never been much of a fan of tea, but after one sip of the sweet brew, I'd found my new favorite drink and enjoyed several swallows before answering.

As I set the glass down onto the coaster, my finger tapped out the catchy jingle onto the tabletop "*Shave and a haircut, clip clip,*" then I leaned back on the couch.

Tammy fixed her gaze straight at me, tilted her head, and nibbled on her lower lip.

Somehow, I managed to skate my way through her reasonable concerns before tossing two heavy-duty questions. She asked, "Okay, what would you like to know about the Lafayette treasure?"

"As you know, Louisiana is a hot bed for treasure hunting enthusiasts. My associate Kevin, who, again, is unable to join us today and—"

"Yes, Adam called me earlier this morning and said you wanted to discuss this. Again, my apologies for hanging up on you."

*That was nice of him.*

I waved a hand at her. "Not a problem, totally understandable." She scanned me, looking up and down. "Anyway, the Lafayette treasure. Let's start with your understanding of how the gold came into existence. The legend of the treasure."

She crossed her legs and used a hand to smooth out the top of her skirt. "My husband—my first husband—was obsessed with the darned thing. He found out about it from an archaeologist on a flight back from Africa. My husband was a pilot, a Vietnam vet, and an absolutely wonderful, caring man." She looked up to the ceiling, smiled, and exhaled. She pressed her fingers to her smiling lips. "Spent countless hours doing research at libraries all across the southern U.S. and talking with various descendants to uncover clues."

I scribbled down some notes to at least pretend to be a legit reporter. "Your first husband was?"

"Jack Bachman, Adam's twin brother."

Confirmation of hearing Jack's name mouthed by his widow, someone who I'd envisioned as a young boy, should have provided a certain level of comfort for me. A confidence booster, but no, instead I felt fear. Like I was heading into a dense, dark forest, hungry wolf howls bouncing off distant tree tops. Part of me wanted to get up and run out the front door.

But I stayed put and continued.

"And the archaeologist?"

"Ironically, he died on that same flight."

# CHAPTER 42

Tammy rolled her eyes, smiled, and continued. "I know this sounds melodramatic, but Jack said the old man shared information about the treasure, literally with his dying breath. Was amazing to hear him tell the story."

Her Louisiana accent continued to sound pure, like Mozart on a perfectly tuned piano.

I nodded and continued scribbling gibberish. "This is good stuff. Will make an excellent piece. Did he give you any details about the treasure?"

She looked to the ground, shifted her jaw and said with a slow nod, "If I recall correctly, the sheer amount of gold would have been worth hundreds of millions of dollars back in the seventies. So, I'd imagine the entire lot would easily be worth more than a billion dollars now. It was rumored there were thousands of gold doubloons in the chest, which was, again if I'm not mistaken, made from mahogany wood and reinforced iron plates. His daughter allegedly buried the trunk next to some abnormally giant tree, near the shore of one of the local bayous off the Mississippi, or on an island."

Tammy batted her eyelashes.

"You said 'his daughter', I'm assuming you're talking about the daughter of the Lafayette guy," I said.

"Yes, I'm sorry. Jacques Lafayette was her dad. According to the legend, his daughter was raped by Fatale, Jacques found her and killed the rapist, but the ghost of the dead guy haunted him for months. Both Lafayettes wanted to sail back to France, but the dad had a heart attack and died. Apparently, at the hands of the ghost. The daughter hid the treasure, but she was killed, too, during a hurricane. Never found her body. Terrible tragedy all around. And the treasure's never been found."

"This was all in the nineteenth century?" I asked.

"I believe sometime in the 1840's."

I nodded my head and continued writing. "Fascinating." As I wrote, I twirled my pen around my thumb and whirled it through my fingers, sometimes chewing on the end as I thought.

When I looked up to ask Tammy the next question, she was staring at my hand and pen. She tilted her head once more, nibbling on her lower lip again.

I hesitated, then gave her a tiny nod. "I'll bet the ground-water level around here is pretty shallow? Probably goes up and down every day. What made your husband assume the treasure wasn't underwater?" I asked.

"Good question, it might well be, but according to the legend, she sealed the wood and iron treasure chest inside a custom-built granite box. The problem is if one of the many storms over the years happened to damage the old tree, it'd be impossible to find. Trees come and go, y'know."

"Interesting." I switched subjects. "You don't happen to have any pictures lying around do you? Of Jack?"

She tightened her lips, looked up, and placed her teacup down on the tray. "I'll be right back." She stood and hurried up the staircase, which reminded me of my mom doing that same thing two days earlier.

Her stares were intimate and intense, which had made it challenging to interpret her body language. But if Kevin were here he'd say something like, "For an older chick, I'm getting some pretty hot vibes coming off her."

A heightened sense of relaxation wrapped around my body, nullifying any remaining anxiety. Finally, for the first time since the skiing accident, a sense of normalcy came over me. I felt grounded, with no internal pressure. No irregular heartbeat. No adrenaline surges.

Oddly enough, while in another man's house talking to his wife, a wonderful feeling of joy topped me off like placing the missing piece into the jigsaw puzzle of my life. Confused, I pushed the pleasant thoughts aside and refocused on the treasure.

Tammy entered the room carrying two picture albums. The spiritual attraction to her reignited in full force.

She sat next to me on the couch, opened one of the albums, and the scent of her perfume floated by. For a split second, I swear I lost consciousness.

A black and white image of two people standing at an altar took up most of the area of the first page. I recognized the woman as young Tammy in her early years and this image matched perfectly to the one in my head. I felt my face becoming flushed. The man holding her looked like a younger, thinner version of Adam, but with hair on top of his head.

Quite the handsome couple.

"This is me and Jack on our weddin' day. 1975."

If any part of the reincarnation theory were true, I was looking at pictures of my former self, the last body my spirit had occupied prior to the current one.

She turned page after page, revealing pictures of people who, logically, were strangers to me but at the same time relatives of mine whom I somehow recognized. When I looked at each person, not only did I see their names in my head, but memories of various family get-togethers, conversations, and emotions.

I picked up a faded Polaroid picture of both Jack and Tammy standing in front of a small home, with red brick fascia and a row of gardenias. More memories rushed in.

"Here we go. This is one of the last pictures of Jack before he was murdered," she said, pointing down at another full-sized image of Jack standing on a tarmac next to a DC-9 airplane, outside a set of air-stairs. He wore a crisp pilot's uniform, with epaulets on the shoulders of his pressed white shirt, black slacks, and a captain's hat.

Heat radiated from Tammy.

"Hold on. Murdered?" I asked, playing dumb, which I was getting pretty good at, acting like an idiot. Seemed to come naturally to me.

She stared out the window for several seconds, then back to me. "Yes. Someone murdered him. But nobody ever found his body. Only his arm. Or what they thought was his arm because his pilot's ring was still on a finger." She took in a long, heavy breath and exhaled slowly, rubbing the tops of her thighs, rocking. "But me, I think he was too close to finding the treasure. Ya know there's some curse that's supposed to be associated with the whole darned thing, which sounds more like some weird conspiracy to me."

"Any idea who killed Jack?"

She took a sip of tea. "I have my suspicions."

"You're married now to someone else, correct?"

"Yes, Scott was Jack's best friend from high school. Two peas in a pod, those two. They did everything together. After coming back from Vietnam, they reconnected. Both became commercial pilots. In fact, once Jack found out about the treasure from the dying archaeologist, he told Scott everything and they both became obsessed."

The doorbell rang.

"Excuse me," she said, stood and walked to the front door. A minute later she returned with a small cardboard box in her hand. "Something for my husband." She placed the box onto a wood end table, but her knee bumped the table with her tea and knocked the whole thing onto the plush, cream-colored carpet.

"Oh dear," she said, raising her hands to the sides of her head before running into the kitchen to grab a wet rag and returning to the mess, blotting up the tea from the carpet. Most of it, anyway. I offered to help, but she refused.

"So you married your second husband a few years after Jack's disappearance, correct?" I asked.

"Not disappearance. Murder," she corrected. "Scott turned on the charm a few years afterwards and we got married in 1982. We have a grown daughter, Jenny, who lives nearby with our two grandbabies, Andrew and Josh. We tried to have some children of our own, but my husband didn't seem to have enough soldiers in his little army, if you know what I mean."

"Hmm," I rubbed my chin. "So your husband's not the biological father of your daughter?"

"Nope. He's a pilot, gone a lot. You know the fly-boy type." She looked to the ground. In a monotone voice and with a deadpan face, she said, "He's been a good provider for us."

Before I had a chance to ask more about the baby-daddy, I looked back at the pic of Jack on the tarmac, mesmerized. "Mind if I snap a quick photo of this for the article? This is a good one of him." She said she didn't mind, so I took a shot with my phone.

While sliding the phone back into my pocket, I saw an image on the opposite side of the page, one of Tammy holding a small child, but she turned the page before I could get a better look.

In the next photo, I recognized the older man leaning against a '50's model car. "This looks like your Uncle Joe," I said with a chuckle. "Man, that guy had the funniest laugh, he—"

She narrowed her eyes and turned the page again. Several shots had been taken from the street of an old house, with similar houses on each side. An old subdivision, perhaps.

My verbal filter disappeared.

I blurted out the first thing that popped into my head as I pointed to the picture. "Oh, hey. The Kaluzas lived there. I remember them, they were super nice. They—"

She snapped the book shut, stood tall, and looked down at me. "Somethin' fishy's goin' on. Who on God's green earth are you?" she demanded with a scowl, her hospitality clearly wearing thin.

"I, uh, well, we—"

"Doesn't matter, I'm not comfortable with this." The blood drained from her face. "I think it's time for you to leave, Mr. Bastian." She pointed to the door.

# CHAPTER 43

**Scott Jones**
*November 22, 2016*

Later that afternoon, Scott arrived at their Westminster home. He parked across the street and tried to sneak in by jogging to the back door, but two reporters spotted him and shouted out questions.

"The hero has returned," he said melodically, entering and closing the door, like a king returning victorious from a battle.

Tammy walked through the kitchen, strolled up to her man, and gave him the usual hug and kiss on the side of his face, both of which felt forced. Something had happened. He had a way of reading his wife, seeing right through her.

He peeled off his dark gray windbreaker, placed it on the coat hook nearby, and crossed his arms. Shifting his stance, he said, "Tell me what's wrong."

"You know what." She turned to walk back into the kitchen, but he grabbed her arm, stopping her cold.

"That's not what I'm talking about."

"Fine. A man came by here today asking about—"

"About what? One of the reporters?" he said, veins pulsing his temples.

She looked him square in the eye. "No. A journalist from Silver and Gold. He wanted to know about the treasure."

He shook her loose, then walked in a small circle. "Great. Just wonderful. Babe, what the hell are you doing? You know I'm days—maybe hours—away from finding the damned thing. How could you be so stupid? Tell me who this clown is."

"He said he was writing an article about the treasure."

Cogs churned in his head. He threw his arms up.

"And so you just, what, let him come on in to our house? Jesus fucking Christ, Tammy."

She crossed her arms, looking down at the carpet.

He stepped toward her, standing face to face, glaring down. "Tell me right now who this guy was or so help me God, I'm gonna—"

"No."

Seething, he chuckled while grinding his teeth, trying to figure out how to deal with her insubordination.

"You will tell me his name. Right now."

With a trembling chin, she replied, "No. It doesn't matter. You're a hero, go outside and be famous, talk to some of those reporters."

He huffed, walked toward the nearest wall, and kicked a hole through the drywall.

"Everything is on the line here and today of all days, you decide to finally shut that trap of yours? I've had it with your crap." He set his face directly in front of hers, noses an inch apart. He blinked twice, said, "Jenny's not gonna make it to her next birthday if you don't tell me this asshole's name."

She spoke, emotionless. "You wouldn't."

He stood perfectly still, enjoying her reaction to his slow, calculated grin.

"You think I'm gonna let her come between me and my treasure? You're a lot dumber than I thought."

She took in and exhaled several short breaths.

"Bob. He said his name was Bob," she said.

"Goddammit, Tammy." He grabbed her shoulders, shaking her in frustration like a floppy doll. "How many times I gotta tell you not to lie to me? Huh?"

As a second-grade teacher she barely made enough to scrape by, let alone enjoy life. She'd be nothing without Scott. He had given her stability, extra spending cash for travel, and a comfortable home to live in.

"John. His name was John," she shouted, grabbing at his hands, trying to free herself.

Scott let her go. She collapsed to the ground as he nodded his head, thinking, rubbing his gold nugget before blazing away through the kitchen and heading outside.

# CHAPTER 44

**John Bastian**

*November 22, 2016*

**D**riving back to the hospital to check in on Kevin, I stopped at a nearby restaurant recommended by the motel manager to grab a quick bite. I continued to berate myself about the failed meeting with Tammy. Honestly, since I had no actual plan to begin with, the fault was entirely my own. Kevin, a gifted actor who on any given day was one of the most talkative people alive, could have made a huge difference.

Billy's Grits and Fried Goodies offered fried food like I'd never seen before. Since I had thrown my healthy diet out the window after the accident, I ordered whatever sounded yummy.

The fried alligator bites tasted like chicken. I also ordered a plateful of crawfish, crabmeat boudin, and sole, all with Cajun spice. Finished with the delicious meal, mouth ablaze, I gulped down a gallon of cold water.

The waitress plopped a slice of fried watermelon on my plate and smiled. "Our specialty," she said. Hunger still raged strong in my belly, so I downed the yummy after-dinner treat.

Sitting alone at the table in the restaurant, I tried to figure out my next move, but the pieces were not falling into place like I hoped. I twirled my knife in my hand like a drumstick. The waitress asked if I wanted anything else and I replied, "Two shots of whatever bourbon you have."

After draining those into my belly, I waited for the effects to kick in and, on a whim, called Tammy.

She answered.

Pressing my palm to my heart, I said, "Tammy, I want to apologize for what happened earlier."

After a pause that felt like weeks, she replied, "John, we need to talk." She inquired about my location.

I told her the name of the restaurant, but she wanted to meet somewhere more public and suggested the LSU Museum of Art.

We agreed to meet there in half an hour, at 5:30, plenty of time before the museum closed.

Google Maps gave me directions to the address. Rain had started to fall, so after I parked two blocks away, along the Mississippi, I donned my rain jacket, walked toward the museum and waited in the gray-striped brick courtyard, near a cluster of agapanthus plants in desperate need of attention. According to the time on my phone, Tammy was running five minutes late. A reasonable delay, with the rain and all.

Ten minutes later, staring at the purple Lily of the Nile flowers and contemplating my existence and the purpose of this trip, I noticed a reflection in a tall windowpane of someone standing next to me.

I felt a tap on my shoulder and turned around.

An invisible shroud of Charlie perfume engulfed my entire body. Amazing. The familiar scent flooded my brain with more memories from the past, and her smile warmed my heart.

She stepped to me and, even though we'd barely met, gave me a warm, caring hug. Not just any old hug, the type of embrace you give someone you haven't seen in forty years. A true-hearted, long, loving squeeze.

Odd.

Good, but odd, completely unexpected.

My arms wrapped around her and something inside me officially clicked, the way the handle to an old bank safe unlocks after you spin the right combination.

We ended the brief embrace and she looked deep into my eyes, studying them like a cat trying to figure out how to catch a laser dot. I expected my eyes to dart away, but instead, they maintained their contact with hers without any issues whatsoever and dammit, it felt right.

"What do ya say we go inside and get out of this nasty weather?" she asked.

I tried to verbally agree to her suggestion, but nothing came out.

Inside the museum, she shook off her umbrella onto a damp carpet, purchased two tickets and handed one to me. "You owe me dinner, mister," she said with a gleam in her eye. I nodded, snatched the ticket and we wound through various hallways washed in white paint, all showcasing wondrous works of art. Tammy led the way, walking with purpose, like she'd visited the museum many times.

Plus, she seemed eager to get somewhere specific.

We passed the Clementine Hunter exhibit, beyond the *Art in Louisiana Exhibit -- Views Into the Collection* area showcasing oil paintings of prominent women in history. A glass enclosure of a silver tea set from the year eighteen something-or-other caught my eye and a few yards beyond, Tammy stopped in front of another painting.

A few words squeaked out from my mouth. "I'm assuming at some point you'll want to talk about my botched interview?"

"Yes, of course, but first I thought you might like to see the man who started the entire legend," she said, motioning her arm to the portrait of a man.

I leaned toward the painting and read a gold engraving below: *Mr. Jacques Lafayette - 1842.*

Someone had painted an exact image of the ghost I saw, the one from Adam's house.

The same top hat. The same bulbous nose and deep, miserable blue-green eyes, with reddish facial skin, and obtrusive, thick, curly eyebrows. The same black, graying beard. And the stoic look of a confident, wealthy Frenchman.

"This is the man who killed his daughter's rapist. The man with the gold."

I continued studying the painting up and down.

Beneath the gold engraving, a second plate read: "Donated by the Estate of Amr Abubaker."

"Reminds me of someone I knew a long time ago," she said, pointing to an oil portrait to the left of the Lafayette image. "This was his daughter, Bridgette."

No way the two human beings portrayed in front of me were related. Ocean- and desert-level differences. The daughter looked like a famous movie star. Anne Hathaway. Bridgette could easily have been a modern fashion model. To say she was gorgeous would be an understatement of epic proportions.

Tammy turned and glanced around the corridor. "Anyway, I wanted to show you these two paintings."

In the corner of my eye the picture of Jacques morphed into a 3D hologram, lifelike and breathing. I jerked my head to get a better look, but the image snapped back into the original two-dimensional space. My imagination. Or another hallucination. Or ghostly vision. I turned back to Tammy.

"Not sure I follow," I continued with my reporter ruse. "These portraits won't help anyone find the gold unless, perhaps, there's a map on the back side like they always have in the movies." I motioned toward the corner of the image of Jacques and leaned forward, but she yanked me back.

Playfully, she said, "You're going to get us kicked out of here. Don't touch anything." She scanned the other end of the corridor, half smiling.

"Sorry," I said with a wink.

The Jacques painting whispered to me, a string of indecipherable words, standing my forearm hair at full attention.

# CHAPTER 45

**Scott Jones**
*November 22, 2016*

Four different times, Scott had set up the meeting with the crazy old witch lady, cancelled, and re-scheduled. Fresh waves of headache pain rumbled through his head.

Over the years, he had met and paid two separate vendors for so-called original Le Trésor Fatale maps. Each con artist had been genuine, sincere, and knowledgeable with the history of the treasure. But unfortunately, each map had been an inaccurate forgery.

In fact, nobody had provided details of how the unique tool—the wooden compass—worked, until recently when Scott had met with the assistant of the dying archaeologist—Amr Abubaker—who had originally given the actual map to Jack back in the seventies.

If Jack had simply shared the goddamned map with Scott instead of burning most of it, Scott would probably have found the treasure decades ago.

Scott had to get his hands on an accurate version of the original map. Desperate, on many occasions he had visited the murky depths of the dark web, offering cash and a ten percent take of the treasure as a finder's fee to anyone who could help him procure an original map.

Scott's long-time associate in Milan turned out to know an old lady named Ms. Petitpont who claimed to have one of the original maps. Not a forgery, an original, like the one Jack had been given. Scott paid off his friend and went about setting up the meeting with the elusive woman.

Now, on the rescheduled night of the appointment, Scott arrived at the harbor behind Deer Island in Biloxi, Mississippi, about a hundred and fifty miles east of Baton Rouge, where the woman had docked her yacht. He parked, strolled down the slippery concrete path soaked from the driving rain and gusty winds, out onto the harbor dock, where hundreds of moored boats bobbed up and down. Scott managed to find space R-2, painted black on the white walking wood-planked platform, before scanning the exterior of the impressive vessel, a Sea Ray Sundancer hard top express, which looked to be about fifty feet in length. Not at all what he expected from how his associate had described the witch.

Scott climbed onto the rear deck, envy running through his veins. He pondered what type of boat he could buy once the gold was securely in his vault.

He hollered "Hello" into the darkness. Nothing. Without warning, a crusty old lady appeared in an opening below deck. Easily in her nineties, with a worn-out sun-leathered face, she wore all black, a silk dress shirt and baggy pants and cape, all coordinated with her full head of waist-length hair as white as snow. Hand tented on her forehead to block the rain, she stared at Scott through horn-rimmed spectacles and waved him below.

He stepped down the wooden stairs, out of the storm, wiping streams of water off his bald head.

They made each other's acquaintance before she asked him to sit. Stained wood covered the interior walls and furniture, all of which gave off a calming varnished scent. Beige leather seats surrounded an oak table in the middle of the main hull room.

He assumed a simple transaction: he'd pay the lady, get the map and dart off. But apparently, she had other plans, so he played along.

"I must admit," Scott started, "Impressive. Wasn't expecting a boat of this caliber."

"Of course not," she said, a hint of French accent mixed into her words.

"When you told me ya lived on a boat, I pictured more of a sailboat. Something smaller than this." He continued studying the vast interior.

She nodded. "I decided to meet with you because of what you did yesterday, Mr. Jones. With the airplane full of passengers. That bastard. You're a national hero."

"Don't feel like one," he lied. "Just did what anyone else would have done in my shoes." Inside, he enjoyed the flattery.

She poured herself a glass of Chardonnay and sat. "You look like a whiskey man."

"Please. Neat." She poured a double shot into a clear Mardi Gras glass and handed it to him.

"Aside from being modest, tell me about yourself," she said with a wonderful grin.

"Not sure how that's relevant."

"When you get to be as old as me, Mr. Jones, doing business such as this gets boring without the pleasantries of establishing relationships. Tell me what it is you seek."

Scott petted his goatee, rubbed his ear, and looked around, considering her request.

"Well, as I mentioned to you in my email, I'm a commercial pilot, married for over thirty years, one daughter, and I'm a part-time treasure hunter. My intention is to purchase the map ya allegedly have and—"

"Not allegedly. But continue. Please." She sipped her wine, eyebrows raised.

A clap of thunder boomed outside.

"Of course. After I purchase your map, I intend to find the treasure and share the wealth with the community of Baton Rouge, perhaps making several generous, yet anonymous donations to LSU," he lied again, grabbing and rubbing the gold nugget on his necklace unconsciously.

She treated him with a coy smile. "You know the treasure is rumored to be worth over a billion dollars. I'm curious what you're willing to pay to be the one who'll finally find something that's been in a state of obscurity for over 170 years."

"The map's worthless without the other piece. I'm sure you know that." He knew his weak negotiating position, but tried to stay firm with the old witch. "I've been burned before. Twice. Not even sure ya got what you say you got. Ain't no way to know ya haven't already given a copy of it to someone else."

She cackled. "I assure you I have not."

"Ya came highly recommended, but forgive me, ma'am, your assurances honestly mean nothin'." He turned hardball on the lady. "In fact, if you ain't able to produce the map in the next thirty seconds, I'm afraid I'm going to have thank you for the whiskey and leave."

She fully opened her black eyes, smiling, the wrinkled skin tightening at the corners of her mouth. "Of course, you are free to do as you please, Mr. Jones. But if you leave now, I guarantee you will never find the treasure."

# CHAPTER 46

**John Bastian**
*November 22, 2016*

To give my ear a better angle to the Lafayette painting in the museum, I turned my head and leaned toward the wall.

"Something wrong?" Tammy asked.

"Nope. Nothing. Perfectly fine."

She darted glances between my face and the painting without moving her head. "You sure? You look like you've just seen a ghost."

How cliché, I thought. But true. I closed my eyes to focus the noise and as the gibberish repeated over and over like a broken 8-track tape, words started to form.

*Look inland? No. Look inward? No.* I leaned in closer. *"Look on the island,"* the ancient, whispering, strained voice said.

"Do the words 'Look on the island' mean anything to you?" I asked Tammy, but as I opened my eyes, the image of Jacques metamorphosed back into a life-like hologram of the nineteenth century French merchant. I jumped back, leg muscles flexed and ready to run. I pointed to the picture of Jacques, noticing a substantial mole on one of his cheeks.

"John?"

With my head in a virtual vice, I moved only my eyes, speaking as slowly and calmly as possible. "Please tell me this exhibit has a hologram. Like a video or something?"

The entire head of the man oozed out of the frame, all the way to the base of his neck. "*Look on the island. Look on the island,*" the ghost said now with perfect clarity.

Eyes squinted, she shook her head once and put her hand on my shoulder. "John, there's nothing there. Just a painting."

All moisture in my mouth had vanished. *I must be going nuts.* With clenched fists, trying to keep a grip on my sanity, I said, "You're right," then the ghost retracted back into the painting, vanishing. I blinked several times, scanning the entire wall, corridor, and floors. Nothing unusual, totally normal and quiet.

"I'll bet you just need some food. C'mon. I'm starving." She tapped my chest with the tip of her index finger. "Plus, you owe me some answers, bub." She cradled my hand and led me back out to the museum entrance. "There's a great bistro around the corner. Let's walk in the rain."

Although I'd just had some food, my stomach signaled that I needed more.

She stretched open her umbrella and shared it with me as we headed toward Art's Bar and Bistro two blocks away along, oddly enough, Lafayette Street. The walk helped me catch my breath, which helped settle my heart down. She was quiet the entire time, deep in thought, I assumed. Once inside the restaurant, I helped her remove her black wool coat and we sat at a round booth table.

She wore a black sleeveless chiffon dress with faux leather trim. Another unexpected move by her. *Was she planning on seducing me?*

No way.

And with her bright red hair styled in a wavy bob with heavy fringe, those amazing blue eyes popped. She turned toward me, gazing into my eyes and time slowed, my senses immediately infused with her essence.

A server arrived and Tammy ordered a PBR beer, my favorite. I did the same.

"So," I started. "You wanted to talk."

"You're not with a magazine, are you?"

Caught. I shook my head, hunching my shoulders. "Guilty."

"I've talked with a ton of reporters and journalists in my day, before I was a schoolteacher. You didn't fit the bill, but for some reason, I went along with your little ruse," she said, with a smile and constant eye contact. "Not bad, actually."

I curled my lips and smiled. "You don't look like a schoolteacher."

"Oh no? Tell me what schoolteachers look like."

Like a dope, I shrugged, tried to mouth a few words, pushed my lower lip out, and shook my head. "No idea."

"Exactly. I worked as a server for the Bright Star Restaurant in Bessemer, Alabama for a few years back in the eighties." She straightened the fork and knife so they were both parallel to the edges of her napkin. "I knew I didn't want to do that my whole life, so I went back to school in eighty-two and got my BS in Elementary Education from the University of Alabama, Lafayette. Unfortunately, they weren't hiring teachers at the time, but I managed to get my foot in the door as a public relations manager and handled all the press releases for the district and any inquiries from the press. Did that for three years. Once a teaching position opened, I snatched it up and have been teaching elementary school for the last thirty-one years. Getting ready to retire soon."

Our beers arrived. She swigged down half her pint. "You seem to drink like some insane, primitive hominoid maniac," I joked.

"See? That's the type of stuff I don't understand. That's the same phrase I used to say to my . . ." She looked at her beer, setting the mug on the table and furrowing her brow.

An urge to stretch and yawn came over me, but as I raised my right arm, Tammy stared at the upper inside, below my bicep, where I had a small purple birthmark in the profile shape of a rabbit head.

She leaned in, tilting her head. "Let me see that birthmark, if you don't mind."

I lifted my arm further, she scooted over toward me and deliberately lowered her head, studying me. She found my eyes and stared.

"What?" I asked.

She grabbed her beer glass, drained the rest of her brew, and panted.

"Who are you?" she asked.

I took a beat. Time to put up or shut up. I'd traveled all this way for this moment of truth, waiting since the first images—memories—of this woman entered my mind.

After fishing out the clay figurine from my jacket pocket, I stared at the tiny piece for a second, studying the light-blue dress with white trim and the big, happy smile pasted across the doll's face, and handed the figure to Tammy.

She frowned. "What's this?"

"I lied about the magazine. But my name is John Bastian, I'm a commercial real estate broker, and I live in Newport Beach, California, and . . ." I thought about telling her about the skiing accident, the coma, and the visions, but decided not to. "I was married for ten years, she had an affair, and we've been divorced for three. Been doing a lot of skiing lately, burying myself in work, trying to move on with my life."

She shook her head and squeezed her eyebrows together. "That's not what I meant."

I took a swig of beer, trying to wash down the growing anxiety. *Now or never.* "I'm not sure exactly how to say this, but . . ." I gulped, waving to the waitress for another round of beers. "Go on."

A song started streaming through the ceiling speakers. My parents used to listen to it when I was a boy. The melody of the Paul Davis song "I Go Crazy" had always stuck with me, making me feel emotional in my gut whenever I heard it. I looked up and paused, continuing to listen. She reached across the table and cradled my hand.

*She knows. She must know, or at least suspect something.*

"Wow, this song brings back mixed emotions from '77 and '78," she said. "Right around the time I lost my first husband." She closed her eyes and mouthed some of the lyrics.

With my trembling hands, I caressed her fingers and brought her hand close to my heart.

"Have you ever noticed how everything in nature occurs in cycles or vibrations, all with frequencies that have relevance to time?" I asked.

I half-expected her to be confused, but instead she looked down, paused, and gave a slow nod.

I continued. "For example, our breathing, pulse, sleep and wake cycles, the rotation of the earth around its axis, the rotation of the earth around the sun, which gives us days and nights, seasons, and more, this stuff all happens in cycles."

"Hmmm . . ." she said, biting her lower lip as I took another sip of beer.

"Science is basically shedding more light on how stuff works at a quantum level. You got molecules made up of atoms, which are electrons, protons, and neutrons, all made up of what they call sub-atomic particles, but at the super small level, these pieces are not little balls like we were all taught in chemistry class, it's all actually waves of vibrating energy and, like, over ninety-nine percent is made up of pure nothing."

"You're sayin' everything happens in cycles."

I gently squeezed her hands and scooted closer, nodding, glad my rapid rambling hadn't turned her away.

"Even sex. In and out. Rhythms."

She bit her lower lip.

My heart raced as I continued. "We use cycles when we walk, run, or bike. The moon, which controls the tides, is also cyclical. Electromagnetic radiation, like visible light, travels in waves. Energy in the ocean travels as waves. They've discovered, recently, that gravity also travels in the form of waves. The list goes on and on."

"So what's your point, Mr. Bastian?" she said with a smile, intrigued.

"If everything in nature occurs as cycles, vibrations, or otherwise, why would we assume humans are born, live, die and go to heaven or hell? One and done?"

She rubbed her thumb along the top of my hand, said, "Not consistent with nature."

I leaned in even closer, noses almost touching. "Speaking of crazy, this is going to sound off-the-wall nuts, but, I . . ."

She blinked, staring into my eyes. "Go on."

My entire body felt light and tingly. I drew in a deep breath. "That doll is made of clay and I made it when I was four years old." Her eyes told me she wanted to know more, so I decided to tell her. "It's you."

She squinted, trying to process my unearthly comment.

I continued, enjoying her scent. And the fact she hadn't run away yet. "Fact is, Tammy, I feel some kind of bond, this weirdly strong connection to you. Can't explain it. Not like some stalker, weirdo obsession, but a warm, loving, familiar attachment. I feel like I've known you my whole life, even though we've barely met, and . . ."

The tips of our noses touched, then she placed her hands on both sides of my jaw. For a second, I thought she might try to snap my neck and run away, but instead, she planted her lips to mine. I felt the spark and another magical click falling into place, similar to our earlier hug, but with ten times the intensity. My soul stirred from a powerful, internal joy, and tears welled in my eyes. My entire body tingled from a single kiss.

I felt alive.

Blissful.

The waitress brought two more beers and we ended the kiss. Tammy sat back, chugged half her beer again and stared at me. I did the same with my drink.

"I know what you're doing. I know why you're here," she said.

I gulped.

"And?" I scooched back, up against the seat.

She tilted her head and said, "This is totally crazy. You knew my family members. You know things about my first husband nobody else could know. You do things out of habit that he used to do, like twirling your pen. You knew the name of our neighbors. You say phrases he used to say. In fact, I know the words you're gonna say before you say them."

We moved in close to each other, touched our nose tips together, gazed deep into each other's eyes and continued the kiss for another few seconds. More tingling sensations filled me to my core.

She continued. "The phrase 'insane, primitive hominoid maniac' is *our* phrase. Jack's and mine. I used to call him that for fun. Nobody else on the entire planet knows about that." I felt paralyzed. "And you have the same little birth mark he did. In the same exact place under your arm."

This is not how I'd envisioned our evening going. I expected her to be angry that I lied to her, but now I found myself kissing this woman twenty years my elder? *Is this normal? Either I'm crazy or we're both nuts.*

Still embracing this amazing woman from Louisiana, I sensed the family sitting next to us staring but I ignored them.

Tammy fanned herself, then nibbled on my ear and whispered, "I want you. Right now." Never in my wildest fantasies had I contemplated getting intimate with a woman so much older than me, but my stomach felt heavy and my heart raced with a weird sort of spiritual eroticism. Our age difference was immaterial.

"No. You're married," I said, pulling away, which felt like driving a dagger into my spleen.

She blinked and nodded. "Yes, but I married him more out of sympathy and the fact my daughter needed a male role model, or at least that's what people had told me at the time. Now Jenny's all grown up, and the fact is Scott is an abusive spouse. Our marriage has been over for a long, long time, but I just haven't had the strength to end it."

Until now.

# CHAPTER
## 47

### Scott Jones
*November 22, 2016*

Scott took a sip of bourbon, shifting his stance inside the yacht cabin.

"You sound like you got one of the original maps, but trust me, I've heard this bedtime story before. Twice. And both maps ended up being fake, somethin' was missin'. Totally useless." He set the glass on the table and leaned in. "So tell me, right now, why the hell I should trust you. Prove it to me or I walk."

Another clap of thunder struck outside. Scott felt the yacht rock back and forth, more than when he arrived, and he scanned the inside of the cabin.

Scott expected fear in the old lady's eyes, but instead he only sensed growing confidence as she smiled. "I'm afraid you can't trust me, Mr. Jones. We've barely met, after all." She sipped her wine. "But I will tell you this: I have something better than the original map that Bridgette Lafayette, the amazing and brilliant mathematician and daughter of Jacques, drew all those years ago."

"Bullshit. You got ten seconds."

"My friend. I have what the original map and compass led to, which was a letter Bridgette had written to her uncle many years ago. Guess what's on the back side?"

"No way. Can't be that easy."

"The complex map requires the use of a wooden compass, and when used properly will lead you to a location where I buried another clue: a simple code which, if read by a learned man, would lead to the location of the treasure. Where the proverbial X marks the spot, as they say. But I assure you, dear sir, this letter has been in my family since day one."

Her dull, black eyes spoke volumes.

Scott's mouth dropped open, but he quickly realized his tell, closed his mouth, stood straight and said, "You said 'I'. What the hell do you mean you buried another clue?"

She smiled.

Cogs churned in Scott's head, pondering various probabilities and scenarios. He continued. "Impossible. You talk like you're one of the Lafayettes or something. You're crazy."

Her smile grew big as she cocked her head. "You say these words without knowing all the facts."

He furrowed his brow. "C'mon, lady. Don't con me with some crap about how you're related to Jacques Lafayette."

She took several more sips of wine, forcing Scott to wait before he stood and took one step toward the exit. "Indeed, sir. I am."

He stopped dead, turning. "How so?"

"Mr. Jones, the French word for bridge is 'pont.' My last name, Petitpont, roughly translates to small bridge, or Bridgette."

She paused as her words soaked in.

His mind told him this was a waste of time and he considered leaving. But something in his gut made him stay.

"You're telling me you're Bridgette Lafayette? *The* Bridgette Lafayette?" He let out a deep, bellowing laugh. "I gotta say, you look pretty good for two-hundred and whatever years old you are."

He swiped his glass and took another sip of whiskey.

She stood.

"The curse of the Lafayette treasure is real, Mr. Jones. After watching my father whack off the head of Fatale, the man who raped me, the scene played over and over in my mind, his warm blood pouring from his neck onto my face, the dead weight of his body, my inability to breathe, the horror of it all. At the brink of losing my mind, and in great anger to punish the soul of that evil man, I confided my story to one of our longtime slaves. A woman rumored to have voodoo powers. Black magic. She offered to invoke a powerful curse against Fatale, telling me he'd suffer for as long as I lived. I agreed.

"I asked her to add extra protection for my family, specifically our gold. She complied. But I now regret my decisions. My anger has brought death to many otherwise unworthy males, and that same voodoo has given me an extended life. From their deaths, I have lived. But over the years I've realized living forever is not a blessing. It is a curse all on its own. And Fatale visits me in my nightmares. Every. Single. Time I fall asleep."

Scott squinted, remaining silent, taking all this in.

She continued. "Or you may choose to believe I'm simply the great-granddaughter of Bridgette and voodoo is nothing more than tricks to scare children."

He sat in a chair, crossed his arms, and chuckled. "Okay, enough with the history lesson. Let's say I'm totally nuts and believe that you are, in fact, old and ancient or whatever. I've seen the letter you're talking about. And the code on the back. My best friend had an original back in the seventies, but most of it was, um, destroyed."

She held her sinister smile. "You're clearly unaware a map and compass were stolen by one of my greedy crew members and eventually made their way into the hands of an archaeologist named Amr Abubaker who, with his dying breath, gave the package to a man named Jack Bachman—also a pilot, like you."

Scott jerked his head back. "Jack's dead."

She raised her eyebrows. "The original letter has been in my possession this entire time and is here. On this very boat. Right now."

Scott narrowed his eyes, saying and revealing nothing, only pressing his lips together. "You don't believe the treasure exists?"

"Oh, my gold is out there. Somewhere. No doubt about that," she motioned with her wine glass. "I nearly died when my ship went down, changed my name and made up the story about being drowned."

"Legend says your ship went down a few miles off the coast of the Panhandle."

"You know your maritime history, Mr. Jones. Impressive." She lowered her gaze. "So, this leads us to where we are today. You seem to be of the opinion that the treasure exists and a map will lead you there. I'm merely informing you of the strong possibility the treasure has been moved or erased from existence by mother nature." She shot him a strong stare, which he returned. "Now back to my original question. What are you willing to give up in exchange for the location of the treasure?"

A bell rang several times in the distance, the boat's rocking intensifying as a fog horn blasted through the howling wind outside.

"If you think the treasure's buried somewhere in Baton Rouge, not lost at sea as the rumors say, why don't you try to find it?" Scott said, pointing westward. "We could find the treasure ourselves, split the gold, and you'd become a rich woman."

Bridgette frowned, shook her head, wagged her finger, and took a step closer to Scott. "No, no, no, Mr. Jones. First, I am already a rich woman. I've traveled the world many times over, given my share to the poor and needy, and have lived my life, nightmares and all. What I need, I'm afraid money cannot buy. Second, I am unable to control the voodoo. There's a reason the gold is called *Le Trésor Fatale*, which, translated from French, roughly means 'the deadly treasure.' If you're as smart as I hope and you find the treasure, you will inherit the brunt of the curse, which will likely kill you, unless of course, you . . .'"

Scott steepled his fingers. "Not sure what you mean. If you're already rich, what else could you want?"

The thought of wanting anything more in life than gobs of gold and cash boggled Scott.

"Peace, Mr. Jones. Death will bring peace to my spirit and an end to my nightmares. Only someone with a loving heart can find the treasure and break the curse. Then, and only then, will I find what I need. You, being the national hero right now, saving those passengers, are someone with such a loving heart, are you not?"

Scott stroked his goatee again, considering the weight of her words, wondering how he'd be judged if it came to that. "That's all well and good, Miss Petitpont, or Lafayette, or whatever your name is, but I don't believe a word you're saying." He retrieved his nickel-plated thirty-eight special from inside his jacket. "Time's up. Show me right now where the treasure is. You have five seconds. Four. Three—"

"Well played, Mr. Jones, but unfortunate," she said, setting her glass down with a sigh. With Scott's gun pointed at her face and not breaking eye contact, she reached down underneath her chair and retrieved a brown leather portfolio. After carefully putting the package onto the wood table, she unclasped the lock and, with a steady hand, extracted a single piece of ancient parchment, faded and creased much like her skin, from years of oxidation. She slid the letter along the polished wood tabletop, toward Scott's whiskey glass. "Here you go, the location is on the back. No compass needed. Do as you please, but I've warned you of the curse."

He stood and aimed the gun downward, keeping the barrel aimed at her chest. He leaned over to get a better look at the letter, flipped it over and read a series of letters and numbers:

*T.10S. R.13E.*

Scott's mind flew back in time to 1978, to the incident with Jack, when his friend had tried to show him numbers like this and explain, before he burned it.

"Your family will be upset with you for giving me this information," he said, still pointing the gun at her.

"You're a pilot. I assume you know what those numbers mean?"

Scott nodded.

"Good. I have no family left. I am the last of the Lafayettes and welcome death with open arms. You can shoot me with your little gun, sir, and yes, I will die for a short while. But I will rise again. And I will haunt you as Fatale has done to me all these many years, even after your physical form devolves into nothing more than dust."

She stared at the floor, deep in thought.

Scott pulled out a crisp hundred-dollar bill from his wallet and held it high near the ceiling. "This bill's gonna float down. It lands Franklin up, you die right here, right now. Independence Hall, I keep the letter and you keep your trap shut."

Bridgette sat and crossed one bony leg over the other. "You don't have to pay me, Mr. Jones. Because of your heroic efforts, I planned on giving you the map without asking for anything in return so you could hunt the treasure void of any potential repercussions from the curse. But it appears I have made a gross miscalculation."

He loosened then retightened his grip on the pistol, considering his options.

She continued. "On my honor, I give you my word as a Lafayette."

"Today, God's gonna decide your fate." Scott winked at her and released the bill.

Floating down, the paper fluttered and spun before finally landing on the low pile, waterproof carpet.

Ben Franklin stared up at them.

"Shoot me now and you'll be dead within seven days," she said with a smile, zero fear.

"Nice knowin' ya, lady." He pulled the trigger twice, putting two rounds through her chest. His ears rang deaf. Blood splattered onto the seats and ceiling before she collapsed onto the floor. Crimson red flowed from her body into a puddle, flooding the area under the table and drowning the bill in blood.

For a brief moment, out of the corner of his eye he thought he saw a guy wearing a black top hat and tuxedo, standing a few feet away from her. He jerked his head to get a better view, but the image disappeared.

Panic swept through Scott. He needed to get as far away from the damned yacht as possible. Careful not to step in her mess, he scooped up the paper and turned it over, where a bunch of French words were scribbled in the format of a letter to someone, then slid the item back into the leather folder, ran up the stairs, and rushed out into the driving rain. He stuffed the package underneath his jacket, exited the boat without looking back, made his way up to his Mercedes and fled the crime scene.

He dialed Mike.

Struggling to catch his breath, Scott managed to say, "I know where the treasure is."

"You better not be shittin' me."

"Don't worry your pretty little panties off. I'm headin' back to Baton Rouge, but my old lady's having a hard time with all this."

"I took care of those two guys. The black guy should be dead, but for some reason, the poison didn't do nothin' to that son-of-a-bitch John. I'm closin' in on him, though."

Scott turned his windshield wipers on high as he merged west onto the interstate. A strong wind jerked his car sideways.

"I brought you on because you're supposed to be a bad-ass Miami coke smuggler and could handle this kind of shit. Sounds like you're tellin' me I made a mistake."

Mike paused. "Fine. I got some guys in New Orleans I'll bring up. Get this done faster."

Scott missed a yellow moving van by inches as he swerved into a different lane on the freeway. A loud horn echoed inside his car. He hammered his steering wheel twice with the butt of his hand. "Move over, you stupid shit."

Mind racing, Scott pondered additional details about digging up the treasure and the logistics needed to get away clean. And the merit of the curse.

Hogwash.

# CHAPTER 48

## John Bastian
### *November 22, 2016*

Throwing all sense of caution aside, I stood, threw down more than enough cash to cover the tab and rushed alongside Tammy through the rain to my parked car a couple blocks away. Soaked to our bones, we hopped in and zoomed east toward the interstate. The familiar tickle of her fingertips on the nape of my neck made my heart race. With one hand gripping the steering wheel, I took her hand into mine, kissing the back and inhaling the scent of her perfumed wrist, all the while feeling like we'd danced this foreplay game before. Many times.

We exited the freeway, quickly spotted a tall, four-star hotel, parked, and with my arm around her, hurried to the front desk to check in for one night.

Once inside our second-floor room, she slammed the door shut and unzipped the back of her dress.

She reached down, grabbed hold of my rear and moaned with approval. I kissed her neck and massaged her shoulders. She smelled incredible. Familiar. Her rapid, shallow breaths increased my desire for her.

She jumped onto me, wrapping her legs around my waist. We continued kissing and I swear, miniature lightning bolts zapped between our lips. My lips touched her cheeks and I nibbled on her upper neck before making my way down to her soft shoulders. She arched her head back, shaking her silky hair loose.

Several hours into the unexpected, epic lovemaking marathon, we took a breather. The digital clock on the nightstand read: 10:05pm. My head had unfortunately developed a pinging sensation in front, likely from dehydration caused by too many beers combined with an extensive loss of bodily fluids.

With a few pillows propped behind me, I leaned back, and she cuddled against me, with her head resting on my chest. With joy flowing throughout my entire body, I quickly fell asleep.

The next morning, I awoke to the sensation of warm drops of liquid landing on my nipple, beneath her eyes. I leaned my head forward. Tears.

"You okay?" I asked.

She twisted the ring on her finger. "The entire time we've been in this room, you've touched me and behaved, intimately, the same way he used to. Either you're a hell of a con man, or—"

My eyebrows rose. "I'm not a con man. I wouldn't even know where to start."

"Are you sure? The spirit of Jack Bachman is inside you. Reincarnated, but I have no idea how. How in all that's natural can you explain that?"

I took a beat, shook my head and shrugged. "Can't."

She sat, staring at me, then wiped her cheeks, sniffling. "So you're you, John Bastian, but you're also him somehow. I don't understand how this is even possible. My heart, my mind, my soul all agree that it's true, that it's happening, that I'm sitting here in a hotel room with my once dead, now somehow alive husband. I can feel it. But it makes absolutely zero sense."

I gently pulled her into me and inhaled pure peace.

"Tell me about him."

She smiled.

"This is crazy freaky."

"I know."

"Jack was an amazing man. We were soul mates from the beginning, when we first met."

I paused, trying to remember any details. Nothing.

"Sorry, I don't recall. Give me a hint," I said.

She took my hand and kissed my palm. "Las Vegas."

I closed my eyes and waited. Images rushed in from the dream several days earlier, the one of an airplane and a young version of Tammy, with her bright red hair, glowing eyes, and skin as smooth as cream. The memory provided me with more details than I could have asked for.

"Yes! You met him on that flight to Vegas," I said. "You were flying with your family. You were twenty-one." I closed my eyes and remembered more. "You talked and found out you both had beagles named Pepper, right?"

A big, beautiful smile erupted on her face and she nodded. "No way. Wow. This is unreal. I fell in love with Jack on that flight. His eyes, his sense of humor—both of which I see in you—everything."

"I also remember a whole bunch of letters. Old school, before texting," I said.

"Yes. We wrote to each other constantly. Back and forth for the next two years. Calling was ridiculously expensive, but we did talk occasionally. I turned twenty-three on March 5, 1975. Do you have a memory of what happened six months later?"

I paused again, reaching down deep into my memory bank. "Wedding. You were married on September 27, 1975, right?"

She nodded with excitement.

"Your dad's name was," I paused and looked up to the popcorn ceiling, "Robert Schroeder. And he wore a black and white tux to your wedding."

"Yep, three months after I graduated college, but we didn't care. We were in love," she said with a deep, longing, familiar gaze into my eyes. "I can see your soul, John, Jack, whatever your name is. I know you're in there."

"I read online that Jack went missing three years after you guys married," I said, searching for more of those answers I came to find.

Her eyes turned away to the window near the rear of the hotel room. A distant stare. Her smile disappeared. "Yes. On his birthday, too. Never found his body. Police referred to the case as a missing person, but I knew in my heart he was murdered. No body, no murder they said. No murder, no murderer. So they never charged anyone. No way he just disappeared on me. As of last year, the police still have his disappearance listed as an open cold case. Gosh, it's been over thirty-eight years since that happened. If only we had a time machine or something that could see into the past."

She tilted her head and narrowed her eyes.

"That's the same age I am. Thirty-eight. Born November 8, 1978."

She let out a tiny yelp. "Oh my God! That can't be a coincidence. That's the day after Jack went missing. Last time I saw him was November 7th, 1978. He kissed me goodbye and said he was going out for a few hours. Something about a fresh lead on the treasure."

I nodded my head slowly. "Interesting."

"Well, if anyone on the entire planet could find the treasure, I'd put my money on him, I mean, you. He had the map and the wooden compass he needed to pinpoint the location."

"Was wondering about that. I have a crystal clear image of the map in my head. In fact, I drew a replica based on memory."

I rolled my pale, naked body out of bed, scooped up my jeans from the floor, dug out a folded piece of paper from my pocket, and spread open the sketch onto the bed sheet.

Her eyes widened and her lips parted. "This is nuts. I remember this," she said with her mouth gaping open. "Holy B'Jesus. Y'all know how this is supposed to work, don't ya?"

"Something about a compass?"

"Sort of. What you do is—"

Someone banged five times on our door. Hard.

"Open this damned door, Tammy. I know y'all are in there," an angry man shouted.

# CHAPTER
## 49

**John Bastian**
*November 23, 2016*

Inside the tiny hotel room, a look of panic spread across Tammy's face. Her frightened eyes bored into my heart.

Our peaceful moment had disintegrated, replaced by pure, unadulterated fear.

"Open up, Tammy, goddammit," the man outside barked, still beating the door. "I know you're in there with that son-of-a-bitch Californian."

I held her nude body tight, moved close to her ear and whispered in as calm a voice as possible, "I got an idea. Get your clothes on. Quick."

Amidst the thundering noise, like the door would bust open any second, we jumped out of the bed, grabbed our clothes and got dressed. I tied my shoes while the man outside kicked and clobbered the cracking, splintering wooden door.

"There's a window in the bathroom," I said in a small voice, pushing her toward the rear of the room. Pointing to a non-existent watch on my wrist, I whispered loudly, "Go. Go!"

She shook her head, "No way. I can't. I lost you thirty-eight years ago, I'm not gonna let that happen again."

I stepped toward her, squeezed her in my arms, and landed a passionate kiss, inhaling her essence, an intoxicating blend of gardenias and sex. The banging on the door intensified. She turned to putty but her shallow, rapid breathing gave me pause before the door burst open with a loud rupturing noise and Tammy pushed behind me, screaming.

A squat, bald man wearing jeans and black boots stepped through the doorway.

"You dirty ass son-of-a-bitch," the man yelled in a deep, gruff voice.

"No, Scott, no," she yelled.

Every instinct in my bones told me to stand my ground and fight to be with Tammy no matter what the cost. I needed her. My thirty-eight-year absence was finally over and running away from some angry man and the potential consequences was dead wrong.

Tammy stood behind me, hands on my shoulders, as Scott accelerated towards us and took a wide swing at my face, but I ducked and rammed my left shoulder into his gut, thrusting his body back toward a side wall. His back slammed against a wall-mounted flat screen TV. I dropped low and planted a solid punch to his groin, forcing Scott to fold in half.

Turning my head, I said to Tammy with more of a grunt than well-enunciated words, "Get outta here," before standing and coming down onto his upper back with my elbow. He let out a painful cough and dropped to the floor. I turned, holding out my hand, to follow Tammy as she bolted toward the door, but before I could take a second step, he grabbed my ankle and twisted, bringing me to the ground. Quick as a cat, he stood, took several steps towards the open area of the bedroom, and whipped out a pistol. I crept away from the door, trying to draw his aim away from Tammy, who stood in the doorway, but Scott aimed the gun back and forth between Tammy and me.

Out of breath, he said, "Goddammit." He wiped saliva from his chin.

Tammy disappeared down the hallway. Scott took a shot through the wall, where she might have been in the hallway, and I heard a short scream.

With Scott distracted, I planted my foot at the base of the wall and launched my body towards him, grabbed his gun arm, pushing upwards, then rammed his body backwards against the wall. Another shot rang out before I hammered his hand against the wall, forcing him to drop the weapon. But he kneed my groin, doubling me over.

With a final shove against Scott's waist, I pushed him onto the ground, away from the gun, but his body ended up between me and the door. With no option to grab the gun or follow Tammy, I raced into the bathroom.

My head pounded harder each step, but I managed to swing the bathroom door closed and set the lock. I flung open the window, kicked out the screen, and looked down two stories below at a grassy area sloping downward from the base of the hotel. You gotta be kidding me. The drop was at least fifteen feet.

Out of breath and in full animal panic mode, I stuck my arms and head out the doggy-door-sized window opening and squeezed the upper half of my body outside.

After wiggling my legs through the window into the damp, dark, dreary morning drizzle, I dangled by my arms from the windowsill and thought of Blake Lynds, how he'd hung this same way from the gondola. The sound of footsteps approached the bathroom, then more door banging, more doorknob jiggling. The outside stucco scraped against my forearms and chest before another explosion in the bathroom and what sounded like kicking open of the door.

I shot a glance below, let go of the ledge, made the drop and in less than a second, crashed my feet against the wet, soft, slippery grass. The jolt buckled my knees and forced me to roll. Dirt and clippings of torn, ripped grass roots clung to my hands.

I got to my feet and raced away from the building, further down the slope toward the asphalt parking lot.

Scott's angry voice boomed from my escape window. "Get back here you goddamned—" Four rapid fire gunshots echoed throughout the tree-lined area, as I hunched behind a blue Ford F-150 parked several dozen feet away. He fired three more shots, several of which pierced the metal siding of the pickup.

A fragment of one of the rounds grazed the skin on my right shoulder.

The sensation of a red-hot knife slicing through my flesh forced me to the ground.

My brain revved into high gear. *Maybe Tammy made it out to the front parking lot.* If I could get to my car parked in front of the hotel, we might have a chance of escaping this lunatic. The thought of her meeting her demise at Scott's hand made my stomach churn.

Blood soaked through my polo shirt and dribbled down my shoulder onto the ground.

I peeked above the hood of my automotive shield. Scott had retreated from the window.

But from inside the room came a scream, a flash of light and another gunshot.

Thoughts flipped round and round through my head. *Go back inside and help Tammy. No weapon. Call the cops. No, the sheriff is Scott's buddy, probably in on Kevin's poisoning.*

I dashed around the side of the hotel to the front, but as I turned the corner, Scott darted out through the front glass doors, spotted me, and popped off another round. He missed.

With no way to get into the hotel, no way to find out what happened to Tammy, no way to help her, I ran to my car, jumped and slid across the hood, dripping blood along the way. Inside, I fired up the engine and tore out onto the wet street.

I zigzagged right and left around the next few corners in an amateur move to cover my tracks.

But after a few blocks, a black, late-model Mercedes appeared in my rear view mirror. I floored the gas pedal with no destination whatsoever, racing through various neighborhoods. The car continued to follow me and the distance between us narrowed. I entered the Interstate 10 north and drove as fast as possible, swerving in and out of traffic like a maniac, dodging slow-moving trucks, and zipping past old clunker cars. Two gunshots fired from behind me, the second one exploding my left mirror into a thousand pieces.

With both hands on the wheel, white knuckles, and blood streaming from my shoulder, I passed a sign that read "Baton Rouge Metropolitan Airport - 3 Miles." *Maybe I can get near a security office or police station there and ditch this guy.*

I exited to Highway 408 and skidded my way around several corners to the southern end of the airfield, guided by a mystery force.

On pure adrenaline, I blasted through an unmanned chain link security gate and skidded my car to a stop near the tarmac, knowing I had no clearance to go further. The area felt familiar, so I jogged to a door labeled "Pilot's Lounge," and heard the screeching tires of Scott's car coming to a halt not fifty feet away. Inside the mostly empty waiting area, I hurried past two seated people, toward a rear door that led to the open airfield. Outside, rain poured down from the black sky. Overhead lights illuminated the scene and because of the minimal security, nobody bothered to ask me any questions. Of course, had anyone truly stopped to look, the amount of blood all over my clothes would have probably shocked them.

Feeling compelled to hustle to space "C-4," I ran, out of breath, into the darkness, looking down at each of the painted space numbers on the wet asphalt below. C-2, C-3, C-4. Got it!

Scott yelled from behind me. "Get the hell away from my Cessna."

Scott caught up to me, but stood, also out of breath, on the opposite side of the plane, and we darted back and forth like a lion and hyena around some African boulder.

Someone had left a crowbar on the ground near the tire of an adjacent plane. On instinct, I scooped it up with my left hand, but realized the thin metal object would do me little good against Scott's pistol. Scott put his hands on his knees, pumping air in and out of his lungs, face soured and tired.

I tried to run, as fast as my legs would churn, back toward the shelter of the Pilot's Lounge, but Scott was too quick. He tackled me from behind, my legs collapsed, and I dropped the crowbar. My shoulder screamed with pain.

On my back, with Scott straddling me, I found myself face-to-face with his pistol.

I felt around for the crowbar. Got it. Held a firm grip.

"This is what you get for fucking my wife, you cock-sucker," he said.

Images of Tammy, my dad, my mom, and Kevin all montaged in front of me. My entire body shook.

"No, Scotty Potty," I said. "You don't get to do this to me again."

Those words stunned Scott long enough for me to sweep the crowbar across his face with my left arm, landing in the sweet spot on his jaw, knocking him to the ground.

He lay on the tarmac, dazed, semi-conscious and bleeding.

The Lafayette ghost appeared out of the darkness. Stoic, he casually pointed to Scott's jacket.

I stepped toward Scott and rifled through his jacket pocket. An extra mag. Full. Keys. Airplane. The ghost nodded and faded away, disappearing as quickly as he'd emerged.

Pelting rain continued to soak me.

I scooped up Scott's gun from the asphalt, popped out the empty mag, jammed a fresh one in, and stuffed the weapon into the rear waist of my pants. After jogging to the white airplane with two blue stripes, which was a combination float plane with wheels—one that could take off and land on either land or water—I kicked the wheel chucks out and stepped toward the door. Somehow, I knew the tarnished blue key would unlock the door. Yes. I entered the cramped space inside and sat in the pilot's seat on the left side. The only experience flying a plane I had until that point in my life was playing the flight simulator games on my PC. No actual flight time.

But somehow, I knew how to step through the process of priming the engine and firing up the power plant. A few moments later, the engine roared to life, spinning the prop. I pushed the little black throttle knob inward and the plane inched forward. With my right foot, I pushed in the right rudder pedal and the plane turned to the right, heading toward runway 31. I tuned the COM1 radio to the tower frequency and was about to put the headset on to speak to the tower, when a sharp thudding noise came from the door.

Scott.

*This guy with all his banging! Jesus.*

Eyes half shut, blood poured down the side of his face from the gash in his head, mixing with the fresh water from the rain. He threw open the door and dragged me out of the cockpit. With the chopping of the spinning prop in the background, I fell to the asphalt. He kicked my ribcage. Twice. He spit on my face and ran after the plane, which had rolled—pilotless—along the tarmac thirty feet before he took control.

My midsection cried out in pain as I lay in a pothole of water in the asphalt tarmac. Blood flowed from my shoulder. Scott slammed the airplane door shut and the engine revved, whooshing massive air and horizontal water drops onto me before he disappeared into the windy, wet darkness.

# CHAPTER 50

Weak and dizzy, I stood, put my hands on my knees, caught my breath and thought about finding and chasing after Scott on the tarmac, firing at him with the pistol.

No. Instead, I stumbled back to the now vacant pilot's lounge, made my way back to the Beemer, tossed the gun under my seat, entered the Interstate, and sped back to the hotel while thoughts muddled around inside my brain. *Did he shoot her? Is she still alive? Is there anything I can do to help?*

Bright images of Tammy and our time together flowed through my mind.

But flashing red and blue lights splintered the darkness, reflecting off the building, trees, sheets of rain and parking lot. Four cop cars sat in front of the hotel entryway. A black van had parked near the cop cars, the word "CORONER" on its side.

*Did Scott kill Tammy?*

My eyes filled with tears, my chin trembled, and I hammered the front dash with my open palm so many times my left arm went numb. I considered walking over and poking around, but with blood on my shirt and my California accent, I'd be locked up in a cell in less than two seconds.

Something told me to run, so I did. After driving east for ten miles, I exited to a twenty-four-hour RiteAid and threw on my lightweight jacket to conceal the throbbing wound.

Beads of sweat trickled down my forehead as I walked inside, bought some first aid supplies, and headed back to my car to patch myself up. I hoped I could remember the details from those first aid classes I took back in college.

I doused the wound with alcohol. Fortunately, the gash appeared to be a relatively minor cut. Just a flesh wound, so I poured on some *WoundSeal* powder to stop the bleeding and placed a bandage over most of my outer shoulder. I gave myself a nod for quality workmanship and set my mind next on what to do about the pain.

Not only the damned pain in my shoulder, but also the aching in my heart. For Tammy. I remembered watching a video of a honeybee stinging a victim. When the drone tried to fly away, the barbed needle had stuck so deep into the flesh of the victim, the stinger acted as a heavy anchor, preventing the bee from taking off. The entire guts of the bee were ripped out from inside and the flying insect died a moment later.

I felt like that honeybee. Forced to leave Tammy at that hotel had ripped out my insides.

I needed to be with her. I had no idea what Scott had done. The thought of her getting hurt—or worse—felt like drowning.

After making a U-turn, I drove a few blocks, pulled into the parking lot of a seedy liquor store, purchased a fifth of Jack Daniels and eventually made my way to an old abandoned barn in a rural area outside Dutch Town. Under an ancient oak, I parked my car and sat, my mind a swirling mess of worry, doubt, and angst. Rain drops pelted my car.

Wouldn't be the first time an angry, jealous husband took out his frustrations on his wife. Playing with fire, here, for sure.

A sense of grief came over me, like she'd already been taken away to the great beyond.

I twisted off the bottle cap.

My mind homed in on the noises coming from the radio. Something about a hurricane. I turned up the volume and listened.

*". . . mandatory evacuations are now in place on the southern coasts of Louisiana and Mississippi. This massive storm is expected to hit land as a Category Four hurricane. Residents of these areas are strongly encouraged to pack their bags and head to one of the many shelters being set up inland. More information can be found at . . ."* I turned off the radio and returned to my inner dread.

Less than an hour since the last peaceful moment with Tammy, my heart pounded as though decades had passed. Dark gray clouds loomed strong on the entire southern and eastern horizons. I needed to call my mom and check in on my dad, but instead, guzzled a third of the whiskey down into my gullet. The liquid burned, grating along my esophagus, but I didn't care.

I closed my eyes, needing the enjoyment and comfort brought by visions of Tammy. But nothing appeared. Not a single image.

I tried focusing my thoughts, energy, and mind on her. For weeks, my curse had been to see everything as clearly as if I were watching a movie. Now, nothing. No Tammy. No treasure map. Only a black, empty canvas void of anything helpful. I needed a plan, but the magic had vanished.

Kevin lay sick in a hospital. Tammy was probably dead. I tried calling her, but the call went straight to voicemail. I sent her a text asking her to call me. I needed to know she was all right. Or at least alive.

A few hours ago my half-baked plans had started to come together, but now, everything had gone to hell. I had no idea what to do next. Head to Tammy's house with the gun I swiped from Scott?

No, that wouldn't work.

My luck, he'd shoot me dead.

I hoped Kevin was getting better, but the doctor had told me to wait for his call.

I leaned over to the rear seat and grabbed one of the reincarnation books Dr. Carpenter had given me.

After reading the first few pages of the book and skimming through the remainder, the skeptic in me waned a bit. Or the alcohol might have kicked in.

The author wrote about a scientist who used the scientific method to gather and analyze data, trying to debunk fantastic stories of kids who claim to have lived past lives. Sometimes he could explain the stories with logic and reasoning, but other times, there appeared to be no other scientific explanations for why the young children said they were other people, departed.

One story caught my attention. Apparently, back in 1985, a five-year-old boy in India had horrific night terrors in which he was shot three times in his belly by a soldier on a mountain peak and died during the Bangladesh Liberation War. He made several pencil drawings of the dream that included a chicken neck and specific details of the murder, including the type of weapon, the name of the soldier, and the same name of the deceased.

When the boy turned seven, his night terrors stopped, and his memories of the dreams faded. But his parents traveled to the border of India and Bangladesh for answers.

The outer reaches of the alcoholic buzz hit my brain, kicking in the numbing process. The tips of my fingers tingled. Angry, menacing, gray clouds stared back at me through the drenched windshield. Continuous drops of water splattered the roof of the car.

I continued reading.

After extensive research into various local archives and discussions with residents, the author discovered that there was indeed an Indian with the same name who was shot and killed with three rounds in his belly from the same type of rifle by a man with the same name in an area known as the "Chicken's Neck" because of the shape of the land.

*How the hell did this boy know all these details? Five-year-old kids aren't supposed to experience murder and death and war.* I closed my eyes and arched my head back.

The possibility of having lived hundreds of previous lives freaked me out, mostly because the notion flew straight in the face of my thirty-eight years of religious and social programming about why we humans exist on this planet. Our purpose. At the same time, after skimming through the second book, a sense of calm washed over me.

Somehow, from a certain perspective, reincarnation could be possible. Even inevitable. Would make death something to look forward to, not fear. I imagined how peaceful my life could be without the fear of death.

My phone vibrated.

"Sorry, Mom, I was just going to call you."

"Honey, something's happened to your father."

I straightened up, rubbing my eyes, but the world outside started spinning.

"I thought the doctors were waiting for him to wake up. He's going to be fine," I said, trying to sound strong, but fighting the urge to pass out.

"No, honey. Early this morning he had a massive stroke and . . ." Wailing noises came through the speaker.

I paused. Nothing came to mind. No idea what to say. Frozen.

She continued with a trembling voice. "Honey, we had a massive earthquake today and I'm not sure if that's what caused your father to, well, he's gone. He did wake up during the quake, and stayed awake afterwards, but just long enough to have a brief chat with me before passing."

Time slowed to the viscosity of molasses as I studied the bottle before bringing it up for another swig.

# CHAPTER
# 51

Fantastic memories of now departed Dad flooded my mind: playing catch with a baseball and gloves in our backyard, teaching me how to play the clarinet, sitting on his shoulders in the pool, watching Fourth of July fireworks on his lap, his seventies-style mustache, his strong hands with thick fingers, playing hide-and-go-seek when mom was away, eating pancakes for dinner, fishing trips, his attempt at the Catholic version of 'the sex talk' when I turned nine, and more.

For some reason, one afternoon in particular stood out.

A shiny wood pipe clung to his lower lip, cantilevered, puffs of smoke billowing out every few seconds. On the back porch, he sat with legs crossed in a poolside lounge chair completing a crossword puzzle, the scent of Captain Black tobacco everywhere. My nine-year-old self approached him holding two baseball gloves and an old beat up ball. I asked if he wanted to play catch. To my surprise, he set the puzzle aside, picked me up by my underarms and answered, "Of course I do, big guy. Maybe today you learn how to throw a curve ball. You're already pretty good at the fast ball."

The smile on my face stretched from ear to ear as I followed him over to the side yard. We warmed up, throwing back and forth at a close distance and within a few minutes, we had moved further apart to forty-five feet, the Little League distance between the pitcher's mound and home plate.

He punched his glove several times as he squatted down, knowing how much I enjoyed pitching to him. He gave me the sign for "fast ball" with his free hand. On my imaginary mound, I wound up, and zipped one down the pipe. "Strike," he yelled with a booming umpire voice before tossing the ball back to me. Two more like that and I had struck out our imaginary batter. My dad jogged over to me.

"Nice job, son. Now here's how you throw a curve ball." He showed me the two-fingered grip and how to twist my arm and wrist as I came down on the release. "Gonna take some practice, but we'll get ya there."

No idea why, but curve balls fascinated me. Too young to understand the Magnus effect—the reason baseballs magically shifted direction in midair—my undeveloped brain believed I was witnessing true magic when something headed in one direction suddenly pivoted a different way simply because of spin.

My first try flew up onto our roof, but after several dozen attempts, I had those pitches curving like a pro.

"Okay, last batter," Dad said. He assumed the catcher position and gave me the sign for a curve ball. I shook my head. He changed his sign to fast fall. I nodded.

I put my hand behind my waist, gripped the ball, wound up and let the orb fly. The sphere floated through the air at fifty miles an hour, or faster, approaching my dad. He put up his glove to make the catch. Had we known the net of his glove had a substantial tear, we could have fixed it beforehand.

But we had no idea.

So, when the ball struck the mitt, the leather ripped apart, the ball broke through the glove and struck my father's left eyebrow, gouging a massive two-inch gash into his forehead.

The ball dropped to the ground. Blood spilled from his head. He touched the wound with his fingertips and saw crimson. I assumed he would probably need to go to the hospital. Worried and filled with guilt, I ran toward him to help.

But instead of my loving, caring father, I met an angry part of my dad. The monster. With a red face and blood trickling onto the entire side of his cheek, down his neck, he threw his glove onto the sidewalk. "Goddammit, mother fucking son-of-a-bitch—ugh."

He yelled at me, the sky, and the ground before stepping toward me with his fist raised like he was going to beat my face, but instead turned and punched the wood fence behind him, snapping the top foot of the board clean off. I flinched and crouched down, afraid. "Get the hell outta my sight you little shit." He pressed his hand onto his brow and jogged inside.

Young boy tears streaked down my cheeks as I picked up his glove, sat on the ground and wailed to the world, confused.

At that point, mixed emotions inside me raged. One moment the man was my loving father, my god, my idol. Someone I trusted to keep me safe. The next, an angry man full of hatred exhibiting behavior which apparently, as I learned from my therapist, he had picked up from his old man, my grandpa. Apparently, extreme anger and losing one's temper was a learned behavior, something boys picked up from their fathers and other men. Throughout my adult life, I have lost my temper many times, something I had my dad to thank for. But knowing this, I made a vow to myself long ago to be a better father to my children and never, ever lose my temper. I refused to let my kids know a short-tempered man. Only a kind, gentle, loving, guiding, supportive father.

Of course, these feelings and memories only made me feel worse as I sat there in my Beemer, buckets of raindrops pounding down on the roof and hood. *I hear about my dad's death, and the first memory that comes to mind is one of his failures as a father?* Guilt piled on top of my confusion.

*What good is this knowledge of how to be an awesome father if I'll never find someone to love, and be one myself?*

The bottom of my soul plummeted down into a dark, eternal abyss.

# CHAPTER 52

"No. No. He can't be gone. No," I said to my mom through my speakerphone. Tears welled up and broke free, one after another streaming down my cheeks and falling onto my shirt.

"He apologized for not being a better father—his words—and wished you nothing but happiness in your life."

Phone in my left hand, whiskey in my right, I swigged another long draw from the bottle.

"How big was the quake? Are you alright?"

"I'm doing a hell of a lot better than some. Houses collapsed everywhere, huge mess, look it up on Google. The only damage to our Beaumont house is a few stucco cracks."

*Hurricane in Louisiana, earthquake in California. What the hell?*

"Glad you're fine, but he was an awesome dad. He did the best he could, especially raising a boy as messed up as me." Words to the 1973 Jim Croce song, "Time in a Bottle" played in my head.

*... if I could save time in a bottle / the first thing that I'd like to do / is to save every day, 'til eternity passes away ...*

"Oh, Johnny, you're not messed up."

I sniffled, chugging another few ounces of juice as my vision went double.

"But now you need to drive home, Johnny. We need you here. The news is saying there's some big hurricane headed your way and all flights have been cancelled over the next day or two."

"That can't be good." My speech started to slur, and I hoped Mom couldn't tell, but if anyone would understand my need for the bottle, it was her. Outside, a cluster of trees blew like an angry mob.

Between sobs, she managed to change the subject. "I'm not sure if this is good news or bad, but Karl Cannon came to our house today. Said he's been trying to get a hold of you. Something about that big real estate deal you guys were working on."

The sky lit up bright as day for a split second, then went dark again. Rain poured down hard and a second later, thunder rolled through my bones.

"Kevin was poisoned, he's in the hospital, but should be recovered by tomorrow. I promise I'll get back to California and help, but I need to make sure he's alright first. I'm just so confused ..." I couldn't finish my thought.

The blood on my shoulder had continued to cake dry.

"Poisoned? Like food poisoning?" I heard the strain of concern in her voice

"No." I explained the Waffle House incident, really only wanting to empathize with her and what losing a spouse must feel like. Horrible, I thought, now regretting telling her about Kevin. She already had enough stress.

"You make sure Kevin's alright, he's a good friend and—

"I know, mom."

A long, drawn out exhale came through the speaker. "Fine, then I'll get started on planning the funeral, you come home once it's safe and Kevin's better."

I purposely held back details of my time with Tammy and almost getting murdered by Scott.

We said our goodbyes, hung up, and by then, the liquor had kicked in big time. The world spun faster and I welcomed the numbness.

But the negativity void in my belly only grew stronger. I'd never grieved for two people simultaneously. In my inebriated and upside-down mental state, I called Karl.

"Dude, I've been trying to get a hold of you for, like, days. Business partners need to be transparent, we discussed this, and—"

"I know, man. So sorry," I said, slurred, then pushed the remaining air from my lungs. "Something important came up and I had to take a few days off. I just found out my dad passed away. Please tell me the deal closed."

"Oh no, man. I'm super sorry to hear about your pops. I remember seeing him at the Fourth of July party at your place." He paused. "Can't believe he's gone. Was a good man."

He took another beat. A gust of wind rattled my car, shaking everything inside. My ribs and ankle throbbed and I wondered if my ribs were cracked or bruised. I coughed, shooting out jolts of pain from my upper right chest.

Karl continued. "Dude, I wish I had better news, especially with your dad passing away and all." My heart climbed up into my throat. "You know we had a huge earthquake here centered over Newport Beach."

"I heard—"

"Eight point three. I drove by your home. It's toast, dude. Nothing more than two of the four primary walls still standing."

I squeezed my eyes shut, trying to will this nightmare away. I thought about my cat, Jazzy, and wondered if he was still alive. My mind floated over the mountain of tasks needed to deal with my house: insurance adjustors, clean up, reconstruction, permits, possible sale, et cetera, but then instead tried to focus on the positive. If only we could close the deal, I could afford to buy three new houses.

"Since the quake was in Newport Beach, the Dana Point property might be—"

"I know where you're going, bro, but unfortunately no. You know how these things work. We're talking a severe quake that shook most of Southern California. Hard. The whole area is like some goddamned war zone. The commercial property suffered significant damage."

I needed positive news.

"Please tell me the deal closed before the quake hit."

He paused. Again. Shit. Here it comes.

"The deal is teetering, almost sunk. The frickin' lender wants to turn down the financing, the buyer is scared about the potential damage, the insurance, the lawyers. I need you back here right now to help me keep this afloat. Without you, the deal is as good as dead."

The urge to run away consumed me and without saying goodbye, I hung up on Karl, puckering my lips and inhaling another hefty draw of whiskey. The inside of the car spun fast and I passed out in my seat.

# CHAPTER 53

**R**ain pitter-pattered the roof of my car, nudging me awake. Hunched over, I opened my eyes, but when I tried to straighten, a loud explosion went off inside my head. The world twisted and a wave of nausea hit me. Hard. I shoved my door open and puked half-digested whiskey onto the wet grass as rain poured onto the back of my head.

After slamming the door shut, the faint memory of the brief conversations with my mom and Karl popped into my mind, sending a whole new wave of depression through me.

The rain pounded harder. Louder. What I would consider a thunderstorm in California. Sheets of water splattered down on my car.

The word "failure" flashed in bright big, red, bold letters. Failure at business. Failure at love. Failure at having a family. Failure at being a son. Failure at being a friend. Failure at finding the treasure.

My head pounded and the nausea forced me to sit still, waiting for the hangover symptoms to subside.

I must have dozed off again. Apparently, I was not as skilled a medical technician as I thought. The chemicals had failed to seal up the blood from the gunshot wound. Too deep a cut. My life-juice did not coagulate enough to stop the bleeding. I'd probably lost several pints of blood over a period of multiple hours. The alcohol made things worse. Or better.

In a daze, varied glimpses of two elderly folks hovered above my body as I lay on a couch somewhere. Pain rang out from my shoulder, but I pushed it back down as I jolted awake.

With an I.V. stuck into the top of my right hand and the tube wound toward a bag hanging on some medical prop, I yanked off an oxygen mask from my face.

"Relax, dear. Ya need to rest," said a woman with a thick Louisiana accent and kind, worried eyes. She looked down at me, but my gaze averted hers, darting instead to an old wooden chest with a creamy white doily, oil paintings of what I assumed were family members, and a grandfather clock tick-tocking away in the corner.

A man stood behind her, arms crossed on his chest.

She had curly white hair, smelled of mothballs, and wore a light blue polyester shirt. The man had short white patches of hair on both sides of his head and thick gray caterpillar eyebrows.

I tried to sit up, but she nudged me back down. "You stay put," she said. Her touch felt abnormally strong, forceful.

Breathing hard, I asked, "Where the hell am I?"

The man piped up. "We found ya in a fancy car parked out next to our barn. Thought you was dead, laying there in yo' seat, blood all over the place and on yo' clothes."

"And the liquid you're giving me—"

"Relax, son, my wife here's a retired nurse," said the man, exuding confidence with each word.

"Don't worry," the woman said, "if you were in hypovolemic shock, you'd have different symptoms. We volunteer for the Red Cross, so lucky for you we got extra saline solution to help with fluid resuscitation, to keep you hydrated."

"Name's John. John Bastian," I said, wincing from bone pain in my shoulder, ribs, and ankle. I leaned back into the couch.

Not having the physical energy to argue and fully depleted mentally, I closed my eyes and the couple introduced themselves before I drifted back to la la land.

At a quarter past twelve, my phone rang, startling me out of my semi-dozing state.

Kevin's doctor told me my buddy was awake, alert and asking about me. I told the doc I'd be over in a few minutes.

My two elderly lifesavers entered the room and stood next to me as I spoke.

After they helped remove the IV from my arm, I stood, waited for the dizziness to wear off, excused myself from the old couple, and walked to their living room for some privacy. I texted my mom about Kevin.

When I walked back into the TV room, the old couple stood next to my pseudo-hospital bed and crossed their arms.

"I'm sorry to have come into y'all's lives like this and run," I said with my best, thick Louisiana accent, not knowing what else to say. "Thank y'all for your help, hospitality, and generosity." They both frowned.

"You still don't look so good. Have a seat."

I sat back on the couch and put my head in my hands.

"Son, you look like you could use someone to talk with," said the old lady, pulling up a small chair and taking a seat. "Tell us what's going on."

"Y'all wouldn't believe me if I told you." I looked at the ground.

Someone knocked at the door.

The old man whisked toward the entryway and opened their front door, a scented trail of Old Spice wafting past, reminding me of my dad. Outside, red and blue alternating lights flashed. Two other men stood on the porch.

"Sheriff Cook, thanks for comin'," said the old man.

I thought about Scott's gun hidden underneath the front passenger seat of my car.

"Hey Earl, understand y'all got some hippie dippy city slicker up in here causin' problems," the sheriff said, switching his gaze to me. He was the same guy from Adam's house two days ago, the one who met with Mike. A fire erupted in my gut. *Something's off.*

"I'm sorry, John," the old woman said, embracing my upper left arm. "We thought you might have been some drug addict or Satan-worshiper parked on our property, so we called the sheriff." She turned to the two police offers and leaned forward. "Sorry to waste y'all's time, gentlemen, but everything's fine up in here."

Unconvinced, the sheriff blew past Earl, barged inside the house and walked toward me, one boot thud at a time on the wooden floor. With him came a strong odiferous blend of chewing tobacco and coffee. "Hope ya ain't causin' no problems for these good folks up here. Had a murder at a fancy hotel downtown just a few hours ago. Y'all don't happen to know nothin' 'bout that?"

I looked down at the ground and spoke, still with my Louisiana accent. "No sir, just trying to get a move on, that's all. Who died?"

He scanned the room, then brought his focus back to me. "Ya from around here?" he asked.

"Yessir. Grew up just north of here, in Baton Rouge. I'm applyin' for a professorship up at LSU. I teach real estate and business classes, y'see, and—"

"What happened there to your arm?"

"Bar fight, outside the alley of Waffle House. Just a scratch, though, sheriff, nothin'. Me and him, we worked it out."

"Okay, okay. We thought you might be someone else we been lookin' for."

Earl asked, "Sheriff, who died at the hotel?"

"Unknown female. Caucasian. Late-fifties, early sixties. We doin' the investigation now. Y'all hear anythin' you be sure to let me know, okay?"

My shoulders rounded, taking on a slumped posture, I clenched my jaw, trying to hold the rising pain inside my heart.

*What color was her hair?* I wanted to ask, but figured the sheriff would become suspicious. Wanting this guy gone, I swallowed my words.

Sheriff Cook, apparently satisfied with my lies and non-existent threat to the community, turned around and headed back toward the front door, tipping his cap as he walked by the old man. "G'night, Earl."

The two officers walked toward their patrol car and Earl shut the front door.

"Thanks again, folks, but I gotta be going," I said with a cracked voice, needing to leave and continue investigating.

"You seem like a nice young man, but need ya to stay off people's private property from now on, y'hear? And get to a hospital soon to get y'self checked out," said the old man.

I agreed, we shook hands, they walked me to the front door, and I exited back out into the storm, covering my head with my blood-soaked jacket as best I could. My right shoulder failed to move as instructed, so my left shoulder did the heavy lifting.

Back inside my car, I pushed back into my seat, trying to catch my breath. Then I leaned over and felt for the gun. Still there.

After driving a couple blocks north, I parked on the side of a suburban street to gather my thoughts. Initially, my intentions were to get back on the highway, head back up to Baton Rouge and pick up Kevin. But that plan quickly dissolved. Instead, my eyelids folded closed and I sat in my car on that dark, tree-lined street, the rain falling hard. I dozed off again, but this time into a deep, depressed slumber.

# CHAPTER 54

**Scott Jones**
*November 23, 2016*

$A$ proud Baton Rouge native for his entire life, Sheriff Cook considered himself a Louisianan through and through. Twice divorced, he now enjoyed the full benefits of bachelorhood at his residence located along the Mississippi River, which he'd told Scott on more than one occasion gave him a sense of peace in an otherwise chaotic world. His family had lived in the area since the early days the white man came over from Europe, when Rene-Robert Cavelier, Sieur de La Salle claimed the land for France in 1682. The settlers had named Louisiana after King Louis XIV, and Scott knew Sheriff Cook had visions of becoming a king himself, at least in Baton Rouge.

At Scott's urging, Adam had given the sheriff both names of the two new treasure hunters, and the sheriff ran background checks. Scott arranged a meeting at the sheriff's house, and intended on playing a fun little game he liked to call Blackmail.

Scott trudged through the driving rain and threw open the sheriff's front door. The sheriff grabbed them each a cold soda and the two men proceeded to sit in the sheriff's wood-paneled home office. The sheriff kicked his feet up onto an oak desk and leaned back in his leather chair, fingers locked behind his head. Behind the desk, various mounted deer and moose heads hung lifelessly on the wall.

Scott restrained himself, allowing the sheriff to enjoy his power spot, where he brought people to work them over. To negotiate.

"Finished the background checks on them two California bastards," the sheriff started, sipping his diet cola.

"My people dug up some stuff, too, but some of it don't make no sense."

"'Fore we get into dealin' with them two idiots, we need to talk." The sheriff crossed his arms and tipped his baseball hat back on his head. "'Member couple days back, when we was in the bayou, you said you was just out fishin', and I asked if y'all had heard any gunshots?"

"Yessir."

The sheriff slurped down another swig and over-exaggerated an exhale. "Well, today we found a body out there. Tied down. Apparently, the gators had a feast, but we did recover enough pieces, including a hand with viable fingerprints, to make a positive ID, which we'll have soon." His stare penetrated deep into Scott's eyes.

Scott raised his eyebrows and blinked as slow as possible, not wanting to show any sign of fear. "I'm sure there's a point to this."

Someone knocked on the door. Scott turned, spilling a few drops of soda onto his t-shirt. "You expectin' someone?"

The sheriff stood, walked out of the room to the front door while Scott remained seated, sipping his beverage. A moment later, the sheriff walked in with Mike, who sat next to Scott.

The sheriff paced the room, apparently thinking about what to say next. His phone rang. He listened for a minute, said thank you to the caller, and hung up.

The sheriff crossed his arms again, alternating his view between the floor and the two men seated in front of him.

"That there was my medical examiner," the sheriff said. His phone pinged and he gazed down at the screen. "Got the file right here. Amazing what these new-fangled gadgets can do these days." He scrolled on his phone screen. "Okay, here it is. The body in the bayou, or what's left, has been tentatively ID'd as David Brickheimer." He leaned his hefty, wide butt against the desk, glancing down at his phone. "Sorry, *doctor* David Brickheimer. Blah blah blah. PhD in archaeology from University of London. Apparently, he's a friend of Mr. Bixleton's here." He pointed a finger toward Mike.

Scott darted his gaze at Mike.

"Sheriff, sorry to hear about this man's death, but you ain't tellin' us nothing we don't already know," Scott said.

The sheriff set his phone on the desk. "See, Scott, that's the trouble. When y'all signed me up as part of your little plan here to find the treasure, ya ain't mentioned no kinda cover up for murder. For the five percent ya offered, I figured I'd help you sort out a few of my department resources, getcha some backhoes for digging, extra security when needed to help ensure nobody done steal the treasure when y'all finally found it. But now someone's going around killing folks, and well . . ."

Scott rubbed the nape of his neck and stole a glance at Mike, who had nothing but an arrogant smirk on his face.

The sheriff continued. "Plus there's this whole publicity business of you being on the national news lately. Got ourselves an honest to goodness hero in our midst." The sheriff raised his arms above his head like a southern Baptist preacher. "Be a gosh-darned shame if them fine reporters were to find out y'all had anything to do with this here Brickheimer fella. I'll bet—"

"Hold on sheriff," Mike interrupted. "If the treasure is worth a billion dollars, five percent is five million dollars. That should be plenty for—"

"Fifty million, ya ignorant dope," Scott corrected. He turned to the sheriff. "Either way, that's more than enough to be worth it for you to keep your trap shut about any kind of— how shall we say—unsavory work that needs to be done."

The sheriff walked around to the back of his desk and sat. He retrieved another folder from a drawer, spread open the manila cover and without looking up, said, "Of course there's this issue of one Bridgette Petitpont, some sorta direct descendant of Jacques Lafayette himself. Mr. Gold Treasure." He looked up at Scott, most likely to get a read on him. "We found her body just this mornin' on her boat a few miles east of here. Not sure y'all know anything 'bout that." He paused, eyebrows raised, staring back and forth between Scott and Mike. Scott shot a glance at Mike. "They found a brand new, crisp hundred-dollar bill nearby. When they run the bill for fingerprints, I wonder what they might find. And the security video from the dock the night she was murdered. Supposed to be comin' my way any minute now. What do y'all s'ppose we'll see when we watch that?"

Scott stood. "Okay, okay. Jesus."

The sheriff chuckled. "Son, I ain't even mentioned the fact we got two eyewitnesses sayin' they saw someone matchin' your description firing several shots from a window and out front of a fancy downtown hotel early this morning. Don't suppose ya know anything 'bout that?"

A thick, awkward silence filled the air as each man contemplated his next move.

Finally, the sheriff slapped both hands on top his desk. "I could haul both your asses in now, beat a confession outta ya for any of this, and find this damned treasure myself." He arced a toothy grin on his smug face. "But," he licked his lower lip,

"I'm feeling generous today. Y'all deserve a tiny tad of good ol' fashioned southern hospitality."

Scott stole a glance at Mike, who nodded.

"Ten percent," Scott said. The sheriff laughed.

"Boys, I ain't sure what y'all's arrangement is, but I'm gonna get half. Fifty percent. Take the deal or rot in jail. Your choice."

# CHAPTER
## 55

Anger erupted inside the sheriff's home office. Hands flew up.

Mike stood, pulled out his 0.45 and pointed the pistol at the sheriff. "My turn," Mike said with a grunt, cocking the hammer of his pistol. "Yo' fat ass is goin' to get fifteen percent. Or a lead slug through your ugly. Pig. Face. Take your choice."

The sheriff laughed again, loud and bellowing as he motioned with his arms for the other two men to sit. "Boys, settle down here. Y'all don't even know what you're talking about. I got the missing piece to the equation here."

Mike and Scott exchanged confused glances, but Mike kept the gun aimed at the sheriff's head.

Scott said, "We know exactly where to dig. Flew over the area this mornin'. But I came here today to give you instructions on where to start, not get fucked in the ass."

The sheriff pounded his open hand onto the table and kept laughing. "That's all well and good, son, but you boys is missin' one thing. Those two pieces only work together if you have the correct sized hinge."

"Bullshit. Our compass has a hinge," Mike said with a cold stare. Scott let him talk, curious to see where the conversation would lead.

"Of course. But that ain't the correct one," the sheriff said. "Whoever gave you that compass screwed y'all. Mine has the correct angle. Y'all gonna be off by a mile. In any direction. Maybe more."

Mike uncocked his pistol and lowered his arm. "Scott, tell me what the hell this asshole's talkin' about."

Scott looked at the orange carpet, rubbing the top of his head. "Twenty percent. You make the murders disappear. I mean bury them. Help us with the excavation and press. Keep the questions to a minimum."

"You being a national hero and all for taking on that dumbass terrorist the other day, I guess I might be willing to cut you two fellas a break. Forty percent."

"Thirty."

The sheriff put one hand on his hip. "Thirty-five."

Scott took a beat, thinking about the gold and the island it's on, all based on the letters and numbers from the back of the letter.

The sheriff walked around from behind his desk, stood between his two guests, leaned down and put his hands on his knees.

"And I'll throw in some free gas for the backhoes. No extra charge," the sheriff said with a grin.

Mike and Scott exchanged glances again, each nodding to the another. "Okay, sheriff, you got yourself a deal, but only if you get the digging equipment in place today. Need to beat this hurricane."

The sheriff strolled back behind his desk.

Scott continued. "Nobody outside this room knows about our plan. We need to keep it that way."

"One more thing," the sheriff said, wagging a loose finger as he stepped toward his chair. "Our two friends, John Bastian and Kevin Traylor seem like a couple of average Joes, but Kevin appears to be some kind of wannabe comedian, a minor celebrity of sorts, so we'll need to be careful with him."

"Already handled that, Sheriff," Mike said. "Poisoned them at the Waffle House."

Scott shook his head at Mike's lie.

The smile fell from the Sheriff's face, his eyes turned cold, dead, flat. "They both survived, you moron. John wasn't affected and Kevin's still at the hospital and totally fine, might have been released for all I know. Thanks to our wonderful medical community, I'm told they saved his life, got to him before too much of the poison stopped his heart. He's gonna be in pretty bad shape for a while, but he's very much alive. Worse yet, my deputy spoke with the waitress who gave him the poison. She described your face to the guy, said that you told her something about a prank. Then she said some guy chased her into an alley, which I'm assuming is this Bastian fella. Every hour he's alive, there's more risk. For all of us."

Scott spoke. "Either way, John knows more than he should. He knows little details and stuff about Jack that nobody else ever knew."

"Jack? Your buddy you whacked back in the seventies?" Mike asked.

"Shut up." He slid his hand back across his scalp. "To make things worse, I found John bopping my wife, which I can't even comprehend. I tried to blow his head off, but . . . I don't know, there's something creepy about him. Can't wrap my head around it." He looked back down at the floor, ideas swirling in his mind.

The sheriff glanced into one of his folders and shuffled some papers inside. "Background check shows the little prick's divorced, no kids, some kind of real estate broker, lives in Newport Beach, California, wherever the hell that is. Kind of a loner, not a lotta of friends." He snapped the folder closed, then intertwined his fingers as he set his hands on the desk. "Now that the prize money's all divvied, I suggest you boys work together and remove this variable from the equation. Needs to be clean. No loose ends."

# CHAPTER
## 56

**John Bastian**

*November 23, 2016*

Maybe the stars and planets all came into alignment. Maybe the universe was trying to nudge me forward, to get on with my life.

Details about Jack's killer, the gold, Lafayette—all of it—rolled into my head like an avalanche of boulders. Same as before, but this time with countless details filling in the cracks. Now, the complete picture came into view.

Finally.

My headache was gone and a raging hunger for waffles had replaced the nausea. Energy flowed through my veins. Jack's visions and memories were all readily available every time I closed my eyes.

I finally knew the precise location of his murder. Without a doubt. I also knew, absolutely with a hundred percent certainty, where the murderer had buried the body from my previous life. I grabbed one of the drawings from my childhood and pinpointed the location with a pencil.

Instinct told me to get moving, to get the hell on the road.

First step: get Kevin out of the hospital. I floored the gas pedal, peeled out of the muddy, grassy shoulder, hopped on the interstate and sped north to Baton Rouge. But five miles into the drive a new vision hit me so hard, I nearly passed out. My breathing rate skyrocketed, my heart leapt out of my chest, and stars flashed in front of me. My vision blurred, which was too much to take while driving, so I pulled over. Again.

Eyes closed, the entire murder of Jack Bachman now played in front of me like a high definition movie.

Somewhere near the Mississippi at Point Clair, in one of the many Louisiana bayous, the night air clung to my skin like a wet dishrag. Crickets chirped, frogs croaked.

November 7, 1978.

Evening.

A fight had ensued between me and my best friend, Scott Jones. On a whim, I'd figured out how the map and the compass worked together, the ones Abubaker had given me. They pinpointed a location in the backyard of an old house a few hundred yards inland of the Mississippi, at the base of an ancient tree. I started digging and before long, my shovel clunked on a granite box structure. After clearing the edges, I slid off the lid, found an old leather briefcase inside, and opened it. A single piece of paper. A letter, written in French. With handwritten, cursive letters and numbers on the back. From my backpack I grabbed a fresh piece of bond paper and copied the code and handwriting as best I could.

Abubaker's words rang in my head.

*Find love. Do something great in this world. The treasure chest full of gold is yours. But beware of the curse of Le Trésor Fatale. Your friends will turn on you.*

I folded my version of the letter and secret code, stuffed it into my pocket, then put the original letter back inside the leather pouch, and buried everything the way it was before I'd arrived.

Excited to share the new discovery with Scott, we met near the Mississippi, but the normal, friendly version of my buddy did not show up.

Instead, Scott accused me of scheming with someone to remove him from the hunt so I could keep the treasure all to myself.

"Look at me when I'm talking to you," Scott had demanded, following behind as I hiked through muddy terrain. He grabbed my right shoulder from behind, whipping me around, and we stopped.

"Not sure what you want me to say," I said, hands on my hips. "We've been searching for this treasure for years. *We*. Not I. Not you. *We* have. It's beyond comprehension that you think I could turn my back on ya like that. I thought you trusted me. In fact, I had a breakthrough today, I got—"

"We've known each other since, what, third grade?" Scott asked with furrowed brow.

Inside my pocket, I wrapped my fingers around the folded letter, waiting to share with Scott.

*The curse. No way Scott would behave this way.*

"We've been together through all the highs and lows of life. We graduated high school together. We dated the same girls and played football together, for God's sakes. We served two tours in Vietnam. I owe my life to you, Jack, but now you have to go and try to find the treasure without me?"

I turned to continue walking, wrapping my fingers tightly around the letter and map in my pocket. We were so close to finding the treasure.

Maybe neither of us were worthy? Maybe the treasure was never meant to be found? Maybe the gold was some sort of black hole of death, put on Earth for the sole purpose of sucking in the lives of greedy men?

Who knows, but in order to save Scott, I needed to destroy our only link to the treasure and stop the hunt. I needed to do something I'd probably regret later on.

I withdrew a lighter from my pocket.

"Don't you fucking ignore me, man," Scott said before sucker-punching me from the rear, a jab to my right kidney, knocking the wind out of me and out of instinct, I flicked the lighter onto the ground. Bent over and in a coughing fit, I tried to grab the lighter, but Scott lifted his elbow above me and hammered down his entire weight onto my upper back, forcing me to the ground. He kicked my torso twice while I was down. Probably broke several ribs. I had seen his anger before—the hidden rage—but never directed toward me.

"I followed you today. I know you found somethin' in that old man's backyard you ain't tellin' me about, you son of a bitch. A traitor and a backstabber. The treasure's mine, Jack. Mine! You fucked with the wrong guy."

As I coughed, blood spewed across the sand and grass. "Let me explain." I wiped the red liquid from my mouth then grabbed the lighter while trying to stand from one knee.

"You know somethin' and ain't tellin' me."

"Yes, but I'm tryin' to tell you, but the curse ain't letting you listen. I figured out how to use the map and the compass and found another clue today and was usin' it to find the treasure for us. But I realize now, there is no us. And there won't be no treasure."

I stood hunched over, hands on my knees, writhing in pain, spitting blood onto scattered dry leaves. As Scott meandered over to a nearby wood pile, I flicked on a flame, extracted both the original Abubaker map and my version of the letter with the code on the back—fully aware of what the letters and numbers referred to—then proceeded to light both cursed papers on fire.

It was the only way to save Scott. I had no choice.

But Scott grabbed an axe, ran back to me and pushed me down. As I fell onto my back, the flaming letter floated to the ground. He placed the butt of the axe on my throat.

I strained for oxygen. My eyes bulged. Pain and burning sensations throbbed throughout my entire body, rendering me paralyzed. Bubbles of saliva oozed down the side of my face as I stared up at my former best friend. His fiery red eyes blazed deep into my soul and he tightened his lips, teeth fully exposed, breathing like a mad man.

"We were gonna change the world, man. You and me," Scott said, veins popping from his forehead as he stomped out the tiny flames. "This was our chance to make things right. I was gonna find love with this money. Real love, like the kind you and Tammy have. Now you've gone and stole it all away from me."

I shook my head and grabbed at the base of the axe, gasping. "Stop. Please. You're not yourself right now."

Breathing like he'd just finished a marathon, Scott glanced around. No sane man would act that way. I had questioned my choices up until that point in life. Instead of my twin brother, whom I'd become estranged from over the last few years because of his drinking problem, I chose to spend a lot of time with Scott and had brought him in on the treasure hunt because he was my best friend and I wanted a second set of eyes to help discover the lost gold. Somewhere along the line, I must have made a mistake. Trusted him too much. Or the guy was psycho from getting beat by his angry dad all those years.

I pondered all this while sucking in my last few breaths on earth as Jack Bachman.

"You're never gonna stab anyone in the back again," Scott said, raising the axe high above me. The blade was coming right at my head. With the last of my energy, I connected my shin to his groin and knocked him slightly off balance. Instead of hitting my face, he brought the axe blade down onto my right shoulder, tearing through flesh, bone, muscle, and cartilage. A sharp pain, stronger than any I'd ever endured, raced through me. I convulsed, turning my head to the right, as blood spurted from my shoulder onto the severed limb. I tried in vain to will my arm back into place, but my world became dark. A circle of light closed inward, collapsing my field of vision.

The man standing above me dropped the axe. A look of dread had replaced his anger.

"You stupid idiot," Scott yelled. "Look what you made me do! I was only going to scare you. Why'd you kick me? Oh Jesus." He picked up my arm and set the dead, twitching, bloody limb next to my body, as though magically reattaching my arm would stop the bleeding.

Time stopped, memories shifted and flashed in my mind to Jack's life with Tammy.

A day before Jack's twenty-ninth birthday, standing next to his smiling, proud mom, Elaine Bachman, back in their home in Thibodaux, Louisiana. Memories of Jack's twin brother, Adam, and all the happy times we shared growing up together, like working part-time as a mechanic at the local airport while in high school.

Then memories of trying to have a child with Tammy, but failing. Her face, her sweet, loving, caring face and those eyes, had me wandering in an endless loop of pure joyful bliss.

Visions of the treasure map, Jacques Lafayette, and all the research that went into finding the truth about the tragic events of that man's life. My entire existence as Jack summed up in an instant, an infinitesimally tiny speck of time.

Then the circle closed. My life as Jack Bachman ended.

Everything I had seen on TV, read about in magazines and in library books led me to believe that when you died you saw a bright light. You were supposed to walk toward the light and heaven would magically appear.

But when I died as Jack, nothing like that happened.

Rather, my body felt weightless. All the pain disappeared. Once I had died, time stopped and every fear and worry evaporated into nothingness. I existed only as pure delight. Nothing but joy. And I saw everything in the entire universe, anything that had ever happened, anything that will ever happen, all at once.

I wondered how people could fear death when the experience was so impossibly amazing.

Perhaps I had traveled into a dimension unknown to man, where Scott—where anyone—could no longer see me. Between realms. I somehow had full awareness of him and his life force. His emotions of sadness, regret, hatred, jealousy, and fear. But not only him, I sensed the trees, the grass, the fungi and various tiny creatures living on and beneath the surface of the saturated soil. The intertwined energies of life all merged together, but each one simultaneously remained unique.

The universe appeared both small and infinite.

My soul floated above the grisly scene below, all several hundred yards inland from the Mississippi River. In my spirit state I floated in and explored 1978, following Scott as he dragged my former body to a deserted construction site nearby. An unfinished new building. Reinforced concrete walls for a basement had been recently constructed inside a deep hole in the ground. Timber was used as forms while the concrete walls cured. Construction workers had left some tools between the finished walls; however, on the exterior of the walls, the existing soil had been over-excavated and partially backfilled with decomposed granite, a special type of sand used to backfill underground structures.

Scott rolled an empty, black fifty-five-gallon drum toward my body, pried off the lid, lifted and stuffed my corpse into the drum, and replaced the top. He rolled the makeshift coffin next to the top of the sloped hole.

I read his thoughts.

He wanted to bury my body in the sand. This way, when the construction crews returned to work, they would unknowingly continue to bury my body. Scott carried out his plan, digging a ten-foot deep hole in the backfill sand next to the concrete basement wall, and heaving the cylinder with my limp, dead body into the pit. He then shoveled soil onto the drum until it was completely covered.

Afterwards, he walked with the shovel back to where he murdered me, then scraped up and mixed all the blood with soil. Before long, the murder site gave no clues to what had happened. The entire landscape had been wiped clean of the crime.

Except in his haste, he forgot to hide my severed arm, which lay partially hidden among the dead leaves.

Scott wiped sweat from his brow and returned the shovel before walking away from the scene like taking a stroll through a park.

The Lafayette ghost appeared in my dream and convinced me to wake up, to come out of the vision and get back to reality.

I opened my eyes.

Everything vanished.

No more Scott. No more ghost. Nothing.

Only detailed memories remained, like they'd happened yesterday.

# CHAPTER 57

**Scott Jones**
*November 23, 2016*

**B**ack at the sheriff's house, Scott and his two accomplices agreed to their updated terms. Mike and Scott exited the front door and walked through horizontal rain and gusts of wind that nearly knocked Scott over.

They hopped in their cars and drove two miles to their favorite bar. On their way in, Mike kicked a puddle.

"Goddamn that backstabbing asshole," Mike said. He hammered his open fist on the outer bar wall, making grunting sounds barely audible over the noise of the howling wind.

"You said you were gonna take care of Bridgette's body," Scott said, stepping in front and getting in his face. "Tell me how in God's name he found out about her."

"Was gonna tell you, boss. I swear." Mike said. "By the time I got my cleaning crew there, the cops were already there swarming the area. No way in hell we could've gotten to the boat."

"You should've told me. We got railroaded in there. I should blow your skull apart right now."

Mike jammed his face up against Scott's. "You do and your fat pig daughter dies."

"You'd be doing me a favor."

"And your dog."

Scott squinted at Mike and bit his tongue.

"Yeah, that's right," Mike said. "You think I'm too stupid to have an insurance policy? I don't check in with my buddy every hour from now 'til we find the treasure, they're both history."

"Calm down." Scott changed the subject. "We got this guy right where we want him."

"Not if he's taking a third of our loot. Our loot!" Mike said, stabbing his index finger on his own chest.

"Only if he's alive to take it."

Mike stepped back, staring at Scott and wiping his drenched hair sideways across his scalp, before blinking twice and smiling.

Scott continued with a nod. "We use him for what we need. Maybe he has an accident he doesn't walk away from. You hear me?"

Cogs slowly turned in Mike's head. "Ahhh. Okay."

"You go track down that Bastian bastard, figure out the status of his little black buddy, and eliminate them. I'm going to fly my chopper out to that island bayou on the Mississippi to find this damned treasure once and for all. You come out in a couple hours."

Mike turned and walked into the dimly lit parking lot, as sheets of rain pummeled them. Scott hustled to and hopped inside his car, carrying some rain with him. He slammed the door shut and fired up the engine to warm his cold bones.

A thought hit him that at first he tried to ignore, but as he drove south, toward the place where the treasure was supposed to be, the thought gnawed at him more and more: John Bastian and Jack Bachman were connected somehow.

Uncle and long lost nephew?

He shook his head, focusing his energy on finding the treasure, then gunned the engine as he merged onto the highway toward the airport.

# CHAPTER 58

**John Bastian**
*November 23, 2016*

Eyes closed, the white noise of rain filled my head. Stars in my vision faded away and, blinking, clarity returned to my vision. I shook my head like a cat waking up from a nap, flipped on my turn signal and merged back into traffic, headed to the hospital.

I remembered images of the Lafayette ghost, complementing a strong sense of lucidity resonating in my core. Now, I knew exactly what needed to be done. Every cell in my living body spoke, motivated to unearth Jack's dead body, prove that Scott murdered him, then find the treasure.

For Tammy. God rest her soul.

I traveled north, exited the freeway, arrived at the hospital, and went straight to Kevin's room.

Sitting on the side of a gurney and fully dressed, he alternated between tying his basketball shoes and sipping orange juice through a straw from a plastic cup. The instant we made eye contact, I knew he would be alright.

I gave him a hug, the kind you give your best friend who almost died.

"Glad you're still here in the land of the living," I said.

"Right back at ya. Dude, we gotta stop scarin' each other like that," he said.

"I agree. I'm sorry, man. Listen, a lot's happened since the Waffle House."

He leaned forward, eager for information. I got him up to speed on who probably poisoned him, the entire Tammy experience, the love-making, getting shot by Scott, the coroner's van at the hotel, the skirmish at the airport, my dad dying, and the real estate deal falling apart.

Everything.

I added, "... and, I know where my previous body is buried."

"Say what?"

"You look like you're good to go," I said, nodding. "We don't have much time, let's hurry out of here and notify the police."

"But the doc said I gotta take things slow."

With the hurricane approaching, I wasn't so sure that would happen.

Kevin and I made our way down to the lobby, ordered some not-so-high-quality Joe from the vending machine, sat on two colorful plastic chairs with a view outside, and I opened up my laptop. The trees bent to the point of snapping in half as the wind and rain howled hard.

As a real estate broker, we had to study land surveying, law, sales and a bunch of other useful stuff, but I'd found a ton of value using Google Earth. I opened the app and searched for an area along the Mississippi that might match my visions.

Kevin studied the map I'd drawn and asked several questions.

The building with Jack's body buried outside the basement walls could be a one, two, or perhaps a three-story structure. To be honest, I was less than a hundred percent sure what exactly to look for, since the vision only showed me the basement. Some clues I had to work with were the relative size of the building footprint—about fifty by thirty feet—and the year the building was constructed: 1978.

Google Earth failed. Too many buildings. Too much land.

I logged in to the county records site and searched for commercial buildings constructed in Baton Rouge in 1978. I downloaded the list into a spreadsheet and searched by square footage and location. This narrowed the list down to three possible buildings.

I gave Google Earth another shot. As creepy as ever, while I tried to plot all three locations, the Lafayette ghost appeared again. This time, outside the window, standing, hands straight down at his side, with a killer poker face. When the man's lips moved, I heard him whisper something with a thick French accent so heavy I could barely understand, but as though he were mere inches away from me.

*"Building. Right. Sunshine."* I pointed to one on the map displayed on my laptop. *"No,"* he said. *"South."* I pointed to a different structure. *"Oui. Go. Find what you are looking for."*

Although convenient, communicating with a ghost raised the hair on my forearms and tested my resolve as a sane person. But my options at that point were running thin. When I turned my head toward the ghost to thank him—is that normal when communicating with a spirit from the great beyond?—he had already disappeared.

Kevin had been watching over my shoulder the entire time, with no clue as to what I'd just seen. I pointed to the winning location. "This is it. This is where Jack's body is buried."

I questioned myself for putting so much faith in following the advice from a ghost. It could have been a hallucination, something from my subconscious. Either way, I felt like I needed to trust where we were headed. Faith, as it were.

"C'mon now, oh resurrected one, let's get a move on. Let's go find us a dead body."

With my windshield wipers on "high" and the wind threatening to roll our car over like a toy, we drove to the site, located in the unincorporated area of Sunshine, and parked. Waves of wind and rain pummeled the lush trees and green grass everywhere as we stared at the two-story building sporting a beige stucco exterior and river rock fascia along the bottom five feet. The building resonated with me, along with a sense of deja-vu. A strange warm feeling traveled from my toes, up through my legs, and into my gut.

*I've been here before.*

Kevin turned to me. "We need to strategize. We can't go charging into some building and tell them we're lookin' for a dead body."

I rubbed my chin, scratching the three-day-old stubble. "I know." An idea hit me. "I read an article in Broker Monthly a while ago about a new ground-penetrating radar machine that could peer through walls and see, more or less, what's on the other side. Was designed for use on horizontal surfaces like roads, but these guys were using the contraption along retaining walls. It was for building inspectors."

"Fo' real? Things these engineers be comin' up with these days."

"Yeah. I'm thinking we somehow talk our way into the building, set up the machine in the basement and start scanning."

"That ain't never gonna work."

"It has to. Stay positive, man."

"First of all, we don't got no damned x-ray machine. Second, how the hell we gonna talk our way into a perfectly good building?"

Two valid, logical points. With my wi-fi hotspot and back online, I searched for ground penetrating radar machines. A few minutes later, I had secured a local company that does the work—they referred to the process as GPR for short—and put in an order to rent a unit and a technician. They told me that with the approaching hurricane and the rain, their next two days were empty, so they could come out right away for an extra fee. I gave them directions, my credit card info and confirmed the order.

"Okay, my friend," I told Kevin, "one issue down, one to go. Need to figure out a way into the building."

"Hmmm." Kevin's creative mind went to work. He rested his chin on a fist, squinting. "Sign on that door says National Insurance. I wonder if they might be willing to—"

A clump of several dozen people exited the building. I darted a glance at Kevin, and he shrugged. We both exited the car and walked toward the front of the building into the group of people, all sporting umbrellas.

"What's going on?" I asked a woman.

"They makin' us evacuate the buildin'." She rolled her eyes in disgust, then continued walking toward the parking lot.

"C'mon," I said to Kevin and we made our way past a couple dozen more people as they exited, then we entered the building. A damp, musty smell permeated throughout, but the inside looked clean. I searched for directional signs and found one that had a staircase logo and a downward-pointing arrow. I pointed to the sign and looked at Kevin.

*Basement.*

We hustled into the stairwell and stepped down to the lower floor. A pile of folders sat on a desk. I picked a few of them up, realizing we were officially trespassing and breaking a host of privacy laws, but Kevin did the same. A man walked around the corner, staring at his phone. As he walked past us he stopped and said, "Y'all can't be down here. Evacuation orders."

I replied with my best Louisiana accent. "We're comin', don't y'all worry. Gotta get these filed real quick, but we'll be out in a jiffy. See y'all up there." I turned to walk away and apparently that did the trick. The man went back to his phone and strode up the stairs.

We wandered around the basement, mostly around the perimeter. I looked around for places we could set up the GPR machine. I also hoped one of my memories would confirm we were in the right spot because theoretically at that point, I could be mere feet away from the corpse of the body of my previous life.

Or not.

The lights went out and darkness consumed our entire world. I assumed someone had cut the power to the building once everyone had left, but we still had a few minutes until the scheduled arrival time of the GPR technician. Using our phone flashlights, we fumbled our way back upstairs and sat in a couple of chairs in the lobby. Enough charcoal gray, gloomy light from outside soaked in through the front windows for us to see and talk. Thick rain and wind continued slapping the trees along the now-empty parking lot, with several claps of thunder rattling the building.

A white minivan with a logo "GPR Experts" pasted on the side arrived in the now empty parking lot. A rotund man in his late twenties wearing circular-rimmed glasses and a yellow raincoat exited the vehicle, shuffled around to the back and opened the rear doors. He extracted a beast of a machine, which seemed more like a small spherical nuclear weapon the size of a truck engine, with shiny stainless-steel parts and gauges welded onto the exterior. He placed the GPR onto a roller, then pulled the hefty mass toward the front door of the building. My plan was to open the front door like we owned the place, but when I pushed on the glass door, nothing happened.

Locked.

Fortunately, I found a knob on my side of the door, which I rotated to unlock the dead bolt, then pushed open the door in time for the technician to come inside. I scanned the outside. The workers had abandoned the area.

The power came back on and overhead lights shone brightly down on us.

"How'd the power go off then back on just when we need it?" Kevin asked.

I shrugged as the tech rolled through the doorway.

"Wally. GPR Experts," he said with a half-smile, looking up toward the ceiling. "I understand there's a wall or something we need to examine?"

"Sure, I'm John, I'm, uh," I stumbled, but quickly stepped into the broker role I've played a bazillion times. "I'm the listing broker for this building. Represent the owner. C'mon in. Power keeps going in and out. Let's go down to the basement."

He told us there's no way the stairs would take the behemoth of a contraption, so we found the elevator and he was soon set up in the basement.

"Tell me how this bad boy works," I said.

"Be happy to," he said, adjusting his glasses. "This is a revolutionary technology that does with concrete and dirt what the sonogram did for expectant mothers. This thing allows us to see in real time what's up to twenty feet of dirt inside and behind up to an eighteen-inch reinforced concrete wall, depending on the type of soil."

I raised my eyebrows, patting the hefty man on his back. "Not bad. Sounds like we hired the right guy."

He rolled the device along the perimeter hallway, then pushed it up against the first of four walls.

"I'm guessing you move the machine along these walls here to scan and create the images?" I asked.

"Yep, exactly. While I move around, the machine takes twenty-four HD images per second. I flip the 'on' switch, set the parameters for this scenario, and pull the machine along at about one foot per second. Once we're done, we pop out this tiny Micro SD card right here and I'll go out to my van and upload all the images to our proprietary software which stitches everything together to make a 3D model for us."

"Wow."

"Mind if I ask what we're looking for here?"

"To be honest, we don't know," I said, half-lying. "I'm guessing the buyer wants this done to make sure the water table is not too high. Either that or he thinks there's a dead body buried somewhere." I gave my best fake laugh.

The man tried to force a smile, gulped and continued dragging the machine along the floor.

"You guys don't have to be here while I do this. It'll just take a few minutes." He pulled out a helmet with a clear plexiglass shield and placed it onto his head.

"This is radar, so I'm assuming it's not radioactive," I said.

"Well, I'm just a technician, so I'm not sure. You can watch, but your kids might end up with three heads." He laughed and snorted like a pig. "Technician humor. Just kidding." He waved a hand at us and pulled his pants up to his navel.

The lights went out again.

*Dammit.*

The man turned on a flashlight.

A spark zapped between my ears. The location of my former body popped into my head, telling me which wall to search to find the corpse. Like Superman's x-ray vision. I pointed to a wall on my right, the one covered with chipped white paint and black mold in the upper corners. "Just do this wall."

"10-4, chief," he replied, confirming the area along the wall. "If there's no power to the building, we've got a problem, though."

"So that's it, then," Kevin said. "We ain't gonna be able to get this sumbitch to work?" Kevin asked.

"No, we will. Got a generator in the van. Extra charge, though."

"No sweat," I said, staring down at him. He stood still, glaring back at me, apparently not impressed. "Okay, we'll pay an extra hundred bucks. Cash."

He smiled, agreed, then hurried upstairs and out to the parking lot, backed up his van to the front door and ran a heavy-duty extension cord from the generator downstairs to the machine.

Game time.

"Make it quick. That hurricane is getting closer."

Kevin and I headed back upstairs and started working up a backup plan in case the radar didn't pan out.

The elevator pinged, the doors slid open, and the man wheeled out the device.

"All done," he proclaimed, pleased with his handiwork. I jogged to the front doors and pushed both, half-expecting to get drenched outside, but the rain had stopped. For now.

From the east, a dark sky spoke as the black swirling ooze told me it had much more in store for Louisiana.

Kevin and I followed the tech guy to his van, then helped him lift and load the machine.

"You said you can do the image processing here?" I asked.

"Yep. Give me a few minutes and I'll have some printouts of where the dead bodies are," he said, giggling.

Light droplets started to fall as the sky lit up several times, followed by rolling claps of thunder that echoed through the parking area and nearby fields.

We watched over the technician's shoulder as he opened his software, clicking several buttons and the system ran computations to create ghostly images. Finally, he printed out four grayscale photos and laid them on the carpeted floor of the van. He stood, crossed his arms, proud. "Okay, all done,"

"What am I looking at?" I asked, fanning the photos out to get a better look. He was right, they did look like baby sonograms. I remembered because Karl's wife had a sonogram for her baby.

But the same way you need an obstetrician to interpret the human embryonic parts shown on a sonogram, we needed an interpretation from someone with experience reading the GPR images. Two white, hyperbolic shapes were in the center-right area of two of the images, which, according to the tech guy, meant something.

He pointed to several spots of the images. "Here are pieces of rebar . . . and these are rocks . . . and this is where the water table is."

I pointed to an odd-shaped, cylindrical outline on the paper. "What's this?"

"Hold on a sec." From his pocket protector, he grabbed and donned a different set of glasses before moving the paper closer to his face for a better look. Squinting, the man said, "That looks like a . . ."

A ear-piercing boom erupted from the building, shaking the ground, along with several flashes of light. Instinctively, we all ducked.

A lightning bolt had struck the building and now flames licked the exterior walls near the doorway.

"Seriously?!" Kevin yelled to the sky.

Black and gray smoke hurled upwards toward the sky. I turned and faced the building, wondering how this would affect our search. My thoughts turned to Tammy, and my assumption she'd been killed, the need to mourn her growing stronger, but I buried the feelings and promised myself I'd deal with that later.

Now's not the time.

I stepped to the technician, picked up the printouts in my hands, and said, "Talk to me."

The technician nervously licked his lips, somewhat shaken. "As you can see, there's a set of bones arranged in a fetal position inside what appears to be a cylindrical container, maybe a 55-gallon drum, about eight feet away from the reinforced concrete basement wall."

Kevin chimed in, rotating one of the photos. "Now I get it." He pointed several white spots in the photo. "Here's a skull, backbone, ribs, an arm and I think two legs."

*The same place my new memories said they'd be.*

My breathing rate and pulse increased, and I rubbed my face, struggling to discern reality from a potential dream. Kevin put his arm on my shoulder, "Dude, you don't look so hot. Here, sit down," he said, motioning to the rear bumper.

The light rain had turned to a mild mist.

In the distance, a siren pierced the air, increasing in volume. Within seconds flashing red lights from a fire engine flooded the area.

"I'll bet the cops are on their way, too," I said with the pressure of panic rising inside me. I whispered behind my hand to Kevin, "We're totally trespassing here, man."

Sure enough, as we headed toward my car to leave, a vehicle with flashing red and blue lights approached the scene and skidded to a stop in front of us.

County Sheriff.

# CHAPTER 59

**P**arked less than five yards away, the Sheriff rolled out of his vehicle and stood straight, assessing the fire, the van, my car, me, Kevin, and God-knows-whatever else. Hands strapped to the front of his belt buckle, he moseyed toward us and recognized me in an instant.

"Holy Mother of Jehovah. If it ain't Professor Real Estate. You seem to be gettin' around these days, son."

Kevin tilted his head, narrowing his eyes at me.

"Don't ask," I told him.

"Got a call from the building owner about someone talking about a non-existent listing, possible trespassers. And now I find y'all here. And a fire. You boys mind telling me what happened?" he asked, head cocked backwards, looking down at us.

The thought crossed my mind to lie like 007 and spin a story of how we were minding our own business when the vacant building exploded from the lightning bolt. After all, there was a shred of truth there.

But hell no.

I knew the bones of my previous body were buried about a hundred feet from where we were standing.

"I'm going to be honest with you, Sheriff, we—" I said.

"That's a good start, son. You best be honest," he said, cutting me off while his lower lip protruded with chewing tobacco from his fat face. He spat off to his right, licked his lips and cocked his head back again.

"We—"

"What the hell you doing out here in the sticks? Y'all are a long way from home, ain't ya? What's with this van here? GPR? The hell's that?"

"Well, sir, we were doing some—"

He cut me off a third time. "Y'all better not been the ones who started this here fire. You been inside this building?" Kevin, the technician, and I stared at each other in silence. "Well? Have ya?"

"There's a body buried right there," I said, pointing to the spot on the ground where we needed to dig. The arrogant smile disappeared from the sheriff's face. I grabbed the printout photo and explained to him about the GPR machine and the findings. He stared at me, then Kevin, then back at me.

"You shittin' me. Ain't no body buried nowhere."

"Here's proof," I said, shaking the photo.

"It is a body, sir," the tech said.

The sheriff furrowed his brow, looked up and winked at me. "Hmph. Well I s'ppose we best get us some digging equipment and find out what's what. You boys stay right here," the sheriff said before walking to his squad car.

Soaked and dizzy, I leaned against the rear of the van.

Eventually, several more squad cars arrived, all skidding to a stop, one with a Bobcat backhoe in tow, and a dozen people with spade shovels.

"You tell me where you say this here body is buried," the sheriff said with a smile. I led him to the location outside the wall and estimated, based on the GPR printouts, where the body would be.

"My guess is about six feet down from this point right here," I said. The sheriff put his arm in front of me and pushed me aside.

"Okay boys, right here. Start diggin'," he said.

Inch by inch, the backhoe dug a hole eight feet by eight feet and between three and four feet deep. The sheriff never took his eye off us. He knew we were hiding something.

With shovels, the workers hopped down into the hole and dug until one of them hit metal with the shovel tip and yelled, "Got something."

The makeshift forensics team, essentially deputies wearing yellow and blue plastic jumpsuits, slid down into the muddy hole carrying several toolboxes. They carefully cleaned the mud from the area surrounding a rusted fifty-five-gallon drum.

I half expected to see a bunch of bones, but my jaw dropped when they popped off the lid and slid out the contents. At the bottom of the excavated area lay a grayish-brown, dirty, raggedy-clothed corpse. Bloated skin, brown hair on the sides of an otherwise bald head, wearing a pair of blue jeans and a light blue, long sleeved flannel shirt. The deceased only had a left arm. A short stub, caked with brownish-black, dried blood, protruded outward through a torn shirt, where the right arm should be. The team snapped hundreds of photos of the limp carcass, some placing various pieces of evidence into baggies and boxes.

The sulfury smell of death permeated the entire scene, reeking of rotting flesh.

A technician reached inside the drum, extracted something flat, a torn piece of paper, encased inside clear plastic. He stumbled his way up the slope, out of the hole, and stood next to the sheriff.

"Found this, sir," he said.

I leaned in, peeking over the sheriff's shoulder. Stuffed inside a clear plastic cover was the remnants of a fancy hand-written letter on yellowed parchment, with burn marks on the entire perimeter. Three inches square. A signature in cursive letters: *LAFAYETTE*

The sheriff shooed me away, folding and tucking the arti-fact into his inside jacket pocket.

I wandered over to the van next to Kevin. He said, "I'm hungry."

"Not me. Seeing Jack's dead, rotting body gave me the willies. Turned my insides over a few times."

"Still. I need a burger or something. Go ask your sheriff friend if we can go get us some food," he said.

The technician asked about the bill, I gave him a hundred bucks and my credit card info, and he split.

By now, the coroner had arrived on scene and was working down in the hole.

Giant, dark clouds continued to gain momentum, still swirling in the sky above us.

My phone rang, probably my mom.

I stared at the number. Hold on.

*How could that be?*

My mouth went dry, like an empty desert pool as my heart climbed into my throat and pounded.

I showed the phone screen to Kevin, who puffed out his chest, shoulders back. I jostled the phone but dropped the darned thing onto the wet asphalt, and then inadvertently kicked it into a wet, oily puddle of goop.

Scooping up my phone, it magically continued to ring as I held it up, pinched between my thumb and index finger, drip-ping brown liquid.

I hesitated.

*The call must be from Scott or someone using Tammy's phone.*

I replayed the events at the hotel and shook the phone before wiping the screen half-dry with my jeans. Swallowing down my anxiety, I swiped a wet finger across the answer button and put the call on speaker, but said nothing. Kevin stood at my side, staring at me.

"John?" a female voice said fast, in a questioning, scared tone.

Tammy!

"Oh my God, I thought you were . . ." I gulped hard, my mouth completely void of saliva. "How—"

Her breathing sounded shallow, fast. "John. John, listen to me. Scott's had someone following me since the hotel, I would've called earlier but—you don't know what you're getting into with this treasure hunt. It's too dangerous."

"Not sure I understand, Tammy, but I'm just really, super glad you're alive and I—"

"Scott's completely lost it," she said. "He killed a maid at the hotel. She saw us fighting, saw his gun, and he didn't even hesitate. Right in her heart, too. He'll stop at nothing to get to the treasure. Now he's coming after you guys and wants to kill you, too."

"I thought he shot, I mean—"

"He's a murderer and—that poor maid, she was innocent and—"

"Where are you?"

She didn't seem to hear. "Deep inside, I think he thinks of himself as a good guy, but whenever someone or something gets in the way of his treasure hunt, he turns into a different person."

"Are you alright? Where are you at?"

"I didn't get a chance to tell you about the wood compass."

"Never mind, screw the treasure, I just want to see you and help you stay safe. An hour ago, we found Jack's body. If we can find proof Scott killed Jack, we can—"

"But—" She paused. "No, it's not worth it. None of it is. You need to go back to California."

Kevin gave me a terse nod.

"As long as you're alive and safe and Scott's still out there, I'm not going anywhere."

A long moment lingered. "Fine, I'm at home, but whatever you do, do not come here. Scott has me on lockdown, not allowed to go anywhere. He's got someone parked out front watching. Says if I leave or anyone shows up, he'll know about it. If he found out I'm calling you, he'd kill me. I hope you guys aren't anywhere close to my house," she said.

"I'll figure something out. Maybe cause a distraction out front and pick you up out back and get you somewhere safe. Away from Scott."

From the crime scene twenty yards away, the sheriff jerked his head towards us, raising his eyebrows, holding something in his hand.

"This is important," she said. "Scott has the compass to find the treasure, but I don't think he has the map. If he does, he hasn't told me. You have the map you drew, but not the compass. I'm texting you a picture of it now." Silence hung in the air, then a few seconds later my phone pinged with a message and an attachment, which I opened.

The wood compass reminded me of one of those tiny metal ones we used in geometry class, not the kind you'd use to find north. With the pointed needle on one end and a clasp to hold a pencil on the other so you could draw a perfect circle or determine a distance or triangulate a location. I determined it was actually two compasses combined into one, with two different preselected distances, all connected in the middle with a brass hinge at the top. The wood and brass object had a smooth, stained finish. I showed the pic to Kevin.

"That's dope, yo. I got an 'A' in geometry class. I'm pretty good with a compass."

"We might be able to make one of these, if only I knew the actual size."

"Look at the ruler in the background so you can determine the scale of the thing," she said.

Indeed.

The sheriff cleared his throat loudly and started heading toward us with the burned letter in his hand.

"I gotta run," I said. The words "I love you" wanted to leave my lips, but instead only, "See you soon," came out as I tapped the red end call button.

The sheriff approached.

"Sheriff, my friend and I were wondering if—"

"Wondering what? If y'all was gonna get away with murder? Hell no, son. Not on my watch. Turn around and put your hands behind your head. Y'all under arrest."

"Murder? I'm the one who told you where the body was buried."

"Exactly. The coroner says this body only been dead for a couple years. Means you and your black friend and me gonna have a nice chat. You have the right to remain—" He almost had one hand cuff on my hand when I lost it, shoving his fat ass, with all my strength, into a muddy pothole. He slipped on the edge, dropped the letter, and fell in with a splash.

Despite acting on pure survival instinct, I picked up the letter and ran to the Beemer with Kevin. "Get in. Get in. He thinks we murdered that guy!"

We both jumped in, I gripped the wheel and peeled out, spewing a huge, high muddy mess from the rear tires.

"Great. Now we're fugitives," Kevin said, out of breath.

# CHAPTER 60

The rain started again. But with a vengeance. Fat drops streaking horizontally amidst a driving wind.

Kevin and I held tight as my BMW cat-tailed out of the parking lot onto the slickened roadway. Multiple firecracker bangs popped behind us, with one of the gunshots exploding my passenger side mirror into oblivion. Now both my side mirrors had been hit by bullets.

A moment later, my rear view mirror showed several red and blue flashing lights. Sirens screamed.

Speeding and splashing our way inland, away from the river, we plowed through puddles and swerved around cars, potholes and a yellow moving van.

"Quick! Get a map and tell me where to go. I have no clue what I'm doing," I said, jerking my view between Kevin and the road. He'd pushed himself backward into his seat, arms extended in front, palms on the dashboard. The swooshing noises of frantic breathing came from his puckered lips.

I slapped his chest. "Now!"

"Right. Right. Sorry, man. I just, I never been in a car chase before," he said blinking rapidly. "Always looked so mellow on TV. Crazy real when you're—" I swerved hard right onto a side street and floored the gas. "In one."

He dug into his pocket, retrieved his phone, and after a few seconds told me to turn left at the next signal.

"We need a plan to ditch these cops," he said. Fortunately for us, the entire surrounding area had turned pitch black. Rain crashed onto my windshield like a fire hose, and angry wind gusts threatened to roll my entire car every few seconds. A hefty challenge to my driving skills, but if I was having a tough time, so were the men in blue chasing me.

"We gotta use this weather to our advantage," Kevin said. "Ditch the car somewhere. Make a run for it."

"No way I'm ditching my baby."

"Then I guess we both goin' to jail."

"That's the kinda crap you see in movies. This is real," I said, stating the obvious.

"You think of something."

But my friend had a solid point. The car was old. And going to prison was not my idea of fun.

"Find me a place along the Mississippi. Maybe a pier."

We zipped past an old rust bucket of a tractor plodding along the road in the rain as Kevin struggled to scroll, zoom, and pan his tiny phone screen. Finally, he found something. "Got it. Turn right here and head down Highway 75 for a couple of miles. There's something we can use there."

Sirens and flashing lights all continued blaring from at least three cop cars following us.

I yanked the steering wheel hard right, screeching around a tight corner onto Highway 75, then opened her up and sped south, the red and blue lights in my rear view shrinking. For a few minutes hail pelted my windshield so hard that the sirens stopped. Traveling south on the highway, we approached an old grain mill transport contraption, as the mighty Mississippi flowed parallel a hundred yards on our right, on the opposite side of the huge levy. A gravel road appeared within my headlight view, ahead on our right, sloping up the side of the levy at an angle and presumably leading down toward the river on the opposite side.

"Turn here. Turn here," said Kevin, jabbing his finger into the air.

We careened off the pavement, splashing through a puddle, kicking up gravel and sand, then wound our way up over the levy and back down the river side of the earthen mass. Half the distance to the river the road dead-ended into a wood-planked pier.

No cops in my rear view.

I slowed to ten miles per hour, looked at Kevin and nodded. We shared the same thought so I pointed the car at the pier–dead straight ahead–shifted to neutral, grabbed Scott's loaded gun, then looked again at Kevin and shouted, "Now."

We each opened our doors and fell out of the BMW, rolling out onto the deck as buckets of rain dumped everywhere.

I landed on my elbows. My chin smacked against the ground. I stood, jostled my jaw, and with headlights leading the way, watched as my car—my baby since college graduation, the vehicle that brought us to Louisiana—crawled down the deck toward the Mississippi, toward certain death by submergence.

The Beemer continued another hundred feet before diving front-end first into the river, dousing the lights and drowning my now former ride.

And the box full of items I'd made as a child.

And my phone. With Tammy's number.

*Dammit.*

I kicked myself for not thinking to grab these. In the panic, my brain had let me down big time.

Rain soaked my clothes. Kevin looked like he'd gone swimming in his jeans and t-shirt, but he had something hidden underneath the front of his jacket, protected.

"Tell me you grabbed the shoebox," I said.

He smiled.

*Whew.*

"How about my cell?" I asked.

He shook his head. "Just the iPad."

*Better than nothing.*

I crouched. Kevin motioned for me to follow before the cops caught up. I tucked the pistol into the rear waist of my pants, then we hustled into the nearby brush and continued away from the scene, in stealth mode, wading through the weeds in a southerly direction along the river.

I wondered if gators prowled the riverbanks, if my ignorance would get us eaten, a thought that helped my legs move faster as I double-checked to make sure I still had the weapon, just in case.

We were a hundred yards downriver before four flashing sheriff's cars arrived on scene. A total of six officers exited vehicles, guns drawn, waving flashlights, and walking in marching fire position to the end of the pier. With the front two-thirds of my car submerged, stuck in the river mud, the ass end protruded upward to the thundering night sky.

Unseen, we exited the reeds and jogged south in the rain for another couple of miles toward Point Clair. Several patrol cars whizzed by us on a dirt road, in the opposite direction, but with the downpour and low visibility, we blended into the night like two dark gray chameleons resting on a black boulder.

Without the digital map on Kevin's phone we would already be in jail.

Rain crashed down, but the relatively dry area under the generous canopy of a grand oak tree off some random side road provided a bit of shelter, so we dialed Adam's cell.

"I ain't supposed to talk with y'all," he said.

Kevin piped in. "Tell him we need more info about Jack."

I covered the lower part of Kevin's phone, shushing him. Lightning flashed, illuminating clouds and the surrounding area, followed by an immediate crack of thunder.

Pain throbbed from my shoulder and swollen ankle, but I transformed it into strength to continue moving forward with my quest. I still had so many unanswered questions.

"Please, we need to talk more about your brother, Jack, and the treasure and more details about his murder. I have a copy of the map."

Adam was silent for a beat.

"That's impossible. There's only one copy of that godforsaken paper."

I narrowed my eyes and wiped the drips of water sliding down my forehead. "A wood compass somehow complements the map. We need the compass to find the treasure."

Nothing but static.

"Hello?" I asked.

"Tell me where to meet y'all."

I gave Adam instructions to meet outside a residence off Highway 141.

He said he'd be there in a bit.

Kevin and I huddled under the oak tree. I wanted to talk with Tammy, tell her what had happened and make sure she was safe. But her number was stored in a phone at the bottom of the Mississippi.

Eventually, Adam rolled up in a beige, eighties-model Cadillac, and motioned for us to get in.

With the doors open, we drenched the interior of Adam's car. The scowl on Adam's face hinted he hadn't slept in days.

"Show me the map," he said to me as I settled into the front passenger seat, soaked, before slamming the door shut.

I tried to keep water off the drawing as I slid it from my pocket. But as I unfolded the paper, Adam snatched the map out of my hand.

With a lost gaze he said, "Impossible."

"Not sure what you mean."

He grunted. "This is exactly like the original, but it's a copy." He turned the paper over. "I've seen the original and this one is different in texture, shading, and how these here lines are drawn."

I stuck out my lower lip. "How 'bout that."

Without warning, he dug out a lighter from his jacket, flicked it to life, and held the tiny yellow flickering flame to the map corner.

Kevin leaned forward from the rear seat of the car and swiped the map out of Adam's hand. "Dude! What the hell?"

"The treasure's cursed," Adam said, holding the still flaming lighter in his hand. "Trust me. I'm doing y'all a favor. Nothing good can come from this map. My brother died because of the damned thing. My life's a toilet bowl full of shit because of this map. And that's the tip of the iceberg. You two have no idea what you're doing. Hand it back. We gotta destroy this thing."

I looked away from Adam, out the passenger side window into the howling wind and rain, with darkness staring back at me. The light scent of burning paper filled the air.

"I want to know more about the wood compass," I said. "Details."

"Won't do you no good without the map. Y'all need both pieces. Give it back."

Kevin folded the map and stuffed it into his pocket.

Adam released the lighter button, darkness swept through the car interior, and he leaned his head back, looking up at the cracked interior ceiling.

"Amuse me," I said. "Assume we don't have the map and tell us about the wood compass."

Adam contemplated my suggestion, licked his lips, then said, "Okay, what the hell." He tossed the lighter onto the center console. "The wood compass would be like any other mathematical compass, except it's, well, unique. They called it a double compass. There are two letters, 'W' and 'E', and two numbers, '180' and '360' inscribed on the side. You line up the letters on the compass with the letters on the map and draw a semi-circle arc. Then you do the same with the numbers. The point where the two arcs meet, that's supposedly the location of the treasure."

I nodded slowly, picturing the images in my head. "You've never seen the compass."

"Hell, yeah, I have. In fact, I had the damned thing. Until yesterday. Scott offered me a wad of cash and to pay off the balance of my house if I gave him the compass. O'course I jumped at the chance, but if he's got a way of getting the map, he'll be close to finding the treasure. If the gold even exists. But then he'll be the one gonna have to deal with the curse."

"The treasure does exist."

"Hold on a minute there, son. How the hell y'all know that?"

"Same way I knew which items in your house belonged to Jack. Same way I made a sketch of the map you just tried to torch. I can't exactly explain how or why I know these things, and there's no easy way to tell you what I'm about to tell you."

Adam stared at me. Somber. Blank. No response.

"Back at your house, you nailed what's going on here," I said. "I realize how crazy this sounds, but Jack's spirit lives inside me, reincarnated somehow. I'm John, but a skiing accident unlocked a ton of Jack's memories. They're inside my head like an extra hard drive."

Adam pushed himself against his car door, eyes as wide as golf balls. He looked down, blinking. "If you're trying to tell me you're some kind of back-from-the-grave version of my brother, you're fuckin' nuts. No way in hell."

I shifted in my seat, leaning towards Adam. "Relax, I'm not your brother, but I'm telling you, this spirit inside my body is Jack's. And he's telling me the treasure is real."

He continued his stare for a moment, then a smug look came over him. "Okay mister spiritual miracle, answer me this: when Jack and I were five years old, we were playing out in our backyard and he did something to me. Gross. Describe that scene to me. Only Jack would know."

"It's not like that, Adam, I can't just—" A thought hit me. A memory.

"You can't just what?"

"Pee in your mouth," I said, looking out the front windshield, dazed.

"Say what?" Kevin asked from the back seat.

"When we were five, Jack peed in your mouth," I said, turning back to Adam.

Adam covered his forehead with his hand. "Holy. Fucking. Shit. Tell me right now how the hell you know that. Nobody knows that happened."

"Like I said, I have no idea how this all works. But I have all the memories from when your twin brother walked this earth. His spirit is inside me. Or something."

Adam pointed at me. "Shit. If the treasure wasn't cursed, we could all be rich."

I smiled. "I don't believe in curses."

Kevin apparently had the same idea as me because we both nodded simultaneously. "We could actually go after this shit ourselves."

"I got an idea." Adam fired up the ignition, backed up, slammed on the brakes, and put the gear shift handle into drive. "We gotta go."

# CHAPTER 61

"**Y**our brother's dead," I told Adam as he drove way faster than he should with the approaching hurricane.

"No shit."

*Get a grip on yourself!*

"I mean, his body, or at least what we think is his body, almost fully intact, skin and everything, was excavated an hour ago by the sheriff's forensics team."

He shook his head. "No way. If he died back in '78, he'd be nothing but a bunch of bones by now."

"I know what I saw. He was sealed in a fifty-five-gallon drum. Maybe the moisture and bugs and things were unable to decompose the body, which looked like you, but . . ." I scanned Adam up and down, "about fifty pounds less and preserved, like a body that had been dead only a few years. Tight, gray skin. Similar hairline." My stomach turned over again as I pictured the body.

Adam rubbed his hand across the length of his shiny head. "Having a hard time with this."

"He looked peaceful, like he was taking a nap," I said, lying to help keep his focus on not getting us killed in some tragic car crash.

"Y'know, at one time, Jack had the map," Adam said. "And the compass. Both pieces to the puzzle. I told him not to talk about the treasure with anyone. Some people get weird when they talk about money. That's a fact. Greed has a funny way of getting under the skin of most folks. Probably the reason the gold is cursed. But he trusted his buddy, Scott. They'd been searching for over a year by the time he got his hands on both pieces, in fact, after we graduated from Thibodaux High School back in '67, Jack went to work as a mechanic at the local airport and got his commercial pilot's license within a year. Fascinated with airplanes and anything that could fly. He met Tammy on a plane. She was twenty-one and he was twenty-four and—"

"I know all this," I said, interrupting, and waving my hand for him to get on with whatever point he was trying to make.

"Well, short story long, fast forward three years to 1976. Some rich guy hired Jack to fly a chartered flight round trip from New Orleans to Paris and Cairo. Some archeologist named Amr something-or-other."

"And?"

Adam switched his windshield wiper speed to "high" and continued. "So the story went that while they was over in Africa, something happened and the guy needed to make a quick escape. Apparently, as Jack told the story to me, the military was shooting at them as they was takin' off. They all escaped, but the old man took one to the chest, a lung I think, as he boarded the plane. Jack tried to patch the guy up with the on-board first aid kit, but he needed a hospital. No joke, his dying words were, and I'll never forget this: *Find love and do something great in this world, and the treasure chest full of gold is yours. But beware of the curse of Le Trésor Fatale. Tell no one. The map is behind an oil painting of Jacques Lafayette in my Baton Rouge home. I have no heirs.'* Then he told Jack he had permission to break into his house and steal the map, *'but whatever you do, don't let the witch know.'* It sounds clichéd, but the dude handed Jack a crusty old leather satchel, spit out some blood, and keeled over right there on the floor of the plane."

"Let me guess. The satchel had the wood compass inside."

"Bingo."

I nodded my head. "That's how he found out about the curse."

"Yup."

The front left tire of Adam's Cadillac smashed into a massive pothole, splashing water up under the wheel well, slowing us down.

"And the map—I'm assuming he got hold of it somehow."

"Not exactly."

"Jack returned to Thibodaux, where we was both livin' at the time and called me up and we talked, but didn't tell me none of the details. Drove me nuts. But then he dragged me out to a local bar and we met with Scott and told us the whole story, everything I'm telling y'all now, except the part about the satchel and the compass, only the map. He left the part about the compass out, but told me later. Scott offered to break into the old man's home and get the map from the safe, but Jack told him not to go alone. He was afraid he'd magically invoke the curse, but Scott thought the curse was a bunch of hogwash. After watchin' that archeologist die in his arms, Jack didn't want anyone else to die, let alone his best friend."

"Interesting."

"Somehow, Jack and Scott figured out where the old man's house was, broke in, found the painting of Jacques Lafayette, busted open the safe behind it, and stole the map. Remember, there was no internet at the time, so they had to do research, as best they could, by using the local libraries and interviewing a ton of people who knew folklore surrounding the treasure."

"Did Jack ever show the compass to Scott?"

"Good question. I don't think so. He gave me the compass to hold for safe keepin'. Told me to make a replica and keep both hidden, as an insurance policy, in case the curse came true. But somehow Scott found out decades later I had the compass. Somethin' inside me wanted to give the damned thing to him, especially after causing me so much heartache over the years, so yesterday I figured what the hell. If I could live the rest of my life without a damned mortgage payment, so be it. I sold the compass to him."

Speeding south in Adam's Cadillac through driving rain, I closed my eyes, desperate to figure out our next move. Images flashed again like a slideshow. Tammy. Gold coins. Treasure map. Scott's contorted face as he murdered Jack. Slow, unraveling emotions mixed together, swirling, like melted wax crayons overflowing a simmering black kettle.

Fingers snapped in front of my face. "Hey. Hey. Wake up, dude. We're here."

I jolted awake, we exited the car. Kevin grabbed the shoebox and followed me to the rear.

Adam popped open his trunk and extracted a folded blue and white beach towel. He looked at Kevin, then me. Rain pelted my hair and back side, dripping off my nose as I nestled the shoebox inside my jacket, safe and dry.

Adam unwrapped the towel, revealing a wooden object like the image Tammy had texted me.

"Holy shit," Kevin said.

"C'mon," Adam said, motioning us to walk, while also protecting the compass under his leather jacket.

We hustled several blocks to The Bulldog, a cold, dark bar, but before I walked inside, I stood on the sidewalk, staring up at the restaurant sign through steady rainfall.

An odd feeling bounced around in my gut.

Adam skidded to a stop next to me. "Whatsamatter?" he asked.

"Roberto's. This used to be Roberto's Bar and Grill. But the building is . . . different. Used to have more windows on the front," I said.

Adam nodded. "Amazing. Jack and I hung out here all the time when it was Roberto's. But that restaurant burned down in the eighties. They built this place in the same footprint and changed the name a bunch of times since then, but yeah, it used to be Roberto's and there were, I think, four or five windows in the front. Freaky."

We walked into the place. Stone dead. Except for a honey of a bartender cleaning beer mugs with a rag.

"Howdy, Adam," she said, waving. Adam guided us into an otherwise empty back room, except for the big screen television hanging in the corner and pool table.

"Here's the compass," Adam said, handing the object to me. "I'll be right back." He disappeared back out to the bar area.

I set the shoebox onto the pool table, lifted the lid, dug around inside, found my youthful drawing, and carefully laid the map onto the felt. Kevin fished out the more detailed map and set it next to my crayon drawing.

Identical.

I set the wooden compass on top of the detailed map as Adam walked back into the room with three beers, then placed them on a nearby table.

I overheard the newscast on the television and looked up.

". . . body of a man found outside the evacuated National Insurance building off Highway 141 near Bayou Goula. The sheriff's office is searching for this man . . ." The television showed a low resolution, blurry picture of me, apparently while making my escape from the dig site. ". . . for a possible connection to the alleged murder. Police say the man they are looking for is thirty-eight-year-old John Bastian, along with his accomplice, up-and-coming comedian Kevin Traylor, both of Newport Beach, California. Police say Mr. Bastian knew exactly where the body was buried, but when they tried to arrest him, both men escaped.

*of the Mississippi, but Mr. Bastian and Mr. Traylor's bodies were*
*nowhere to be found and they are assumed to be alive, armed and*
*dangerous. If you have seen either of these men or know of their*
*whereabouts, you are urged to call . . ."*

I shook my head, dumbfounded.

"Ha ha. They think you murdered yourself," Kevin said.

My heart pummeled my chest. Fast. The room started spinning.

"Dude, you don't look so good," Kevin said. "Your face is all pale. Here, man, you sit down on this here chair. You need something to drink." He reached down and handed me a cold beer. Crazy thirsty, I drained the brew in three gulps then wiped my lips with my forearm.

"Thanks, man." I stood straight, took a deep breath, and leaned over the pool table.

"Here," Adam said, tossing some pencils onto the map. I slid a pencil into each of the two holes in the compass. Adam reached out a closed fist to me. "You're gonna need this." He rolled open his fingers, revealing a hefty brass object. I remembered the shiny hinge from my visions. After retrieving the metal piece from his open palm, I slid the wood parts together. Everything fit snug, like a properly torqued lug nut.

With the map and wood compass in our possession, I placed the wood pointer on the dot next to the 180, drew an arc with the pencil, then repeated the same procedure for the number 360 with the other side. The two arcs joined in the lower area of the map, in the middle of what looked like a snake, which I initially thought might be some satanic symbol.

But no. Not a snake.

The Mighty Mississippi.

In seconds, I had correlated the exact shape to the Google Map on Kevin's iPad, which pinpointed the area of Sunshine.

"No, can't be. That's too big of an area," I said, mostly to myself. "Must be several square miles."

Adam chimed in. "Correct." He smiled and narrowed his eyes. "But you need to use the other part of the compass, too. Not many people know this, but this bad boy is two maps blended into one. Here, let me show you."

He pointed to the upper right corner of the document, which I had assumed was part of the overall map, but in fact showed an inset, or zoomed-in portion, of the bigger map. He folded the map, creating a "new" map. Now that we knew the main area represented Sunshine, the folded inset would tell us the precise location of the treasure.

Or so we hoped.

With shaking hands, Adam took the compass from me. "Watch this." He paused. "I've been waiting thirty-nine years to do this." He drew two separate arcs, this time using the opposite side of the compass and the two points next to the "W" and "E" indicators. Sure enough, they crossed. I picked up the map to study the details.

The eastern side of Sunshine had several houses located off Route 991. I compared Google Maps to the spot indicated on the treasure map. If the treasure existed, the location pointed to a recessed area in the backyard of one of the properties. I showed the location to Adam.

He nodded. "Yup. That's where the old wagon trail used to be. Been there forever. They built Route 991 more or less right on top there." He looked closer at the Google Map, going back and forth between my phone screen and the treasure map. "That's where the old Stanwick Mansion was, but they tore that down several decades ago and built a couple of new houses. Big deal, all over the news back in the day."

"I think we should hunker down and wait for this hurricane to blow over, that's some serious wind outside," Kevin said.

"We don't have time. I can feel it," I said, stuffing the map back into the shoebox, grabbing one of the clay voodoo dolls and jamming it into my jeans pocket.

"Fine, but if I die, you deal with my mom. She gonna be pissed," Kevin said, snapping both pieces of the compass in half and tossing them into a trash can. "Don't need that no more."

The three of us hurried out to Adam's car, needing to head north a few miles to where the Stanwick Mansion used to be.

Through the driving rain we wound our way up the deserted two-lane paved highway, parallel to the Mississippi, then stopped and pulled off into a drainage swale caked with overgrown grass. The front tires kicked up buckets of water as we parked on the opposite side of the road in a gravel turn out. I stared east across the road, to a white picket fence and the black gloom beyond. Several lightning strikes hit in succession, illuminating the entire property. I was able to make out a plantation house set back on the parcel about a hundred yards away, at the end of a winding gravel driveway. Two brick pilasters, with glass gas lamp lights affixed to the top of each, sat on either side of the driveway entrance.

"This is it," Adam said.

"Whatchoo thinkin' we gonna do? Just walk out there into someone's backyard in the middle of all this dark storm and what? Dig for a treasure that may or may not be there?" Kevin asked.

My friend had a point.

Adam reached behind him, pulled out a backpack from the rear seat, opened it, reached in and pulled out a fancy GPS unit.

"Here." He handed the device to me. "Use this to pinpoint the exact location of where we need to focus."

I cross-referenced the location from the Google Map to the paper treasure map. Adam was correct. I punched the coordinates of the location on the GPS, which gave accuracy within a five-foot radius. If the map read true and our coordinates were accurate for the treasure location, there should have been a large tree somewhere beyond the house, in what I would have referred to as the backyard of the property, which could easily have been several dozen acres.

Adam exited the Cadillac, opened the trunk and pulled something else out. Curious, I walked to the rear of the vehicle.

A shovel lay on the ground next to two long, black flashlights. Adam held a metal detector in his hand as he slammed the trunk closed with a splash. He smiled. "Tonight's the night, brother. We're gonna need these."

"That thing's not gonna work in the rain," I said, pointing to the metal detector.

"You bet it will," Adam replied. He walked across the road toward the driveway.

Kevin sat inside with his arms crossed. I knocked on the window and he cracked open the door. "This is crazy, I know," I said, "but I have to do this. I really wish you'd come."

I waited a few moments. He uncrossed his arms, pushed opened the door, and exited into the rain. "Fine. And they call me the crazy one." He put his hand out and I gave him five, shooting massive pain through my right shoulder, which I tried to ignore. I hobbled along across the street, nursing my left ankle.

We caught up to Adam and continued walking in the dark with flashlights lighting our way across the wet, grass-covered front yard of God-knows-who's house. No lights were on inside the house. Nobody home, or so we thought. We passed several small fruit trees and since there were no property fences, we easily navigated into the backyard.

"Hand me that GPS," Adam said. I complied and he followed the display map on the GPS unit.

We walked around for five minutes. He stopped.

"Should be right about here." He handed the GPS back to me, turned on the metal detector, and started waving it back and forth in an arc pattern a few inches above the soaking wet ground.

A slow, steady beep—nothing—pulsated from the device.

"We better find the damned treasure here, with all these maps and machines and shit." Kevin said.

Damned fine point.

I shrugged, scanning our surroundings. Nothing special. Only deep, dark rain and the steady push of a strong easterly wind.

Adam continued pacing back and forth in a strategic pattern, fanning the metal detector. Then, the frequency of the beeping increased. He homed in on a spot near a large oak tree. "Here we go. Somethin's down there. Start diggin'," Adam told Kevin.

Kevin rolled his eyes. "I see how it is. The black guy does the digging," he said, joking, as he swiped the shovel from me and started clawing through the saturated soil, which was relatively soft to chew through. As he dug, I noticed something odd about the hole, as though someone had dug here recently. Several two-inch-diameter roots had been severed by something sharper than our shovel, possibly an ax. And the deeper Kevin dug, the more I noticed a variation in the soil striations, which confirmed the dirt had, in fact, been dug previously. Sure enough, two feet down, Kevin clanked something metallic with the shovel.

"Got something," he said.

"Keep digging around the edges," Adam said, shining his flashlight down into the hole to illuminate our find.

A rectangular object began to take shape, the rain cleaning off the surface as he dug. A box with metal bands clasped around the perimeter—a foot and a half long—rose up from the mud. Kevin sank the shovel blade underneath and pried the mass from the grasp of the earth with an odd slurping, suctioning noise, as though we weren't supposed to remove it from its place of rest.

Adam stepped down into the hole, bent over, and examined the clasp. Holding the lock with his fingertips, he looked back up at us.

"Already unlocked."

He cracked open the box, then reached down and extracted what looked like an antique briefcase, the kind with two leather straps buckled shut. There was nothing else in the box.

Flood lights blazed awake from the rear of the house, shining bright onto the rain, grass, fruit trees, dirt, mud and, of course, us. We scurried behind the large tree to hide, but Kevin had left the shovel sticking up out of the hole.

Through the rain we heard an elderly man yell out, muffled. "Whoever the hell y'are, better get off my property. Already called the sheriff."

"Run," Adam said, pushing us out from behind the safety of the tree. We high-tailed it across the lawn back toward our car, with Adam in the lead and Kevin and I following close behind. My ankle shot pain every time my foot landed on the soggy soil. A muzzle flash boomed from the rear porch of the house, probably a shotgun.

After slogging through the rain and darkness, we finally arrived back at the Cadillac. Adam tossed the briefcase to Kevin. "Here."

Adam fired up the engine and we peeled out north. The owner's final shot blasted the my door with an ear-piercing noise that rattled my brain. Fortunately, the outer metal of the Cadillac prevented the pellets from penetrating to the interior.

But I nearly peed myself anyway.

# CHAPTER
# 62

**B**ack on the road, Adam said, panting, "We need to open that briefcase and see if the treasure is inside."

"This thing? No way," Kevin replied.

He wrinkled his nose. "The hell y'all talkin' about?"

"He's right," I said. "Le Trésor Fatale is supposed to be hundreds of gold doubloons, there's no way all that's in that leather thing. It weighs like five pounds and is probably empty. This whole thing has been a huge waste of time."

Energy sapped, disappointment ran through me before my thoughts turned to Tammy, wondering if we should use Adam's phone to call, how she was holding up, if she was crying, if she was sad, if she was still alive.

"We got one way to find out," Kevin said, snapping open his trusty pocket knife, and sawing through leather straps.

"Wait," Adam said. "There might be something danger-ous inside."

"But we gotta see," Kevin said.

I held a flashlight on the object. He inhaled a long, drawn out breath. "Moment of truth, gentlemen." He finished slicing the second strap, peered inside, reached his forearm in and pulled out a yellowed, stained envelope with frayed edges. He checked inside the case. "Nothing else, only this old paper envelope."

I clicked off the flashlight.

Kevin tossed the briefcase on the floor, leaving the envelope in his wet hand.

Adam and I exchanged glances. "Hurry, open it up," Adam said, swerving us back into the center of the lane.

Kevin repositioned the knife, sliced through the top of the envelope and with his fingertips, carefully slid out a single, folded piece of paper. Smiling, he unfolded the parchment.

"It's a handwritten letter," Kevin said.

"Read it," I said.

"It's in French."

"Wait a minute," I said, reaching into my pocket and retrieving the clear plastic container with the partially burned letter I'd stolen from the Sheriff, the one from inside the drum with Jack's body. Kevin handed me the full letter and I held both papers next to each other.

An identical match.

Adam spoke up after clearing his throat. "They make us take French here in Louisiana. I'm a bit rusty, but I got a translation app on my phone."

A clap of thunder shook the entire car and we all glanced outside into the darkness.

Adam pulled off to the side of the road, Kevin handed him the letter, then Adam read the message to himself, moving his lips with slight whispers as he typed the entire French message into his phone. A minute later, he said, "Okay, y'all gonna like this."

He nodded and continued.

"Best I can tell, in a nutshell, the message says, in formal terms: *Dearest Uncle Jerome, as you may have heard, we have decided to move back to France, as the economic climate here in the U.S. is not optimal. It is imperative I provide you with the location of our family's fortune my father left behind, in case, God forbid, we do not make it to France. My hope, should this tragedy befall us, is that you may one day continue his legacy of helping to ease the suffering of sick children around the world. No doubt you have used the map I drew, along with my unique double-compass design to find the location of this letter. Once the gold is in your capable hands, please do as I wish. It is what father would have wanted. The chest is located two-hundred and twenty paces due north from the southernmost tip of the Towhead located within the area found using the land survey information on the back of this letter, which pinpoints the precise location of the gold. Yours truly, Bridgette Lafayette-Stanwick.*"

Adam flipped both papers over.

"There's something written on the back of both, but not much on the small piece." He studied the papers for a moment and nodded his head. "A towhead is an island. But I don't know what these letters and numbers are." He handed the letter to me and the back was written:

*T.10S. R.13E.*

Having studied land surveying as part of my real estate licensing program, I quickly realized these were township and range coordinates, which would give us a thirty-six square mile area to narrow the search. I pulled up a USGS quad map on my phone, zoomed in on that particular township square, and showed it to Adam.

"The Bayou Goula Towhead," Adam said, pointing to an island in the Mississippi. "I know exactly where this is, but I haven't been there in decades." He paused, stroked his thick, ruffled goatee, and looked back at the map. "We need to get there before the brunt of the storm hits."

As he explained the location to us I studied the small, burned piece of paper, remembering why Jack had burned it.

"I don't understand. The storm's already here," I said.

Adam chuckled. "This ain't a hurricane quite yet, son. This here's only the rain and thunderstorms from the outer bands of the storm. The extreme outer bands. The welcomin' party for the actual event. This hurricane is gonna get fifty times worse before the night is over. If the treasure is where I think it is, we have to get there before the storm surges up through the Mississippi and buries the location underwater."

"Let's go then," I said.

"Wait," Adam said.

I stopped, looked at Kevin, and stared at Adam holding the letter in his hand, shaking his head.

"The hurricane's not our only problem."

"I don't understand. What could be worse than the hurricane ruining our chances for getting the treasure?" I asked. The night sky lit up brightly before another clap of thunder.

"Dammit," Kevin said from the back seat. "I say we get the hell inside. Somewhere safe."

Adam grabbed the flashlight from me and shined a bright beam in my face.

"I'm, uh, not gonna be able to join you fellas on the island," Adam said.

"Bullshit, we're a team now. You're coming with us. C'mon, let's get out of here," I said, motioning to the wet road outside.

"Can't. My daddy drowned on that island. Our daddy, or whatever."

Silence filled the Cadillac. I swallowed hard.

That meant the dad of my previous life, Jack Bachman's father, died right next to where the treasure was.

*An interesting coincidence?*

Adam shook his head. "Good news, though. Tammy knows the island well. Y'all need to go to her home and tell her what we know, but whatever you do. Do. Not. Tell. Scott."

But now that we had figured out several key pieces to the puzzle, hearing Tammy's name forced me to focus back on her. At that point my mind, heart, and soul tugged at Tammy. Whatever I did at that moment, whatever action I took needed to be a part of helping me get me back to Tammy. Adam's suggestion about bringing Tammy in on the hunt suited me just fine.

"No worries. Kevin and I will sneak into Tammy's place, make sure she's okay, then see what she knows about all this. There's something she's not telling us," I said.

With a furrowed brow, Kevin said, "That's a bad idea. She specifically told us not to go there, man."

"She's been married for over thirty years to the only guy on the planet who knows more about the treasure than we do," I said. "We have to ask her more questions. Plus, she knows the island, like Adam said. Worth the risk, as long as we're careful."

"Dude, we got the letter and the instructions on where the treasure is. We don't need a tour guide. We don't need Tammy. We need to get to higher ground," Kevin said.

"I'm being guided—by what, I have no idea—to go see Tammy right now. Call it gut instinct. Something else is going on here. If my gut says to go to her house, we need to listen."

"Need to listen to the hot air coming out your mouth," Kevin said. "Dude, the man who shot you lives there. Cops are after us. A hurricane is coming. You be trippin'. Ain't no way I'm going there. Uh uh."

"Adam, I say you come with us to Tammy's house," I said. "We park around back, you walk out front, distract whoever Scott has guarding the place, we sneak in through the rear of her home, break Tammy free, ask her questions, get the answers, whatever they are, meet you a block away, we bolt to the island in the bayou and find the treasure. You're the only one with a car, mine's in the Mississippi, and Scott has Tammy's car. We need you all in on this."

Kevin looked at me with unblinking eyes.

"Screw it," said Adam, as he sped us back onto the highway. "But only to Tammy's. Ain't goin' on that damned island."

We drove to Tammy and Scott's home and cruised along out front. With the hurricane approaching, the reporters must have had other stories to cover. The front yard was deserted, except for one car.

Adam parked two blocks away. We split up, with Adam walking toward the front yard and us walking toward the back.

Thick raindrops pelted my face as Kevin and I jumped over their backyard fence, then hustled to the back door. Instead of Tammy, though, we found a middle-aged brunette with pretty, perfectly round eyes and a cute nose standing in the rear doorway. I immediately sensed a connection to her.

I expected her to freak out. After all, two strangers just appeared from the dark at her back door. But no, she only smiled and introduced herself as Jenny. "My mom said you might try to come by," she said, inviting us inside.

Kevin and I stepped into the kitchen, shook off the water, and Jenny promptly motioned for us to follow her into the same living room where, less than twenty-four hours ago, I had met Tammy and enjoyed an engaging conversation. Until she had given me the boot.

"So, John, Adam said you and your buddy are hunting for the same treasure my dad's been looking for," Jenny said. She had a tattoo of a cross behind her ear and one of a heart on her left wrist.

"I'm sorry, but is Tammy here?" I asked.

As if on cue, Tammy came down the staircase. I stood to give her a loving embrace, but seeing the woman I'd recently assumed had been killed at the hotel, my knees wobbled and I almost fell. Holding me up, she felt warm and trusting and familiar, like an old family member I hadn't seen in ages.

But I needed to get us to true safety. If Scott barged in, he wouldn't think twice at a second chance to take me out. I touched my fingers to the gun in my waist, to reassure myself.

A dog barked upstairs, then a moment later, a golden retriever shuffled down the shag carpeted stairs. He stopped at the bottom, looked at us, and barked again. Twice. He backed up.

"No, Charlie. No barking inside. Stop it," Jenny told him, snapping her fingers.

He made that whining sound dogs make when they are confused, but then he cocked his head to the side and ambled toward me, head down and tail wagging. He licked his black lips as he headed toward me.

"Interesting," Tammy said. "He normally barks at strangers until they leave. Not the friendliest dog to outsiders. Great guard dog." She petted his back as he came within biting distance, sat in front of me, and made more whining noises.

I moved my hand up to his head, allowed him to sniff, then petted him. He started panting and wagged his tail faster.

"I've honestly never seen him take to someone like this before. He's treating you like family," she said.

Without moving my head, I glanced to Kevin and shrugged. "Seems like a friendly pooch to me," I said with a cautious smile.

The resemblance of Jenny to her mother struck me as uncanny. She looked nothing like Scott.

"Like you said earlier," I said to Tammy in a hushed voice, "something bigger than the treasure is hovering over us. That probably sounds creepy and I honestly can't explain it any better than that, but can you come with us right now? We need to get you two out of here."

She looked up at the ceiling and slumped her shoulders forward. "I can't possibly be of any help."

Some rustling noises came from outside, mixed with wind and rain.

At risk of offending Jenny, I asked about her father, Scott.

But she chuckled. "Scott's my step-dad. I never knew my real dad, Mom doesn't like to talk about him much, other than something about this month being the same month he died. Thirty-eight years ago, right mom?" Tammy nodded. "Eight months before I was born."

"I'm probably getting way too personal here, but I'm assuming she lives here with you guys?" I asked Tammy.

Before Tammy could respond, Jenny said, "I help out with their cleaning." She looked at her mom. "Call me a part time maid, but I also work as a lab tech at a local cement factory." She paused. "Me and my kids live a few miles from here. Husband kicked the bucket three years ago. Liver failure. Loved his liquor. But good riddance."

I stared at Jenny, thoughts running through my mind.

The doorbell rang.

Shit.

Jenny stood, walked to the door, checked the peep hole, squeezed her eyes shut, and covered her mouth. She took a step backwards, glaring at Tammy. "He's not supposed to be here," she said.

"Who?" Kevin asked.

"Dad's friend, Mike, he—"

The doorknob exploded. Mike stormed in and pushed her aside. "Where the hell's that Californian son-of-a-bitch?" he demanded.

He looked at the three of us, arms flared away down his sides to make himself look bigger, like some bodybuilder moron. "Well, well, well. Who do we have here with you, Tammy? These clowns are the two fuck-os getting in the way of my treasure."

I stole a glance at Tammy, then Kevin.

"Get the hell out of my house," Tammy said, stepping toward Mike.

Mike lifted his "Geno's Bar & Grill" t-shirt, revealing a matching silver belt buckle and wood-handled eight-shot revolver tucked behind. He snatched the weapon from his crotch, cocked the hammer and fired off one round toward Tammy.

# CHAPTER 63

In a split second, we all dove in different directions of the family room to avoid being hit by Mike's thirty-eight.

To my shock, he missed Tammy, shattering a crystal lamp into a thousand shards.

"Next one ain't goin' over your head."

The dog barked.

Mike shot toward the dog, striking Charlie in the leg, who winced and hobbled upstairs, leaving a blood trail.

I thought about firing back with Scott's gun, but other instincts took over. With Mike's attention focused on the dog and since I was closest, I barreled toward him, lowering the boom of my left shoulder—my strong, working shoulder—into his gut, tackling him onto the wood floor. His gun popped out of his hand before he had a chance to fire another round.

"Run!" I yelled to Tammy, Jenny, and Kevin, as I stood and kicked the gun away toward the kitchen, at least fifteen feet away from the man lying on the floor, groaning. My cohorts raced into the kitchen and disappeared around the corner.

Mike started to stand, but I kneed him in the ribs, knocking him back onto the floor. I sped toward the kitchen, scooping up the revolver on my way.

The back door flopped open in the wind, rain pouring in the darkness outside.

A distant muted voice called to me through a gust.

"C'mon!"

Kevin.

I zoomed through the doorway, following shadows around the side of the house and back out to the front. A sixty-six Ford Mustang sat parked next to Adam's Cadillac. His hefty body waddled along through the rain to the driver's side. We all slid inside, slammed our doors, and Adam floored the beast forward.

Speeding away in the Cadillac, past the front yard, I turned to see Mike stumble out the front door before firing three more rounds at us.

All misses, thank God.

"That's the second time tonight I've been shot at in this damned car," I said mostly to myself, covering my head with my arms. "Real winner, that guy, carrying around two loaded guns. And you say he's a friend of Scott's?" I asked Tammy, who nodded from the rear seat.

I peered out the rear window between Kevin and Tammy. Within seconds, two headlights appeared behind us. Gaining speed.

"Wait," I said. "Where's Jenny?"

"She stayed behind," Tammy said. "That bastard shot Charlie and now he's coming after us. She's a big girl and has a ton of friends close by. She'll get Charlie to a vet and find somewhere safe to ride out the hurricane."

*Good.*

"Faster. Faster," I said to Adam, glancing down at the revolver and popping out the cylinder. "I managed to get the gun, but there's only one bullet left."

Both panting in the rear seat, Tammy and Kevin struggled to catch their breath.

I turned to Tammy. "We know where the treasure is, but aren't sure exactly how to get there."

Adam said to Tammy, "The treasure's buried on the Bayou Goula Towhead, where, I believe you told me once y'all used to do summer explorations as a girl with your parents at a nearby rental house. That creepy, haunted old island in the middle of the Mississippi. The one with that forest of tall, dark eucalyptus trees."

She furrowed her brow. "I don't believe you."

"It's true," I said. "I need you to trust me. Jack would have wanted you to help us find the treasure."

She shifted in her seat, leaning forward and staring into my eyes, like she was trying to find Jack inside my head somewhere.

A moment later, we turned right onto a highway.

"But the hurricane's here and we've got Scott's right-hand man on our tail," she said, pointing her thumb backwards. "That son-of-a-bitch Mike Bixleton. He'll do anything to—"

Mike's Mustang plowed into our rear right fender. We spun out. My stomach turned over several times before we skidded to a stop. Adam shook his head, trying to gain his balance. A bright bang and popping noise came from our right. A window exploded.

"Get us outta here," I yelled as Adam floored the gas again, spitting up mud behind us, and for a second, I thought we'd lost Mike.

But no. He appeared again. Right on our tail.

Adam turned a hard left off the highway, onto a dirt road.

"Hope you know where the hell we're going," I said.

"Just takin' a little detour," he said, white knuckles gripping the steering wheel. He pressed his lips together, then hunched his shoulders forward.

We finally came to a fork in the road, bounced back onto a paved highway and accelerated, with Mike still close behind us.

The brightness of blurred city lights became greater until I realized we were back in town. Mike's car rear-ended us again. My head whipped back. "Hold on," I yelled.

The late hour and approaching hurricane meant a deserted, evacuated town and no witnesses to see the madman chasing us. All the smart people were back home safe in their beds, patiently waiting for the hurricane to leave.

Out of nowhere, the Lafayette ghost appeared in our headlight field, facing us and waving his arms as though saying "stop" in slow motion. Adam slammed on the brakes and skidded, driving right through the geezer.

I jerked my head around just in time. Mike tried to miss the man, too, but overcorrected to the left, jamming his front tire into a curb, rolling the Mustang several times before sliding, upside down, into a depressed section of highway full to the rim with flood waters like a small lake.

Adam skidded to a full stop. Mike's car melted into the water, disappearing within seconds like a swallowed pill. Lafayette had disappeared.

I turned to Adam. "You saw that man. Tell me you saw that man."

He shook his head, looking around. "I saw something jump in front of us, maybe a big dog, or deer, or somethin'."

"At least Mike ain't gonna be shooting at nobody no more," Kevin said.

Tammy chimed in from the rear seat. "Fine. I'm all in. Let's go find us some treasure. Screw Scott and his sick friends once and for all."

# CHAPTER 64

Rain poured down hard, like firehose hard, with an intensity stronger than my California eyes had ever seen.

"I'll drive," Tammy said. "I know this area better than any of y'all." She gave Adam a convincing smile and he complied without haste. Once she sat in the driver's seat, he closed the door for her.

Raising his voice to be heard over the downpour, he said, "Y'all're on your own. My brother died because of the curse, the treasure, Scott, whatever. I'm too much of a chicken shit to keep going. Y'all don't need me. Good luck."

Tammy gave him an understanding look without uttering a word, put the Cadillac into gear, and drove the tank like she'd had ten thousand hours of practice. With Kevin in the rear and me up front, she plowed down Highway 141 past bending trees, through the rain, lightning, and gusts. Within seconds we sped up and over the huge earthen levy and down to a boat dock on the shore across from, according to her, the Bayou Goula Towhead.

Tammy parked, turned to me and said, "Show me what you got."

I slid out the old yellow letter and flipped it over so she could see the rear. "See here, this is the island, and this is apparently where we think the treasure is buried," I said, pointing to an "X" where we marked the approximate location of the two hundred and twenty paces north of the southern tip.

"Scott has no idea of this?" she asked.

"Not that I'm aware of."

"Good."

From Adam's trunk we retrieved three shovels, the metal detector, and a knotted mess of thick hemp rope, then followed Tammy down onto the dock, which bobbed atop the surface of the wave-strewn, white-capped Mississippi. The heavy rain shot down sideways from the darkness beyond, which made looking out over the river impossible. Fortunately, lightning struck so often, we made our way to the boat with barely enough light to avoid falling into the river.

"Get in," Tammy said, pointing to a SunCatcher V322 pontoon boat. She untied the line.

"I ain't gettin' in that thing," Kevin said. "It's black as shit out here, there's a hurricane comin', and we can't even see where the hell we goin'."

I shared his sentiment.

"I know you can't see the island, but now it's your turn to trust me," Tammy said. "It's only about a thousand feet straight out from here. Been there a million times."

The dock rocked back and forth, making standing difficult. Giant claps of thunder boomed and roared from the angry clouds above.

Kevin conceded, saying under his breath, "Puttin' my damn life in your honky hands. Again." He climbed aboard and I patted his soaked back.

Tammy fired up the engine, engaged the transmission, and pushed the throttle full forward. After lurching into the inky black beyond, I lost my balance and fell to my knees. Kevin sat on the outer edge, looking straight ahead.

I stood, grabbing on to the railing, and stepped toward Tammy. "I assume this is your boat."

"Nope. But we're just borrowin' it," she said.

"Great. Another felony."

*But a damned sexy one.*

Tammy handled the boat like a pro.

Each time lightning struck, massive trees appeared and disappeared from behind the black shroud in front of us. The island slowly became more visible, growing larger with each passing second.

Tammy throttled back and after slowing, inched us into the island dock at the southernmost tip before killing the engine and tying down the boat next to a white floatplane with two blue stripes.

*Scott.*

Several small animals, possibly fish—or something else entirely—whirled around in the water, rustling just beneath the surface.

We each took a flashlight Tammy found in a box under the control panel. I held the metal detector and the map. Kevin carried the shovels and rope.

"C'mon," she said. "I know exactly where to go."

Through the driving rain, overgrown grass, and a forest of dense bayou trees, we hiked, slogging through mud, counting each step as a single pace until reaching two hundred paces inland.

"Should be up ahead about twenty more yards," she said.

But as we approached, a well-lit clearing appeared. I pushed aside a soaking wet branch to get a clear view. Situated in front of several construction lights, a silhouetted man was sitting in the operator's chair of a black backhoe that had large letters "SHERIFF" painted on its side, digging his way down into a three-foot-deep hole at the precise location where we needed to be, according to the map.

"Shhh," I said, motioning for them to crouch down.

"We need a plan," Kevin said.

"Scott," I said to my two partners.

Tammy nodded.

"How the hell did he know where this place is?" Kevin asked. "We only knew because of the letter we found in the backyard of that shotgun-happy property owner."

"He had the compass, but not the map. But even with the map, he should've already found the briefcase with the letter. He must've found out or gotten a copy of the letter from someone else. Taken a shortcut."

Before fear could take hold, a growing strength had caught fire in my belly. "There's the man who killed Jack," I said, touching the gun in the back of my waist, then regripping Mike's revolver, popping open the chamber and confirming the single loaded round. Two guns. "I'll be right back." I started to stand.

"No," Tammy said, grabbing at my jacket, pulling me back down. "You do that and you're a dead man." She scanned the area, huffing for more oxygen. "Wait. Say that again."

I pointed to the man on the backhoe. "That guy right there's your husband, right? The man who barged in on us at the hotel?"

She nodded.

"And his name is Scott Jones, right?"

She nodded again, confused.

I studied her face, scanning every line, every feature. "You didn't know he killed your first husband in November 1978."

She stayed in her crouched position, glaring at me, wheels turning in her head. "Holy. Shit." She blinked rapidly, glancing between my face and my right shoulder. "I had my suspicions, but no proof. Dammit, how could I be so naive? I don't know why I didn't see it before. Perfect connection. Wonderful, I spent the last thirty-plus years married to a murderer." Flames raged behind her eyeballs. "I'm gonna kill the son-of-a-bitch myself." She stood and took a step toward the backhoe, but I grabbed her arm and pulled her back down next to Kevin in the weeds.

My heart pounded in my throat, but I managed to place my hands gently under Tammy's jawbone before leaning in, almost touching noses, and staring deep into her gorgeous green eyes. "I've always loved you, Tammy. Can't explain how, but I have, and I always will, no matter what time or place, no matter what age difference we now have. Please let me deal with this guy. He hurt you. You lost your husband. But when he killed Jack, he killed the man of the spirit somehow miraculously living inside me now. Jack's death is on Scott. Scott needs to pay. This is something I have to do. For Jack."

# CHAPTER 65

Tammy tilted her head to the side, wrinkled her dripping wet nose, and said, "Okay. I don't understand, but I'm gonna trust you."

With a total disregard for the approaching hurricane, the threat of death by a murdering bastard a few dozen yards away, and the total ignorance for our overall safety, I kissed Tammy. The world stopped. No more rain. No more lightning. An annoying stress inside me lifted. Weightless, floating on a cushion of air, my body enjoyed a warm sense of love rippling through, with electric sparks surging up my spine. My own form of internal fireworks exploded inside my abdomen, resonating through my core and all four limbs. We were one. A montage of images of Jack's life flashed before my closed eyes. Time was everywhere and nowhere, the same way it was in my coma. A feeling of invincibility came over me.

I pulled away from her lips, breaking the spell. She smiled, biting her lower lip.

"Here. Hold this," I said, handing her Mike's revolver with the single bullet loaded in the chamber. "I'll be right back." I turned, swiped a shovel from Kevin and marched toward the digging machine.

My shoe hit a soft spot and came off, disappearing in the mud. But I charged forward anyway. I needed revenge. For Jack. For Tammy.

My new purpose: take the life of the man who took the life of my spirit the last go-around. Revenge would even the score.

Images of Scott's angry face flashed before me. I wanted to watch him bleed to death, needed to put him through the same hell, to witness his life extinguish.

I tip-toed up to the rear of the backhoe, next to a giant, slow-spinning tire. I extended the shovel and nudged Scott's back with the tip of the spade to get his attention. Completely unaware of my presence, he whipped his head around. "What the hell?" He slowed the engine to idle, climbed down off the machine, shaking his head with disbelief.

I took a single step backwards, raising the shovel like a base-ball bat, ready to swing for my murderous home run of revenge, thoughts turning to the loaded gun in my rear waist.

He walked toward me, determined, confident, cocky, fearless.

But I stood my ground. "Looks like you're doing a bit of digging," I said, twisting my grip harder on the shovel handle.

He stopped, studying my every move, looking at me up and down before glancing around the site. "John Bastian. The bastard who fucked my cheating bitch wife." He nodded. "Son, you're a long way from California."

He stared, grinning, the many years of sun damage crin-kling the skin around his eyes. "This treasure's mine. Always has been." He took another step toward me.

*One more step and I'll pretend to swing, then pull out the gun and blow him away.*

I stepped to the side, matching his arcing path.

"You're lucky I ran out of bullets at the airport. Not this time, though, I got me plenty. Ought to waste your pathetic loser-ass right now." He took another step toward me.

"Like you did with Jack thirty-eight years ago?"

He stopped, gazing at my face, down at the ground, then back up at me. A hint of fear, or perhaps uneasiness. "The hell you talkin' about?"

A flash of lightning stunned the entire clearing. Thunder crashed a second later, echoing off the forest of eucalyptus trees.

"Jack Bachman. Your best friend. 1978. You murdered him."

He straightened his stance and put his hands on his hips, scanning the area again while puffing out his chest. "Damned right I did. Like I'm gonna do to you right now, fuckin' pesky little cocksucker."

He pulled a revolver from behind his waist. Before he could point the weapon at me and with no time to grab my gun, I went Babe Ruth on him. He put his arm up to block. I connected the flat side of the spade with his forearm and heard the crack of bone as the gun fell to the muddy ground.

I dropped the shovel, took two quick steps toward him, and buried my left shoulder hard into his gut, same as with Mike, driving him back several paces before slamming him into the backhoe tire.

Grunting like cavemen, we collapsed onto the ground.

I tried to get a punch in, but he belted my face with an uppercut. A loud clunk rattled my head. Dizziness overcame me. He pushed me off him and I landed on my back in a puddle of mud.

I shook my head to get my bearings, thoughts turning to my gun, but he kicked my ribs. Pain jolted up from my chest.

"You son-of-a-bitch," he said. "How dare you come here and threaten me. Me!" He tried to kick me again, but I caught his foot with both hands and twisted his leg. Fast. He fell backwards onto his front with a splash.

With pain shooting from my ribcage and with Scott on all fours, I rose and, from behind, clobbered his groin with a full-strength kick. He collapsed again, kneeling. I jumped on him, grabbed his right wrist with both my hands, and twisted with every ounce of strength, turning him around, dislocating his shoulder with a loud crack. He cried out into the darkness.

"That's for killing Jack. And this is for trying to kill me," I said as I held onto his twisted arm and shoved his face down into a muddy puddle, air from Scott's lungs bubbling to the surface.

I ground my teeth, with every intention of killing this man. For revenge. In self-defense.

Seconds away from becoming a murderer myself, an odd sense of calm came over me. A higher level of consciousness. Peace. Serenity. An unexplained force deep inside my soul ordered me to stop.

I grabbed a clump of his hair and extracted his head from the puddle. His chest pumped in and out for air. "Stop. Stop. I'm sorry. Y'all can have it. The treasure's yours. Don't kill me. Please."

"I got him," said a voice to my right. I swung my head to the side. Tammy held two guns: Scott's gun and the one I had given her. Both revolvers pointed at his head. Kevin stood at her side.

"You can let him up now," she said, cocking one hammer.

I climbed off his limp body and stood, struggling for air, vision spinning, forcing me to lean over and put my hands on my knees.

"Put them guns down, baby," Scott said to Tammy, also out of breath, mud dripping down his face.

She shook her head and cocked the second gun's hammer. "You killed Jack. I want to know how a sane man could murder his best friend and then marry his widow. And pretend to be a father to our daughter all these years." She squinted her eyes, filled with rage, lips tight. "Tell me right now or I swear on my mama's grave . . ."

Scott blinked, sucking and pumping out air. No response. Blood dripped from his nose, diluted with rain.

Out of breath I managed to say, "You get to live with the guilt of killing Jack. That'll be worse than death."

The sheriff with the same black baseball cap emerged from among the eucalyptus trees and strolled toward us, with a pistol in his left hand, aiming at Tammy, then me, then Kevin. His left hand was draped over his massive silver belt buckle as if he'd done this a thousand times.

Tammy spread her arms, aiming one gun at the sheriff and the other still at Scott.

The sheriff put his left arm up, stopping several paces away from Scott, before turning his head and spitting chaw onto the mud.

Rain drenched down on us all. More lightning. Thunder.

I put my hands up, so did Kevin.

"You said you'd bring back-up," Scott said to the sheriff, spitting blood into the mud as he wiped his eyes with muddy hands.

The sheriff put up a hand toward Scott, but stared at me. "We thought you and your little black friend here drowned in the Mississippi tonight," he said with a smile. "I'm the law 'round here and I say y'all got some explainin' to do."

"Sheriff, I'm sorry I pushed you in the hole, but I panicked and, well, I didn't kill the man in the barrel. His name was Jack Bachman and this man," I pointed to Scott, "killed him. They were best friends, hunting for a treasure. Scott got greedy."

"Boy, you ain't much older than thirty-five. They ain't no way you know all this for a fact. Nobody in they right mind gonna believe a word you sayin', son." He turned toward Tammy. "Little lady, you best put them guns down. The law's here now. Everythin' gonna be just fine."

Tammy ignored his request. "It's true, sheriff. But you don't give a shit 'cause you're in on this, aren't ya?"

Scott shot a look at her, balling his hands into fists above his head. He glanced down at her mud-soaked tennis shoes and bared his teeth.

"I found the ax in our shed a long time ago," Tammy said. "The one with the blood and mud caked on. I didn't think much of it at the time, but now I think I knew deep down you murdered Jack. And now you've admitted it to everyone. We're witnesses and can testify."

The sheriff glared at each of us, continuing to point his gun at Tammy. "The coroner worked with our friends at a lab at LSU, put a rush on the fancy carbon dating and sure enough, they confirmed the year: 1978. His initial assumption that the body was dead only a few years was incorrect. Something about the soil being dry or some fancy scientific crap and the combination of the depth of the body and being inside the drum, prevented it from decomposing at the normal rate. Preserved the body in pretty good shape all these years." He grabbed his walkie-talkie from his utility belt. "Seven Mary Six, where you at with that backup?"

Someone crackled back on the walkie-talkie, broken, tin-can-sounding. "Ain't coming, sheriff, can't fly in this wind, just like I told ya before."

The sheriff bent his neck backwards, face to the sky, allowing the rain to pelt his face.

More lightning.

Gun still aimed at Tammy, the sheriff grabbed his handcuffs from the back of his utility belt. I assumed he was going to arrest Scott, but he stepped toward me.

"Ms. Jones, put down them weapons. You a schoolteacher for God's sakes." He apparently assumed Tammy was not a threat. "Let's try this again, Mr. Bastian, you under arrest. You got the right to remain silent, anything . . ." He started to read me my Miranda rights, but before he had me in cuffs, Tammy stepped away from the crowd, backing up towards the forest.

"This ain't right," she said, still pointing one gun at Scott, the other at the sheriff.

Thunder clapped.

I blinked and the sheriff had now crouched down, gun pointing at Tammy, ready to fire.

But Scott kicked the gun out of the sheriff's hand and the pistol went flying into some nearby shrubs.

"Moron," the sheriff yelled as he dove in the bushes.

The rain dumped down hard on us, which blurred everything. But not enough for me to ignore the long, thick, wagging gator tale poking several feet out of the shrubbery. A second later came a loud shriek and the sounds of cracking bones.

# CHAPTER 66

Tammy took several steps toward the bushes, but Scott put his arm out and blocked her. "Gator's got him, baby. Leave 'em be."

Tammy stepped back, now pointing both guns at Scott, who fell to his knees, closed his eyes, dropped his head and started crying.

"You've been an asshole for almost four decades," Tammy said, clearly enraged. "Give me one good reason I don't put a bullet through your lousy skull right here, right now."

Scott took a beat, continuing with his self-pity. But I questioned whether he was truly genuine. More likely, the sneaky man was planning something.

Water rained down all around his head. Kneeling, he sat back on his lower legs, slumped in the mud. "I'm sorry."

Three shots rang out.

Neither of Tammy's guns.

Behind me in the bushes, a hungry gator had enjoyed the sheriff for dinner.

Or so we thought.

Kevin aimed a flashlight toward the gunshots.

The sheriff, standing waist-high in the bushes, fresh blood covering most of his body, a thick chunk of his neck dangling above his shoulder with blood draining down his chest, flickered his eyes between consciousness and death. His right arm pointed straight toward Scott, his stance rocking, struggling to maintain balance.

Smoke wafted from the gun held in his hand, swallowed quickly by the rain and wind.

Scott fell onto his side, one wound to his chest and another to his head, eyes staring up at the night sky, open, wide, filled with death.

The sheriff collapsed like a limp voodoo doll. The head of the gator appeared for a moment, chomped on to the midsection of the sheriff, and pulled the limp corpse back into the bushes to finish the meal.

Tammy collapsed, supported only by her arm, hand buried in the mud, then knelt and tossed both guns. She covered her face with her hands and let out a heart-wrenching wail. I ran and embraced her. Kevin followed and knelt.

"The sheriff shot Scott," Kevin said with an impatient huff.

Without turning my head and barely able to hear myself, I said, "The hurricane."

Tammy said, "Can't stay here. This whole area's gonna flood any minute with the surge."

The rain continued to pummel us.

"Anyone know how to use this thing?" I asked, pointing to the backhoe.

Tammy looked up to me, wiping water from her eyes, possibly tears but no way to tell, and stood.

"Jenny showed me. She uses one at the cement factory, not that hard," she said, pushing her wet bangs back. "I'm not super good at operating one, just the basics."

"Get up there and dig like you've never dug before," Kevin said, pulling her up.

"Or we can leave now and live," I said. "Without the treasure."

"If this hurricane hits us with full force," Tammy said, "it'll wipe us and the treasure clean off the face of the planet."

"I'm in if you guys are," I said, darting glances at each.

With a fast nod, Tammy climbed into the operator's chair of the digging beast. Kevin and I grabbed shovels and cleared the perimeter around the hole as she dug. The bodies of Scott and the sheriff continued to plague my mind and I turned the various shooting pains in my ankle, shoulder, and ribs into energy needed to dig.

Kevin leaned into me. "We got two dead bodies here. Cursed deaths numbers twenty-nine and thirty, right?"

I nodded, remembering twenty-eight men had already died searching for this treasure.

Kevin continued. "We can bury them in this big ass hole we diggin.'"

The thought lingered in my head until a loud metallic clunk erupted from the belly of the crater, bucking the backhoe upwards. "Got something," Tammy yelled through the rain.

Using the backhoe bucket, she cleared the area around the object while Kevin and I cleared the edges. Within minutes, the earth gave birth to a cracked, chipped concrete enclosure. The rain helped clean the top, but mud crept in around the sides. I shone a flashlight on the box, which measured four feet long, about two feet tall. Kevin and I continued digging until we'd removed all the surrounding dirt. Water flooded the hole from the rain, but Tammy scooped out massive volumes with the bucket.

I jammed the tip of my spade into a crack on the top of the box and yanked down with all my weight. "Won't budge," I said.

Kevin did the same with his shovel, heaving down with me. With the leverage and our combined masses, the lid snapped open with a crack. We pushed the top off, sliding it off the side with a muddy splash.

Tammy jumped down from the backhoe and climbed down into the hole with us. Together we leaned over, amazed at the contents centered in the concrete box: an ancient, wooden chest, shackled with iron brackets.

"Jackpot," Tammy said with an air of reservation, sharing a look of incredulity with me.

Kevin and I each grabbed a hold of a bracket and tried to lift the wood box, but were unable to even nudge the darned thing. The chest, wood rough and half-decomposed, felt welded or bolted to the bottom of the concrete enclosure. Or the sheer weight of the gold held everything in place. Gravity could be a real bitch.

"Get that rope," I told Kevin. "Wrap it around the chest and tie everything to the loader bucket."

Kevin complied. Tammy climbed back up into the backhoe, rotated up the stabilizer legs and turned the backhoe around, so the loader bucket hovered over the chest, then she nudged the various hydraulic levers in tandem to raise the backhoe arm upwards, lifting the object up from inside the concrete box.

The wet, mud-strewn treasure chest dangled by the rope attached to the bucket, at my eye-level, swaying in the wind, dripping brown water.

*Finally.*

So far, so good, but I wondered how much more we should push our luck, if the curse would allow us to remove the infamous Lafayette treasure from the island. If the box fell apart, too much force for the rotting wood to hold together, I would not have been surprised.

Two dead men already. Numbers twenty-nine and thirty. Would there be a number thirty-one?

"That thing's gotta weigh a ton. Literally," I said.

With the hurricane even closer, the gusting winds made standing upright almost impossible. We had no time to open the box and peek inside. Safety first, but definitely a huge risk either way.

And no time to hide the bodies, either.

"Tammy, drive that thing back to the dock. It's the only way we're gonna carry the gold out of here before the swell hits."

I dug out the voodoo doll from my pocket, stepped over to Scott's dead corpse, knelt down beside him, and placed the clay figure atop his blood-soaked chest. I had an odd sense his spirit was watching me. "May you find peace in your next life, my old friend," I said, before hustling over to the departing backhoe, trailing behind.

Tammy crawled the backhoe toward the dock, treasure chest dangling from the bucket, Kevin and I standing on the rear, hitching a ride.

A lightning bolt struck a sturdy eucalyptus tree thirty feet away, splitting the base into multiple slivers. The clap blasted my eardrums with a high-pitched ringing noise.

Tammy stopped. The muted sound of sizzling and snapping wood came from the falling tree, but between flashes the area went black. I ran around to the side of the backhoe as the giant eucalyptus tree rotated downward toward us.

"Look out!" I yelled, helping Tammy jump down off the rig to her left. Kevin dove toward the rear. A split second after we had cleared, the tree crashed down onto the machine. Fortunately, the rope held. The treasure swayed and bounced among the leaves and branches.

"Move the backhoe 'round the tree," Kevin said. Tammy climbed through wet, wind-strewn branches, back into the driver's seat, put the hoe in reverse and, with the front two tires buried a foot in mud, maneuvered out.

Kevin and I climbed back aboard the rear of the backhoe, and we continued the reverse direction along the path we had originally walked through, toward the island dock.

More thunder ripped through the night sky. Lightning lit up the forest, the trail, and the grass and shrubs on the ground.

Rain blasted our faces like sand. We eventually found our way to the dock, where the boat bobbed up and down, slamming hard against the wood planks. The winds had already flipped Scott's floatplane.

"The treasure's gonna sink that little boat. Ain't made for that kind of weight," Kevin said.

*Excellent point.*

Assuming the chest held together.

"Only one way to find out," I said.

# CHAPTER 67

Tammy continued inching the backhoe down toward the dock. Kevin untied the boat and brought our aluminum vessel closer to the loader bucket. With the center of the boat directly beneath the chest, Tammy lowered the thing into the hull, which shoved the entire boat downward into the water, inches below the railing. If we boarded the craft, our combined weight would force river water to breach the upper edges and sink everything.

"Only enough capacity in the boat for one, maybe two of us," said Tammy. "Plus we have no way of getting this thing out of the boat once we dock on the mainland."

My mind drifted to the curse.

*This thing was simply not meant to leave the island.*

Pure and simple.

"We're out of time," she said, looking down at a weather app on her phone, shielding the device with her hand from the horizontal rain. "The hurricane's gonna make landfall any minute."

The gusting winds continued to blow like a freight train, growing faster by the minute, and had knocked me to my knees several times. California earthquakes were bad, but this hurricane blew with such fierce intensity, I changed my mind about the gold.

*Ditch the treasure and run to higher ground. Whatever it takes to help Tammy stay alive.*

The force of the wind and rain pushed against me like a moving wall, stronger than anything I had experienced back home. By far. Water whipped up from the river, splashing onto us.

At that point I only cared about Tammy and Kevin. The way Tammy took charge of the situation amazed me, her knowledge of the area. What an absolutely stunningly strong woman. My admiration for her grew exponentially, which fueled my connection to her.

"I say we leave the treasure and get to high ground fast," I said. "The money won't do any of us any good if we all drown."

I thought about Adam's dad drowning in the same place back in the 60's. *Jack's dad.*

A bright spotlight approached us from the north, through the driving rain. A tugboat erupted from the darkness. I aimed my flashlight at the captain and smiled.

Adam.

He slid the massive vessel into the dock, ramming against our tiny fishing boat.

"Thought y'all might need a hand right about now," he yelled through the downpour, with a massive grin.

"You said you couldn't come here," I said.

"Can't go onto the island, but nothing can stop me from pulling into the dock." He pointed to an area toward the center of his boat. "Drop that chest right there. We need to get the hell outta here."

Tammy revved the backhoe engine and lifted the bucket, treasure dangling and attached with rope, swaying, twisting.

She relocated the hoe and extended the hydraulic arm, lowering the chest onto Adam's boat, which easily handled the extra weight.

Before I had an opportunity to board the large boat, squeaking noises and the sounds of tiny feet lapped in the water surrounding us. Something pecked at my ankles, biting. Tammy screamed through the rain. I looked down. Chills ran up my back.

Hundreds, no, thousands, of twenty-pound rodents–the size of cats–were running onto the island in droves, a cross between a beaver and a New York sewer rat.

"Nutria rats," Adam yelled. "Scared shitless. Runnin' to higher ground. Y'all better get aboard. Now!"

Tammy fired off three rounds at the beasts. I retrieved the pistol from my waist and fired off six rounds, all of which forced them to scatter, allowing us to climb aboard. One nutria bit into my ankle, but I shook the damned thing off into the water.

Tammy tossed both guns into the river and I did the same with mine.

Adam reversed away from the dock, then thrust our vessel forward on a northerly heading, against the flow. The motor propeller churned through dozens of the nutria in the process.

*Lucky it's dark outside.*

"The mainland dock's back that way," I said, pointing my thumb across the Mississippi toward our original launch point.

"Ain't going there," Adam yelled. "Not big enough to park this bad boy. I got a better place."

We headed up the Mississippi. Past Sunshine. Past Addis. Into Port Allen in downtown Baton Rouge.

While pulling in toward the dock, something hit the boat from underneath, jerking the side of the craft upward and knocking Tammy off balance.

She screamed, tripped against the side rail, and fell backwards into the raging, wave-strewn Mississippi.

In that instant, I had to make a split-second decision between staying alive on the boat with over a billion dollars' worth of gold or jumping into the cold, dark, violent river, risking my life to save the woman I loved.

*No brainer, really.*

I grabbed two orange life vests from underneath the boat seat, yelled to Adam, "Come 'round and get us!" and jumped in after Tammy.

My head hit the water first. The cold pounded my skull like a jackhammer. Fear encased my entire body but I had a purpose.

Find Tammy.

Nowhere to be seen.

Then, "Help me! John!" Tammy screamed to my left, downstream. I jerked my head toward her voice. My legs and core shivering, arms churning the water, I kicked hard and fast. Multiple pulses of sharp pain came from my shoulder and ribcage, but I overcame the stabs, focused only on saving Tammy. The water smelled of moss and wet dirt. I only had seconds to make this happen before my muscles cramped up and we both froze to death.

More screams came from the darkness beyond. I spotted Tammy, five feet away, arms flailing, struggling to keep her head above the choppy waves.

I took a deep breath to calm myself and focus on the task at hand, then kicked stronger and harder toward her. My arm bumped Tammy's hand and I grabbed a hold, yanking her toward me.

"I had no idea you enjoyed swimming so much," I said, placing the vest over her head. She wrapped her arms around my neck and squeezed.

# CHAPTER 68

The sweet sound of a high-revving boat engine approached, a wake of water pushing us sideways.

"Grab 'hold of the ladder in back," Adam said. The rear of the boat glided past us as we drifted downriver. Kevin leaned over, reaching down to grab us. Flashes of lightning struck nearby. Thunder clapped.. He heaved Tammy up onto the boat. I forced my numb fingers to wrap around the water ladder and squeezed hard, knowing any slippage would result in my death.

Struggling each step, I climbed up, then threw my leg over the side rail, balanced myself for a moment on the boat deck before collapsing and curling into a fetal position. A repetitive beeping sound, faint and small and distant, captured my attention. Adam whirled us away back toward the dock. Kevin hustled over with two wool blankets, one for Tammy and one for me and my trembling bones.

Adam scooted our boat up against a covered dock, with a loading arm off to the side, tied down the boat, and ran to us.

"You two are freezing." He looked up at Kevin. "We gotta get them inside and out of these wet clothes. Now."

"You got some wheels parked 'round here somewhere?" Kevin asked.

Adam nodded. "Here, help me get 'em up." They grabbed my blanket and underarms and I stood, lower lip quivering nonstop. The hefty winds blew right through me, sapping valuable heat. I felt less like a human, more like a block of ice.

We hobbled to a black Ford F-350. Adam opened the rear door, Tammy and I climbed in, then he hustled around to the driver's side, started the engine, and cranked up the heater full blast.

"Stay here while we transfer the treasure chest," Adam said. "Get out of those soaked clothes." He ran back to the boat, found four more blankets—dry ones—and handed them to us. "Get warm."

I looked into Tammy's eyes. I leaned in and kissed her tears away. "I'm sorry you're sad. I'm sorry—"

"John, I'm not sad. I'm happy. I haven't been this happy in God knows how long. But Jesus Christ am I freezing!" She started to unbutton her wet, white blouse, while I slid off my shirt and helped her out of her jeans. Before long, we were both sitting in the back of Adam's truck shivering and wearing only our underwear, huddled together beneath thick blankets, trying to recapture the heat we'd lost during the rescue in the mighty Mississippi.

We turned around and looked through the rear truck window at the dock behind us. Kevin was operating the main controls of the loading arm. Adam attached the rope to the rocker arm, then Kevin lifted the box off the boat, and swung the object toward land as our gold swayed in the rushing wind. Adam climbed into the truck, then backed up closer to the loading arm. The treasure chest dropped onto the truck bed with a hefty thud, weighing down the rear of the truck several inches. Adam hurled the tailgate shut, waving for Kevin to get in.

"There's no way Adam could have put all this together last minute," I said to Tammy.

"He's had years to secretly plan for this moment. Like an apocalyptic prepper. Just in case. He thought he'd be doing this with Scott, but since Scott stabbed him in the back a couple months ago . . ." She shrugged through another set of shivers.

Adam pulled the truck away from the dock and onto a dirt road before asking how we were doing. We told him we were getting warm but weren't there yet. The quivering of my lip waned.

"Good. Wasn't sure we'd ever get this far with the treasure, so I hadn't planned out a final place to open it," Adam said.

"Let's go to my place," Tammy said in a raspy voice before clearing her throat. "Scott has, or had, a ton of tools in our garage and he obviously won't need them anymore." She turned to me and under her breath, so only I could hear, she whispered, "Hope that crooked sheriff rots in hell."

We shared the details with Adam of what happened on the island.

"The gators are probably enjoying him right now. A tasty midnight snack," Kevin said.

To Tammy, I asked, "You alright?"

Her eyes fell to our trembling, clasped hands, then darted up to my eyes again. "I think Scott loved me at one time. But that love died long ago. Now he's gone and I feel . . ."

I squeezed her tight and as I re-wrapped a blanket around her, I realized how unafraid I felt. All my fear had melted away, replaced by a growing strength deep within.

*Fear is weakness.*

Adam drove us through hurricane-strength winds and horizontal rain, eventually pulling into Tammy's driveway.

Still no reporters.

"Turn around and back up into the garage," she said, climbing down from the truck, a blanket wrapped around her.

She opened the garage door, then waved Adam inside. "C'mon John, let's go up to my room and get us some warm clothes."

I followed her with a blanket wrapped around me, too.

While Kevin and Adam used a hydraulic hoist to unload the chest into Tammy's garage, I found myself upstairs in Tammy's bedroom wearing only my wet underwear.

She handed me a stack of clothes. "Here. You and Scott are about the same size, or were, or whatever."

"This feels weird," I said. The chills returned, wind howled outside, slamming buckets of rain against the windows. "This guy just died and now I'm putting on his clothes." I slid off my wet underwear. Tammy handed me a fresh pair.

The clothes felt warm on my skin and the internal ice started to melt.

Once dressed, I slid on a black and yellow ski jacket. Tammy tossed me a wool beanie and ski gloves.

Within minutes we were dry, fully dressed and inside Tammy's garage.

The hurricane winds pummeled the sturdy brick house.

The chest hovered several feet above the ground, hanging by the rope attached to the engine hoist.

"Almost got her," Adam said, lowering the chest.

But the chest made a cracking, snapping wood sound, the rope slipped, and the treasure chest slid out from the bindings, crashing down onto the ground and busting open most of the ancient wood panels.

Thousands of sparkly gold doubloons splayed out all across the concrete floor.

Tammy put her hand over her mouth and screamed with excitement.

"Holy jackpots, Batman!" Kevin said.

I shook Adam's hand, then gave Kevin a strong bear hug before squatting and picking up one of the doubloons. The gold piece shined bright, with a hefty weight and felt smoother than expected, as I brought the coin to my face, pressed it to my lips, closed my eyes in deep appreciation and kissed it.

When I opened my eyes, the Lafayette ghost was standing in the shadows, floating toward us, sleek, deliberate, unhurried, and into the garage lights. He stopped in front of me and gave a crisp nod.

# CHAPTER 69

Without moving his lips, the ghost spoke to me, *"I've been waiting a long time."*

I cocked my head. "I don't understand."

Kevin looked at me, around the garage. "Who you talkin' to?"

The apparition floated closer toward me. *"My gold now belongs to the spirit of Jack Bachman."* My mouth fell open. *"Share with the unfortunate. Enjoy life with Tammy. Now I can move on to the next realm."*

I wondered why this guy hadn't spoken this clearly before. Would've been helpful. Perhaps because I still had to prove myself.

"What about your curse?" I asked.

Another ghost appeared, floating up from behind Jacques. The young woman from the painting at the museum, the daughter.

Bridgette Lafayette.

She spoke with purpose. *"We invoked the curse to ensure a worthy soul would find treasure. One who loves others and the world above himself."*

As I nodded in understanding, Kevin nudged my shoulder. "You okay, dog?"

I leaned down and picked up a handful of the shiny gold doubloons, but when I looked up to thank the apparitions, they'd already disappeared.

Glancing at my companions, I said, "This gold needs to be split up. Twenty-five percent each." They confirmed the agreement. "I'm going to give most of mine away to charities. I know that sounds crazy, but my being here is crazy." I looked at Tammy and, from the relative safety of her home that had withstood countless hurricanes in the past, she smiled. My heart melted.

A clap of thunder rattled the garage.

# CHAPTER 70

*November 25, 2016*

The hurricane ended up killing dozens, swallowing the bodies of the sheriff and Scott, and causing billions in damage across a huge swath of Louisiana. For us, we all considered ourselves fortunate to be alive.

Maybe we experienced divine intervention.

Or maybe we just got lucky.

The bullet Mike shot at Tammy's pooch, Charlie, ended up grazing the skin near his hip. Vet said he'd make a full recovery.

By all accounts, the Trésor Fatale legend and folklore that had built up over the years indicated there would be roughly ten thousand gold pieces. But over the next two days, as we hunkered down at Tammy's house, it turns out there were more. A lot more. By my count, the chest held exactly 55,672 beautiful, shiny discs. According to my research, each of the twenty-two karat gold pieces weighed about six grams, or one-fifth of an ounce. Adam suggested we melt the gold into bars and sell them, but when we did the math, the coins would lose over ninety percent of their value because they were ancient artifacts, all minted the same year, and in pristine condition. I held one in my hand and inspected it, impressed by a shine beyond shine.

Online searching yielded a ballpark value for each piece: between $25,000 and $45,000 US dollars, depending on how many we released at a time, whether we kept them all as a set, the spot price of gold at the time, et cetera.

We split up the loot evenly amongst the four of us and I placed my 13,918 coins into empty single-gallon paint cans.

Kevin had a hard time lifting his two cans. "These babies be fifty pounds each. Little suckers are heavy."

Over the mild howl of a strong wind outside–remnants of the storm–the same repetitive sound, faint and small and distant continued beeping in my ears.

As I rested in Tammy's living room, my phone vibrated.

"Dr. Willis," I answered, standing and covering my other ear with my palm, while stepping out into a corner of the garage near a workbench full of tools.

"I'm sorry to bother you again, John, I promise I won't call you again. Out of fear and anxiety, I hung up on you last time we spoke. Please accept my apologies. But I do have one final question for you."

Picking up a 1/2" crescent wrench and twirling the metallic object through my fingers, I said, "Shoot."

"I can't explain why, but I feel like you were going to give me an answer, but since, well, okay, here's the question: you said my son wanted me to know something . . . what do you think that is?"

I thought about telling her what Mark had whispered to me, how Scott had essentially killed Mark by sharing the story of the treasure and the Jack Bachman murder, but now that Scott was dead, I decided against it. But she did need to know Scott was dead.

Wanting to break the news to her with as much empathy as possible, I said, "Not sure how exactly to say this, so I'll just come right out with it. Mark's dad, Scott Jones, was shot and killed.."

A loud gasp came through the phone.

I continued. "Yep, two days ago."

She asked about the details, so I gave her the Cliffs Notes version.

Through various weeps and sobs, she responded. "Thank you, John. You're a good man and I'm happy to know you. Thank you for your honesty. I feel like soon I'll finally have some closure."

"You're certainly welcome, Dr. Willis."

Beep. Beep.

Every second or so, the damned noise continued.

I ended the call.

Beep. Beep.

I darted my eyes to Adam, who had just finished loading cans brimming with gold into the rear seats of his truck, apparently oblivious to the beeping noises.

Only wind. And rain.

The beeping stopped. A new hurricane warning system for a second hurricane?

Tammy and Kevin joined me, we said goodbye to Adam, and he drove away.

Tammy invited Kevin and me to stay at her place until we were ready to make the trip back to California. Of course, we gratefully accepted.

Early the next morning, after another night of restless sleep on Tammy's couch while wearing Scott's clothes, I awoke to the aroma of fresh espresso.

And more of the distant beeping sounds.

Beep. Beep. Beep.

And Tammy's amorous gaze.

"Today's Thanksgiving," she said, bending down to hand me a full cup of joe.

I rubbed my eyes, propped myself up on my elbow and took a sip.

She continued. "I'm going to show you some good ol' fashioned southern cooking."

We spent the day talking, sharing Jack's memories, and working with Kevin to prepare the most delicious, juicy turkey dinner I'd ever had, at least in my life as John. Kevin must have the same food genes as his mom because I couldn't get enough of his shrimp gumbo.

The beeps continued every few minutes throughout the day.

After the late afternoon meal, Tammy pulled me aside and said, "Come with me, mister. Kevin's watching a football game and I told him we'd be back in a bit. I have somewhere I'd like you to see."

"Can you hear those beeps?" I asked.

She stopped, rested her hands on her hips, stared down at the floor for several seconds, and said, "Nope. All I hear is the game."

I shrugged. The noises stopped. Again.

We locked our buckets full of gold safely in her upstairs gun safe, called an Uber and went for a drive.

We pulled up next to a small two-bedroom stucco house on the corner of Ferndale Drive and Orchid Place, in a quaint neighborhood of southern Baton Rouge. As the Uber driver sped away, I picked up a wrapped newspaper from the concrete driveway.

Staring at the dirt front yard, a vision entered my mind. I glanced at Tammy, furrowed my brow and said, "Not sure why, but I feel like this place used to be made of bricks. And had a row of gardenias out front. And a dark charcoal gray roof. Two trees out back. With a hammock strung between."

"Freaky.. But amazing," Tammy said with a smile, wrapping her arm around me from the side, putting her head onto my shoulder. "All true. The bricks are still there, but we covered them with stucco a long time ago."

I turned, gazing into her crystal green eyes. "I don't understand."

"Yes, you do." She smiled, then gave me a peck on the cheek and locked her arms around me. "This was our home, where Jack and I first lived together as a married couple. My family ended up paying off the mortgage a few years after Jack disappeared and we've had this place as a rental ever since. It's vacant right now."

Another memory filled my noggin . . . carrying Tammy over the threshold and through the front door, she'd worn a conservative white bridal gown . . . while kicking her feet, one of her shoes had fallen to the ground.

I told her about the memory. She nodded, patting my upper arm. "C'mon. Let's go inside and see what else you remember."

As we strolled to the front porch, I yanked off the rubber band from the newspaper and read the headline: HERO PILOT MISSING

While Tammy fished out the key from her purse and worked to unlock the chrome deadbolt, I quickly scanned the article about Scott's disappearance, then folded the paper and stepped up onto the front porch. The door creaked open and the interior, furnished with minimal items, gave off a musty, old wood scent. A set of maroon and brown wingback chairs sat strong in the corner, a fridge in the kitchen stood against a yellow wall, and in one of the bedrooms a sheetless double bed lay next to an oak dresser sporting a four-foot oval mirror affixed to the top.

I closed my eyes, allowing the moment to sink in, when an idea hit me. I tossed the newspaper aside, hustled into the bedroom, rolled the dresser away from the wall, and studied the back side.

Writing.

Tammy came in and leaned over next to me.

In the center, in black permanent marker, someone had drawn the shape of a large heart with the words "Jack and Tammy – Insane Primitive Hominoid Maniacs." I craned my neck up toward Tammy.

"You wrote those words our first day here, right after our wedding," she said, tiny pools of tears welling up in her soft, caring eyes.

I stood, brought her close and joined in a long, passionate kiss. With our lips locked, we shuffled to the uncovered mattress, fell on top and made love in the same room she and Jack had done so many times before his untimely death.

But afterwards, lying in each other's arms, as I tried to enjoy the calm of the moment, those darned beeping noises returned. Only this time, each beep sounded louder, closer, as if coming from loudspeakers in the living room.

Before I could ask Tammy if she could hear the beeps, my phone vibrated.

Karl Cannon. Probably more bad news..

I turned to Tammy. "Sorry, it's my business partner."

"Dude. You're never going to guess what just happened," he said.

I chuckled, said, "Right now, nothing could possibly surprise me."

He laughed. "The commercial deal is back on!" His voice had a level of excitement I hadn't heard in years. "We brought in a civil engineer, a structural expert, and it turns out the earthquake damage wasn't as bad as we'd originally thought. Plus, since so many other buildings were damaged, the demand for similar properties has skyrocketed and prices are up across the board. The earthquake was a blessing in disguise. Unbelievable. The buyer's desperate and wants to pay cash and a premium on our commission to close this week. Oh, and we found your little cat. He's staying with me, totally fine."

The beeping noises stopped.

A huge weight fell off my shoulders. "Outstanding," I said, nodding, but confused. "That's great. Keep me posted. I'm headed back next week and we can celebrate once escrow closes."

After ending the call, I set down the phone and kissed Tammy on her forehead. "I'm getting a two-million-dollar commission next week. The money was supposed to help get me back on my feet financially, but now that we have at least a billion dollars in gold, doesn't seem like that much. Weird, huh?"

"You don't need it. Any of it. Money doesn't buy happiness."

She was right. I'd heard people say that clichéd phrase before, but it had a completely different meaning to me now.

"We don't need money to have this. Right here. You and me."

We embraced again, shared love flowing through every cell of our bodies.

I thought about giving the commission away for a benevolent cause. A logo with an apple at the center popped into my head. I had seen their television ads running recently and had read somewhere that teaching reading to young children was of critical importance to a society. Pulling out my phone, I went to Google and searched for "reading red apple fun" and at the top was the site I had seen in the ads: Red Apple Reading. I decided to donate money to help a million children all over the world learn to read, then told Tammy about my idea.

She kissed me.

"This is going to be a wild ride for us," she said.

"Switching subjects back to the gold, we need to figure out what to do next. Sell to dealers? Sell all of it? Some of it?"

"I'm worried about theft. Need to get the whole thing insured."

She brought up several other risks I hadn't thought of. After pondering her comments and worthy questions, I said, "I have faith everything will turn out. Heck, to me it already has. Gold or no gold, I couldn't be any more content than I am right now with you in my arms."

Later, while getting dressed, my phone rang again, but when I answered, only the sounds of beeping noises came through, like a heart monitor had married a fax machine.

I ended the call, staring at my phone screen.

Another call.

The beeping noises came back. Loud. Close. Deafening. I looked at Tammy, completely unaware as she finished putting on her top. The doorknob to the front door jiggled. Curious, I walked to the front room and stopped, waiting to hear the noise again, but the front door exploded open.

A man wearing black leather biker gear stood in the doorway. With eyes cold, hard, flinty, he withdrew a pistol from behind his silver Geno's Bar & Grill belt buckle, and stepped toward me with a limp. He had white gauze covering his forehead, wrapped around his entire noggin. A vein twitched on his temple.

Mike Bixleton.

Frozen stiff, the air rushed from my lungs.

Beep.

Silence.

Beep.

"Heard y'all killed Scott," Mike said.

Tammy appeared next to me and let out a tiny yelp.

"Good," he continued, deadpan. "More for me." Another limp closer, now two yards away. He lifted his arm and aimed the gun at my face and cocked the hammer.

Tammy nestled her body against mine as I wrapped my arm around her and squeezed. No words came to mind.

Beep.

Beep.

I focused my eyes straight into Mike's as he inhaled slowly. "Tell me where the gold is. Now."

*Fear is weakness.*

"No," I said, not caring what happened to me, only wanting to protect Tammy.

"I get the gold. She lives. You die either way." He took another step toward us, then bared his teeth.

Tammy pulled me even tighter.

Beep.

"Fine," Mike said, smiling, before pulling the trigger and firing a shot directly at my skull.

# CHAPTER 71

After an instant of inexplicable pain, my entire field of vision, Mike, the dresser, the window, Tammy, all twisted and swirled and darkened into a tiny ball, then vanished. A warm feeling wrapped around me like an electric blanket, swooshing sounds filling the air.

A sense of calm.

Joy, even.

Blackness.

Beep.

Beep.

Slow, calm, inhale.

Exhale, slow.

Beep.

Beep.

Lying on my back, I cracked open my eyes and gripped bed sheets.

Massive, rapid inhale.

My heart pushed upward into my throat. The frequency of beeps increased. I jerked my head to the right, left, up to the ceiling.

Panic replaced the sense of joy.

Another hospital room.

*If I never set foot in one of these places again, it would be too soon.*

I quickly inventoried the room: heart monitor, tall window, groovy, flowery, orange and yellow and lime green wallpaper, clean white bed sheets, an I.V. needle stuck into a vein in the top of my right hand, and a bag of clear liquid hanging above me.

Someone standing at the foot of my bed wearing a pressed white outfit and nurse hat. Old school nurse outfit. "Shhh. Shhh. Shhh," she said, taking several steps away before leaning out the door and yelling down the hallway with an echo, "He's awake, Dr. Willis."

Panting like an Olympic sprinter crossing a finish line, I tried to lower my pulse by controlling my breathing. In. Out. Slow.

The frequency of the beeping noises relented, but only a tad.

Despite the groggy mind, I remembered the little ghost boy.

A doctor entered my room.

His thick, wavy black hair, peppered with white and parted to the side, drew down to long, chunky sideburns. He approached, wearing a white overcoat and checkered pants with bell bottoms, leaned in and flicked a flashlight into and away from my eyes. He smelled of Old Spice cologne. Below his fat, dark caterpillar eyebrows pointing upwards in the center to a "V", his deep brown eyes stared at me, prominent, serious, and concerned.

With a low pitched, raspy, smoker's voice, he said, "I'm Dr. Willis. Are you able to hear me?"

I nodded.

"Good," he said with a squint, thinking for a short pause. "You've been in an accident and are in the Baton Rouge hospital. Do you remember anything about what you were doing before now?"

"What day is it?" I asked.

"Saturday. November 11th."

I closed my eyes, searching for memories, answers, clues. Tammy's face appeared in my mind's eye. So did the bedroom in Baton Rouge. Scott. The gold. Mike and his gun.

"The hurricane," I said, looking outside to a cluster of eucalyptus trees through the small hospital window.

"I'm sorry?"

The nurse furrowed her brow.

Between breaths, I said, "Hurricane Carl. My house. Scott. Adam. Kevin. The bayou. The—"

"Mr. Bachman, you're not making any sense," the doctor said. "Take a deep breath and listen to me. Very carefully."

My eyes widened, pulse skyrocketing again, out of breath.

He continued. "A man named Scott Jones tried to kill you with an axe. You've lost a lot of blood and have been in a coma for three days. You almost lost your right arm, but we were able to save it. You're lucky to be alive."

I closed my eyes again, searching for answers.

Wait.

I forced open my eyes, then looked directly at the doc.

"You said Bachman."

"Yes," the doc said, parting open a manila folder, then glancing through papers. "Your Louisiana driver's license says your name is Mr. Jack Richard Bachman. You live here in Baton Rouge and have a commercial pilot's license."

I pushed myself up into a seated position against the pillows, shaking my head.

Something was wrong. Seriously wrong.

"No. I'm John Bastian. I live in Newport Beach, California. I was just in a coma a couple weeks ago. Woke up in a hospital in California, similar to this place, but without the weird flowery wallpaper. Was treated by Shauna Willis and she—"

"Hold on," the doc said, holding up his hand to stop me. He took a step closer, bending at the waist, staring deep into my eyes. "Did you just say Shauna Willis?"

He turned to the nurse, who shrugged, then back at me.

I nodded rapidly.

The doctor leaned toward me, studying my face. "How in God's green earth do you know the name of my daughter? She's only ten."

My right arm rested in a sling, but as I wiggled the fingers of my right hand I tried to move my heavy arm, pain jolted from my shoulder. Rubbing my forehead, I asked, "Where's Tammy?"

"Just relax, Mr. Bachman," the doc said, gently pushing down on my shoulder. "We'll get this all sorted out."

I darted my eyes around the room, from the doc, to the antique-looking medical machines, to the nurse, to the door, to the window.

"No," I said, huffing, barely able to get words out. "It's Thanksgiving and I want to know what the hell's going on."

The doc gave an understanding nod, scooted closer, and said in a gentle tone. "Don't worry, Mr. Bachman, your assailant is in custody and, according to the sheriff, has confessed, said he lost his temper, but called for help once . . ." The doc let out a small chuckle. "Said something scared him, said he saw some kinda ghost wearing a top hat. Lafayette something-or-other."

My gaze fell downward, toward the white sheet covering my legs, and memories montaged.

*No way.*

He continued. "More importantly, your wife, Tammy, has been in the waiting room this entire time, but not ten minutes ago I told her to go and get a bite to eat. Wasn't sure when you'd regain consciousness."

Images of Tammy surrounded me with her smile, her spirit. That gorgeous red hair. Those eyes. I shook my head. "I want to see her."

"You're on a hefty morphine drip, not sure you're ready for visitors and—"

"No, give me my cell phone right now. I need to text her—"

"I'm sorry, cell what?" he asked with a frown, squinting.

"Hold on, doc," I said, raking my fingers through my hair, taking a slow breath. Something clicked and at that moment, everything made sense. Complex and completely bizarre for my human mind to wrap around, but I was okay with it. All that remained was to confirm my suspicions.

I took my time with the next question, wanting to ensure each word was said with the utmost clarity so there was absolutely no mistake in what I was asking Doctor Willis. "What year is it?"

He folded his arms across his chest, glanced at the nurse, back at me, dumbfounded.

"1978."

*THE END*

# EPILOGUE

**Jack Bachman**

*November 25, 2016*

**W**ell, that's my story. Hard to believe, I'm sure.

I can say that I've thought more than a healthy amount about visiting my parents. Well, John's parents, out in California. In fact, according to county records, no John Bastian had ever been born, but they did have a child. A girl, a daughter, now a grown woman with her own family. She works as a real estate broker. Go figure.

I'd watched, with great curiosity, how the world evolved from 1978 until now. Most of the memories I had as John Bastian remained in my mind, stuck on a human hard drive like a duplicate set of life events, but without a delete button, and I'd spent considerable time trying to figure out what exactly happened. Having memories of future events helped out immensely, especially from a financial standpoint.

I mean, what would you have done if you knew four decades of key future events?

For me, I invested heavily in Microsoft back in '86 before Windows had been invented. Then sold off a few million dollars and bought a ton of Amazon stock in '97 when some guy named Jeff Bezos had a crazy idea for an online bookstore. Then parlayed a huge chunk of my wealth into Google in 2004 when it was just another search engine. And Tesla in 2010 when everyone thought all electric vehicles would be a sure failure. And a bunch of other investments along the way.

Despite the accumulated wealth, I still had no clue how my life as John could just disappear like that? How that version of the future could cease to exist? My best guess is that I was given another chance at life as Jack.

But why?

My investment success has afforded me multiple unique opportunities to hire the best scientists available to study quantum entanglement theories and alternate universes and timelines. Maybe that's what happened. Or maybe reincarnation is, in fact, something that exists and I was the one guy on the planet with a glitch. After spending ungodly sums of money trying to look at all this from a scientific perspective, I honestly can't tell y'all for sure, unfortunately.

However, assuming I was reincarnated and then somehow the universe gave me a do over by preventing Scott from killing me the second time around, there are gobs of loose ends. Thinking about it too much makes my Southern head spin. I'd been living under this assumption for the last forty years because it's the only reasonable, logical explanation I can wrap my arms around. But to be honest, not fully. Because my journey has had its pros and cons. I can tell y'all, though, acceptance has been the key to keeping my sanity in spite of not knowing what or why I was sent back into Jack's body in 1978.

And, of course, my sweet, beautiful, kind-hearted wife, Tammy—who's been with me the entire time—was there for me every time I needed someone to lean on. Since '78, our love has flourished to inexplicable levels—you might even call it an unwavering spiritual connection. Our oldest daughter, Jenny, had two girls and two boys. Our other two kids, Amy and Brent, each had two sons, so it's been an absolute joy to not only raise three children—something I'd always wanted and absolutely knew was missing from my John Bastian life—but having eight grandkids has been the best part of all. I'd give up all the money in a heartbeat if anything were to ever happen to them.

Tammy and I have enjoyed countless epic discussions and discovered how ridiculously mind boggling it is to know most of what the future holds for the world, who will be elected to power positions, which stocks will rise, what technologies will surface, when wars and other tragedies will take place, et cetera.

On countless occasions, I'd considered reaching out to Kevin who, by the way, did make it to the Tonight Show. He killed it. But how would I approach him? From his perspective, he never had a friend named John Bastian, never knew me as Jack Bachman. Of course, I'd made other friends since '78, ones who wouldn't have known me had everything not happened the funky way it did.

And John's mom, my goodness. From what I can tell, she never actually remembers a John Bastian, so all the heartache I'd apparently put her through with my autism as young John, the night terrors, the stress, the crying . . . none of that happened in the current version of events. Good for her, but I still remember her love, her kindness. I can still taste her home-made macaroni and cheese. And for several years I mourned her. And my dad. And Karl. And my sweet little kitty cat. Sure, the hefty wealth is a terrific perk, but this journey has not been a cake walk. Again y'all, ups and downs.

But the fact that Tammy and I consciously chose not to take advantage of our knowledge in terms of unearthing the treasure—it's still out there on that Bayou Goula Towhead, as far as I know, and I could tell y'all the precise location, should you choose to risk your life—has given us an amazing life full of joy and pleasure. We have become two of the most giving philanthropists the world has ever known, which has been quite liberating. Our foundation has helped sick children all across the globe, taught millions to read, created clean drinking water for countless, and righted a lot of man-made wrongs.

Fear is weakness and I've learned to be strong, a trait I'll need now more than ever as we head into the unknown. Today, time has caught up to us—today is the day Mike shot me as John, in the alternative history—and I'm nervous, but excited to spend however many years I have left on Earth with Tammy. We no longer know what the future holds, so there are no expectations other than a solid grounding in my belief that when it's finally my time to die, I know in my heart that something extraordinary will happen to my spirit.

And Tammy's.

Exactly what, I've got no idea, but no matter what, I ain't afraid.

# THANK YOU

Thank you for taking the time to read *Echo From a Bayou*! I hope you enjoyed it, and if so, please consider leaving a review at the store where you purchased it and tell your friends about it. I also have author profiles on Goodreads and BookBub – please stop by and leave a review there as well!

As an author, getting the word out about my book is vital to its success.

Visit my website and subscribe to my email list:

**www.jlukebennecke.com**

Follow me on social media:

**Instagram, Facebook, Twitter: @jlukebennecke**

**YouTube Channel: @jasonlukebennecke**

The third installment of the Jake Bendel thrillers, *Blackout*, is finished and making its way through the publishing process. Subscribe for email updates on my website to get news on its release!

If you haven't already read my Jake Bendel thrillers, *Civil Terror: Gridlock* and *Waterborne*, then please look for the ebook, paperback, and audiobook versions on Amazon. The first chapter of *Civil Terror: Gridlock* is included here.

# OTHER BOOKS BY J. LUKE BENNECKE

*Civil Terror: Gridlock* is a thrilling novel that explores the dark side of self-driving cars, as civil engineer Jake Bendel must partner with the FBI to stop a terrorist group from weaponizing the new national self-driving car network and carrying out a devastating attack.

*Waterborne* is a fast-paced thriller where civil engineer Jake Bendel once again teams up with the FBI to stop a group of vengeful terrorists from weaponizing California's water supply with genetically modified viruses.

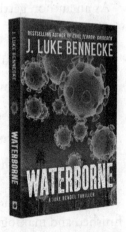

J. LUKE BENNECKE

CIVIL TERROR

# GRIDLOCK

A JAKE BENDEL THRILLER

# CIVIL TERROR
# GRIDLOCK

A JAKE BENDEL THRILLER

## J. LUKE BENNECKE

# FACTS

**1.** Every year in the United States, traffic congestion causes over $450 billion in lost economic productivity.

**2.** 93% of all fatal car accidents in the United States are caused by human error.

**3.** Between 30,000 and 40,000 people are killed in car accidents in the United States every year.

**4.** As of Spring 2019, there are at least forty major corporations working on self-driving car technologies.

## May 6, 2023 – Los Angeles Times

*Statewide Traffic Collisions Kill Nearly
1,800 Motorists in California*

*Los Angeles, CA* – At least 1,800 people died yesterday in traffic accidents across California in what Caltrans officials are referring to as a "technical glitch," according to a representative from Governor Fairchild's office.

"At approximately four o'clock yesterday afternoon, what appears to be a freak technical glitch in the Statewide Intelligent Transportation System (SITS) caused over 7,000 traffic accidents throughout the state," the state representative added. "The timing of tens of thousands of signalized intersections throughout California, typically handled by local agencies, was taken over two months ago by the SITS. The Super Six are looking further into this unfortunate and regretful incident."

The Super Six, led by civil engineer Dr. Jake Bendel under the direction of the US Department of Transportation, are responsible for the implementation of a separate, nationwide self-driving network known as the "Sûr System," or SS, and are generally considered the "Top Gun" of transportation, legal, ethical, and psychological experts in the country.

Dr. Bendel, who resides in Upland, was unavailable for comment.

# CHAPTER 1

**June 9, 2023**

*Los Angeles*

Deep inside the Federal Building, FBI Special Agent Jose Cavanaugh huddled with several other agents around a flat screen TV, listening to the distorted ramblings of a female reporter as crackled audio came and went. The bottom of the screen displayed an ABC-7 logo and read 4:09 p.m. The Sky-7 copter, which provided the source of the feed, swerved right to avoid hitting one of the other dozen aircraft hovering above the unfolding freeway scene in West Los Angeles, mere blocks away.

"Carnage," reporter Nicole Freemonte said. "From up here, we're looking down at an apocalyptic scene of twisted metal, smoke, and chaos along seven miles of the 405 freeway." Her voice, normally pleasant, comforting, and professional, had deteriorated into that choking sound people make when they experience gut-wrenching pain, trying not to break down at the sight of true terror. "Thousands of vehicles lie in a mangled sea of destruction that is, from what I'm told by our fact-checking crew, incomparable to any traffic accident in the history of the US."

Cavanaugh shook his head. *First the statewide SITS nightmare, and now this.*

People struggled, crawling over lifeless vehicles, waving their arms to garner attention from the souls suspended above them.

Nicole continued, "To get a better sense of the magnitude of what appears to be a terrorist attack on thousands of innocent civilian drivers using the new Sûr System, let's turn it over now to our reporter on the ground, Bobby Jones. Bobby?" She sounded relieved to pass the attention to a different reporter.

The reporter stood on the shoulder of the 405 freeway, facing south, wearing a white dress shirt and blue tie with slicked-back hair and thin-rimmed glasses. The bloodbath behind him filled the majority of the frame. Sweat trickled down his brow, and he wiped his forehead. A woman cried in the background. A shriek rang out from an unseen man, "Help me!"

"Nicole, the scene down here is pure chaos. In all my years of reporting, I've never—" A truck-sized fireball exploded a few hundred yards behind the reporter, rattling the camera. Bobby ducked, turning his head. A fraction of a second later, a booming clap of thunder forced him to his knees.

"Jesus, that's the second explosion in five minutes," Cavanaugh said, leaning forward to turn up the volume on the TV.

The cloud behind Bobby mushroomed as he straightened up and looked around, smudges of charcoal on his right shoulder and left cheek, his microphone shaking in his hand. "We, uh, sorry, I . . ." he cleared his throat, laughing under his breath. "We're here on-site at what reminds me of"—he paused and raised his eyebrows— "a war zone. That explosion came from one of dozens of tanker trucks caught in the pileup." He extended his trembling arm. "Miles and miles of tangled cars and trucks sit motionless here on the 405 freeway. The scene is like one giant junkyard of death and destruction. Emergency crews are skirting the perimeter, trying to tend to the wounded, but I'm told they're having a difficult time getting to the inner lanes."

The camera panned away from Bobby and zoomed in to an upside-down green Smart Coupe with a caved-in roof. At first, the shot appeared fuzzy, but when the cameraman focused the lens, it revealed the partially decapitated head of a woman. The camera jerked away, back to Bobby.

Cavanaugh muted the TV, shook his head. "Too late."

***

August 10, 2023

Jake designed the Sûr System to save lives, but some bastard had gone and weaponized the damned thing.

The SITS nightmare three months ago was only the beginning. The terrorists cloaked themselves well. Even the papers reported it as a glitch. Jake had a theory. SITS had been a test run. A warmup.

It made the second attack in June, the one using the Sûr System, that much worse. And, when no one had answers, they needed someone to blame. So Jake had ended up here.

Wherever 'here' was.

From brilliant engineer to suspected terrorist. Just like that.

The interior of his eight-by-eight room reminded Jake of a prison cell, with gray paint flakes clinging to the tops of the walls. A fly buzzed, landing on Jake's nose, but he remained still, his mind focused on how to stop the killing. He knew the Sûr System inside and out. Someone must have set up a back door into the code.

Jake's mind shifted focus to Cynthia, his wife of twenty-five years. He missed the way her hazel eyes sparkled when she smiled. They had never been apart longer than two days. Until now.

The fly buzzed away, then Jake sat upright on the clumpy, two-inch thick mattress and inhaled the scent of charred wood from the sooty dress shirt he'd worn since his arrival six days ago. Feeling abandoned, he assumed the FBI had forgotten to get him a change of clothes. Or they didn't care.

Standing, his back cracked as he stroked his stubble. A sense of determination devolved into frustration, made its way down to his hand, and balled into a fist before he punched a hole through the drywall. *Pain is good*, he thought, craning his head downward to his bloodied, shaking fingers.

After closing his eyes and leaning against the wall, clouds of depression swirled inside his tired brain, mixing with distant memories of his wife dancing in her favorite yellow dress, the curls in her hair bouncing whenever she tipped her head back to laugh. With his palms pressed against his eyes, he imagined the faces of the thousands of people killed by his Sûr System.

He resumed doing calculations in his mind, imaginary code floating in front of his face, like a personal hologram, courtesy of his semi-photographic memory. A gift and a curse. As a member of the Super Six, he'd worked countless hours on the algorithm, with his memory protecting key pieces of code.

Sirens suddenly screamed throughout. With emergency strobe lights flashing, Jake hustled to the door and yanked on the handle.

"Roger that, getting him now," yelled the ex-football-playing, beer-gutted agent jogging toward Jake's room.

Jake put his hands over his ears and yelled. "Looks like I finally won the lottery."

"Bomb threat. Gotta move your ass down to the basement."

A bruise on Jake's upper arm jolted with pain as the agent clamped on, manhandling Jake down the hall. Sleep had been hard to come by, with unresolved issues colliding in his brain of the SITS nightmare, his family, the Sûr System attack and the reasons behind his pseudo-incarceration. The passageway turned right, taking both men down several flights of stairs before dead-ending at an oversized metal security door. A box near them buzzed, and the massive steel door clicked.

The agent swung open the door, but Jake hesitated, darkness staring back at him. "In you go, Dr. Bendel," the agent said, shoving Jake, who staggered into the bunker, tripped, and crashed down into a small wooden table, hitting his head.

"For your own safety." Lights flickered on before the door shrieked and slammed shut, jolting Jake's bones.

After shaking his head, a floating image appeared in the air above him of Cynthia, wearing her yellow dress. He briefly wondered how hard he'd hit his head but decided he didn't care and spoke to her shakily. "Help me, baby. I need you more than ever."

"You know what you need to do, sweetheart. But wait for the right time," she said, her voice as smooth and calm as ever.